Leaving Home

Book One in the Caston Teacher Series

Margaret Standafer

Leaving Home - Book One in the Caston Teacher Series

By Margaret Standafer

ISBN-13: 978-1734800814

Cover Art: Kristin Bryant, kristindesign100@gmail.com

FOR MY PARENTS

Mom, my biggest cheerleader, my constant source of support and encouragement, and my best marketer. Thank you for always believing in me!

Dad, who had possibly never read a fiction book—certainly never a romance—before I published my first, and who has read every one since, even when it meant holding a magnifier to do so. Thanks, Dad, it means the world to me!

And thank you both for providing a happy, fun home, for a childhood full of adventure, and for a lifetime of unwavering love.

A VERY SPECIAL THANK YOU TO:

My nephew, Tim, who ensured his musically challenged aunt made at least some sense when writing about a musical character.

Kristin, for another perfect cover.

Phil, for putting up with me at crunch time.

And all my readers who patiently waited for this book to see the light of day. It was a long wait.

1

It was only one link. One thin strip of red paper, hardly more than a scrap, but more important to Ellie than if it had been made of gold.

Ellie's eyes moved past the red link to the blue one next to it, to the green, the yellow, and the dozens and dozens that followed. Draped along the walls of Ellie's bedroom, it seemed impossibly long. Ellie's fingers itched to tear off that first link, to drop the total by one, so she clenched those fingers and turned away.

When she caught a glimpse of her face in the mirror, a face so pale she hardly recognized it, she told that face, "You can do this."

Ellie might have believed herself if it hadn't been for the sweaty palms and the quavering voice. But she needed to believe herself. If she didn't, how would she ever get through the coming nine-hour day, the four more nine-hour days that week, and the one hundred and seventy-seven that would follow?

"You can do this," Ellie repeated, but even as she said the words, her eyes drifted again to the paper chain.

Silly maybe, but something Mama had done with Ellie and her brothers and sisters as a way to count down the days when they'd been eager for a holiday or a special occasion. The twin to the one that hung in Ellie's bedroom was eight hundred miles away, draped over the posts of the bunk beds in her youngest brother's bedroom. They'd made them together a week earlier during a video call, both dreading the start of school, but for very different reasons.

As much as she may want to tear off that first link, she'd wait. Her plan had been carefully crafted, and she wouldn't veer from it. Every day when she came home, another day behind her, she'd reward herself with the satisfaction of hearing the paper tear, of making the chain one link shorter. And she'd imagine her brother doing the same.

It was something she'd planned on doing with her kindergartners, and it's what she'd once done as she'd counted down the days to her wedding. Now she'd count down the days until her first year of teaching language arts to one hundred and eighty middle schoolers was behind her.

Her knees threatened to give out, so she smoothed the skirt of her favorite dress, an A-line splashed with pink and yellow flowers, and sat on the foot of her bed. She looked longingly at her guitar, propped precisely next to her reading chair, but Boomer was at her knees in a flash. Her lab plopped his head on her knees and turned his big, brown eyes on hers, so instead of letting her guitar soothe her, she let Boomer.

"I know, sweetie, it's a hard day for you, too, isn't it? But you're ready for this, and you can do doggie day care. I know you can. We're both going to be amazing on our first days, right? Because we're smart, we're strong, we're brave, and in ten hours we get to come back home."

A strangled sob escaped Ellie's mouth before she could stop it. Boomer joined her with a lament of his own.

"No need to cry, baby, it will be okay."

She held up her palm and Boomer bumped it with his paw. Ellie smiled her first smile of the day. Then, because she glanced at the clock and figured she had a few minutes to spare, she reached for her guitar.

She strummed, no longer surprised by the A minor chord her fingers found. After a moment, her voice joined the sad melody.

I wonder if you know what it feels like
When he smiles and takes your hand
I wonder if you know what it feels like
To be in the arms of the perfect man…

Only a few cars dotted the parking lot in front of the school district's administration building. Ellie checked the time. Twenty minutes early. She hadn't been sure how long it would take to drop off Boomer at day care, so she'd allowed herself plenty of extra time. Boomer had balked a bit, but once she'd led him inside and he'd gotten a look at the other dogs, then at the fenced-in yard complete with a swimming pool, he'd darted from Ellie's side without so much as a backward glance.

Ellie frowned a little as she twisted in her seat and scooted from her car. Part of her, the selfish part, had hoped Boomer would be more reluctant to stay, maybe even refuse at first, but the sensible part was glad it hadn't been more difficult dropping off her trusted companion. For the dog, anyway.

Ellie hustled inside and went in search of the ladies' room. She had twenty minutes to fix her tear-streaked face.

In an effort to keep her eyes open, Ellie had taken to studying everyone in the room. Sixteen new teachers. More than she'd expected in a district the size of Caston's. Six men, ten women. Best guess, nine were older than Ellie's twenty-five. Five were dressed as Ellie deemed appropriate for the first day of work: dresses or skirts on the women, dress pants and shirts with ties on the men. The rest wore jeans, a scattering of t-shirts with slogans, even shorts. Ellie'd had to look twice at that to be sure her eyes weren't playing tricks on her. At the beginning of the session, seven had looked as nervous as she felt, wide-eyed and furiously scribbling notes. She figured they, too, were starting their first-ever teaching jobs. As the morning wore on, sixteen were fighting yawns. Talking policies and regulations could only hold a person's attention for so long.

"And that wraps up our morning. Thank you for your attention."

Chairs scraped and zippers zipped.

"Lunch is on the back table. Feel free to eat inside or to take your lunch outside. We'll meet back here at one o'clock."

It felt good to stretch her legs. As Ellie wandered to the back of the room, she dug in her bag for her phone. One quick call to check on Boomer seemed reasonable. She scrolled through her contacts searching for the number and bumped into the tall woman with sleek black hair she'd noticed earlier.

Ellie gasped. "Oh, heavens, I'm so sorry. Please forgive me. I was so busy with this silly phone that I just about bowled you right over."

The woman looked down at Ellie from under raised eyebrows. Perfectly arched eyebrows, Ellie noticed, but the sort of perfectly arched eyebrows that came naturally. Ellie fought the urge to run a finger over her own uncooperative brows.

"I can't imagine you bowling over anyone. What are you, five-two?"

"Five-four," Ellie answered, straightening her already ramrod straight spine.

The woman's eyes traveled to the floor, and she laughed. "In those heels, maybe."

"Yes. Well, anyway, I apologize."

The woman waved a hand. "Don't worry about it." Then she

extended that hand toward Ellie. "Max Simmons."

Ellie dropped her phone back in her bag and shook Max's hand. "Ellie Hawthorne. Max? Is that short for Maxine?"

"It is, but I'd caution you against using that name."

Ellie grinned. "So noted, Max."

They walked together to the table holding a row of boxed lunches, bottles of water, and carafes of coffee.

"So, Ellie, where're you from?"

"What makes you think I'm not from Caston?"

"Oh, let's see. Maybe it's the fact that you looked terrified and sat so straight in that folding chair I swore you were tied to it. Or maybe it's the fact that you didn't laugh at the superintendent's lame hockey jokes, didn't look like you even understood them. Or maybe it's the dress and heels and make-up and hair that make you look like you belong on the cover of some debutante magazine. And then there's that accent. Ellie, you've got about as much Midwest Farmer's Daughter in you as I have Southern Belle in me."

The tiniest wrinkle appeared between Ellie's brows. "You were watching me?"

"I had to do something to stay awake. Trying to figure you out kept me busy."

"I see. And for the record, I don't have an accent, you have an accent."

Max threw her head back and laughed.

"It's not that funny," Ellie said. "And Oklahoma. I'm from Oklahoma."

"Let's get some lunch, Oklahoma, and you can tell me how in the world you ended up in Caston."

That would take a while, Ellie thought. "I have to make a quick phone call. Is it okay if I join you in a minute?"

"Sure. Take your time. I'm going to head outside." Max pointed to a group of picnic tables. "I need some fresh air."

Ellie smiled, deciding Max was going to be her first friend in Caston. "I'll be just a minute."

Once Ellie made the phone call and assured herself Boomer was okay, she gathered up her lunch and bottle of water and joined Max at a table just outside the glass doors of the conference room. The sun was hot and high in a cloudless sky. The umbrella shielding the table provided a welcome relief from the rays that were, in late August, still brutal.

Before Ellie could get herself situated, another woman approached the table.

"Do you mind if I join you? I asked, and it appears there are three new middle school teachers this year." The woman pointed at Max, then at Ellie, then at herself. "One, two, three. I figure we may as well get to know one another."

"Is that right? The three of us? I had it all wrong, it seems." Then Ellie remembered her manners and held out her hand. "Ellie Hawthorne. This is Max Simmons. Please, join us."

"Nicole Emerson" Nicole sat down then looked at Ellie. "You had what all wrong?"

Ellie flipped her wrist and blushed. "Oh, just me being silly. I was looking around the room during the talks this morning and making guesses as to who'd be teaching elementary, who looked like a high school teacher, and who would be braving middle school." Ellie gave an involuntary shudder.

"And where did you have me?" Max asked.

Ellie paused. With Max's long, athletic build, her sleek, black hair styled in a glossy swoosh, and her intense green eyes that, Ellie guessed, missed nothing, Max exuded confidence. Ellie had decided Max must be headed for the high school. She hoped saying so wouldn't get her off on the wrong foot with Max.

"I guessed high school for you."

"Why's that?"

Ellie tried to read Max's expression, but it was surprisingly blank.

"Oh, I don't know, I just thought, well…it seems I was wrong about everyone."

Max laughed. "You thought I looked like I could kick some butt, right? Good. That's the look I was going for."

Ellie's jaw dropped, but she caught herself and clamped it shut. She turned to look at Nicole, hoping for a reprieve. Nicole just looked from Ellie to Max and grinned.

"Ah, relax, Oklahoma. I'm just giving you a hard time," Max said.

"Um hmm," Ellie mumbled, and dropped her eyes to focus on unboxing her lunch.

"I suppose you'd better tell me where you placed me," Nicole said. "I'm curious."

Ellie felt her face heat, and it had nothing to do with the weather.

"I don't know that I got to you."

Nicole laughed, a rich, musical laugh that made Ellie think of the string quartet that had been… She caught herself and turned her attention to Nicole.

"To tell you the truth, I didn't think you looked much like a teacher at all. I hope that doesn't offend you, as that's not my intention, but you look…"

Ellie paused and tilted her head, studying the no-nonsense woman with the intelligent brown eyes, the golden hair a couple of shades darker than Ellie's that cascaded over her shoulders. Nicole wore a snappy skirt and blazer and, Ellie realized, looked as out of place as she herself did. "You look like you belong in a law office. My daddy's a lawyer. You have the same look about you."

Nicole blinked and drew back just a bit. If Ellie wasn't mistaken, some of the color drained from Nicole's face. "Oh. Well. I see."

"Not that you aren't a brilliant teacher, I'm sure you are, but you look like you're used to being in charge, and of something, or someone, other than a room full of thirteen-year-olds."

Max nodded. "I have to agree with Oklahoma. That suit screams board room, not middle school history room."

Nicole regained her composure and sat up straight, pulling back from the table and moving herself from the shade of the umbrella into the glaring sun. Ellie couldn't quite convince herself that the heat was to blame for the washed out look on Nicole's face.

"History classroom?" Nicole finally said. "Why do you say that?"

Either Max hadn't noticed Nicole's unease or she was choosing to ignore it, because she continued, undaunted. "I figure Oklahoma's right about the lawyer thing. I've known a few lawyers. Not my *daddy*," she said as she cut her eyes toward Ellie and grinned, "but I've been acquainted with a few over the years. Law school likely means an undergraduate degree in history. It fits."

Nicole blew out a breath that sent her loose strands of hair fluttering. "I…yes. History." Her shoulders slumped, and she cast her eyes downward to her lunch.

She didn't want to talk about it, that much was clear to Ellie. Why not remained a question, but as curious as she was, Ellie told herself it wasn't any of her business and pushing for information wasn't the way to make a friend, so she changed the focus of the conversation.

"I'm teaching language arts. I've studied what I'm required to teach, but there's some room for me to make a few choices of my own as far as which books the kids read, how we tackle the poetry unit, that sort of thing. How does it work with history? The curriculum is based on facts. Is there leeway?"

"Sure, the facts are there, there's no changing what's happened in history. That's what I like most about it. But, it's still open to some interpretation. People view history in different ways depending upon their backgrounds, their beliefs, their own personal histories. I've been researching techniques teachers are using to make history more interesting and relatable for their students." Nicole shrugged. "Some seem promising."

"All I remember about history class is memorizing dates," Max said. "Seemed pointless."

"I rather enjoyed it," Nicole said, "but I know I was in the minority. It seems I'll have to come up with ways to motivate the kids other than simply making flash cards with dates and events."

"Then you've never taught before, either?" Ellie asked.

"I haven't, aside from student teaching, of course. You're also brand new at this?"

"I am," Ellie said, "and nervous as a long-tailed cat in a room full of rocking chairs."

"A what?" Max asked. Then she shook her head and rolled her eyes. "Never mind. And it's my first year too. Math and a couple of intro to engineering classes for me."

"So we're all new." For a moment, Ellie was disappointed. She'd hoped for guidance, advice, and above all, a calming voice or two when she teetered on the edge of despair, but then she decided maybe it was for the best. They could learn together, they could fail together, and hopefully more often, succeed together. "It should be a fun year."

"Fun. Right," Nicole muttered, convincing Ellie that Nicole would rather be just about anywhere else.

"Fun. We'll see," Max said, but unlike Nicole, Max looked determined and ready for a challenge.

2

The week was long. It was, at times, boring, and at times confusing. It was a week filled with introductions and instructions; with passwords and prep work; with meetings and more meetings. For as terrified as Ellie was at the idea of a classroom full of twelve- and thirteen-year-olds, by Friday, she was almost looking forward to facing the kids if it meant a reprieve from the barrage of HR paperwork and the endless calls and emails back and forth with IT to get her access to all the websites, portals, and drives she needed.

With the last meeting wrapping up at eleven o'clock that morning, the rest of the day was hers to put the finishing touches on her classroom. Ellie had to fight a pang of sadness when she hung up a poster explaining literary devices in the spot that would have been perfect for a weather chart with smiley-faced suns and gloomy dark clouds. Then again later when she filled bins with paperbacks written by authors like Gary Paulsen, Lois Lowry, and Jerry Spinelli instead of brightly colored books by Dr. Suess, P.D. Eastman, and Margaret Wise Brown. She reminded herself over and over that she was doing the right thing, that she could handle it, and that it was all for the best. She tried hard to believe the words as she started muttering aloud in her attempts to convince herself.

She had to admit, though, that the room was inviting. She hoped the kids would agree. In one corner, she'd set up a cozy reading nook complete with a soft, blue couch she'd found at a second-hand store, two beanbag chairs, and a dozen oversized pillows in different shades of blue, green, and yellow all scattered over a fuzzy teal rug. The floor lamps cast a soft glow. Ellie imagined her students settling in and flying headlong into a world of witches and wizards or embarking on a journey into the past. As much as Ellie loved the fun rhythm and rhyme of books for the younger set, she'd fallen in love with the tales she'd devoured over the past few months getting acquainted with the authors and stories her students would read, and she was eager to discuss them to get the kids' take.

Eyes scanning the room, Ellie wondered how the teens, or almost teens, would respond to the choices she'd made. Popsicle sticks with their names in color-coordinated jars lined a shelf near her desk. While she wouldn't require her middle schoolers to find their stick and tuck it into a pocket on a chart reflecting their mood for the day, she would use the sticks to call on students to answer questions or to place them into random study groups until she learned their names, and learned who shouldn't be grouped with whom.

A large bulletin board, covered in backing paper decorated with tiny shooting stars, was blank except for one lone pink star. The first project in each of her five sixth-grade classes would be a 'Get to Know Me' assignment. Once the kids had completed their stars with an important or unique fact about themselves written or drawn in each of the five points on the star, Ellie would hang them on that bulletin board, joining her pink one, and together, they'd learn about one another.

Tiny white lights twined around the perimeter of the room and crisscrossed the ceiling. In between those lights dangled chains with clips on the ends of them. A few were already decorated with book cover images of some of Ellie's favorite books: *Harry Potter*, *The Hobbit*, *Little Women*, *The Giver*. Most, though, were empty and were waiting to be filled with more book covers after a student read a book and presented a good argument on why that book deserved a spot among the stars.

She'd push her students, and she'd expect their best. The two teachers she'd spent time with during her student teaching stint had different philosophies and practices. One was easy-going—too easy-going in Ellie's opinion—and while the idea to let the students have some say in what they studied, what they read, and how they were evaluated had merit, they'd had too much free rein and the result had been near chaos. The other ran a tight ship. She'd been teaching for years and still used most of the same methods she'd used thirty years ago. While the result was a quiet, attentive group of students, Ellie had gotten the feeling it stifled the kids. Most of them had been full of interesting and often unique ideas and perspectives, but had little chance to express them. Ellie would fall somewhere between those two teachers, she hoped, adopting the strategies she felt worked the best from each, but she wasn't naïve enough to expect things would always run smoothly. She'd have to be flexible, she knew that, maybe even altering the rules and expectations a bit from class to class, depending upon the dynamics of a particular group.

Ellie used the clipboard she was holding to fan herself. No matter how prepared she felt she was, no matter how much she'd read and studied, she was a nervous wreck. Hiding that from the students might be her biggest challenge.

Sipping at her water and popping an occasional pretzel in her mouth, Ellie studied the student files she'd received from the special education teacher, the school counselor, and the dean. Some of her students would travel to her class under the watchful eye of a paraprofessional. Some would be pulled from class occasionally for special services. Some would need an extra push to achieve their potential, some a gentle reminder that school was a safe place. Ellie's heart ached as she read about the issues facing her students, issues no child should ever have to face.

She snapped the last folder closed and, leaning back in her chair, closed her eyes. She knew the facts by heart. Come Tuesday, she'd find out if she was up to helping those who desperately needed someone to care.

"Sleeping on the job, Oklahoma?"

Ellie sat up with a grin. "Sleeping? I wish. I feel like I haven't slept in weeks and I don't expect that to change soon."

Max's mouth turned down in a frown. "What's up? Nervous?"

"That's putting it mildly. Aren't you? Aren't you afraid you'll bomb in spectacular fashion?"

"Nah. I can handle a bunch of kids. What are they going to do? Mutiny?"

"Probably."

"You're the boss of them. You'd do well to remember that."

"It sounds easy when you say it. Believing it when I'm facing them is another matter entirely."

"You can do this, Ellie, and you have to believe it because if you don't, the kids never will. It's important to get off on the right foot. You need to be confident, or they'll sense weakness and move in for the kill."

"Thanks. I feel so much better."

"Glad I could help."

Max dropped into a chair, then pulled another close and stretched her legs out and onto it. Her eyes roamed around the room and Ellie spotted the grin Max tried half-heartedly to suppress. While Max studied the room, Ellie studied Max.

Her short swing of black hair was hidden beneath a ball cap, but what escaped looked sweaty. Ellie knew Max had been wearing a pair of white linen pants and a red blouse that morning. Because their meetings were completed and the afternoon had been devoted to carrying boxes and hauling furniture, Ellie forgave the cut-off shorts and T-shirt boasting a picture of a motorcycle that Max now wore. The legs that extended for miles from the frayed hem of the shorts were tanned and toned. As were the arms.

At first glance, Max looked in control, but when Ellie looked a little closer, she spotted the tiniest bit of doubt, a hint of fear even, in those eyes that were a deeper green than Ellie'd ever seen before.

"You're nervous too."

"Nervous. No. I told you, I can handle a bunch of kids," Max said, but Ellie noticed Max avoided eye contact.

There was something, Ellie knew it, but she wasn't sure if she felt better knowing that even Max had concerns or just the opposite: If Max was worried, Ellie should be petrified.

"What is it? What's bothering you?" Ellie asked.

Max yanked off her cap and swiped her arm across her forehead. She fidgeted and fiddled with the cap, first twirling it around her finger, then tapping it on her leg.

"You can tell me. I don't know that I'll have much advice, but I'll listen, and I'll try to help."

Max looked at Ellie, but not before slumping lower in her chair.

"Fine. You're right. I suppose I'm a little nervous, but not for the reasons you think. I can handle a room full of kids. There's nothing they can pull on me I haven't pulled on a teacher. If there's a book somewhere with tips on getting away with stuff in school, my name's on it. No, it's not the kids. It's just, well…" Max turned and stared out the window. When she looked back at Ellie, her expression was desperate.

"What if I can't teach? What if they don't learn anything? What if my lessons don't hit home and they're bored senseless? Algebra? Engineering? I know that stuff backward and forward, but how to explain it so it makes sense? So a bunch of kids want to learn more? I don't know. I don't think I know how to do that."

"Oh, Max, listen to yourself. You're passionate. That's the most important thing. You love what you're teaching and you'll make the kids love it too. Just wait until you get in front of those kids. All those years of dreaming about teaching, about imagining yourself setting young minds on fire with the desire to learn, you'll be doing it. You'll be—"

"All those years of dreaming about teaching? You're kidding, right? You think I've spent…" Max's eyes rounded. "Oh, geez. You're not kidding. You mean you've always wanted to do this? Always wanted to be a *teacher*?"

Ellie tilted her head, confused. "Of course. Since I was a little girl. I played school with my friends, my siblings, my dolls. I even asked for desks for Christmas one year so I could set up a school in our playroom. Mama found these old-fashioned desks, you know, the ones with the wooden seats and desktops and the wrought iron sides? I got four of them, and a blackboard with a pointer."

But Max didn't know. That much was clear.

"You didn't?" Ellie squeaked. "Really?"

"No. Definitely no. Not even a little. No way."

"But then, why—"

"Max, you beat me. Did she say yes?" Nicole breezed into the room. Ellie heard her, but couldn't seem to tear her eyes from Max.

"Haven't asked her yet," Max said. She turned her head toward Nicole, but her eyes stayed fixed on Ellie.

"What's up with you two?" Nicole asked. "I know it's been a long week, but Ellie, you look like you're ready to keel over." When neither answered, Nicole continued. "Whatever it is, happy hour will make it better."

"Happy hour?" Ellie finally managed.

"Yes. Happy hour. It's this thing people do after work, especially after a long, hard week of work. Max and I talked this morning, thought it would be a good idea, and decided you need to come with us."

Ellie focused on Nicole. Her golden hair was pulled away from her face in a neat braid, and though Ellie was sure Nicole had worked as hard as anyone else, no one would know from looking at her. Her pants still held a neat crease, her silk blouse was tucked in and unwrinkled, and with her shiny leather briefcase slung over her shoulder, she looked as though she was heading *to* work rather than ready to head home.

"I don't know about happy hour," Ellie said. "I have to pick up Boomer from day care."

Nicole's jaw dropped. Max blinked and sat up straight in her chair. At the same time Nicole said, "Day care?" Max asked, "You have a kid?"

And for the first time that week, when Ellie laughed, it was a laugh without restraint.

"So, you take your dog to day care?" Max asked thirty minutes later when Ellie joined Nicole and Max at Scooter's Sports Bar.

"Just a couple of times a week. At least that's the plan. He's not used to being alone for such long stretches. I feel bad for him."

"He's a dog," Max said.

"I'm aware he's a dog. It's possible he's spoiled, but he's, well, he's important, and he just looks so sad when I leave him."

"Again, he's a dog," Max said.

Nicole waved at the server and pointed from her glass to Ellie. "If she wants to take her dog to day care, she should take her dog to day care."

"Thank you, Nicole," Ellie said. She reached for popcorn from the basket in the center of the table. "I've never been here. Looks nice."

They sat around a high-top table. Several more dotted the middle of the room while booths circled it. The floor was dark wood, nicked and scarred, but polished to a shine. Exposed ductwork, painted black, ran along the high ceiling. Warm, light brown brick softened the look. The windows sparkled, the bar looked spotless, and as Ellie let her eyes wander, she spotted an employee sweeping up a popcorn spill.

"It's so clean and feels, I don't know, friendly, I guess. Do y'all come here often?" Ellie asked.

Max chuckled. "There's your Oklahoma again."

"My Oklahoma?" Ellie's forehead creased as she looked from Max to Nicole. Nicole grinned and gave a quick nod.

"Y'all doesn't exactly scream Caston."

"Oh, darn. Did I say that again? I've been trying so hard not to."

"Why?" Nicole asked.

"Because I'm trying to fit in, not stick out like a sore thumb."

"You're going to need to do more than just lose 'y'all' from your vocabulary before you fit in, but I agree with Nicole. Why try to fit in? Be yourself."

Herself, Ellie thought. That's exactly who she didn't want to be.

Eager to change the subject, she asked again, "Anyway. Have you been here before? I've only driven by."

"Once," Max answered, "but just to grab a takeout order. They make good burgers."

"About a thousand times," Nicole murmured, almost more to herself than to Ellie and Max.

"Really? Then you're from Caston? You grew up here?" Ellie asked.

Nicole closed her eyes for a moment and seemed to will away the memories. "I did."

"Why didn't we know that?" Max asked. "Do you have dirt on anyone we're working with? Maybe that snooty little secretary who sighs and acts like I'm asking her to move heaven and earth when all I need is a green highlighter?"

"Sorry, I don't know Cynthia. She wasn't around when I was. A lot of the faces are the same, though. It's unnerving. Have you met Mr. Haggerty? Chemistry teacher?"

Max nodded, but Ellie shook her head.

"How old do you think he is?" Nicole didn't wait for an answer. "He told me to call him Clem. I can't call him Clem! He's Mr. Haggerty, just as he was Mr. Haggerty when he taught me middle school chemistry, and just as he was Mr. Haggerty when he taught my dad high school chemistry."

"He taught your dad?" Max asked. "I figured he was old, but holy cow. Why doesn't he retire?"

Nicole shrugged. "He's not the only one, but it's hardest with him. He's an institution around Caston. Mr. Haggerty this, Mr. Haggerty that. Everyone knows him and everyone calls him Mr. Haggerty. Clem? No way."

"But how sweet that you're teaching in the school you attended," Ellie said. "It must be like a dream come true for you. I assume you always wanted to be a teacher?"

"Always wanted to be a teacher?" Nicole's burst of laughter was bitter. "No. That wasn't exactly the plan."

Ellie lifted a hand and slapped it on her leg. "Well, I'll be. Teaching wasn't the first choice for either of you. That's so strange. I assumed y'all would have spent your childhood playing school like I did."

Ellie watched as Nicole, who looked both uncomfortable and curious, studied Max. Just when Ellie thought Nicole was going to ask questions, she instead bit her lip and lifted her glass.

"Regardless of how we all got here, we're here. Here's to surviving a week of training and to hoping we're ready for what's coming next week," Nicole said.

They clinked their glasses and sipped.

"Do you still have a lot of friends in town?" Ellie asked after a minute.

"No. My close friends have all moved away. Most still have parents here, so they visit, but that's about it. Those that are still around were never close friends, and the years seem to have made them even less so."

Nicole didn't seem to want to discuss it further, so Ellie moved on. "Tell me about Caston. What's the town like? I've driven around, looked around, stopped in some shops, but I don't feel like I know the place yet."

"I guess maybe the best way to describe it is that it's a small town that's not so small anymore. Some things around here have an old-fashioned, small-town feel, but there's also the sense that something's about to burst. That Caston is on the brink of something, some kind of change.

"For example, there are families here that can trace their histories back generations to some of the earliest residents, and those families sometimes think that makes them somehow better than others. It can be cliquey. I didn't notice it so much when I lived here, but coming back, it's clear. Looking over my class rosters, there weren't that many names I recognized, so there's definitely a wave of new families moving into town. Still, it's a nice place to live. Most people are friendly and welcoming. We've got mom and pop stores where the owners will get to know you and treat you like family, but then we've got Walmart just outside of town. Lots of folks are worried it's just the start, that other big box retailers will follow and will drive those mom and pop stores out of business, but so far, they're coexisting. I guess it's a good thing to be growing when so many small towns are dying out, but it makes for an odd dynamic."

"Hmm. Interesting. It's a bit like home in that respect. A small town with growing pains. But it's different in so many ways. I can't find anyone who knows what sweet tea is to save my life. How y'all get by on these hot days without a glass of sweet tea I'll never understand."

"I don't know, a margarita seems to hit the spot," Max said as she waved down the server. "Another round, please."

"Another round? We have to drive," Ellie said.

"Then we'll order some food and stick around for a while. Is there somewhere you need to be?" Max asked.

"No, not really. Boomer's worn out from day care, so he'll be fine if we don't have time for a walk this evening."

"Will you bring us menus, please?" Nicole asked when the server brought their drinks. "Tell us about Boomer. Is he the only man in your life?"

The quick stab to her heart took her breath away. When would it stop hurting? Ellie wondered. Would it ever? Though her arms felt numb, pressure on her wrist got her attention. When she looked down, she found Nicole's hand squeezing her wrist.

"I'm sorry if I said something wrong."

"You didn't." Ellie swallowed over the lump in her throat, and focused on what was in front of her, not what was behind her. "Yes, Boomer's the only man in my life. He's a yellow lab, just over a year-and-a-half, and as sweet as honeysuckle. He's a bit of a handful." Ellie smiled, and some warmth returned to her limbs. "He's ninety pounds, but still sees himself as a puppy and thinks he should sit on my lap. And sometimes he gets excited if he spots a squirrel when we're out on our walk and almost pulls me right over, and he likes to chew TV remotes and eat socks, but we're working on those things."

"Ninety pounds? Then he weighs more than you. Why did you choose such a big dog?" Max asked.

Ellie chuckled. "I didn't know he was going to be quite so big. His mama wasn't all that big, and he was just a skinny little ball of fur when I brought him home." Ellie tilted her head and sighed. "I had a few people—okay, more than a few people—warn me he was going to be huge once he grew into his floppy ears and those catcher's mitts where his paws were supposed to be, but by the time I realized they were right, I was in love with him. Big is okay. What about ya'll? Any pets? Or boyfriends?"

Ellie realized that while the three of them had been in the same place every day for the past week, and while that week had felt more like a year, and even though they'd spent a great deal of time talking, most of their conversations had revolved around work. Between training, meetings, and setting up their classrooms, there had been little time to get to know one another.

Max and Nicole looked at each other for a moment before Max used her hand to make a sweeping gesture in Nicole's direction. "The floor's all yours."

Nicole shifted in her seat. "There's not that much to tell. As you already know, I grew up here, I left to go to school, now I'm back. My dad still lives in town. One brother, but he's in the middle of a three-year assignment in Japan with the tech firm he works for. No dogs, no cats, and no boyfriend. All fine by me. Dogs and cats are messy. So are boyfriends."

Max laughed. "Agreed. Although some dogs are cute, at least."

"Does that mean you're single as well?" Ellie asked Max.

"It does." Max lifted her glass. "To all the single ladies."

"To all the single ladies," Ellie and Nicole replied in unison.

"Did you always know you'd come back to Caston?" Ellie asked Nicole.

Nicole was suddenly interested in the water droplets on the table. She swirled her finger through them and shrugged instead of answering. She then asked Max, "How did you end up in Caston?"

Max's eyebrows arched in Nicole's direction, telling Ellie she wasn't the only one curious about Nicole, but Max answered the question.

"There was a job opening, I applied, I was hired. Here I am."

"But why Caston? Is it close to home?" Nicole asked.

"It's as close as anywhere."

Nicole looked like she wanted to ask more, but turned her attention to Ellie. "And you, Ellie? Why Caston? Wisconsin is light-years from Oklahoma."

And wasn't that the best part of it? Even if she wound up disliking everything else about her new home, it would have geography going for it. But she wouldn't be sharing those feelings just yet. If Nicole had something she'd rather not share, if Max did, so did Ellie.

"No, not close at all. I needed a change. Needed to push myself. Besides, I have an aunt who lives in the state, so I was able to stay with her while I did my student teaching and got my Wisconsin license in order."

"How was your student teaching experience?" Nicole asked. "Both of you. Did you enjoy it? Did you feel it prepared you for what's ahead? Did you think it was long enough? Too long?"

"That's a lot of questions," Max said. "I still say you should've been a lawyer."

Ellie noticed Nicole stiffen at Max's words, but Max didn't seem to notice. She plowed ahead.

"It was okay, I guess. And long enough, I guess. At first, I appreciated having an experienced teacher there with me in case I had questions, but after a while, it bugged me. I think she sensed it, because she backed off and more or less let me run things, but I suppose that's the idea. See if a new teacher can handle it on her own, right? Do I feel as though I'm prepared? Probably not. How could I? It's a new job. New jobs always have a learning curve, no matter how prepared you think you are."

Nicole nodded. "I don't feel prepared either, at least in the sense that I know what's coming my way. Organized, yes. But prepared? No."

"Yet you both seem so calm," Ellie said. "I've been a nervous wreck all week. The closer Tuesday gets, the worse my nerves get. I'll probably worry myself sick over the weekend and won't be able to teach come Tuesday. I wish I had y'all's confidence."

"Believe in yourself and remember you're the teacher. You're in charge. Act like it, and the kids will believe it," Nicole said.

"That's what Max told me earlier."

"Then it's got to be good advice." Nicole smiled. "You said you've always wanted to be a teacher. I understand some nerves, but I'd expect more excitement, more eagerness."

"Oh, well, I didn't expect to be teaching…to be teaching so far away from home. I figured I'd know some families and would feel a little more comfortable." It wasn't exactly a lie, more like skirting the whole truth, Ellie told herself.

"I know some families, and I think that makes it worse. More pressure. I know I shouldn't let it bother me and that I should go about my business the same way I would if I didn't know a soul, but there's something inside me telling me I need to knock their socks off, need to show them that even though—"

Nicole stopped, a fiery blush creeping up her neck to her cheeks. Her hand gripped the edge of the table tightly enough to have her knuckles turning white.

No, Ellie thought, she wasn't the only one preferring to keep some things to herself.

"We're all going to knock the socks off everyone," Max said. "The whole town will be sockless. Now, can we order?"

They placed their orders, and for a while, conversation was easy with the new friends discussing the continued heat wave, the bartender who had stopped even pretending not to be staring at them, and a little more about themselves. Ellie noticed none of them seemed ready to provide many personal details aside from the basics. If she were back in Oklahoma, out with the friends she'd had since childhood, very few of those personal details would have been off limits. She wondered if she'd ever get to that point with Nicole and Max. Then she wondered if she hoped to.

"What are your plans for the long weekend? It's supposed to stay hot through Labor Day, likely into early next week, at least," Max said. "What's the beach like, Nicole?"

"Crowded. Always crowded. Families, teenagers, everybody goes there. It's the place to go to beat the heat."

"Beach?" Ellie said. "There's a beach? Where? How did I not know that?"

"Head south out of town about three miles," Nicole said. "Stone Lake. Pretty place, some gorgeous homes around the lake, and a big, public beach."

"I can't believe I didn't know. Any place I can let Boomer in the water?"

"Keep him away from the beach. They're strict about that. Since most of the lakeshore is built up, it's pretty difficult to find a spot for a dog. Take him to Crooked Lake instead. It's just a couple miles farther and for as much as Stone Lake is clear and inviting, Crooked Lake is weedy, shallow, and deserted."

Nicole grabbed a napkin and started drawing. "Go past Stone Lake. After a little over two miles, you'll see a sagging billboard advertising The Rusty Nail, an old supper club that's been closed for years. I tell you to watch for that sign because there's no street sign marking the turn to Crooked Lake. It's a gravel road, probably overgrown with weeds, but it will take you almost to the clearing on the edge of the lake that's perfect for your dog. Park on the side of the road when it ends and you'll see the path through the trees. A few locals use it for their dogs, but most have stopped going there in favor of the dog park in town. Dad tells me it has a small pond, it's maintained, and I guess most people prefer that to the weedy lake. But you won't be disappointed. If your lab loves the water the way mine did, he'll be in heaven."

"You had a lab? Why didn't you say?"

Nicole shrugged. "It was a long time ago."

Something else she was reluctant to talk about. Nicole was a puzzle, Ellie decided.

"But it's legal? And safe?" Ellie asked.

"It's safe. I don't know that it's strictly legal, but it's not illegal. No one's going to bother you. Trust me."

"Thanks. I might check it out."

"And I might check out the beach. Is there a place to run there? I'm always looking for a good spot to run," Max said.

"There's a path that winds all the way around the lake. It's about four miles if you run the whole thing. Lots of people use it, but it's not so crowded that you're running into one another. At least it wasn't when I used to run there."

"You don't anymore?" Max asked.

"Haven't since I've been back. I might try it one of these days. We'll see."

"Besides maybe running again one of these days, any other plans? For the upcoming weekend, at least?" Max asked.

"I'll see what my dad feels like doing. Maybe we'll take a drive, have lunch somewhere outside of town. He likes to do that."

"Your daddy must be thrilled to have you back home." Ellie heard the sadness in her voice. So did Nicole, because instead of commenting, she turned the focus to Ellie.

"You're homesick, aren't you? How long has it been since you've been back to Oklahoma?"

Too long, but not long enough, Ellie thought. She kept her answer vague. "A while." Then, before either Nicole or Max could ask another question, she let herself remember, and grieve, just a little.

"That doesn't mean I don't know exactly what's going on at home. Mama spent today getting ready for the Labor Day picnic. She'll work into the night tonight and then all day tomorrow to get ready for Sunday. This will be the first one I've missed."

"Family picnic?" Max asked. "At your parents' house?"

"Yes, with my grandparents, aunts and uncles, cousins and lots of might-as-well-be cousins. The house and yard will be filled to bursting and Mama will work her fingers to the bone, baking biscuits, cooking beans, and making her famous pulled pork. Everyone brings a dish, of course, but Mama always says that if no one else brings a single thing, she wants to see that no one goes hungry."

"Sounds fun. It was always just my dad and me, so I've never done the big family get-together kind of thing. Do you play all those games like horseshoes and Frisbee? I've seen movies."

"You've never been to a family picnic? I'm sorry." Ellie couldn't imagine a life not surrounded by family.

"Hey, no big deal. Usually in those movies the whole thing blows up with siblings fighting, cousins swearing they'll never talk to each other again, and parents threatening to write kids out of their wills. I figure if

I missed some good, I also avoided some bad. Trade-offs, you know?"

Ellie nodded, not sure if Max believed that or if she was just covering some hurt.

"We do play games. Horseshoes can get pretty heated. There's a homemade trophy and everything. The kids stick to the pool with parents taking turns on lifeguard duty."

"You have a pool," Max said. "Wow."

"We do. Oklahoma's hot. Pools aren't all that uncommon."

Max nodded, a dreamy look on her face. Ellie left her to her fantasy.

"Most of the men, though? They'll spend a good part of the afternoon in my daddy's study. For my daddy, that's the best part of the whole day. The whole year, maybe."

"Cigars and whiskey?" Nicole guessed.

Ellie shook her head. "It goes way beyond cigars and whiskey." She glanced at her watch. "Right now, I can guarantee you that Daddy's organizing bottles of obscure liquor he's collected over the past year. It's become a game. An all-out, you-have-to-swear-to-take-this-seriously kind of game."

Nicole's eyebrows arched as she waited for more, but Ellie had to take a deep breath. She needed a moment before she could answer. Homesickness was as real as the flu or chicken pox, she decided.

"It stems from years and years ago when my great granddaddy and some of his friends had stills in their barns and would get together to judge whose batch had come out the best. Now, years later, it's morphed into a competition to see who can come up with the most bizarre, and I have to say disgusting, liquor. Some of them travel a lot for work, so the event has taken some unusual turns over the years. Mind you, I never take part, but I've peeked in and have heard enough of the bragging to know I'd never want to. One year it was Baby Mouse Wine, which is just exactly what it sounds like."

Ellie shuddered, remembering the bottle with the tiny, just-born mice bouncing around the bottom. "There's been Kumis, which is made from fermented horse milk, Chicha, which my uncle Bobby claimed was made by someone chewing fermented corn kernels and then spitting them out, and any number of bottles housing snakes, scorpions, and other horrifying creatures. Instead of tasting and determining the best, it's more shock value. Who's going to have the nerve to taste this bottle or that bottle?"

Nicole looked green. "Baby mice? Why? And how are they going to top that?"

"Heavens, I'm sure I haven't the faintest idea. I don't know what Daddy has up his sleeve this year, but he took a trip to Vietnam and had a package shipped home that he wouldn't let anyone see, so, darlin', it's anyone's guess."

On her other side, Max laughed. "Your Oklahoma sure shines when you talk about home." Max held up her hands before Ellie could respond. "Hey, it's okay. It's who you are, and like we already told you, you need to be yourself. Fighting it, over-thinking it, is going to make you do it even more often. Now, as far as the bizarre booze? If I ever get to Oklahoma, I might have to be the first woman to crash that all-guy party."

"They'd be happy to have you. They always extend an invitation to the ladies. It may be a bit tongue in cheek, but if someone took them up on it, I don't think they'd mind." Ellie looked Max up and down and then winked. "And I think you could hold your own."

Max rested her elbow on the table, then leaned to drop her cheek onto her fist. She turned her head and eyed the bartender for a minute. "Maybe we should ask him to make us a few of his specialties, and we'll have a little contest of our own. Some of those fancy shots."

"Shots? I don't do shots." Ellie shook her head.

"Neither do I," Nicole scoffed.

"Calm down. You guys don't have to look so horrified. I don't either, as a rule, but how about this? Assuming we all survive next week, we meet here after school on Friday and let him," Max tipped her head toward the bar, "give it his best shot, so to speak."

"One shot?" Ellie asked.

"One shot. Whatever he thinks three teachers who have just survived their first week deserve."

"Deal," Nicole said.

"Deal," Ellie and Max echoed.

Then they grinned at one another, but Ellie didn't think she was imagining it when she spotted the nerves in both her friends' eyes.

3

Ellie had heard about rising to the occasion. She could even pinpoint a few times in her life when she felt she'd done just that, but those times paled in comparison with her first day of school. More accurately, her first day of school as a *middle school teacher*.

When she walked into her classroom and flipped the light switch, she couldn't quite recall how she'd gotten herself there. Her alarm hadn't gone off because she'd turned it off at four-thirty when she'd given up any hope of getting some sleep. She knew she'd made coffee, she'd drunk some of that coffee, she'd taken Boomer for a short walk, and she'd showered, but after that, things got fuzzy.

Somehow, she'd said goodbye to Boomer—much harder for her than for Boomer who, Ellie had to admit, looked thrilled at the prospect of a day romping with the other dogs at the day care—and somehow, she'd gotten in her car and driven herself to school. She thought she might have exchanged greetings with a couple of people as she'd crossed the commons on her way to her classroom, but for the life of her, she didn't know with whom.

Now, as she looked around the room, her confidence plummeted. The bulletin boards she'd thought were cute, cool even, looked silly and childish. The couch and beanbag chairs looked like rejects from the Brady Bunch house, and she was all but certain the idea of hanging book covers from the ceiling would get her laughed right out of the classroom. She was ready to start yanking chains from the ceiling when she heard Max from down the hall.

"You'd better not be in there with a case of the vapors, because there's no way I'm going to fan you and wave smelling salts under your nose."

Despite everything, Ellie laughed. And laughed some more until she had to grab a tissue and dab at her eyes.

"Oh, man, you *are* hysterical," Max said.

"No, no," Ellie fought to calm herself and catch her breath. "You just surprised me and you said exactly the right thing. I don't think it was a case of the vapors coming on, but I'll admit to considering making a run for it. And where did you come up with that? 'A case of the vapors?'" Ellie giggled again.

"Thought it sounded like something *ya'll* might say in Oklahoma. Sort of *Gone with the Wind*, you know?"

"The vapors are more a Georgia thing," Ellie said with a wink.

Max just laughed. "You ready for today?"

"I wasn't. You helped. Thank you."

"Glad I could do my part."

"How about you? Are you ready?"

"Who knows, but there's not much I can do about it now, is there?"

"I guess not. Good luck, Max. I know you'll be great."

"Same to you. Oh. I saw Nicole on the way here. She told me to give you a hug, but I don't want to do that, so let's just pretend I did, okay?"

Ellie grinned. "Okay."

Max gave Ellie a relieved thumbs up, then waved over her shoulder as she loped from the room.

Ellie checked the clock. Fifteen minutes until her first class arrived. She took a deep breath. She was ready.

"Do we get graded on our stars?" The boy with bright orange hair and more freckles than Ellie'd ever seen on one face frowned as he asked his question.

"Not a letter grade. I'll just mark off when you turn it in."

"Then we don't have to do it?" The frown was still there, but it wasn't as pronounced.

"Yes, you have to do it, but it will be fun, don't you think? You can let everyone know a little about yourself."

"I don't like to draw."

"You don't have to draw. You can cut out pictures from magazines, or print images off the Internet, use labels, wrappers, anything you want to decorate your star."

"Decorate it? So it's like an art project?"

"I guess it's kind of like an art project, yes."

"I don't like art projects."

Of course you don't, Ellie thought. The students who hadn't already turned to get a look at the boy who seemed determined to find a comeback to everything Ellie said did so now, so Ellie stood facing the backs of twenty-seven heads and one freckled face that was now smirking at her. She peeked at the clock. Two minutes until the bell rang, ending her first class. Up to that point, things had moved along almost seamlessly. Despite stumbling over the pronunciation of a few names—even though she'd studied and practiced the names over and over again—she was proud of the way she'd conquered her jitters. Other than a couple questions as she'd gone through the introduction to sixth grade language arts, a few comments, a few whispered remarks, the kids had mostly stared, wide-eyed, many of them looking more nervous than Ellie.

Two minutes. She'd been so close. But she wouldn't give up without a fight.

"What do you like?"

"Soccer and X-box. Not school."

There were a few snickers from around the room.

"Well, there you go." Ellie held up a star. "A picture of a soccer ball here," she pointed to one of the star's tips, "and a picture of a player you like here." Ellie tapped the next point. "I know there are at least two soccer magazines in the bin of materials I said you could use for the project if you aren't able to find things at home. Then the Xbox logo here—if I'm not mistaken, it's just a circle with a green X so not much art work required—the name of your favorite Xbox game here, and finally a picture of a school, or even just the word school with a big, red X through it here. Done."

The boy crossed his arms over his chest. His frown was back in place and his lips moved slightly, but he seemed to be out of things he was willing to say aloud. Ellie bit her lip to hide her grin. Round One: Ellie.

The bell sounded. "Thank you for a great first class. I can tell it's going to be a great year. Have fun with your stars, and enjoy the rest of your day!"

A few of the kids said goodbye, a few smiled, a few even thanked her, and all in all, Ellie felt it couldn't have gone much better.

She blew out the breath she felt like she'd been holding for the last forty-seven minutes. She wanted to sit, wanted to jot down notes on what had gone well, what she could have done better, but before she could take another breath, kids were already arriving for the second hour.

One class down, but five to go.

Her second hour class was a bit more talkative as they filed into the room than the first hour had been, and Ellie got the feeling several of them discovered they had friends in this class. Some of the girls linked arms in a group hug and proceeded to jump up and down. A couple of the boys shoved one another, then talked in whispers that didn't stay whispers for long.

The bell sounded and Ellie put on her biggest, most welcoming smile.

"Find a seat, please. I'm Ms. Hawthorne and I'm so excited about the year ahead. I hope you all are too."

And with those words, she had to command her feet to stay still instead of breaking into a happy dance. She'd done it. She'd gotten out 'you all,' two completely separate words. She knew she'd slipped and had thrown in a 'y'all' in her first hour class, but she thought it had been only one. The constant concentrating on every word, though, was draining.

She got her students seated, watched as they made their choices on where to sit, and made mental notes. She'd turn those mental notes into actual written notes throughout the first day and the first week in order to help her put together a seating chart. Ellie was a big believer in seating charts. She may change those seating charts any number of times as the year went on, and likely would for certain assignments, but she felt it was important to help students find the best place. Did they need to be closer to the front in order to see? Did they need to be far from the window in order to minimize distractions? Did they need to be in the center instead of on the periphery to encourage more participation? Many considerations, and it would take some trial and error, but Ellie would work to see that each student was in the spot that would best benefit him or her.

"Middle school language arts is probably going to look a little different from elementary school language arts. Yes, we're going to read books, and yes, we're going to learn new words, but we won't always all read the same books at the same time, and we won't all learn the same words at the same time. Some of what you read and write and the new words you learn to understand and to spell will be up to you. We won't have weekly spelling tests like you may have had in elementary school where I give you a list of words on Monday and you have to know how to spell them by Friday. Instead, you'll choose a topic that interests you, you'll read about it, and you'll come up with a list of words you don't know from what you read. You'll find the meanings, you'll learn how to spell those words, and you'll learn how to use them in your own writing."

There were some confused looks, some hesitant looks, and some downright scared looks. Ellie'd expected that.

"Now, if that all sounds confusing, don't worry about it. We'll take it one day at a time and one step at a time, and in a few weeks, you'll all be pros. We're also going to do a lot of writing in class this year. More than you've done in the past. I know that can sound a little scary, and I know some of you will tell me you don't like writing, but one of my goals this year is to make you love writing. There are all different kinds of writing and together, we're going to find a kind that you like. But, before we get to all the reading and the writing and the spelling and all the other stuff, we're going to learn a little more about each other."

Ellie went on to explain the star project, then handed out a blank star to each of her students. This time, no one challenged her. Instead, there were some eager whispers and some excited suggestions about what they could add to their stars. The group of girls who'd hugged one another and who had all found seats next to one another leaned their heads together and began giggling.

"Okay, quiet down, please." It took a minute, but they did. Several were turning the stars over in their hands. Some were already drawing on them. One boy was trying to make his spin like a top on his desk.

"Does anyone have questions about the star project or about anything else we've talked about this morning?"

A few shook their heads, most just stared, but one boy raised his hand.

"You said we need to read books. When should we start? And what if we already started one over the summer but haven't finished it? Does that book count?"

"I'm glad to hear you were reading over the summer. I hope all of you were. If you're in the middle of a book right now, it will count toward your free-choice reading, and that's something you can start tracking today. Later, you'll select a book from a few options that fall within a certain genre, but you're always free to read other books. I've set up a chart for you to use where you'll be able to track all the books you read, write notes about why you liked a book or didn't like it, whether you recommend it, that sort of thing. Anything you put on your personal page can be linked to our classroom book review page so others can see what you've read and what you recommend. And again, if this all sounds confusing, please don't worry yourselves about it. We'll go over everything step by step. Once we get everything in place, it will be an awesome resource for y'all to find ideas for something wonderful to read."

She heard herself as she said it. Once she got talking and didn't think about every word, it slipped out. Maybe, like Nicole and Max told her, instead of fighting it, she should embrace it. Maybe her students would catch on and before long, they'd all be using the term. While Ellie doubted it, she couldn't help but wish. The way the kids used 'you guys' sounded like nails on a chalkboard to her. Probably the way y'all sounded to them.

"We've got a minute before the bell rings. Any other questions?"

Her chatty group of girls had their heads together again. After a few giggles, one of them raised her hand.

"Yes?"

"Where are you from, Ms. Hawthorne?" More giggles.

"Where am I from?" Ellie peeked at the clock just as the bell rang. "I guess you'll have to wait to find out until we share our stars with each other. Thanks, everyone. Enjoy the rest of your day!"

Once the room cleared out, Ellie collapsed into her chair. She had the next forty-seven minutes to herself and she'd use at least ten of them to do nothing but breathe, that deep breathing the yoga instructor had preached when Ellie'd been desperate enough to try just about anything to calm her anxiety.

She lasted two minutes, then she was up and walking between the rows of desks, picking up bits of paper, broken pencils, a book, countless wrappers, and three water bottles. Two forty-seven minute classes of twenty-some students and the room, in Ellie's opinion, looked like it had hosted an hours-long, all-school party.

Once she had the room back to respectable, Ellie sat down again at her desk, opened a notebook, and started jotting down notes. The first had to do with what she thought she'd done reasonably well, and what she thought she needed to improve upon. Greeting the kids, making them feel welcome, explaining a general outline of the expectations for the year had gone well. As far as engaging her students, making them feel as if their voices would be heard, there she felt she'd fallen flat. Once she'd gotten their attention, she'd fallen into the trap of reciting information as if on autopilot. While maybe not all bad in that perhaps she'd given them an idea of how she expected them to listen respectfully when she or a classmate was talking, she worried she'd left them with the impression her class would be boring, nothing but sitting and listening to her lecture.

Ellie tapped her pen against her chin as she stared out the window. No longer dulled by the early morning fog that had greeted her when she'd been one of the first into the school over three hours earlier, the sun now shone brightly and danced on the windshields of the cars in the lot below her second-story window. A sad sort of half smile tugged at Ellie's mouth. It was the kind of day she and Boomer loved, perfect for long walks, a game of Frisbee, or some splashing at Crooked Lake which, after following Nicole's directions and braving the drive down the deserted, barely there road had turned out to be a little slice of heaven on earth for her dog.

Unable to resist, Ellie grabbed her phone and pulled up the website for the doggie day care. Since she'd practiced several times over the weekend, it took her only a few seconds to pull up the camera where she could watch the dogs running and playing inside the huge fenced-in yard.

It wasn't hard to spot Boomer. He sailed over smaller dogs as he darted across the yard, his eyes on some sort of prize. The unlucky recipient of his attention turned out to be a golden retriever who was happily chewing on a stick. A stick Boomer had decided he wanted. One more leap and Boomer was alongside the well-groomed and apparently much more well-mannered dog. Boomer lunged for the stick. The golden pivoted and blocked. Boomer, confused but undeterred, tried again, this time from below. Boomer dropped to his belly, inched his way forward and underneath the golden, then tilted his head upward, mouth open, and went for the stick. Again, the golden outsmarted him when she raised both her front legs off the ground, turned herself around, and darted away, leaving Boomer to flip onto his back with his legs in the air, and watching his coveted stick now on the opposite side of the yard. Boomer took a minute to scratch, to rub his head on the ground, and then was off again.

"Oh, Boomer, leave her alone," Ellie said to her phone, but she needn't have worried. The golden watched and waited until Boomer was within a couple of feet, then dropped the stick, turned, and strolled away. Boomer pounced on it, tossed it in the air, then dropped to the ground with it between his paws and began chewing. But he was content for only a minute because as soon as he realized the stick was his, it apparently lost its appeal. He left it, and started across the yard at a run, off to torment another innocent victim, Ellie figured.

With a sigh, she shut down the feed and picked up her notebook again. She still had a few minutes before her next class arrived, and she used the time to jot down specific notes on a few of her students.

First up, the boy who'd debated every step of the star project. Bryce, she knew, as she'd heard another student use the name after class ended. *Soccer and X-box. Find out what else he likes, how to keep him engaged.* She didn't yet know all the girls' names from her second hour class, but she knew two. *Linnea, Kylie, and two friends - don't seat together.* After a few more notes, she had just enough time to dash to the restroom before her next group of students arrived.

Ellie hadn't met the paraprofessional who'd be accompanying Talia, one of the students in her fourth hour class. She'd read the file on Talia, she'd met with the head of the special education department, and Ellie felt prepared as far as Talia's needs, but she was in no way prepared for Toby Franks.

He had to be closer to seven feet tall than he was to six. Ellie based her guess on how he tilted his head when he walked in the door, out of habit, like someone who'd learned to do just that or suffer a knock on the forehead. His biceps tested the seams of his fuchsia polo shirt, and his buzz cut screamed military. Soft, brown eyes and a warm smile seemed wildly out of place on the face that looked as if it had been carved from granite with nothing but a chisel and hammer.

Holding his hand out toward her, he crossed the room in two strides.

"Ms. Hawthorne? Toby Franks. Pleasure to meet you."

"And you, Mr. Franks." Her hand disappeared inside his and she had to tilt her head back so far to look him in the eye, she nearly lost her balance.

"Welcome to Caston Middle School. And it's Toby, but you may as well call me Mr. T. All the kids do."

"Thank you, Toby. Mr. T. And I'm Ellie."

"If it's all the same to you, I'll use Ms. Hawthorne when the kids are around."

Ellie nodded.

"I'm with Talia this hour." He angled his head in the direction of the girl seated alone in the far back corner of the room. She was thin, her pale blonde hair nearly blending in with her pale complexion, and she was clearly nervous. As Ellie watched, Talia's hands twisted one way and then the other, and her foot never stopped tapping.

"Most of my time will be devoted to her, but I always tell the teachers I'm sharing space with that if they need another hand, mine are willing and able. Don't hesitate to ask."

"I appreciate the offer. I'll likely take you up on it."

Toby nodded, then turned and somehow maneuvered his giant frame through the throng of sixth graders. Those that had been busy joking or lost in their phones and hadn't yet noticed him froze mid-sentence or mid-click to stare. Toby smiled and held his hand out for a few tentative high-fives before pulling up a chair alongside Talia. Ellie had a moment of panic when she was sure the orange plastic chair would collapse under him, but miraculously, it held. Regardless of how uncomfortable he must have been on the chair that he made look as though it belonged in a dollhouse, he turned and whispered something to Talia. Ellie was certain she spotted a hint of a smile on the girl's face.

Suspected learning disabilities, a very unstable home life, and documented incidents of unexplained rage and aggression. Ellie knew the facts, such as they were, but had a hard time reconciling them with the timid-looking girl who, a moment later, was back to wringing her hands.

With Talia new to the district, Mrs. Martin, the special ed teacher, had pieced together what she could based on the few notes and test scores she'd been able to get her hands on. The parents claimed that prior to fourth grade, Talia was home-schooled, but Mrs. Martin's best guess was that the schooling had been sorely lacking in both content and consistency. Fourth and fifth grade had been spent at a very small school in Idaho, without much in the way of a special education department. After being held back one grade already in an attempt to let her catch up, Talia was a year older than most of her classmates, but likely several years behind academically. She currently lived with her father, her mother was in prison, and an older brother had disappeared, apparently for good, after several run-away attempts. Mrs. Martin's notes said Talia seemed to respond better to men than to women, and after Talia's pre-enrollment screening with the district psychologist, the suspicion was Talia had been the victim of abuse at the hands of her mother.

So much for such a young child to handle. Ellie's heart broke at the thought of it all. She reminded herself she couldn't fix everything, that what she could do was everything in her power to make Talia feel appreciated, respected, and cared for while she was in sixth grade language arts.

As she'd done during her first two classes, Ellie got the kids seated, gave an introduction to what they could expect that year in language arts, and explained the star project. She made an effort to involve her students, stopping to ask questions, share a personal tidbit, or mention a current event. She found she was more relaxed than she'd been during the previous classes. Marginally more relaxed, but she'd been coached to look at the glass half-full.

The kids, while they answered her questions if specifically called upon, were quiet. Much quieter than in her previous classes. There were no whispers, no giggles. She hadn't even spotted any of them sneaking a look at their phones. In fact, they barely fidgeted in their seats. While she'd like to think she'd gotten just that much better in a couple of hours, she wasn't delusional. The behavior had more to do with Toby than it did with her. She hadn't missed the glances the kids had cast toward the back of the room at the man teetering on a far-too-small chair, or the wide-eyed stares when that man had gotten up to sharpen a pencil.

As she wrapped up her explanation of the star project, Ellie began winding her way through the desks and handing out the stars. When she got to Talia's desk and tried giving one to the girl, Ellie was met with thin, scarred arms crossed tightly over the girl's chest and eyes that refused to look up from the desk. Ellie raised her eyebrows at Toby who simply smiled and held out his hand for a star.

"I think if I were to make one of these about myself, I'd have to fill up at least four points with pictures of food. Now which foods? That would take some thinking because I like them all. What's your favorite, Talia?"

Talia's eyes darted to Ellie, but only for the briefest of moments, before she turned not only her eyes, but her entire body in Toby's direction. That was okay, Ellie told herself, she could give Talia all the time she needed.

The sound of the bell caught Ellie off guard. With the class running so smoothly, she hadn't once looked at the clock.

"Oh my, we're out of time already. Remember, lunch is next. I hear the pizza is good. Enjoy!"

Ellie watched the class file out the door, orderly and quietly. She wondered how long it would last. Movement in the corner of the room caught her eye, and she spotted a dark-haired boy—Jack, she was almost certain—still standing near his desk. Before she could say anything, he spoke.

"Ms. Hawthorne? I don't remember my locker combination and my lunch is inside my locker. I don't know—"

His voice cracked, and as he dropped his gaze, his cheeks turned pink.

Ellie walked toward him. "Do you know that I forgot my way home from school the other day? Honest to goodness. I got into my car, drove out of the parking lot, and couldn't remember which way to turn." Ellie put a hand on the boy's shoulder and directed him toward the door as she continued talking. "It was my third day here, and I'd driven to and from the school a couple of times before that to make sure I knew where I was going, but there I was, sitting in my car, looking down the street, and I was all mixed up. Just goes to show, we all forget sometimes. There wasn't anyone in the parking lot to point me in the right direction, but I know there are lots of helpers by the lockers today to help anyone who might need help."

"I thought that was just this morning."

"No, there will be helpers for most of this first week. Lots of people forget lots of things at the beginning. The helpers have lists with everyone's combinations, and they can also figure out what to do if the silly locker just doesn't want to open. Here we go."

They had made their way to the sixth-grade locker bay. Ellie waved at a smiling, grey-haired woman wearing a cardigan decorated with a school bus, apples, an old-fashioned schoolhouse, and which boasted the cursive alphabet circling the waist band. Her glasses were on a chain around her neck and Ellie would put money on her having bandages in one pocket and chocolate chip cookies in the other.

"We need to double-check a combination," Ellie said.

"Of course, of course. What's your name?"

"Jack Coughlin."

"Well, Mr. Coughlin, let me take a look." The woman ran a finger down the paper on her clipboard, then tapped. "Here we go. Do you remember where your locker is?"

Jack nodded and pointed. He'd taken a few steps toward his locker when he turned back to Ellie.

"Thanks, Ms. Hawthorne."

"You're welcome, Jack. See you tomorrow."

As they walked away, Ellie saw the woman reach into her pocket and hand something to Jack.

Smiling, Ellie darted her way through the throng of sixth graders making their way to the lunchroom. In her eagerness to help Jack, she'd left her room without the things she'd wanted to grab before heading to lunch herself. By the time she doubled back to her room, gathered up her things, and hiked back to the teachers' lunchroom, both Nicole and Max were there, eating and talking.

"Ellie, we were worried you'd bolted for the parking lot, never to be seen at Caston Middle School again," Max said.

Ellie laughed as she grabbed her lunch box from the refrigerator. "No, not yet. How did the morning go for y'all?"

"Fine," Max said, "but I've only had sixth graders so far."

The ominous tone to Max's voice had Ellie pausing with her apple half-way to her mouth. "And?"

"And?" Max said. "And that means seventh graders are coming up after lunch. Sixth graders are afraid of everything at this point: a new school, a new type of schedule, lockers they can't figure out, a classroom full of kids they don't know. They're too scared to cause much trouble for a while, but seventh graders? They think they've got it all figured out. Sure, some of the teachers are new, but not much else is. They're comfortable and that means the whole 'scared straight' thing isn't going to work."

Ellie set down her apple without eating it. Her stomach threatened to revolt. "I hadn't thought of that. I have a class of seventh graders the last hour of the day."

Instead of biting her apple, Ellie bit at her fingernail.

"Oh, yeah, sorry about that. I forgot you have seventh graders. I shouldn't have said anything."

"Don't let Max get to you, Ellie," Nicole said with a frown in Max's direction. "One class at a time, one day at a time. You'll be fine."

Ellie drummed her nails on the table. "I shouldn't have been so willing to take that class of seventh graders. Do you think I could have said no to the principal?"

"You probably didn't have much of a choice," Nicole said. "When Amanda wants something, it's hard to refuse."

"Why did she need someone so late in the game?" Max asked.

"From what I understand, the seventh grade class is quite a bit larger than sixth and eighth. In order to keep individual class sizes down in seventh grade, an eighth grade teacher was going to teach one section of seventh. Until she found out she was pregnant and decided the extra workload and stress would be too much. Enter, Ellie. Naïve newbie."

Curse that silly desire to please, Ellie thought. It wasn't the first time it had gotten her into trouble.

"Amanda gave me a detailed curriculum in order to take off some of the pressure since it was late when she asked me and since it takes away one of my prep periods. There's a small pay increase, but now I'm regretting saying yes."

"We can compare notes on the kids," Max said. "I'll help you keep them in line if you run into trouble."

"You think I'll run into trouble?" Ellie pushed away her apple. No way she was going to be able to eat anything now.

"Like I said, Ellie, you'll be fine. Don't worry," Nicole said.

Ellie nodded, far from convinced, but ready to focus on something else. Or, at least try to focus on something else. She looked at Nicole. "How was your morning?"

Nicole's forehead wrinkled. "They're needy, aren't they? I wasn't prepared for so much needy."

"They're young. Just before lunch, I had a boy nearly in tears because he couldn't remember his locker combination. Earlier, one asked to use the restroom, left the classroom, but was back a half minute later asking where the restroom was."

"That's what I mean," Nicole said. "I didn't expect that level of neediness. I thought they'd be more grown up. This is like having kindergartners."

A pang, straight to Ellie's heart, had her clutching her hands to her chest. Nicole didn't seem to notice.

"But unlike kindergartners, they're big. Some of them are really big. El, half of them must be taller than you."

Max snorted. "Half? Most, I'd guess."

"Not most. At least not most of the sixth graders," Ellie said.

"My student teaching was during second semester, so I didn't see sixth graders at the beginning of the year. I had no idea." Nicole shook her head. "No idea."

Ellie grinned. "It's my turn to tell you, 'You'll be fine.' Anyway, it's not so bad, is it? Being needed?"

If Nicole answered, Ellie didn't hear because at that moment, her phone alarm chimed and Ellie jumped to her feet. "Five minutes until lunch is over. I want to be back to the room before the kids get there. I hope y'all have a good afternoon."

Ellie shoved her lunchbox back in the refrigerator and hustled from the lunchroom. Three classes to go.

4

Her feet hurt, her voice was hoarse, and all she wanted to do was hug her dog. She'd find some lower heels and some throat lozenges for the rest of the week, no question, but at that moment all Ellie could focus on was picking up Boomer, going home, and having an hour or two during which time she didn't have to think about anything school-related.

She turned the correct way when she left the parking lot. That was a plus. She'd been honest when she'd told Jack about not knowing how to get home from school the week before. Sure, she'd figured it out after a minute or two, but given her current state of exhaustion, she wasn't sure she'd be able to say the same if she got turned around that afternoon.

Boomer's day care was a few miles from school, so she had time to reflect on her day. For the most part, it had gone well. Or at least okay. Passable, maybe. Her two afternoon sixth grade classes had been mostly problem-free. There'd been a bloody nose that had resulted in more embarrassment than anything, and a scuffle between a couple of girls over a seat next to their shared friend, but otherwise, nothing too noteworthy.

Her seventh-grade class had been another story entirely.

Loud and uncooperative, that group was mostly responsible for the hoarse voice. Max had been spot-on when she'd predicted the seventh graders would be far past the nerves and timidity of the sixth graders. The difference had been night and day.

Ellie knew she'd failed spectacularly in setting the stage for what she expected from them. By the time seventh hour had rolled around, she'd been tired and though she wasn't proud of it, had been hoping to coast through the hour.

She'd done anything but.

There'd been raised voices, not all coming from seventh graders. Thinking of it filled Ellie with regret and no small amount of shame. She wasn't a yeller. She'd never been a yeller. Not that she'd yelled, exactly. She equated yelling with scolding and punishing. That she hadn't done, but she'd had to raise her voice several times just to be heard. That had never been her intention, and she vowed it wouldn't happen again. She'd find a better way.

There'd been that brief moment when she'd lifted her hands, ready to clap out a rhythm in hopes of getting her students' attention and having them reply in kind, but she'd caught herself just in time. Good thing, as they probably would have laughed her right out of the room. Still, there had to be a better way than raising her voice.

Promising herself the next day would be better, she pulled into the parking lot at the day care. This had been by far the longest day Boomer had spent at day care, and on top of everything else, Ellie had been worried about how he was doing. As she climbed from her car, she wondered if she could use Boomer to get her seventh graders' attention. Not that she could actually bring Boomer to school—though wouldn't that be fabulous?—but she could tell her class about him. She could show some pictures, ask her students about their pets, and if they responded well, maybe use the first couple of minutes of class every day to give a Boomer update or a funny anecdote about her silly dog.

It might just work.

Her steps were a little lighter as she walked to the desk and tapped the bell. The girl who popped out from the back room didn't look much older than some of Ellie's seventh graders. Her blonde braids swayed as she rushed to the desk. Ellie had met a few of the employees, but Marin, according to her name tag, was a new face.

"Hi! Are you here to pick up?"

"I am. Boomer. A yellow lab."

"Right. I know who Boomer is. I'll go get him."

Marin skipped back through the door and Ellie busied herself browsing through the dog treats, designer collars, and picture frames for sale on the shelves throughout the reception area. It was only a couple of minutes until Marin was back with Boomer prancing alongside her.

"Hi, buddy! How was your day?"

Boomer came toward her, but only when Marin led him on the leash. Odd, Ellie thought. Usually, the employee unfortunate enough to retrieve Boomer had a struggle on her hands trying to keep the dog from bolting toward Ellie.

"Oh, my stars. Look at you, so calm. You must be tired."

Ellie leaned down to hug her dog, but before she got both hands on him, she bolted upright.

"Oh! This isn't Boomer. You must have two yellow labs today."

"This…um…what?" Marin stuttered.

Ellie smiled. "He sure looks like Boomer, doesn't he? I should have known when he didn't pull your arm off."

Ellie waited for Marin to laugh about the mistake, but instead, the girl paled. And didn't move a muscle.

"Marin? Is something wrong?"

"Um…I…just a minute."

Ellie stared after the girl as she flew from the room and through the door.

"Well, what do you suppose that's all about?" Ellie patted the dog's head while he sat obediently in front of her, looking up at her with what Ellie could only describe as a confused look. "You don't know either, do you?"

When Marin came back, she wasn't alone.

"Hello, Ms. Hawthorne."

Ellie was instantly on alert. Ellie had met Tyler, the young man with Marin, a couple of times. He was easy-going, friendly, and seemed to love his job. Right then, he looked tense and as if any job would be preferable to the one he had.

"Tyler. Is there a problem?"

"I'm afraid so, Ms. Hawthorne. Nothing we can't fix, but it seems Boomer isn't here. He, um, he was—"

"Isn't here? What do you mean, isn't here? Where is he?" Ellie's voice rose with every syllable. Next to her, the lab began to whine.

"I'm sorry. There was a mix-up, and Boomer was sent home with another one of our dog parents. He has a yellow lab as well, and the two look practically identical. They're the—"

"Sent home. With someone else. I don't understand." The voice that a moment ago had risen at least an octave, now dropped twice that. Ellie felt her knees tremble and reached out a hand to brace herself against the desk.

"This other dog parent was in only about ten minutes ago. He picked up his dog, and they left. We didn't realize there'd been a mistake. I'm going to call right now."

Tyler walked backward toward the desk. His eyes were round beneath his shaggy bangs and his head nodded ever so slowly, up and down, up and down.

Ellie focused on the up and down and ordered herself to breathe with every movement. In and out, in and out. As usual, it was useless, and she began to hyperventilate.

"I want my dog. You need to find my dog."

It was too much. She dropped the leash she'd been holding and stumbled to a group of chairs along the back wall. She fell into one, leaned her head into her hands, and tried to stop those hands from shaking.

But she couldn't sit. She jumped back up and jogged the few steps to the desk. She held her breath as Tyler dialed the phone.

It was taking too long. Ellie was certain Tyler was being put through to voicemail. What if the man who had Boomer didn't listen to his messages? What if he went home, dropped off Boomer thinking it was his dog, and headed out for the evening? What if Boomer, scared when let out of the car at a strange place, ran away? What if she never saw her dog again?

Ellie felt dizzy. For crying out loud, Max had been right. Ellie had a case of the vapors.

"He didn't answer. I left a message. I'm sure he'll call back in a minute. I'm really sorry, Ms. Hawthorne, we've never had a mix-up like this before."

Of course you haven't, Ellie wanted to say. Who would bring their dog here if word got out that it was anyone's guess whether the dog you dropped off would be the one you went home with? But of course, she didn't. She didn't say anything, just turned and began pacing.

Should she call the police? Probably not. If what she knew from TV was correct, the police didn't classify a *person* as missing until twenty-four hours passed. She figured they wouldn't be putting out an APB on a dog that had been missing for less than one hour. But doing nothing didn't seem right.

"If you give me this man's name and address, I can drive over there and sort all of this out. It's possible he'll be busy with something, won't listen to his messages, and won't realize he's got the wrong dog. We can't take that chance."

"Ah, yeah, I don't think I can do that. Give you his name and address, I mean. That's confidential, I think. I mean, like I said, we haven't had this happen before, but I know I'm not supposed to give out names and phone numbers and things like that." Tyler stood a little taller. "No, I can't do that."

Ellie wanted to scream, but again, she didn't. What would Mama say if she found out Ellie screamed at a teenage employee at a doggie day care? Well, Mama wouldn't actually say much more than 'Eleanore Maureen,' but her tone and her body language would fill volumes. Instead, Ellie ran her fingers through her hair, freeing the long, blonde waves from the royal blue barrette that perfectly matched her royal blue dress.

"It seems as though there are times when policy doesn't apply. Perhaps this is one of those times. Perhaps we could resolve this situation much quicker if you'd give me that information. Sitting here and hoping that this man calls back seems like a poor choice of how to spend our time, doesn't it?"

Tyler looked over his shoulder, probably hoping for back-up, but Marin had long since disappeared into the back room. Left on his own, Tyler's bravado flagged. "I don't know. Maybe I should call my manager."

While Tyler picked up the phone again, Ellie resumed her pacing. She made as large a circle as possible in the reception area, her heels clicking out a sharp rhythm on the tile floor. Her lips moved as she devised and then discarded one idea after the other. She didn't realize until her second lap that Boomer's doppelgänger was at her heel. She stopped and stroked the dog's head.

"Oh, you poor thing. You're just as upset as I am, aren't you? Of course, you are. You're waiting for your friend, expecting to go home, probably to have your dinner, maybe play ball or go for a walk, and instead, you're handed off to a stranger and left to wonder what in the world is going on when that stranger loses her mind."

Ellie sat again, and the dog dropped his head into her lap, his eyes that looked so much like Boomer's, calm and reassuring. "What a good boy you are...um..." Ellie reached for the dog's collar. It was red, just like Boomer's, but unlike Boomer's, the attached ID tag didn't include the dog's name, only a phone number.

"Tyler? What's this boy's name?"

"Bowie. His name is Bowie."

Ellie whipped her head in the direction of the voice. Even though she'd been alternately staring toward the door willing it to open, and the phone willing it to ring, she'd somehow missed the man's entrance.

Tall, she noted, a day's worth of stubble on his face, but that's all she noticed because at his side, jumping and misbehaving at the end of a leash, was Boomer.

"Boomer!" Ellie flew across the room, a swirl of blonde hair and the billow of a blue skirt in her wake.

Ellie crouched and threw her arms around Boomer's neck. He jumped up and down in place, his tongue wagging and connecting with her cheek. "Oh, sweetie, are you okay? Were you scared? It's okay, it's okay."

It wasn't until she felt leather sliding between her fingers that Ellie realized she was still clutching Bowie's leash. She stood and found she barely came to the man's shoulder. That wasn't a surprise, but the eyes that looked back at her were.

Dark. So dark brown they almost looked black, but instead of an intensity that such a color seemed to demand, they were kind, gentle, understanding, and right then, Ellie thought, tired. Very tired. She knew the look because it had stared back at her from the mirror for the last week.

The man held out his hand. "Zeke Fahrner. I'm very sorry for the mix-up."

Ellie wanted to be angry, wanted to demand he explain how he could make such a careless mistake, but now that she had Boomer back, she didn't have any fight left in her.

"Ellie Hawthorne. I'm just glad you got Tyler's message and got back here so quickly. I hope Boomer didn't give you any trouble."

Ellie cringed when Boomer chose that moment to turn his attention away from her and toward Bowie. Boomer jumped and head-butted Bowie who stood stoically, those big brown eyes pleading with Zeke to do something.

"Boomer was fine."

No, he wasn't, Ellie thought, but she appreciated the sentiment.

Zeke pulled his phone from his pocket and looked at it. "I didn't get a message. Looks like my battery's dead again. When I got home with Boomer, he refused to get out of the car. I gave him a tug, and he dug in his heels. That's when I really looked and realized it wasn't Bowie." Zeke rubbed his eyes. "I'm afraid I've had a long day, and I wasn't paying attention when I came to pick up Bowie. It's my fault and I really am sorry."

"It's straightened out now. No harm done." Except a few years off her life.

"Um, is everything okay here?" Tyler stood a long arm's length away.

"I should have realized the dog you gave me wasn't Bowie, but I'm concerned that such a mistake was possible in the first place," Zeke said. "Surely you have procedures in place to ensure the correct dog goes home with the correct owner."

"Yeah, we do. We've never had a problem before and, well, I'm not sure..." Tyler shifted from one foot to the other and wiggled the pen he held in his hand at a furious pace. "My manager is on her way. She can talk to you more if you want to wait."

Now that Ellie had Boomer, all she wanted to do was get out of there. "Maybe another time. Right now, I want to get Boomer home."

She traded leashes with Zeke, or at least she tried to. Boomer twisted and bounded toward Bowie again, effectively tying the two leashes in a knot.

"Oh, Boomer," Ellie sighed.

Zeke took both leashes and performed some sort of magic trick to untangle them, then handed the end of Boomer's leash to Ellie.

"Here you go. I hope you're able to enjoy the rest of your evening."

"Thank you. And thank you again for bringing Boomer back so quickly."

Ellie nodded at Zeke, lifted a hand toward Tyler and was halfway out the door when she heard Tyler say, "We're really sorry for the mistake, Dr. Fahrner."

Doctor. Hmm. No wonder he looked as tired as she felt.

Ellie got Boomer into the car and once they were both inside, he threw himself down on the back seat with an enormous sigh. He was asleep before they were out of the parking lot. Apparently she wasn't the only one feeling the stress of the day.

On her way home, between whispered prayers of thanks that everything had worked out as well as it had, Ellie realized she had one heck of a story to share with her seventh graders.

5

"How could they do that? What a bunch of idiots. What if the other guy wouldn't've ever brought your dog back? Are you going to sue? I'd sue, for sure." The boy sporting a football jersey and a pair of baggy athletic shorts stretched out his legs and laced his fingers behind his head. "For sure."

"It was a mistake. Boomer wasn't ever in any real danger, so even though I was mighty worried about him, and even though I was upset, there's no reason to sue anybody." Ellie bit back a grin thinking about what her father would have to say to the sue-happy boy. William Hawthorne had strong feelings on frivolous lawsuits and was only too happy to share those feelings.

"Are you sure Boomer's okay? Do you think you should've taken him to the vet to make sure he wasn't hurt? Or poisoned?"

"That would have been a good idea if I hadn't known where he was or if he'd been missing for a long time. Since he was only in the other person's car for a short time, I wasn't too worried. Besides…" Ellie flipped to the next picture and a shot of Boomer, curled up in the corner of her couch with his favorite stuffed monkey clutched between his front paws, filled the TV screen at the front of the room.

A chorus of "Aaawwws" sounded from most of the girls. A few of the boys, as well, though they quickly tried to hide their reactions.

"Once we got home, he gobbled up his dinner, then he curled up and went to sleep. I could tell he was fine, Chloe."

Ellie had learned the names of a few of her students, Chloe being one of them. The tiny girl with strawberry blonde hair was wearing a T-shirt with a picture of a puppy and a kitten frolicking together on a patch of green grass. While the majority of the girls in seventh grade

44

were trying so hard to be grown up, a few, like Chloe, were holding on to their childhood. It warmed Ellie's heart, and she hoped Chloe would stay true to herself for a good, long time.

Ellie clicked off the pictures to more than a few groans. "Thank you for your concern about Boomer. It's very sweet. I'll keep you updated on how he's doing." And since the response from her students had been overwhelmingly positive, she knew she'd been right in using Boomer as an icebreaker, of sorts. She had their attention.

"This leads us into our first writing assignment." The groans were louder this time. "What you're going to do is write a persuasive essay about the kind of pet you'd like to have. Your job is to convince me you should have that pet. Maybe it's a puppy, maybe it's a snake, maybe it's a tiger. You can use your imagination, but you have to be able to provide reasons why you should have this pet. You may want to do a little research about what's involved in owning the pet you choose, but I don't want you to spend too much time on that. I'm more interested in how you present your facts and your argument. My favorite part of this assignment is, well, actually I have two favorite parts, but the first is seeing what kind of pets y'all want. When I was a little girl, I wanted a monkey. My daddy thought it would be fun. My mama almost fainted at the very idea."

A hand went up in the back of the room. "Is it legal to have a monkey for a pet?"

"I think so," Ellie said. "At least it was at home. I'm not sure what the laws are in Wisconsin."

"Can we choose a pet even if it's not legal?"

"For this assignment, you can choose whatever you want. We'll pretend it's legal. Any other questions before we talk about what makes a good persuasive essay?"

"What's your second favorite part of the assignment?"

"Ah, you were listening, Michael. Good for you, but I'm not going to tell you my second favorite part just now. That will have to wait, but you'll find out a little later. Okay, let's take a look at some examples."

Ellie spent the next twenty minutes going over some basics on how to write a persuasive essay. She showed her students a few examples of what she considered a well-written essay, and how some of the other examples could have been improved. She didn't go in depth, they'd get to that later in the year, because what she hadn't told them, what her second favorite part of the assignment was, was that they'd do that exact same assignment at the end of the year. For now, her goal was to get an idea of where they stood in terms of their writing. As the year went on and they tackled several different types of writing, they'd grow, they'd improve, and they'd learn. Then, at the end of the year, they'd be able to compare, side by side, the essay they'd written the first week of school with the essay they'd write the last week of school.

She'd been going to tell them that, right up until the moment Michael asked her about her second favorite part of the assignment. All of a sudden, it seemed like a better idea to keep that a secret for the time being. Not that she thought her students were that devious, but she didn't want to tempt them into putting forth a poor effort now in order to show more improvement later.

The students were left with fifteen minutes to get a start on their essays before the bell rang. Once her room emptied, Ellie began her clean-up lap around the room. After two days and twelve class periods, it had already become automatic, and she already had a table in the back of her room devoted to left-behind items. As she deposited yet another water bottle on the table, she marveled at the table's contents: two sweatshirts, seven water bottles, a lunch box, two hats, three books, and one retainer case. She'd given up putting pencils and pens on the table, there were far too many, so she'd added a bin near the door where she dropped wayward writing utensils. If left in her classroom, pens and pencils became classroom property.

Once she was done straightening, she spent a few minutes hanging up the stars that had been turned in. Some were elaborate with glitter, ribbon, and fancy scrapbooking paper letters and cutouts. Others were less decorated, but no less informative. She learned she had students who loved everything from waterskiing to astronomy, from sour gummy worms to kale smoothies. One student had gone 3-D with his star and had attached a complex origami dragon. For the life of her, Ellie couldn't begin to figure out how Kaede had folded paper into something so amazingly intricate.

"Boomer's lost, possibly poisoned, for sure scarred for life, and I hear about it from Chloe?"

Ellie turned as Max sat at one of the desks. "You heard what from Chloe? And do you mean little Chloe who just left my room? The sweet thing with the strawberry blonde hair and big, blue eyes?"

"I don't know what color eyes she has and I'm not sure what strawberry blonde is, but I know she's little, so it's probably the same Chloe. She left a book in my room earlier today and dashed in to grab it on her way to the bus. She was talking a mile a minute to the girl with her and I deciphered enough to conclude something happened to your dog last night. Everything okay?"

"Everything okay with what?" Nicole asked. She sat down at the desk next to the one Max had claimed and looked at Ellie, waiting.

"Everything's okay," Ellie said. "Just a little incident with Boomer last night. When I went to pick him up from day care, they brought out the wrong dog because they'd sent Boomer home with the wrong owner."

"Oh, wow," Nicole said. "It's all straightened out, I assume?"

"All straightened out. I had a few tense moments. Okay, more than a few," she amended when both Max and Nicole looked at her, eyes full of doubt. "But, he's fine. No harm done."

"Maybe not to the dog. To you, I'm not so sure. Did you take him back there today?" Max asked.

"No, but I hadn't planned on it. Once or twice a week to day care. The rest of the time, he'll stay home. That was the plan all along."

"But you will take him back?" Nicole asked.

Ellie hesitated. "I don't know. Probably. Maybe. I don't know."

Max frowned. "How could they mix up the dogs? They must have a system in place so they know which dog goes with which person. What went wrong?"

"The dog they brought out, Bowie, looked remarkably like Boomer. Same size, same color, even the same color collar. I didn't ask too many questions, since all I wanted was to get Boomer home. I suppose when Dr. Fahrner asked for Bowie, the girl working there went looking for a yellow lab. I think she might be new, so—"

Nicole held up a hand. "Hold on. Dr. Fahrner? Sixty-something Dr. Fahrner with white hair, equally white and impossibly bushy eyebrows, and a voice capable of calming the brattiest of kids while at the same time putting the fear of God into them? That Dr. Fahrner? Or Zeke Fahrner with the jet black hair, eyes nearly as black, and who I'd heard was back in town to finish up his residency at the hospital?"

"That's a lot of detail, Nic. This was Zeke Fahrner. He introduced himself. Then his father's a doctor, as well?"

"Yeah. Grandfather too. Maybe further back than that, who knows? Huh. So the rumors are true. Zeke Fahrner's back in Caston. Who would've guessed?"

"You know him?" Max asked. "Old boyfriend?"

Nicole laughed her musical laugh from deep in her belly. "Know him? Sure. Everyone knows him. Or knows of him. Old boyfriend?

That's a big no. Zeke left more than a few broken hearts behind when he left for college. Mine was not one of them."

"A ladies man, then," Max said.

"No, at least not as far as he was concerned. Zeke was three years ahead of me in school, but like I said, we all knew who he was. One of my friends had an older sister in his grade, so we heard all the stories. Smartest guy in school. That was never up for debate. Best quarterback Caston High has ever seen. Also not up for debate. And best-looking guy Caston High has ever seen. That's probably up for debate, but he'd win if put to a vote. Much to the dismay of the owners of those broken hearts, he never dated. At least not that anyone knew of, and in Caston, someone would have known. He focused on school, on football but less so, and talked of being a doctor from the time he could talk, or so the stories go. When he left, most everyone thought it was for good. Now, he's back. Interesting. Did you talk with him, El?"

"We exchanged names and a few words about the dogs, but that's it. The only reason I knew he was a doctor is that I overheard one of the day care employees call him Dr. Fahrner as I was on my way out."

"Guess I'm not the only one who ended up back home," Nicole mumbled.

"It seems to me both you and this Dr. Fahrner should get free day care for life," Max said. "It may have turned out okay in the end, but they messed up. It's like sending parents home from the hospital with the wrong baby. Okay, maybe not quite that extreme, but you know what I mean. Dogs are what they do and they screwed up, big time."

"Carolyn, the owner, left me a message earlier today. She apologized profusely, alluded to some sort of compensation, and asked me to call. We'll see."

"Aside from the day care disaster, how have the first couple of days been?" Nicole asked.

"Pretty good," Ellie said. "My nerves were under control better today than yesterday, so I don't think I rambled quite as much. Yesterday with my seventh graders was something of a nightmare, but that was much better today, too. I told them what happened with Boomer, showed some pictures, and it worked to get their attention. I think 'Adventures With Boomer' will be a regular part of our day. Hopefully, it continues to hold their attention."

"Ah, so that's why Chloe was so worked up about Boomer. Good idea, using the dog. Sharing a little something with them, something they don't see as school stuff, is a good way to connect with them, and to get them to settle down at the beginning of class. Well done, El," Max said.

"Thank you, though I have to admit, the idea was born out of necessity. Yesterday was a complete fiasco. I didn't do anything right."

"I'm sure it wasn't as bad as you thought," Nicole said, "but I'm glad today was better. What about you, Max?"

Max sighed. "It's been fine. I had one kid try to tell me he won't be able to do any homework, probably not even any classwork, for a couple months because he has fractures in both his wrists. He even produced a surprisingly good note. I showed the appropriate amount of concern, asked him how it happened, expressed surprise that it happened to both wrists at the same time, and then asked him why he doesn't have casts or braces or anything else to protect his wrists. He said that, according to his doctor, he's in the middle of a growth spurt and the doctor wants to wait to put casts on until he grows just a little more."

Max shook her head. "I nodded my understanding and told him I thought his doctor was very smart for being so cautious. I grabbed my class lists and said, 'Let me just make a note here that you won't be doing any homework. Oh, and I want you to know that I think you're really brave for participating in that push-up contest I watched in the commons before school this morning. Ignoring what must have been excruciating pain so you could join in and make your friends happy, now that's the sign of a true friend. Okay, when do you think you might be able to do homework?' At this point he mumbled something about another doctor appointment and slunk away to his desk."

Ellie and Max were both laughing long before Max finished her story.

"Aside from the forged note, it was a pretty weak attempt." Max held up a finger as she began to list her reasons. "Far too long a time period to be believable. You never go past a week. Rookie mistake. Both wrists at the same time?" Max shook her head and held up another finger. "I get it that he anticipated my comeback would have been, 'You can punch at the keyboard with one hand,' but both wrists? That makes his story completely unbelievable." She held up a third finger. "He could have at least come up with some elastic wrap for his wrists. The line about casts coming later was ridiculous, of course, but he still needed something on his wrists now. And then, of course, push-ups in the commons? Come on. You have to know someone's going to see you. He's got a lot to learn."

"I wouldn't have believed that story, but I don't know that I have quite the same nonsense meter you do, Max. I had a student today who needed to use the restroom three times during class. I let her, but I had my doubts. How am I supposed to know if they're telling me the truth or feeding me a line, hoping to get away with something?"

"That, my dear Ellie, comes with years of practice. Now, I'm not claiming to have years of practice from the teacher's side of the desk, but I pulled my fair share of bull in school so figure I've seen and heard just about everything there is to see and hear. They'll have a hard time pulling one over on me."

"Really, though, who cares? If they're feeding you a bunch of bull, it's only themselves they're hurting, right? As long as they're not disrupting the class, how much effort am I supposed to put in to figuring out who's lying to me on any given day?" Nicole asked.

Ellie was ready to laugh, certain Nicole was joking, but Nicole's expression had Ellie doubting any of it was a joke.

"I think we have a duty to try to stop inappropriate behavior. A student, as you said, may only be hurting himself or herself, but isn't that part of our job? Making sure they're all getting the best possible education? How can we feel as though we're doing that if we allow them to get away with so much that will interfere with their education?" Ellie threw her hands up and looked at Max, but before Max could respond, Nicole spoke in a rush.

"I didn't mean I don't care. Of course, I care. I'll do what I can to see that they get the most out of my class. I just meant that, well...Oh, I don't know what I meant. It's been a long couple of days."

Ellie looked long and hard at her friend. Nicole appeared to regret her words, but Ellie wasn't convinced those words hadn't been partly true. Still, she knew it wasn't the time to put Nicole on the spot.

"It's been a difficult two days, that's for sure," Ellie said. "I keep telling myself it will get easier as we get to know the kids better and get to know the school better. Being new is hard. It's hard for the kids and it's hard for us. On the bright side, it's a four-day week, so we're halfway done!"

"That means halfway to happy hour," Max said. "We're still on for Friday, right?"

"I'm in, provided I'm still standing by Friday," Ellie said.

"I'm in," Nicole added. "I'll drag myself there if I have to."

It was a relief knowing Boomer was at home. As much as she hated leaving him alone for such long periods, at least she knew the right dog would be there to greet her when she walked in the door.

It had been another hot day, and at four-thirty, it was still plenty warm. While Ellie was no stranger to the heat, she found herself looking forward to cooler temperatures. She had one Wisconsin winter under her belt and though she knew her family thought she was crazy, she was kind of looking forward to another.

She waved a notebook in front of her face as she walked from her car to her front door. Boomer was there waiting.

"Hey, buddy! How was your day?" Boomer nearly plowed her over in his excitement. He jumped on her, ran to grab a toy, then returned and jumped on her again.

"Come on, let's go outside."

Ellie hurried to the back door, and as soon as she opened it, Boomer bolted into the fenced back yard. He rolled in the grass, rubbing his back and stretching his legs toward the sky.

Ellie looked up at that sky. Bright blue without a cloud in sight. While the days were shorter than they'd been at the height of summer, she still had plenty daylight.

"What do you say we head to the lake?"

Boomer's tail wagged furiously. "You'd have the same reaction if I asked you if you wanted to help me clean the oven, wouldn't you, you silly thing?"

Ellie rubbed his head for a minute before she herded him back inside. She dropped her bag, kicked off her shoes and lined them neatly in the closet, then headed to her room to change into a pair of shorts and a T-shirt. On her way out the door, she refilled her water bottle and grabbed a granola bar. After a few steps, she doubled back and grabbed a second bar, figuring if they stayed a while, she could call it dinner and forget about cooking.

Ellie felt herself relax on the drive. Her second day had been better than her first, but that didn't mean she wasn't still tense. As she moved her head in a slow circle to release some of the tension from her neck, she promised herself she'd ease back on her expectations. Magic wasn't going to happen overnight. It would take time to build a relationship with her students, any students, and two days was enough time to tell her that doing so with middle schoolers was going to be a longer process than with younger students.

"Oh, Boomer, what do you think it would have been like if I'd spent two days with kindergartners? Would I feel energized, confident that I was doing the right thing, or would I be even more exhausted than I am now? I guess we'll never know, will we?"

From the back seat, Boomer whined. As much as Ellie wanted to believe it was his way of commiserating with her, she knew the opposite was true. This was their third trip to the lake and Boomer recognized his new favorite playground. He pranced in place and pressed his nose against the window.

"Almost there, buddy, almost there."

When they did get there, and when Ellie spotted another car stopped on the side of the gravel road near the lake, she grumbled, "Well, shoot. I like having the place to ourselves, don't you?"

Boomer didn't care, that much was obvious. Once the car stopped, he leaped to the front seat and nudged at Ellie with his cold, wet nose.

"Okay, hold your horses. We have to make sure it's okay to run and swim, so you're going to have to start with the leash." Boomer pulled his head away when she tried to clip the leash to his collar. "Take it or leave it," she said.

As if knowing it was a battle he wouldn't win, Boomer dropped his head in defeat and let Ellie secure the leash. Once she opened the car door, he jumped and pulled her toward the lake.

"Hold on! You have to be good, or we're getting right back in the car."

Her words fell on deaf ears, she knew that, but for form's sake, she had to try. She needed to work harder with him, Ellie told herself, and needed to practice the commands she'd learned in obedience class. Boomer hadn't been the star of the class, not by a long shot, but he hadn't been the worst, and the instructor had assured Ellie her dog was more than capable of learning. It was up to her, she'd been told. Be calm, be firm, and above all, be consistent. She knew she'd failed to follow through and thereby was failing her dog. In all honesty, she didn't mind the way he jumped on her, the way he got so excited when he saw her that he couldn't seem to control any part of himself, but she knew others didn't see it that way. He was too big to behave like a puppy, and he'd scared more than a few people in his exuberance.

Another thing to add to her to-do list, Ellie thought, as she and Boomer wound their way through the scattering of oaks and maples to the lakeshore. The sight of a man, his arm held high and his hand clutching a stick, and the dog waiting at his side, jolted Ellie to a halt. She hesitated, wondering if it was a good idea to approach a stranger when she was alone in the middle of nowhere.

He hadn't seen her, and Ellie debated turning and leaving. But they'd driven there, Boomer was doing the jumping up and down in place thing again, and she figured since the man was letting his dog in the lake, he wasn't likely to report her for doing the same. And somehow, the fact that he had a dog made him seem less like a potential serial killer.

It wasn't until the man threw the stick and the dog bounded after it that Ellie realized the dog was a yellow lab. A big yellow lab with a red collar alongside an owner with black hair.

Boomer, getting a sniff of the water, was ready to play. He let a single, quick bark fly, causing both man and dog to turn toward the sound. The man paused a beat, but Ellie knew the moment recognition dawned because Dr. Fahrner nodded and lifted a hand in greeting.

"Ellie Hawthorne. We meet again."

"It seems so. How's Bowie? Not too upset after all the commotion last night, I hope."

"Bowie's fine, but he wasn't sent home with a stranger. How's Boomer?"

Boomer couldn't decide whom to greet first, Dr. Fahrner or Bowie, so jumped back and forth between the two of them, kicking up sand and sending it flying. The wet clumps were indiscriminate and landed on all of them. Ellie sighed. "Boomer's Boomer. He's fine."

"Exuberant guy, isn't he?"

"Is that a polite way of saying he's out of control?"

"No, not at all," Dr. Fahrner rushed to say. "He seems to love every minute of life, and I think that's just as it should be."

"You're kind, Dr. Fahrner, but he is out of control. I need to work harder with him. As a matter of fact, I was promising myself I'd do just that as I walked over from my car and he nearly pulled off my arm."

Ellie looked down at Bowie. Like last night, he sat patiently at Dr. Fahrner's side, eyes fixed on his owner and, despite the flying sand and the crazy dog beside him, stoically awaited his next command. "You must have worked tirelessly with Bowie."

"Please, call me Zeke. And yes, I have worked a lot with Bowie, but he comes from a long line of therapy dogs, so I think his natural disposition made my job easier than it might have been with another dog."

"Therapy dogs? Is Bowie a therapy dog? Do you take him to work with you?"

"Sometimes." Zeke tilted his head. "How did you know I was a doctor?"

Ellie felt her cheeks heat. "I overheard Tyler last night on my way out of Top Dog. He called you Dr. Fahrner."

Zeke nodded. His eyes seemed to bore into her, and Ellie fidgeted. Mama would be appalled, Ellie thought. Hawthorne women do not fidget. This time when Boomer jumped and banged into her legs, Ellie appreciated the distraction.

"Do you mind if I let him go? He loves the water, and I'm afraid he's losing patience."

"Of course not."

Ellie unhooked Boomer's leash, and the dog was off like a shot. He threw himself headfirst into the waves. At Zeke's side, Bowie quivered, but stayed put.

"Okay," Zeke said, and with the single-word release, Bowie followed Boomer's trail to the water. Together, the two jumped, splashed, and chomped at the water.

Content watching her dog romp and play, Ellie almost forgot the man who was only steps away until he spoke.

"You know all about me. It seems only fair you tell me about yourself."

Ellie turned to face Zeke, squinting against the evening sun. "I know you're a doctor and that you have a dog named Bowie. I wouldn't say I know all about you."

Zeke smiled, producing dimples on either side of that smile and leading Ellie to recall Nicole's words about Caston High's best-looking guy. It made sense.

"Fair enough, but I know less about you. What do you do?"

"I'm a teacher. Middle school language arts."

Ellie realized it was the first time she'd said the words aloud to someone she didn't know, and the feeling that went with her words was odd and unexpected, almost like she was telling someone else's story. Zeke's reaction, though, was exactly what she expected. He cringed.

"Middle school. God bless you. The fluctuating moods, the raging hormones, the irrational behavior. There aren't many who could do it."

"I'd argue there aren't many who could do what you do. Extreme highs and extreme lows, I have to believe. What kind of doctor are you?"

"Pediatric surgeon. Or I will be. I'm finishing up my final stint of residency."

"And you came home to do that residency." Ellie turned away and squeezed her eyes shut, willing time to turn back to the moment before she'd said those words, before Zeke got all the proof he needed she was some sort of crazy stalker.

Instead of facing him and what would certainly be questions, Ellie turned her attention to the lake under the guise of checking on Boomer. Of course, her dog chose that time to be well-behaved. He paced alongside Bowie in a few inches of water, both dogs staring intently into the lake, poised to lunge at whatever might lurk beneath the waves.

Zeke followed her to the water's edge. "And how did you know I'm back home?"

His voice sounded more curious than suspicious. There was maybe even a hint of laughter, and Ellie breathed a little easier.

"I was talking about what happened last night with Boomer and I guess I mentioned Dr. Fahrner. One of my coworkers recognized the name." Ellie debated how much to tell Zeke. "She was at Caston High the same time you were, but a couple of years behind you, I guess."

"I see."

Now his voice was unreadable. She couldn't say he was angry, but the hint of laughter was definitely gone. Annoyed, perhaps? Maybe he'd been hoping to fly under the radar? Unlikely, based on what Ellie had come to know about Caston and about Zeke Fahrner's reputation.

"She mentioned your father was also a doctor and at first, she assumed that's who had mistakenly taken Boomer. I think she may have been a patient at one time."

"Most people in town were, at one time or another."

Time to change the subject. "She's the one who told me about this place or I never would have known it was here. Boomer loves the water and with this heat that seems to want to hang on, it's been a lifesaver."

Now he smiled again, watching the dogs continue their frolicking in the water. "I think you'd be hard-pressed to find a lab that doesn't like the water. I used to bring my dog here when I was in high school. Joker. He was also a lab, but a black lab. Loved the water and loved to get into trouble. When I came back to town with Bowie, I wasn't sure this place would still be accessible. I'm glad it is."

"I was here twice over the weekend and never saw another person. It's perfect for dogs. I'm surprised it's not more popular. It's not illegal to be here, is it?" Another opinion couldn't hurt.

"I don't think it's exactly illegal. Maybe not entirely legal, but it's a fine line. As long as you're not causing trouble, I think you're safe."

"That's almost word for word what my friend said. You Castonites...Castonians? Castoners? I don't know what y'all call yourselves, but you're of a like mind, aren't you?"

Zeke chuckled. "I don't know that I ever really fit in here, but I suppose, like it or not, the town rubbed off on me, as it does everyone who grows up here."

It took every ounce of willpower she had not to ask him why he'd returned, why he felt as though he'd never fit in, but since she knew what it was like to want to keep certain things to yourself, she reined herself in. He was entitled to his privacy.

"Speaking of growing up here, I don't think I'm going out on a limb when I guess you didn't. How did you end up in Caston?"

It was a logical question, but she bristled nonetheless.

"A job opening and a change of scenery. I have an aunt who lives nearby, so I'm not quite the fish out of water, as I may seem."

"And your thoughts on Caston so far?"

"It's a small town. I know small towns. North or south, there are a lot of similarities. I have a feeling it will take a while before it feels like home."

"And where is home?"

"Oklahoma."

"Oklahoma. Nice place, at least what I know of it." Zeke bent over and picked up a stick. He tossed it into the water and both dogs took off after it.

"You've been to Oklahoma?"

"Briefly, but yes."

"Was it a vacation? Or do you have family there?" Ellie took a turn with the stick when Boomer, who'd outraced Bowie, dropped it at her feet.

"A recruiting trip, actually."

Ellie turned, an inch at a time, toward Zeke. She knew her eyes were wide and getting wider, but she couldn't help it. Nicole told her Zeke played football and that he was good. But *that* good?

"A recruiting trip to Oklahoma? To play football?"

When Zeke nodded, Ellie asked, "Not with the Sooners?" Zeke nodded again. "To play football for the Sooners?"

She hardly recognized her own voice. If she hadn't been aware of her mouth moving, she would have sworn it was one of her middle schoolers raving about the latest pop star, but she was too much in awe to be embarrassed.

Zeke started to laugh, but caught himself. "It wasn't that big of a deal. They invite lots of guys. Besides, I got the invitation because my high school coach had an in at Oklahoma, and I felt I owed it to him to follow through."

Ellie shook her head. "No, they don't. They don't invite that many. Only those they really want. You could have played for the Sooners? Nicole said you were good, but I had no idea."

Zeke's eyes narrowed ever so slightly. "Nicole?"

"Nicole Emerson. My friend at school. She told me you were the star quarterback at Caston High, probably the best quarterback the school has ever had, but back to *the Sooners*. Why did you turn them down? Where did you go to school?"

"This certainly wasn't a conversation I expected to have with you." Zeke grinned, and those dimples were more pronounced than ever. "But then, I didn't know you were from Oklahoma. I guess that changes things."

"I don't believe you answered my questions. Which school did you choose over Oklahoma? And that begs the question, why?"

"I ended up at Northwestern, but football didn't factor into my decision." Zeke held his hands up to his shoulders. "I know, it's probably a crime in Oklahoma, but school won out over football. I was determined to graduate in three years. I never would have managed that if I'd been playing football."

"No, I don't suppose you would have." Ellie shifted her weight to one foot and stared up at Zeke. "But you passed up an opportunity to play for the Sooners. Who does that?"

"Only the clinically insane, I'm sure."

Ellie laughed. "Okay, fair enough. I've heard there are people outside Oklahoma who don't live and breathe football. I wasn't sure it was true until now. You must have really wanted to be a doctor in order to give up on dreams of the NFL."

"I did. Medicine was my dream, not the NFL. Good thing, because I may have been good enough to quarterback a high school team, but college and the NFL? No."

Ellie's nod was slow as she thought it over. "That's admirable, I suppose. My advice, though, is not to lead with that if you happen to meet any more Oklahomans."

"Duly noted."

As they fell into an easy rhythm taking turns tossing the stick, Ellie was lost in her thoughts. Regardless of how Zeke might downplay the whole thing, he had to be an exceptional football player to have been invited to visit The University of Oklahoma. She thought over what she'd learned from Nicole. Smartest guy in school. That fit, based on the fact that he'd chosen school over football and had graduated with what she supposed was a premed degree in three years. Best quarterback in school. That was now fact. Best-looking guy in school. Ellie snuck a peek out of the corner of her eye. Handsome, that was for certain. The sun's rays, now lower in the sky, danced on his black hair and set it to gleaming. He was tall, a few inches over six feet, and the toned arms that flexed when he tossed the stick made it apparent he found time for the gym even with his grueling schedule. The five o'clock shadow she'd noticed the evening before was more pronounced. Ellie found herself wondering if he'd had the day off and chosen not to shave, or if he'd had an early call at the hospital and hadn't made time for shaving, maybe choosing instead to make time for a walk with Bowie.

Unless there was someone else at home to walk Bowie. Ellie stole a glance at the fingers on his left hand. Bare. The odd and unexpected feeling of relief at seeing his hand ring-free was unwelcome. Very, very unwelcome.

"Well, Boomer and I should be getting home." She hadn't intended on it coming out quite so clipped, quite so aloof, but it had, and she knew Zeke heard it as clearly as she did.

"Okay. It was nice running into you, Ellie. I'm glad Boomer's recovered from yesterday. Boomer," he repeated. "Ah, I get it. Boomer. Like Boomer Sooner. The Oklahoma fight song. Is that where he got his name?"

Ellie couldn't help but smile. "Yes, but Boomer turned out to be more accurate than I could have imagined."

"Speaking of Boomer, did you get a call from Carolyn at Top Dog?"

Ellie had Boomer by the collar and was trying to attach his leash. "She left a message. I haven't called her back. Did you talk with her?"

"No, like you, I had a message. She mentioned doing something to make up for their error, which I took to mean an offer of free day care. Do you plan to take Boomer back again?"

"I haven't decided. It's all still a little too fresh in my mind. I think I have to give it a few days. Honestly, though, after making a mistake with our dogs, I have to believe they'd be especially careful and attentive now."

"I think you're right." Zeke had Bowie's leash on him and followed as Ellie started toward her car. "But maybe to be sure, we should coordinate what days we'll be there so there's no chance of taking home the wrong dog."

Despite the internal warning bells, Ellie couldn't tamp down her curiosity. "How often do you take Bowie?"

"I haven't been taking him there long enough to establish a real pattern, but I guess once or twice a week. Usually those days I have long shifts and there's no one to stop by and let Bowie out. How about you?"

No one to let Bowie out. Questions were on the tip of her tongue, but she bit them back. "Boomer's only been there a few times. My plan was once or twice a week just to break up his long days alone."

They reached their cars and Ellie didn't pause, just pulled Boomer past Zeke's car and to hers. "I hope you enjoy your evening," she said as she coaxed Boomer into the back seat. He was wet and dirty, but since she knew he wouldn't stay on a towel anyway, she didn't take the time to cover the seat.

"You too, Ellie. It was nice talking with you. Maybe we'll see each other here again."

"Maybe." Ellie waved and ducked into her car.

On the drive home, she tried to forget about the man who could have played football for the Sooners, who instead chose a career in pediatrics, and who loved dogs. The man who had trained a therapy dog, for crying out loud.

The man who just might be perfect.

6

The next two days passed in a blur and by the time Friday afternoon arrived, Ellie was tempted to find an excuse, any excuse, to get out of happy hour. But then Max and Nicole came dragging into her room. Nicole, whom Ellie had never seen with even the slightest wrinkle in her blouse, had her hair bundled in a messy bun on the top of her head and had traded her perfect blouse and skirt for a faded blue hoodie and ripped jeans. Max, always confident and in control, had bags under her eyes. Eyes that appeared a bit glassy and unfocused.

"Oh, my stars! What happened to the two of you?"

Nicole and Max looked at one another.

"Do we look that bad?" Nicole asked.

"Not bad, exactly, but maybe defeated?"

"Defeated sounds about right," Max said. "I thought I could do this. I was a fool."

"I never thought I could do it," Nicole said. "I've never been more right about anything."

"What happened?" Ellie asked again.

"Middle school happened," Nicole said. "Or more precisely, middle schoolers happened. They never stop, do they? They never stop moving, they never stop talking, they never stop agitating one another. They just never stop." She fell into a chair and dropped her head onto her folded arms. "I have never been this tired in my life," she mumbled into the desk.

"Max?" Ellie asked, afraid of what she'd hear.

"Everything Nicole said. Times two. How long until Christmas break?"

"Sixty-eight days," Ellie answered, picturing the paper chain that hung in her bedroom.

"I'll never make it," Nicole said, her head still buried in her arms.

"Sure you will. We all will. It will get easier as we get used to the routine and get to know the kids better."

Nicole lifted an elbow and peeked out at Ellie. "Since when are you Miss Confidence?"

"Miss Confidence? Hardly. Miss Hopeful, maybe. We're in this for the long haul, ladies, and we can't let them beat us after only one week. I've been telling myself I can improve on one thing every day. For instance, I've stopped trying so hard to keep the room tidy. For the first three days, after every class ended, I walked through the room and cleaned up. Cleaned up scraps of paper, wrappers, all the items the kids left behind. Today I decided I'm done doing that. Sure, I'll straighten up at the end of the day, but I'm not going to kill myself trying to keep the room spotless. I'm hoping it serves two purposes. First, like I said, I won't be killing myself and maybe I'll occasionally find a minute to run to the restroom between classes, but also maybe the kids will start to notice the mess and start to pick up after themselves."

Max bubbled out a chuckle. Then another. "You can't honestly believe they're going to care? Their world is themselves. That's it. They don't notice the mess around them. They don't notice much of anything unless it jumps up and bites them. Or unless it pops up on a screen in front of them. Unless you pile garbage on their chairs, I seriously doubt you'll get their attention. Even then, they'd probably just swipe it to the floor without thinking twice."

"That's possible," Ellie conceded, "but it's worth a try, and that's my point. We'll keep trying until it gets easier. And it will. It has to, or there wouldn't be any teachers left."

"I can't believe anyone actually chooses this job," Nicole said as she lifted her head from the desk with a sigh. "It's so hard."

"It is hard, but all jobs are hard, aren't they? At least, at first?"

"I don't know, El, I can't believe they're this hard." Nicole leaned her head back and closed her eyes. "Maybe I have to quit."

"You can't quit. She can't quit, can she?" Ellie looked at Max, who shrugged. "We have contracts."

For the first time since she'd entered the room, Nicole smiled. "Contracts can be broken. Trust me, I've read every word of our contract and if I want to quit, I can quit. I may not teach again in the district, or in the state, but that's more of a bonus than anything, isn't it?"

"Nicole, you don't mean it, you're just tired. Go home, relax this weekend, and you'll feel better come Monday," Ellie said.

Nicole's only response was a grunt.

"Maybe we should all go home. Maybe it's not the night for happy hour."

Max sat up straighter and looked across at Nicole before looking back at Ellie. "No way, Oklahoma, you're not getting out of it. Not the night for happy hour? I'd say it's the perfect night for happy hour. We need some happy right about now."

"If I go home and have tonight and all weekend to think about it, I'll resign for sure. As appealing as that sounds, quitting isn't my style. You two need to talk me out of this. And you need to talk fast," Nicole said.

"Then happy hour it is," Max said. "I think we all could use a pep talk. Maybe we can lie enough to one another that we start to believe ourselves."

Ellie wanted to argue, she really was exhausted, but part of her knew Max was right. For as much as she'd tried to buoy Nicole and Max, her doubts were far outweighing any confidence she tried to portray. She needed a pep talk as much as anyone.

"Okay. Scooter's it is. I have to stop at home and let Boomer out, but I'll meet you there soon."

Nicole pushed to her feet. "Make it sooner rather than later. That pep talk can't wait long."

Ellie spotted Max and Nicole at the bar when she walked in the door at Scooter's. Curious whether their spirits had lifted, she watched for a minute before joining them. Nicole leaned on the bar with her head in her hand, staring at the ceiling. Max scowled at something the man seated next to her said. It didn't look good.

"Feeling better?" Ellie asked.

"We will be soon," Max answered. "Charlie said he's got the perfect drink for teachers who have just survived their first week of school. He convinced us it will be better than a shot."

"Survived might be a stretch," Nicole said as she twirled a stir stick between her fingers.

"You got through all your classes, you're here, you survived," Max said. "Come on, let's get a table."

Nicole groaned as she dragged herself to her feet, but followed dutifully behind Max as she skirted tables and chairs until she made her way to a booth in the darkest corner of the bar.

"Kind of dreary, don't you think?" Ellie asked.

"It's a bar *and* restaurant. The chance exists that one of our students comes in. I'd rather not have to make small talk," Max said.

"Good idea." Nicole lifted her shoulders, hiding like a turtle inside her oversized sweatshirt. "Maybe we should find a place out of town. Far out of town."

"Don't you think it might be good to get to know the families? Maybe that would help us better understand our students. I think knowing where they're coming from, seeing how they interact when they're not in school, could be very telling."

Max rolled her eyes. "Sit down, Oklahoma."

"Well, fine." Ellie sat, her chin in the air. "I think it's a good idea," she muttered.

"Maybe it is, maybe it isn't, but tonight's not the night to find out. Tonight is about coming up with a plan that gets us all back to school on Monday morning and for all the remaining mornings until June third." Max looked from Ellie to Nicole. "I have to agree with Nicole. The thought of bailing on the whole thing is darn appealing."

"Now, ladies," Ellie said. "We have to stay positive. Let's focus on what went right this past week. Sure there were rough patches, but there were also good moments, moments when you knew you got through to a child. Tell me three. Each of you. Three times when y'all knew you were right where you were supposed to be."

Nicole stared, her eyes like augers, boring, boring until they saw right through Ellie. With a look of triumph on her face, Nicole crossed her arms over her chest and said, "I think, Ms. Hawthorne, your week wasn't quite as wonderful as you're trying to make us believe."

"I don't think I said it was wonderful."

"Forget wonderful then. I don't think it was even good. I think you're putting on a show for us, trying to get us to believe you enjoyed the week, that you felt like you were right where you were supposed to be when, in fact, you're just as terrified, and frustrated, and ready to throw in the towel as we are."

With that, Nicole slapped her palm down on the table and a fire kindled in her eyes.

"Is that true, Oklahoma?" Max asked.

"Maybe my week wasn't perfect, but I never considered quitting. The good moments definitely outweighed—" Ellie gave up when she started to get dizzy watching Nicole shake her head.

"Ellie Hawthorne. Lying is very unbecoming. Why don't you tell us how your week really went?"

"Oh, for heaven's sake. Fine, if you must know, it was tougher than a two-dollar steak."

Nicole nodded one quick nod and huffed out a satisfied breath. "See? That wasn't so hard. The truth always comes out in the end."

Before Ellie could respond, Charlie delivered their drinks to the table.

"Here you are, ladies. I call this A Bad Day at School. It's a take on a drink called A Bad Day at Work, but I put a little spin on it, made it perfect for teachers."

The drinks were red, and each glass was garnished with an apple slice speared with a swizzle stick boasting an 'A+' at the top.

"Now, they're sweet, but don't let that fool you. These babies pack a punch."

"What's in them?" Nicole asked. "No, never mind. I don't want to know. Thank you, Charlie."

"Enjoy! Let me know what you think." Charlie winked and sauntered back to his spot behind the bar.

"Shall we?" Nicole said.

They all reached for a glass. Ellie tilted hers under the dim overhead light and studied it. A couple of maraschino cherries bobbed in the red liquid, adding to the likelihood the drink would be sweet. She smiled at the apple slice and stir stick. A cute touch.

Max held up her glass. "Here's to surviving the first week. Let's hope we don't have to say the same thing every Friday for the next forty weeks."

They solemnly clinked their glasses and sipped. It was sweet and fruity, the cherries doing their thing to soften the blow of the liquor. And it was good, Ellie decided. Really good. She took another sip, a bigger one this time.

"For the record," Nicole began, "I'm not happy that you had a hard week. My only goal was to get you to admit it so we can commiserate. Knowing we're all in the same boat helps. At least it helps me."

"And it wasn't my intention to mislead you," Ellie said. "I've always believed in the power of positive thinking and, believe me, I've had to try everything I could think of to stay positive this week. It's been hard, one of the hardest things I've ever done, but I meant it when I said there were positives as well as negatives. I'll start with my three positives."

Ellie picked up her glass and sipped while she thought.

"Okay, here they are. First, the second day with my seventh graders was so much better than my first, and they've responded so well to the tales about Boomer that I can't help but congratulate myself on deciding to use him as an icebreaker. They do live in their own little world, you're right about that Nic, but there are a few things that get through to them. Dogs, apparently, are one."

Ellie sipped again while Max and Nicole offered congratulations to her for happening upon something that worked.

"Next, the star project is turning out to be a great way to get to know the kids. I didn't know what to expect going in, how much effort they'd put into it, that sort of thing, but most of them have embraced it. Sure, there are a few who haven't turned it in and I doubt they will, but most have and I've tried to spend at least a minute or two with them talking about something they highlighted. I've found that once I get them talking about something they care about, they open up and become interesting little people."

"What about the boy who claimed he didn't like anything except soccer and Xbox?" Max asked.

"He turned in a star with just that: soccer and Xbox. It looks almost exactly like the example I spelled out for him in class, but that's fine. He did the assignment. I'll take it."

Ellie sipped again while she tried to decide whether to share the third thing with Nicole and Max. There was a line between honoring a student's privacy and sharing information that may help the student in the long run. Since her student put the information on her star, even if there wasn't an explanation attached, Ellie decided it wasn't strictly off-limits.

"And the third thing?" Nicole prompted.

Ellie took a deep breath. "The third thing is a bit more sensitive. I have a student who shared something with me and I'm wrestling with whether to share it with y'all."

Nicole's eyes grew serious. "A student's privacy is a tricky subject. Each student is, of course, entitled to privacy, but most often sharing between teachers is not viewed as a violation of that privacy. On the contrary, it's usually beneficial to the student as well as to the teacher if information is shared that will help both the student and the teacher succeed. Now, sharing information with someone outside the school, even if you're convinced there's no chance that person would ever come in contact with your student, is not only frowned upon, it's illegal. FERPA laws dictate that no information, other than basic directory information like name and address, can ever be shared. This means no posting grades, no emailing class scores or other information, and, of course, no sharing of sensitive, personal information."

Max leaned forward and narrowed her eyes at Nicole. "Are you really a lawyer working undercover to spy on the district? Are you taking notes on everything we do and say?"

Nicole laughed, but Ellie could only call it a forced, uncomfortable laugh.

"I'm not a spy. If that were the case, would I care what happened in my classes? Heck no. I'd put in my time and then get away as fast as I could, happy to leave Caston Middle School in the rearview mirror."

Not a spy, Ellie thought, but a lawyer? That claim Nicole hadn't refuted.

"This student put something on her star that caught my attention, so I asked her about it. It was a picture of a couple at their wedding. It was a photograph, not something cut from a magazine, so I asked her if she'd been to a wedding recently. She shook her head and told me it was a picture of her parents. Her eyes teared, bless her heart, and I was ready to let the matter drop, but she told me she thinks they're going to get a divorce, so she put their picture on the star to remind them they used to love each other."

"Oh, wow." Even in the dim light, Ellie could see Max pale. "What did you say?"

"I didn't have much time. I tried to assure her that relationships have ups and downs and it doesn't always mean divorce is inevitable. I told her that no matter what, her parents love her and her siblings, and also that it's not her job to fix whatever she thinks might be wrong. Her job is to be a twelve-year-old, to go to school, and to do whatever other activities she enjoys. I hope I didn't steer her wrong or give her false hope, but the class was emptying as I was talking with her and when we were the only two left, she gave me a hug. Then she smiled and thanked me, so I'm putting that in my positive column for the week. Now, Nicole, before you scold me about touching the students, she hugged me. Yes, I hugged her back, but if a student needs a hug, they're going to get a hug. And I'm glad you're not a spy and won't have to report me."

"That's a lot to deal with," Nicole said. "The thing with the girl and her parents, not you hugging a student who wanted a hug."

"It is, yes, but I feel like I helped, even if only a little, and that's what I want to do. Help those kids however I can. If it's not always helping them with reading and writing, if it's providing an ear if they need to talk, that's fine. I'll do what I can."

"I don't know what I would have done," Nicole said. She picked up her glass and downed a gulp. "I suppose you told us this partly because we have this student in our classes? What if she wants to talk to me? I don't know what to say to her. I'm not a therapist." Nicole drained her glass and looked desperately toward the bar.

"You don't have to be a therapist to listen," Ellie said. "If the time comes, you'll know what to say or what to do. If you're really at a loss, suggest the student talk to one of the counselors. They're trained to handle such issues."

"So, push them off on the counselor? For as much as that sounds perfect, even I know that's going to make the kid feel like I don't care enough to try to help. This is a no-win situation! You have to help me, Ellie, you have to tell me what to say. Who was it? I need to know so I can be prepared. I need another drink. Don't you guys need another drink?" Nicole rubbed her hand up her face and into her hair, pulling it loose from its tie. Once her hair was free, she used both hands to scrape over her scalp and wrap her hair in her fists before grabbing the tie and twisting the golden waves into a fierce knot.

"Geez, Nic, calm down." Max patted Nicole's arm, a little too hard, Ellie thought, but Max seemed as much out of her element trying to comfort Nicole as Nicole was at the thought of trying to comfort a student. "You probably won't have to talk to her. Don't worry about something that's not likely to happen."

"If not her, then someone else. It's only a matter of time until I find myself in a situation I can't handle, where I'm in way over my head. Only a matter of time," she muttered, and dropping her elbows onto the table, pressed the heels of her hands to her eyes.

"I'm getting us all another drink. That was your list of three positives for the week, and look at the result." Max swung her hand toward Nicole. "What in the world is going to happen when we share the negatives?"

When Max headed to the bar, Ellie eased Nicole's hands away from her face. "Nicole. Look at me. You're going to be fine."

"Hah! That's what people say when you're not going to be fine, but they're trying to convince you, anyway. It's what people say when they don't know what else to say."

Ellie leaned back in her chair. "You know, you're right. It's a silly thing to say, isn't it? 'You're going to be fine.' Of course, you're going to be fine, I know that, and deep down, you do too, but that doesn't help right now, does it? Let me try again."

Ellie paused for a moment and drummed her fingers on the table. "How's this? Nicole, I know that right now this seems hard. Impossible maybe, but I want you to know that I'm here to help you in whatever way I can and hopefully that provides some level of comfort. I don't know how much help I can be since I'm floundering, same as you, but together, we'll figure it out. I'm also going to tell you that after knowing you for only two weeks, it's clear to me you are incredibly strong. Stronger than you think. I know this because you're here. You're here after being *there* every day this week. You didn't run, you didn't give up, you faced every challenge, real or perceived, and powered through. And finally, I'm going to tell you to trust yourself. I know that can be hard. Believe me, I know. I've struggled with doing just that and I know what it's like to some days not trust yourself to decide what to eat for breakfast, let alone make decisions on the big things, but in the end, you are the one person you can always trust. Believe in yourself and good things will happen."

Nicole blinked, then blinked again. When Max returned with a tray of drinks, Nicole still hadn't spoken.

"Did you break her?" Max whispered to Ellie.

"I'm afraid I might have offended her." Ellie looked at Nicole. "I didn't mean to. I only wanted her to understand that she can handle this, that she's strong enough to handle whatever comes her way."

Nicole snatched a drink from the tray and gulped half of it, then she waved her finger back and forth in front of Ellie's face.

"You didn't offend me, you surprised me. It's not often I'm speechless."

"It was all true," Ellie said.

"I don't know about that," Nicole said, "but if I hold on to the parts about you helping me and the three of us being in this together, I just might make it another week."

Ellie smiled and clinked her glass with Nicole's. "You got us another teacher drink," she said to Max. "Charlie said they're strong. I should probably slow down," she added as she took another sip. "It's delicious, though, isn't it?"

"I already got us a number for a guy who drives in town. One of those ride share companies, or maybe he's independent, I don't know, but Charlie vouched for him. If we need to, we'll call."

"Who's vouching for Charlie?" Ellie asked.

In unison, they turned and looked toward the bar where Charlie was wowing a group of barely twenty-ones by twirling a bottle in each hand, then lifting them both high and pouring brightly colored liquor into the glasses on the bar. His audience giggled and clapped.

"I suppose they would," Max said, angling her thumb over her shoulder toward the girls. "I hope I was never that stupid."

"Somehow, I can't see you sitting at a bar giggling at the bartender," Nicole said.

"Good. Because I haven't."

"Okay ladies, you're up. Tell me three positives from the week," Ellie said.

"Do we still have to play this game?" Max grumbled. "I don't have any positives. Your turn, Nic."

"Yes, you do," Ellie scolded. "You told us about the boy with the two fractured wrists. You saw right through his story. That's a positive."

"If I hadn't seen through that story, not only should I never walk into a classroom again, I'd have to renounce my membership in the 'Teacher's Worst Nightmare Club' effective immediately."

"Oh, Max, you weren't really that bad, were you?" Ellie asked.

"Bad? No, I wasn't bad, I was good. I was good at getting away with whatever I wanted to get away with. I will tell you in all honesty that I never hurt anyone and never did anything blatantly illegal. As far as skipping school and later producing a note to excuse me, or being allowed to take a test late because of a 'family crisis,' or leaving school early just about every Friday for no reason other than I wanted to, I have no comment."

Ellie giggled and sipped again at her drink.

Nicole rolled her eyes, then pointed at Max. "See? This is one on a long list of things I'm afraid of. What if I have a classroom full of Maxes?"

"Maxes," Ellie repeated. "It sounds funny when you say it that way, like it's a noun you can make plural. Can you? Maxes, Maxeses, Max-is, Max is funny as all get out!" Ellie laughed at her own joke. When she picked up her glass to drink again, she found it empty. "Well, would you look at that. Huh." She shrugged and turned to Max. "Okay, two more."

Max groaned. "I don't have any more." When Ellie pursed her lips and wrinkled her forehead, Max groaned again. "Fine. I had a boy worried about being able to handle Intro to Engineering. I guess I sort of convinced him he could do it. I asked him about his favorite subject and when he told me math, I told him he was in the right place."

"That's good!" Ellie beamed at Max. "I'm sure he felt much better after talking with you. One more."

"You're going to drive me crazy, Oklahoma," Max said, but her grin softened her harsh words. "I helped another boy fix his computer. He'd completely screwed it up by slamming on a bunch of keys at the same time, and he was in a panic. I only had to press a couple of keys and it was taken care of, but he acted like I'd saved his life. He was afraid to go see 'Dragon Lady' who's in charge of the tech lab, said he heard she likes to yell. I don't know if that's true, but he seemed pretty sure he'd have to endure a lecture. Brought me a candy bar the next day as a thank you."

"Oh, Max." Ellie put her hands to her heart. "You got your first present from a student. Isn't that just the sweetest?"

"Yeah, sweet, that's what I was going for."

"You're funny, Max," Ellie said, holding her hand over her mouth as she giggled. "Okay, Nicole, your turn."

"I don't know. I can't think of a single thing I did right."

"There has to be something. Did you help a student with their computer?" Ellie asked.

"I can barely figure out my own computer."

"Okay then, how about pointing a student in the right direction when he was turned around and couldn't find a classroom?"

"No. Once I had to ask a student how to get to the art room, though. Does that count?"

"I suppose it could count," Ellie said. "Did you have a nice conversation with the student? Did you find out anything about him or her?"

"No. I didn't. And it doesn't count. I told you, I don't have any positives. Want to hear my negatives? There are a lot of those."

"We're focusing on positives, remember?" Ellie smiled and patted Nicole's hand. "I know there are some."

"Why were you looking for the art room?" Max asked.

"I needed to ask the art teacher about getting some supplies for a project the kids will be doing on local history. I let them choose, and they wanted to make it more of a visual project than a written assignment, so I wanted to see what I could do as far as providing them with materials."

Ellie threw her arms up with a whoop. "And there you have it. If that's not a positive, I don't know what is. You asked your students for feedback, you listened to their preferences, and you made a decision taking those preferences into account. They'll remember that, and it will go a long way toward forging a bond with them. Well done."

"Seems like a stretch, but if you insist, I guess I'll take it."

"Come on, two more," Max encouraged.

"I didn't yell at a kid when he deserved it."

Ellie frowned. "Nicole…"

"Well, he did deserve it. I handed out an assignment and before I could explain what I wanted them to do with it, one boy had torn and folded his paper into some crazy sort of animal shape."

Ellie nodded. "Kaede."

"Yeah, that sounds right. How'd you know?"

"He attached an origami dragon to his star. Seems to be rather talented."

"Maybe, but I had to give him a new assignment and seeing how we have to jump through hoops to actually print anything, I didn't like seeing one go to waste."

"I say we give her that one," Max said. "We won't ask if she gave the kid a dirty look, we'll just go with the fact that she didn't yell. That's two. One more, Nic."

"I guess it can count," Ellie said. She picked up her glass and tipped an ice cube into her mouth.

Nicole drew in a deep breath and blew it out slowly. "I don't know. I said hi to one of the kids from my class when I walked through the lunchroom."

"Did you use the student's name?" Max asked. "If you did, I say that's three. If not, it goes before the committee."

"I did. Callie. I'm about seventy percent sure it was correct."

Max looked at Ellie, who nodded her approval.

"Then there you have it. Three wins in only four days. Imagine what you'll accomplish next week with five days," Max said.

"Please don't remind me," Nicole moaned.

Ellie swirled the remaining couple of ice cubes in her glass. "Are y'all hungry? I'm hungry. Should we order something to eat?" She held her glass higher. "And maybe another one of these?"

"Three drinks, Oklahoma?" Max's eyebrows shot up and nearly

disappeared beneath her wave of shiny black hair.

"Is that bad? I rarely drink. A third drink seems like a lot, doesn't it? I should order a coke. Yeah, that's probably a better idea. Do y'all think they have Dr. Pepper here?"

"You best remember you're not in Oklahoma," Max said. "If you order a coke here, no one is going to ask you what kind. You'll get a Coca-Cola."

"Oh, that's right," Ellie said. "I made that mistake once already. It's all so confusing."

Nicole ignored the soda conversation. "How about this?" she said. "We each came up with three positives for the week. That equals three drinks. Do the math, ladies. I think that's the only possible solution to the problem."

Max chuckled. "And you call yourself a history teacher, Ms. Emerson. Are you angling for a math position?"

"Very funny," Nicole said. "Even a history teacher can do simple math, Miss Smarty Pants." She stuck her tongue out at Max, then grabbed her purse. "This round's on me. I'll try to find us some menus."

As soon as Nicole left for the bar, Ellie turned to Max. Keeping her voice low, her words were swirled up and swallowed in the tornado of clattering glasses, the slew of TVs broadcasting a baseball game, and the voices of the dozens of customers who had crowded into the bar.

"Why are you whispering? I can't hear a word you're saying," Max grumbled.

Ellie cast a wary eye toward the bar, then raised her voice a fraction. "I said, why do you think Nicole is here?"

"Uh, she wants a few drinks?"

"No, no, I mean, why do you think she's here in Caston? Why do you think she's teaching middle school? I get the feeling it's not what she wants to be doing."

"She's not the only one," Max mumbled.

"What?"

"Nothing." Max shoved a hand through her hair. "I don't know what to think about Nicole. You're right that she doesn't seem very happy, but then, I don't suppose I do either. It's been a rough week, El. Nic seems like the type who's used to having things come easy for her. This definitely hasn't been easy. She's probably just frustrated. And exhausted. Next week will be better."

Ellie leaned back in her chair to ponder Max's analysis. Could be, she supposed, but Ellie had a strong feeling there was more to it. Before she could ask Max anything more, Nicole returned with drinks and a stack of menus.

"Here you are, ladies, another round of Every Day's Bad at School. Or Another Bad Day at School." She shrugged. "Whatever Charlie called it. I told him to skip the fancy stir sticks and save them for the next time we're here crying in our drinks."

"Next time we'll be having one called An Awesome Day at School," Ellie said as she lifted her glass in a toast.

"Hah!" Nicole sputtered. "Doubtful," but she clicked her glass with Ellie's. Max added hers to the toast.

"These are so yummy," Ellie said, as she took a second sip.

"Let's look at the menus." Max pushed one into Ellie's free hand.

"Good idea." Ellie opened her menu and let her eyes scan the list of burgers, salads, and pasta dishes. "What sounds good?"

Ellie looked over the top of her menu at the tables around them for inspiration. The group at the closest table was sharing a pizza loaded with so many toppings, it was a wonder they could lift a slice under all the weight. At another table, an enormous platter of what looked to be a sampling of all things fried appeared to be a hit with the group of men making quick work of it. A server walked past with a tray holding sandwiches, a giant salad, and what Ellie thought was seafood pasta. Nothing she spotted piqued her interest.

Until she looked over Nicole's shoulder.

7

Ellie's shoulders went rigid, and she drew in a sharp breath. Nicole looked down at her shirt, then back at Ellie, before sneaking a quick peek over her shoulder. She fixed her eyes back on Ellie.

"What is it? What's wrong? Did I spill all over myself?" Nicole lifted the hem of her sweatshirt and studied it.

"It's a student, isn't it?" Max asked, fear in her voice. "You got all weird when you looked toward the door. Who is it? Is it someone I have in my class?"

Ellie slouched down in her seat. "It's not a student." Her eyes were glued to the man near the door. "Oh, no, not this way!" She picked up her menu and held it in front of her face.

Max and Nicole stared at her, then at each other, while Ellie hid. She shifted the menu ever so slightly and peeked around it.

"Whew." She dropped the menu back on the table. "He went the other way."

"Who went the other way?" Max asked.

"Zeke. Zeke Fahrner. He walked in here and the last thing I want to do is to have to try to carry on a sensible conversation right now." Ellie picked up her drink and drained it. "I don't think that would be pollisib...pobiss...possible." She threw her hands in the air. "See what I mean?"

"Zeke Fahrner? Here?" Nicole's head whipped around and she scanned the restaurant. "Where?"

"Please, Nicole, don't look," Ellie pleaded.

"Well, where is he? I'd like to get a look at him after all these years."

"He's on the other side of the room. He sat down in a booth with—" Ellie shifted a few inches to get a better look. "With three other people.

I think they're all men, but I can't see one of them very well."

Max put the pieces together. "The guy who took your dog. *Doctor Fahrner*. Why don't you want to talk to him?"

"I just don't."

"I thought you hardly knew him." Max tapped her finger on the table. "You know him better than you let on, don't you? What happened between the two of you?"

"Nothing happened."

"Why don't I believe you?" Max asked.

"Because you're suspicious by nature, I reckon," Ellie said.

"And I reckon sweet little Ellie is mighty upset about something and wants to keep that something all to herself. Isn't it precious the way she goes all 'Oklahoma' on us when she gets her britches in a twist, Nic?"

"Oh, knock it off," Ellie said, but she couldn't hold back her giggle. "And I don't have my britches in a twist, thank you very much."

"Hi! I'm JoJo. Have you had a chance to look at the menus and decide on something? Everything here is good, but I'm partial to the burgers. They're to die for, especially with cheese and fried onions."

Ellie hadn't noticed the bouncy redhead until she was in front of their table. She had to be in high school, no way she could be older, and it appeared whatever she might lack in experience, she was determined to make up with perkiness. She bobbed her head and sent her ponytail bouncing on her back. The smile that seemed permanently affixed to her face showed plenty of straight, white teeth that must have cost her parents a pretty penny.

"What kind of soup do you have?" Nicole asked.

"Just chicken noodle tonight. When it's this warm we don't have much call for soup, so the kitchen keeps it to one choice. If you visit us in the winter, we have lots of different, scrumptious kinds to try. My favorite is tomato basil, and even though we only offer a grilled cheese sandwich on the kids' menu, if you ask, we can make an adult version. You won't find better unless you get an invitation to my grandma's house for lunch."

When Ellie saw Max's eyes glass over and heard her mumble something about JoJo's grandmother, Ellie jumped in.

"I think I'll try one of your burgers. Cheese on mine, please, but no onions."

"That comes with fries, or you can change it to mixed vegetables or onion rings for a dollar more."

"Fries will be fine. Thank you."

"Great!" She turned to Nicole. "And what can I get for you?"

Nicole, who'd been looking over her shoulder, turned her attention to JoJo. "Ah, I don't care. Same thing she ordered," Nicole said with a wave toward Ellie.

"Two burgers. Perfect. And what sounds good to you?" she asked Max.

"Having you stop talking," Max said under her breath. Ellie heard her, but she was almost certain JoJo didn't, as the girl's smile never faltered. Ellie nudged Max under the table.

"Oh, let's make it three burgers, shall we? That sounds like fun."

"Yay!" JoJo bounced on her toes. "You will be happy with your selection, I promise. Those will be out shortly. Another round of drinks while you wait?"

"Ooh, should we?" Ellie said, but Max spoke over her. "How about some water?"

"Of course! I'll put your order in and be right back with your waters."

When JoJo bounced away, Max let out a tremendous sigh. "Did you kind of want to slap her to shut her up?"

"Max, that's not nice," Ellie said. She tried to sound serious, but ended up having to cough to keep from laughing. "She's trying hard to do a good job. Most people appreciate a friendly server."

"Friendly? Remember *Barney*? Remember the kids on that show, always cheery, always dancing and spinning around like a bunch of tops? I was just waiting for JoJo to break into a song about hamburgers."

"They did have a song for everything on *Barney*, didn't they?" Ellie said. "Nicole, did you watch *Barney*?"

"Huh?"

"I asked if you watched *Barney* when you were young."

"The purple dinosaur? Sure." She glanced over her shoulder again. "Wait. Why are you talking about *Barney*?"

"It doesn't matter," Max said. "What's got you so worked up?"

"Nothing. It's nothing."

"I think it's a certain doctor," Max said.

The jolt of jealousy that rocketed through her body came as a very curious shock to Ellie. She didn't care if Nicole was interested in Zeke, did she? Of course not, she told herself. But she didn't quite believe herself.

"No. I mean, yes, I guess in a way it is, but not in the way you're thinking. I don't even know him."

JoJo returned with their waters and chatted the entire time she placed coasters and glasses on the table. To Ellie, it was nothing but a dull rumble.

"You should go say hello," Ellie said, but even as she spoke, she had no idea why she'd made the suggestion.

Nicole finally focused on Ellie and Max. "I told you, I don't know him. Why would I want to say hello?"

"Seems like you're interested. Or curious. Or something," Max said.

"Fine. Maybe a little curious, but only because the guy is practically a legend around here. I'm curious why he's back in Caston after all that...after all this time." Nicole turned again and looked across the room. "Maybe I will go talk to him. Why not? It's not against the law to talk to someone in a bar. What's it going to hurt?"

"Maybe you should drink your water and wait until you've had something to eat. Our food should be here soon," Max said.

"I probably have time." Nicole scooted her chair back. "I want to know what brought the great Zeke Fahrner back to town. I'll bet I'm not the only one who wants to know."

"I think it might be better if you give it a few minutes," Max repeated.

The two debated long enough that Ellie spotted JoJo before Nicole could make up her mind one way or the other.

"Look, Nicole, here comes JoJo. I think she has our order." Ellie breathed a sigh of relief when JoJo skipped to their table.

"It smells so good, I wish I could join you," JoJo said as she placed the plates in front of them. "Anything else I can get you?"

"No, thank you, this looks perfect," Ellie said.

"Then enjoy. Wave at me if you need anything."

Nicole wrinkled her nose at her plate. "Why do I have a cheeseburger?"

"Because you ordered a cheeseburger," Max said.

"Why would I do that? I almost never eat cheeseburgers." She poked at the bun, then picked up a French fry and nibbled. "Hmm. I forgot how good the fries are here."

"Burgers too," Max said over the bite in her mouth. "Live a little, Nic." In response, Nicole picked up another fry.

Ellie debated whether to ask more questions about Zeke or to let it drop, hoping Nicole would do the same. Before she could award victory to either side in her internal debate, Max used a fry to point toward the bar. "Isn't that the man of the hour?"

Zeke stood at the bar, grinning and shaking hands with Charlie. It struck Ellie how good looking the doctor was. He was wearing jeans and a light blue shirt with the sleeves rolled up to just below his elbows, giving her a good look at his toned forearms. She studied his hands as best she could from a distance. Long fingers gave the impression of strength and when Ellie thought of him throwing a football, or even a stick, into the water, it fit. But they also looked like they'd be just as comfortable gliding over the keys of a piano. Maybe the combination made for the perfect surgeon's hands.

When Zeke threw his head back and laughed at something Charlie said, butterflies flitted in Ellie's stomach. So relaxed, but so in control. That was the only way she could describe him as she watched the volley between Zeke and Charlie. Charlie pointed toward Zeke's chest, said something that Charlie himself seemed to find hilarious, then jutted his chin challengingly toward Zeke. Zeke responded with a smile and a self-deprecating nod. He waited a beat, let Charlie have his laugh, then calmly said something that had Charlie scrunching his face in a scowl. The men shook hands again, and Zeke turned to go back to his table. Too late, Ellie realized he'd turned in her direction. He met her stare across the crowded room.

"Now I've done it," Ellie said as she crouched in her chair and wished herself invisible.

"Done what?" Max asked. "Did you remember you don't eat cheeseburgers either?"

"No. Look. Wait, don't look," Ellie hissed, but by the time she finished, Zeke was at their table.

"Ellie. Nice to see you again."

"Yes, you too. Zeke, these are my friends." Ellie put her hand on Max's arm. "Max Simmons," she nodded toward Nicole, "and Nicole Emerson. They teach with me at the middle school. We're celebrating after finishing our first week."

Zeke gave a low whistle. "I see. You know, I have a friend who survived Navy SEAL hell week. I have a feeling what you three just accomplished could rival his feat. The first week of middle school. Wow." Zeke shook his head and took a deep breath. "As a former middle school student, let me extend my apologies on behalf of former middle schoolers everywhere. We're a miserable lot and those of you who are willing to brave our erratic mood swings and irrational, narcissistic behavior day in and day out deserve sainthood."

Ellie started to laugh, then snapped her mouth shut. Zeke looked ready to say something, probably to ask what was wrong, but Max saved Ellie from having to come up with an answer to whatever he might say.

"St. Max has a nice ring to it." She held out her hand. "Nice to meet you, Zeke."

"Likewise." Zeke turned toward Nicole. "And a pleasure to meet you, Ms. Emerson."

Nicole paused and scrutinized Zeke before extending her hand to meet his. "Yes," she managed.

Zeke eyed her curiously for a moment before turning back to Ellie. "You're enjoying your evening, then?"

"We are. We were hoping to compare notes, relax, and bolster one another for the week ahead, far away from anyone we knew. We've accomplished that, more or less."

Ellie could scarcely believe the rude words and even ruder tone had come from her mouth. She was horrified, but told herself it was for the best.

Max made no attempt to hide her shock. She turned her entire body toward Ellie, shielding her face from Zeke. Her jaw dropped, and she lifted her shoulders in a quick, 'what gives' sort of jerk. Even Nicole managed to tear her eyes away from Zeke long enough to cast a curious glance Ellie's way.

For his part, Zeke smiled, but it was a forced smile, frozen in place, and Ellie noted with no small amount of shame that there was a mix of confusion and hurt in his eyes.

"Then I'll leave you to your discussion," Zeke said, recovering his poise. "Enjoy your weekend. You've certainly earned it."

As soon as he was a few steps away, Max flew at Ellie. "What in the world was that? Wow, El, you may as well have slapped him and kicked him to the curb. You were...well, you were rude. I never dreamed you had that kind of rude in you."

Ellie dropped her head. She hadn't ever had that kind of rude in her. Max was right about that. At least, not before. Now? Apparently now Ellie Hawthorne was capable of behavior that would send her mother straight to the emergency room with much more than a case of the vapors.

"I didn't mean to be rude, I just wanted...I thought...I don't know. I'm not sure why he came over here, and I don't know that I particularly liked it."

"Why not?" Max asked. "He seems like a nice guy. He was just being friendly. Or don't people in Oklahoma talk to friends when they run into one another in public?"

"Very funny. Of course, we talk to friends, but I wouldn't call Zeke a friend."

"Okay, an acquaintance, although I'd argue the incident with the dogs makes you more than just acquaintances. If he was half as upset as you were, I'd say you suffered a traumatic event together, and that definitely makes you more than just acquaintances."

Max grinned and Ellie relaxed a fraction. "I don't know that he was quite as upset as I was, although at the lake he said he wasn't sure if he'd take Bowie back to Top Dog."

Ellie cringed when she heard her words aloud. Nicole and Max both pounced.

"At the lake?" Nicole said at the same time Max nearly shouted, "What lake?"

Ellie pinched the bridge of her nose. Three drinks had been a mistake. Any happy and carefree she'd felt a little while ago was rapidly giving way to an anything-but-happy headache.

"It's nothing. I ran into him at Crooked Lake the other day when I took Boomer for a swim. We chatted for a few minutes. End of story."

"No, I'd say that's just the beginning of the story," Nicole said. "Max is right. He was far more than just an acquaintance after what happened with the dogs, but if you spent time together at the lake, talking and playing with your dogs, then it would have been strange if he hadn't come over to say hello. Unless, of course, something happened at the lake that made you want to avoid him."

Max nodded her agreement, and both women looked expectantly at Ellie. She wilted under their scrutiny.

"Nothing happened, and I'm not looking for anything to happen, so I don't want him to get the wrong idea." Ellie told herself she was right, and that she hadn't been rude for no reason. There was no time, no place, in her life for a man, and she needed to make that clear.

"I still think there's something you're not telling us," Max said, "but if you're determined to keep it to yourself, so be it."

Ellie jumped at her chance to deflect the attention to someone else. "Nicole, how come you didn't introduce yourself as being from Caston and tell Zeke that you knew him?"

"Because I don't know him. I've been trying to tell you both that. I knew of him, once upon a time. There's a big difference. And I didn't want to be on the receiving end of one of those glassy-eyed, panicked stares where some guy is desperately trying to place you when he hasn't a clue in the world who you are, then finally just smiles and nods like he remembers that you have this whole history together. It's insulting."

Ellie let Nicole's words percolate for a minute, trying to decide if Nicole was angry, hurt, or simply fed up with being tied to Caston. When Ellie couldn't come to a conclusion, she called it a mix of the three and decided the next change of topic needed to be something completely unrelated to Zeke Fahrner. When she found she had to hide a yawn behind her hand, that change of topic came easy.

"You know what? I'm tired. This was a good idea and hopefully y'all feel a little better about the past week and the weeks ahead. I know I do, but right now I need to go home."

Max stretched her arms over her head. "I have to agree with Oklahoma. I'm beat. I don't know that I even have a run in me tonight. Sitting in front of the TV sounds about as ambitious as I'm going to get."

"Tonight helped. At least, a little. Thank you, both of you," Nicole said. "I honestly don't know what I would have done if I'd gone home tonight and had all weekend to think about everything that was so wrong and so hard this past week. You've convinced me not to hang up my teacher hat quite yet."

"Oh, good." Ellie leaned over and hugged Nicole. "You're going to be an outstanding teacher, I just know it." She turned toward Max. "Both of you. You care. If you didn't, it wouldn't have bothered you that you felt like the past week was so full of problems, and that's the most important ingredient. If a teacher cares, she tries, and she triumphs. Stay strong, ladies."

Max twisted her face in a grimace. "You were a cheerleader, weren't you?"

"Well, actually…"

Max slapped a hand against her cheek. "For the love of everything holy, Nic, we've got a cheerleader on our hands."

While Max peppered Ellie with questions about her days as a cheerleader, they all ate more of their food, drained their water glasses along with the refills JoJo was more than happy to provide, then realized, all at the same time, they hadn't called for a ride.

"It's a small town," Ellie rationalized. "Maybe the driver isn't busy yet at this time of the evening. Try him, Max."

Max shot off a text to the number Charlie had given her. After a few minutes, she got a reply. Her face fell as she read it. "Forty-five minutes to an hour until he can be here."

"An hour? I'm not waiting an hour," Nicole said. "I'm going to go ask Charlie if there's anyone else we can try."

While she went to the bar, Ellie and Max gathered their bags and went to wait by the door. Nicole's face gave them their answer well before she was close enough to tell them out loud.

"There's only one other person who drives, a woman named Rain."

Nicole pointed none too discretely to a woman sitting in a booth. She wore a tie-dyed T-shirt, giant aviator sunglasses, and more long, beaded necklaces than Ellie could count. Her two companions were dressed similarly. "Charlie said she's been there since three o'clock. Evidently, today's the birthday of the original drummer of the Grateful Dead, which makes today some sort of holy day. One of several throughout the year. As you can see, she won't be driving anyone anywhere any time soon."

As they watched, Rain and her friends lifted their glasses in a toast. Their faces were solemn. One of them spoke and the other two bowed their heads before all three looked up and said loudly enough to carry over the din in the bar, "Peace, love, and The Dead."

"No, not any time soon," Max said.

Ellie, Max, and Nicole wandered to the parking lot.

"I could say I feel okay, because I do, and that it's not that far, because it isn't, and that I could drive," Max began, "but instead I'll say it's not that far and we could walk, because that's the responsible thing to say."

Ellie looked down at her pink skirt and matching heels. It wouldn't be the first time she walked in a dress and heels, but she wasn't eager to repeat the performance right then.

Nicole groaned. "No way. I'm too tired. My house is at least four miles from here."

"Mine's only about three," Max said. "If you can make it there, you can crash on my couch."

"This is one of the bad parts about not knowing anyone in town, isn't it? At home, there was always someone around to help. Nicole, I don't suppose—"

"No." She left no room for negotiation.

"Ooo-kaay," Ellie mumbled.

"We could walk to the park and wait around for a while. We should be okay to drive in a couple of hours," Max said.

"Ugh," Nicole groaned again. "Sit in the park for two hours? We really should have planned better. Next time—"

Footsteps and a cheerful greeting interrupted Nicole.

"Calling it a night, ladies?"

The three turned in the direction of the voice, but Ellie didn't need to see Zeke in order to know it was him. He smiled at them while he idly twirled his car keys around a finger of the hand that hung down at his side. Everything about him, Ellie thought with no small amount of annoyance, was cool, collected, and in charge.

"Sure," Nicole muttered, "after we sit in the park for two hours."

"What about the park?" Zeke asked.

They looked at one another, no one wanting to admit they were stranded in the parking lot of a bar at six o'clock in the evening. Finally, after a sigh, Max spoke.

"We all agreed it's not wise to drive, so we were going to wander around the park for a while until it's not so unwise."

Ellie watched Zeke's jaw muscles twitch as he fought his grin. "I see," he said. "I have an early morning, so I stuck with water. I'm more than happy to offer you a ride."

"Oh, no, that's not necessary." Ellie felt panic bubble in her belly and sweat bead on her forehead. No way was she going to get into Zeke's car and let him drive her home as if she were some sort of foolish teenager who had to call Daddy to bail her out.

"It's no trouble," Zeke said. "Come on. I have a feeling the park doesn't hold a lot of appeal."

"It does not. Thank you, Zeke." Nicole was the first to break rank and take a few steps toward Zeke. "Point me in the right direction."

"The black one right over there," Zeke said as he raised his arm and pointed at a shiny sedan near the back of the lot.

"Perfect," Nicole said. She was off before Ellie could get a word out. Max followed with, "Thanks," aimed in Zeke's direction. Ellie heard the beep when Zeke unlocked his car doors with the key fob that was still dangling from his fingers.

"Ellie?" Zeke asked when she remained rooted in place.

"You don't have to do this. I'm sure you have better ways to spend an evening away from the hospital."

"This will only take a few minutes of my evening."

"Still…"

"Come on. It smells like rain. You don't want to get caught in a downpour."

Ellie looked up at the sky. Heavy, grey clouds churned and tumbled over one another. Thirty minutes, at most, Ellie thought, until Zeke's prediction came true.

"It looks like my friends have already made themselves comfortable." She could see Max and Nicole's heads in the backseat of Zeke's car. She jerked her head in a nod. "Thank you."

Ellie spun on her heel and marched as quickly as possible without actually running toward the car. If she got there far enough ahead of Zeke, she'd take a minute to tell Nicole and Max what she thought of them both choosing the backseat and leaving her to sit in the front, and far too close to Zeke, but it wasn't to be. His long strides outpaced her, and he was a half step in front of her when she reached the passenger door. He swung it open for her before she could reach for the handle.

"Thank you." She was getting tired of having reasons to thank him.

Once Zeke was settled, he turned his head to the backseat. "Where to?"

"If you head toward Main," Nicole began, "you can drop me first. I'm a few miles out, right off Main on Maple. It seems my place is the farthest, so you can double back and drop off Max. She's on Third Street. Ellie can direct you to her place from there."

"Sounds like a plan," Zeke said, and started the engine.

Ellie turned and frowned at Nicole. "Got that figured out quickly, didn't you?"

Nicole lifted one shoulder. "It's the route that makes the most sense."

Ellie wanted to ask how Nicole knew that since Ellie'd never told Nicole where she lived, but decided she'd save that conversation for a time when Zeke wasn't seated eighteen inches from her. Instead, she put on her seat belt, stared out the windshield, and wished for green lights.

A few minutes later, when it was just the two of them in the car, Ellie realized it was her turn to direct Zeke. She also realized with all the turns they'd taken, and with all the time she'd spent thinking of ways to get back at Nicole and Max, she didn't know where she was.

"My house is on Valley Lane. I think that's...Um...If you go..."

"I know where Valley Lane is," Zeke said. "I had a good friend in high school who lived on that street."

They waited at a red light for what seemed like hours. With no cars coming in the opposite direction, there was nothing to distract from the fact that they were sitting there, next to one another, in complete silence.

"Did I say or do something to upset you?" Zeke finally asked.

"No, of course not."

"I feel like I did. First, the other night at the lake, it seemed as though you couldn't get away fast enough. Tonight at Scooter's, at your table, you seemed uncomfortable. Then again in the parking lot, I got the feeling you would have preferred walking in the rain to accepting a ride from me."

As if on cue, the first fat raindrops slapped against the windshield.

"I didn't want to put you out, that's all."

Ellie kept her focus straight ahead, but watched Zeke out of the corner of her eye. He opened his mouth, but the light turned green and he closed it again without speaking. Zeke navigated his way through side streets Ellie hadn't ever seen. Before she could think of anything to say to break the awkward silence, they were turning onto Valley Lane.

"Which one is yours?"

"Right up there, the yellow one on the left."

"Really? The yellow one? The Bryant place?"

"Yes, Bryant, that was the name of the previous owners. You knew them?"

"Grandparents of that friend of mine who lived down the road. John and Shirley Bryant. Wonderful people. I was at their place a time or two with Brian. He'd stop in to say hi, to check on them. His friends were always welcome. Mrs. Bryant made the best banana bread I've ever tasted."

"Brian Bryant?"

Zeke laughed. "No, Brian Vaughn. His mom was a Bryant. That's where his first name came from."

"The house was vacant when I looked at it, and I dealt only with an attorney at the closing. The Bryants, they…"

"They both passed away about a year ago. Shirley first, John less than a month later. One of those stories you hear about, married for almost sixty years and when the time came, one couldn't live without the other."

Ellie turned to gaze out the window, not seeing, and not hearing the long sigh that fluttered through her lips. "So sad, but so sweet, in a way. To have that kind of love, a love that endures for decades, it's a wonder. A beautiful wonder."

The car rocked and with a jolt, Ellie realized they were in her driveway. She felt Zeke's eyes on her, and hated how nervous it made her. She dug in her bag for the umbrella she knew she'd tucked inside before she'd left home that morning. Papers crumpled and her water bottle sloshed as she rummaged, searching for the elusive umbrella. She was ready to face what was now a downpour without it when her fingers closed around the silky nylon fabric. Yanking it from the depths of her bag sent papers flying.

"Darn it," Ellie muttered as she bent forward to retrieve those that had fluttered to the floor. That's when she whacked her head on the dashboard. Her next, 'Darn it,' was a little louder.

She felt a hand on her arm. "Ellie." Just one word, two little syllables, but it held a world of comfort and calm. Ellie blew out a breath.

"I'm sorry, Zeke, it's been a long day. A long week. I'm not normally such a train wreck."

"Of course not. I wish I could undo whatever it is I did to make you so uncomfortable. I wish…"

When Zeke paused, Ellie dared a look at him, unsure of what to say, but with one blink, Zeke pulled himself together and the moment passed.

"I hope you enjoy your weekend. I'm sure next week will be better."

She pulled on the door handle but opened the door only a crack. "Thank you, Zeke." Then she was outside. She shoved the door closed, fought with her umbrella, and made a dash through the puddles to her front door. Zeke's car idled in the driveway. He was going to wait until she was inside. As much as she wanted him to leave, she was touched by his gesture.

Ellie fumbled her key into the lock, then opened the door a crack and caught a charging Boomer by the collar. She clipped on his leash, then swung the door wide to let the dog into the yard. Ellie stood in the doorway, one eye on her dog and the other on the car easing out of her driveway and down the road.

Was he headed home? Was someone there waiting for him? Ellie watched until the tail lights disappeared, swallowed by the gloom. The umbrella fell to her side and rain splattered her cheeks. She closed her eyes and tilted her face to the sky until she could no longer tell which were raindrops and which were teardrops.

8

The weekend turned out to be nearly as busy as the week. There were errands to run on Saturday, as well as time spent prepping for the coming week, getting Boomer outside to play as much as possible in between the rain showers, and texting with Nicole and Max. In her first texts, Ellie scolded her friends for leaving her to ride in the front seat with Zeke, but then devoted her next texts to reiterating the positives from the past week and bolstering them for the one coming. On Sunday, when the sun finally admitted defeat and the dark rain clouds won that day's battle, she threw down a tarp, taped off the woodwork, and opened the paint can she'd had since the day she moved in.

The house's second bathroom was an affront to the senses. At least to her senses. While most of the house had been repainted, re-carpeted, and updated, this bathroom had been overlooked. Whether the previous owners had liked it the way it was or just hadn't gotten to it, Ellie didn't know, but she preferred to think it had been next on their to-do list.

A couple of weeks earlier, in what turned out to be a day-long battle wielding a spray bottle, sponge, putty knife, and more patience than she thought she possessed, she had removed the ugliest wallpaper border she'd ever seen. Gold and green with flamboyant birds sporting long, feathered tails perched in all manners of fruit trees, Ellie had half expected to hear it play *The Twelve Days of Christmas* every time she looked at it. Now, with the border gone, the remaining gold paint begged for a facelift.

When she'd been unable to choose between the dozens and dozens of grey shades, she'd gone with the name that charmed her. After a few strokes with the roller, she decided Hedwig Grey looked perfect on her walls. Green floor tile remained, but she'd have to call in an expert, as she didn't think she was ready to tackle that job.

By Sunday evening she was beat, but the bathroom was painted, and she'd only thought of Zeke about a hundred times instead of a thousand. As tired as she was, her nerves were working overtime. Once she'd let Boomer outside a final time and gotten herself ready for bed, Ellie picked up her guitar.

She hummed along as she lovingly strummed *Oklahoma Sky*. Maybe not Miranda Lambert's most well-known song, but one of Ellie's favorites. She slipped seamlessly into a Carrie Underwood hit. She tried to pick up the tempo with *Grandma's Feather Bed,* a song she'd played dozens of times for her brothers and sisters and that never failed to make her smile, but her heart wasn't in it. Without trying, almost without realizing she was doing it, her fingers played the chords and her voice breathed out the words.

I wonder if you know what it feels like
When he smiles and takes your hand
I wonder if you know what it feels like
To be in the arms of the perfect man

I wonder if you know what it feels like
To sit and gaze at the stars
To hear him say 'I love you'
I love you just the way you are...

Ellie's throat closed, her hands stilled. She carefully leaned her guitar against the wall at the head of her bed, then slid down and let her pillow soak up the tears that rolled down her cheeks.

The rain continued into Monday morning. According to the forecast, it would do so most of the coming week. Knowing Boomer would be stir-crazy by the time she got home, and dreading a walk in the rain and mud, Ellie decided to put the unfortunate event of last week behind her and take Boomer back to Top Dog.

It was raining when she pulled into the parking lot. Ellie knew she'd never be able to juggle Boomer, her bag, and the car door while trying to open an umbrella, so she pulled up the hood on her jacket and hoped for the best.

Immediately stepping into an ankle-deep puddle definitely wasn't the best. Sighing, she opened the door for Boomer. While she may hate the rain and the puddles and mud and everything that went with it, Boomer loved it. He loved splashing through the puddles, he loved turning his head up to the sky and snapping at the raindrops, and he loved letting the rain soak his fur then shaking and sending droplets flying to soak everything within a six-foot radius, which was exactly what he did as Ellie dragged him into Top Dog. As she wiped water from her eyes, Boomer danced in place and lapped at the puddle forming beneath him.

"Rain or shine, he finds a way to have fun, doesn't he?"

Ellie didn't have to clear the water from her eyes to know who was behind her. Somehow, his voice had already become familiar. What wasn't familiar—or welcome—was the flutter in her stomach.

"Zeke. Hello." She looked down at Boomer who had moved on to happily sniffing Zeke's shoes. "Yes, he does."

Zeke lowered his voice. "It seems we both decided to give Top Dog another chance. How are you feeling about leaving Boomer here?"

"Okay, I think. I'll be sure to take a good look at him when I pick him up, though. You?"

"Okay. Like you said last week, I can't imagine they'll make the same mistake twice with our dogs."

Ellie nodded. "It was the rain that made the decision for me. It's hard when he can't get outside and burn off some of his energy."

"I know what you mean. Bowie and I ran in the rain yesterday. It was miserable. For me, anyway. Bowie didn't seem to mind."

"They should be tired when they come home tonight." Ellie didn't know what else to say, so she inched toward the counter. "Have a good day," she said over her shoulder just as Zeke's phone rang.

Ellie checked in Boomer with Marin who looked terrified during the entire process. Ellie tried to reassure her, but Marin didn't seem capable of speaking except to apologize over and over. Ellie stopped listening to the apologies when she overheard Zeke.

"No, Blake, it's okay. You get better. Don't worry about Bowie." Ellie turned and saw Zeke rub his hand over his eyes. "I'm sure. Get some rest and we'll talk soon."

Zeke shoved his phone in his jacket pocket and looked up at the ceiling as he drew in a long breath, then blew it out, puffing out his cheeks and ruffling his hair.

Marin had Boomer's leash and was heading to the back with him.

"Marin? Would you grab Bowie for me, please? Plans changed and I have to take him back home."

"Um, okay, but I promise we won't make a mistake again. We'll take real good care of Bowie."

"I know that. This is just a change in plans."

Marin nodded uncertainly as she shouldered open the door to the back.

"Is everything okay?" Ellie asked when they were alone.

"Fine. At least it will be. Blake, a neighbor who sometimes helps me out when I have a long day, is sick and can't pick up Bowie this evening. I won't be done at the hospital until after they close here and I have to be back early tomorrow morning."

"Have you ever left Bowie here overnight? They offer that, I think."

"I haven't. I'd do that, but Bowie is supposed to come with me to the hospital tomorrow. I promised a few kids, one in particular, a visit. If Bowie spends the night here, I won't be able to get him early enough in the morning in order to take him with me."

"So, what are you going to do with him?"

"I'll take him back home."

"But you'll be gone all day and well into the evening from the sound of things. You can leave him alone that long?"

Zeke shrugged. "I haven't before, but there's a first time for everything. He'll be okay."

Zeke checked his watch and looked anxiously toward the door. It was Ellie's turn to look toward the ceiling as if the answer would be there.

"I'll take him," she blurted out. "I'll pick him up tonight when I pick up Boomer." The struggle to keep from hyperventilating at the thought was real.

Zeke smiled. "No, Ellie. I appreciate the offer, but no. I can't ask you to do that."

"You didn't ask. I offered."

"Well, then I can't accept your offer."

"Of course you can. I owe you one after Friday. Let me help you."

"Ellie, two dogs? In the rain? After a long day at work? No."

"Zeke, Bowie home alone? With no way to get outside? For sixteen hours? No."

Zeke grinned. "Well played. Still, thank you, but no. I'll figure out something."

"You already have. I'll pick up Bowie, you come get him when you're off work. Easy as that."

But it wouldn't be easy, Ellie knew. It would likely be hell, but Ellie felt some sort of sense of responsibility, duty, something to Zeke. Or maybe to Bowie, she wasn't sure. Either way, she wanted to help them both.

Zeke looked as if he might be starting to cave. His head tilted ever so slightly and he studied her. "Two big dogs. How will you get them in the car?"

"One at a time, I suppose. One of them, at least, behaves. The other, well, I'm used to him."

This time, Zeke laughed.

"Here's Bowie, Dr. Fahrner."

Bowie sat at Marin's side, looking confused at the change in events.

"Actually," Zeke looked back at Ellie, who nodded. "I guess he's staying. Sorry about the confusion. Ms. Hawthorne will pick him up when she comes for Boomer."

"Oh." Marin looked at Ellie. "You'll be taking both Boomer and Bowie home?" Ellie figured Marin was mentally composing her instructions to leave for whomever had the evening shift, leaving no room for error or misinterpretation. Boomer and Bowie would be in good hands.

"Yes. I'll be here around four o'clock."

"Okay, then I guess I'll take Bowie to play." Marin backed away from them as if waiting for the next change of plans.

"Four o'clock," Zeke said. "I won't be able to get to your house until after nine. You're sure about this?"

Of course not, but that was beside the point. "Yes. I'll be fine."

They exchanged phone numbers, Zeke gave Ellie a few quick instructions, and then they were off in opposite directions.

Facing middle schoolers, Ellie realized, suddenly seemed like the easiest part of her day.

It really wasn't *that* bad. Sure, getting them both in the car, then trying to drive home with Boomer nearly losing his mind over the fact that there was another dog in the back seat with him, getting them both inside, reasonably dried off, and fed had been a challenge, and Ellie had resigned herself to grubby clothes and a ponytail, but it wasn't *that* bad. Once the initial excitement (on Boomer's part) had worn off, and once the entire house was inspected and apparently deemed acceptable (on Bowie's part), things had settled down and both dogs had staked out their spots and fallen asleep. For the last couple of hours, things hadn't been *that* bad.

Ellie managed to get some lesson planning done. The next installment of 'Adventures with Boomer' had written itself, so after snapping a couple of pictures and uploading them to her computer, she was ready for the next day. She turned on the TV and flipped through channels while she waited for Zeke.

He'd called once and texted twice, and Ellie had assured him things were under control. They hadn't been, at least not when she'd gotten the first text, and she'd had to sneak into the bathroom and close the door to block out the noise when he'd called, but she hadn't been forced to lie by the last text. All in all, it wasn't *that* bad.

Nothing she found on TV held her interest, so she turned on some music and grabbed her computer to search for bathroom tile. She didn't know when she'd get to it, but there was no harm in looking.

Except that it was overwhelming. So many choices. Why did there have to be so many choices? Ceramic, porcelain, marble…how was she supposed to know what kind of tile she wanted? To say nothing of colors. If she thought there'd been a lot of different shades of grey paint, there seemed to be even more varieties of tile that were at least partly grey.

Then she made the mistake of moving from the home improvement stores' websites to the home makeover gurus' websites. Should she pull out the old tub and shower combo and replace it with a soaking tub? Maybe a clawfoot tub? Those were kind of cool, but she probably needed a shower, and the hand-held shower wand didn't seem practical. Or maybe no tub? Maybe a larger shower with multiple shower heads, a steam option, a built-in bench. Page after page of stunning before and after photos had her dreaming and forgetting about the second bathroom, instead imagining what she could do with the master bath.

She drooled over rooms that looked almost like spas, with stacks of fluffy white towels, candles, soft, recessed lighting, incredible waterfall faucets, and gorgeous tile on the floor and walls. She acknowledged she didn't have room for a fireplace and let go of that dream. But maybe some open shelves, and a vanity with lots of light, complete with a cute chair where she could sit to do her hair and make-up, with all her things stored in the custom drawers and cabinets.

Ellie was lost in fantasies of relaxing in her soon-to-be oasis of calm when both dogs barked a second before the doorbell rang. Flying to her feet and smoothing her hand over her hair, Ellie scampered to the door with the dogs at her heels.

Once she opened the door and Bowie spotted Zeke, the dog quivered from head to tail. His tail wagged and his front paws lifted a couple of inches off the ground as if he wanted, more than anything, to jump and greet Zeke, but his training had him fighting those wants. It was a marvel to watch.

"I cannot believe how well-behaved he is," Ellie said. "Boomer would have knocked me over by this point."

"I can't take all the credit. Or much of the credit. I took him to a trainer who was a miracle worker."

Boomer decided it would be a good time to play. He ran out into the yard, rolled in the grass, picked up two tennis balls, and ran back inside, dropping them at Ellie's feet, but not before he shook and sprayed everyone and everything around him.

Zeke surreptitiously wiped the water from his face, then added, "I could give you her name, if you're interested."

Ellie sighed and reached for a towel to wipe down not only her dog but her walls and floor as well. "Come in," she said to Zeke, "I'll grab Bowie's leash."

"I hope Bowie wasn't too much trouble," Zeke called after her. "I feel guilty about leaving you with two dogs to care for, especially in this weather."

"Bowie was an angel," Ellie said when she returned with Bowie's leash. "He's no trouble at all. Despite the rain and the mud, I let the two of them out in the back yard for a while. It's fenced so they could run a bit, but both of them seemed tuckered out after a day at Top Dog."

"I never dreamed what a godsend day care would be on days like this. Bowie is so tired when he comes home, all he wants to do is sleep." Zeke looked toward the back of Ellie's house. "I didn't realize your backyard was fenced. Another godsend, I would imagine." He smiled and his dimples creased his cheeks.

"I had it done before I moved in. An expense when I wasn't looking for one, but aside from not having a fence, this house was perfect for us. It's definitely been worth it."

Zeke nodded, and the conversation stalled.

"Well," he began, "I should get going. Early day tomorrow and since Bowie's coming with me, there's a b-a-t-h in his immediate future."

Ellie chuckled. "He must like b-a-t-h-s about as much as Boomer. For as much as Boomer loves the lake, the rain, the snow, even the wet yard, he sure throws a fit about a b–, about those." Ellie patted Boomer's head. "Do you take Bowie to the hospital often? Does someone else handle him while he's there if you're working?"

"Not too often. Unfortunately, I don't have the time, but I take him when I can. He loves the kids, they love him, it's good for everyone involved. And no, I only take him when I can be with him. My shift doesn't start until ten tomorrow morning, so I'll take Bowie over early, let him visit, then get him back home before I report for duty."

Ellie was starting to get a picture of how trying Zeke's schedule must be. And how dedicated he must be. "That makes your day extra long. When do you rest?"

"I find time, but I've gotten used to going without. Goes with the territory."

"Did you always want to be a doctor?" The question was out before she had time to think it through. She'd told herself theirs would be a strictly dog-related, business sort of relationship. No personal questions, no friendly small talk, nothing that might hint at any type of relationship that went beyond seeing one another at Top Dog and maybe occasionally helping one another out with the dogs.

Zeke took a while to answer, something Ellie found odd as she'd expected an emphatic and immediate yes. His lack of response had her studying him. His friendly, relaxed facial expression and posture disappeared, and he seemed to hold tension in every muscle. His eyes were far away, his jaw clenched. She should have kept her mouth shut.

"I always wanted to be a teacher. You know the kid that wants to play school but always has to be the teacher? That was me. I had a playroom full of desks, a chalkboard, even some old textbooks. My brothers and sisters told me I was bossy, but I told them I was only being a good teacher."

Ellie clipped Bowie's leash to his collar and handed the end to Zeke. If he wanted one, he had an out. Instead, he raised his eyebrows and grinned.

"Are you wondering if I'll say I always wanted to play doctor?"

Ellie drew in a sharp breath. "No!" She had to look away, so busied herself with a few drops of water she found on the floor. "That's not what I meant," she added when she was certain he could no longer see her face because she knew it had to be as red as Boomer's collar.

Zeke chuckled. "Thank you again for taking care of Bowie. If there's ever a time you need a hand with Boomer, I hope you'll ask."

Ellie couldn't imagine Zeke having time to help, but she appreciated the offer. "Thanks. Have a good night." Ellie leaned over and nuzzled Bowie. "And you have fun with your hospital visit tomorrow."

"Good night, Ellie. See ya, Boomer."

With a wave, Zeke was out the door, jogging through the rain to his car. Ellie watched as he loaded Bowie into the car, turned and waved again, then backed out of her driveway. This time as she watched his tail lights fade into the darkness, she wondered why her question had been such a difficult one for him.

9

"Do you know anyone around town who does tile work?" Ellie asked Nicole later that week over lunch. The teachers' lounge was deserted except for the two of them. "And where is everyone?"

"Max had some phone calls to make over lunch. Appointments or something. I heard Cindy and Bill talking about grading papers and how they were already behind. I think being that it's the second week of school, work is piling up and a lot of the teachers are choosing to work through lunch." A look of resignation settled on Nicole's face. "I'm giving my students their first test on Friday. I suppose I'll be hiding out in my room soon too. Why do you want a tile person?"

"I have a bathroom with really ugly green tile. I want to tear it out and replace it. And when I say 'I want to tear it out and replace it' I mean I want to hire someone to do it. I managed to paint last weekend, but tiling? That I can't do. I'd like to get an idea of what it's going to cost. Do you have anyone you can recommend?"

"Yes, I know someone." Nicole smiled and Ellie realized it was the first time she could recall Nicole smiling a genuine smile about anything that had to do with Caston. "Jed. Jed Erickson. He can do tile work, or just about any work you need done, and he'll treat you fairly. Tell him I gave him your name and he'll probably give you a deal." Nicole was still smiling.

"How do you know Jed?"

"He lived next door when I was growing up. He raised six boys, coached countless baseball teams, even after his boys were grown, and never stopped wishing for a daughter. Jed was like a second father to me. He owned a construction company which he turned over to a couple of his sons a few years back. Jed still hangs around the office offering his advice, wanted or not, but he also does odd jobs for anyone who asks. I think his boys like it when he's busy so he's not spending all his time looking over their shoulders. And last I heard, he has eight granddaughters, and not a single grandson."

"If he's retired, maybe the job is too much for him. Do you think he does it because he enjoys it, or because he can't say no?"

"It might be a little of both, but if he really didn't want to work, he'd say so. He retired young, mostly to give his boys the chance to run the business, so don't worry about him being too old or too frail or anything like that." Nicole reached in her bag, pulled out her phone, and tapped at it. "There. I sent you his number. I'll call him tonight and tell him you might get in touch."

"Thank you. I'd appreciate that. I like the idea of going with someone you know. Hiring someone to do work in my house based on references that may or may not be legitimate is a bit unnerving."

"You can trust Jed. You should know he likes to bake. If you hire him, count on a pie or two, and fresh-from-the-oven chocolate chip cookies at least once."

"He sounds too good to be true."

"He is. Believe me, he is."

With her sixth graders having selected their first novels of the year and now settled into their book club groups, it had been a day for familiarizing themselves with the discussion outline and note-taking sheets. They'd had some time to read and to become accustomed to watching their stories for literary devices.

With only one hour to go to wrap up her second week as a middle school teacher, Ellie felt pretty good about the way things were going. She'd already fallen into a rhythm as far as her daily routine, which meant she wasn't fretting every minute of the day. It may not go smoothly all day, every day, but having a plan, a sort of outline for her day, made it easier. Kind of like her students and their discussion outlines. Ellie smiled. She could do this.

Then her seventh graders arrived.

Kira was in tears, though she tried to hide it by keeping her head down and walking directly to her desk. That was Ellie's first clue. Kira never went straight to her seat. There were far too many girls to either fawn over her or cower from her, and far too many boys to flirt with, and Kira made it a point to take advantage of every moment. Sara, Josie, and Anna came into the room in a cluster, so close together Ellie wondered how they could walk without tripping over one another. Their fierce whispers carried to the front of the room, though Ellie couldn't make out the words.

The boys, at least the boys that Ellie had determined traveled in the same circles as Kira and her friends, stayed in the hall. Strange, because they, too, rarely passed up an opportunity to either mercilessly tease one another or peek at the girls when they thought their glances wouldn't be detected. They were always detected.

But today, things were definitely off-kilter. Even those students who interacted little with the group in question sensed a disturbance in the force and had their heads together, whispering. Ellie's plan for the day had been to have the students get into groups and play a game with synonyms and antonyms that would test their vocabulary skills. Since they'd wrapped up their first short unit on persuasive writing and Ellie didn't want to start a new unit until Monday, she'd intended the game day as a reward. Based on what she saw in front of her, it would be more of a punishment.

The bell rang. Most students took their seats, some of the whispering quieted, but the group of boys in the hall didn't move.

"Jax, Ethan, Kellan, that was the bell. Take your seats, please."

Kellan and Jax crossed the threshold into the classroom, but it was as if their heads were on swivels. From Ethan to Kira, back to Ethan, then to Josie, and back and forth and back and forth. Ethan acted as though a step across that threshold would cost him everything. He took a step, then drew back, then took another tentative step before sprinting to his desk. Through it all, Kira kept her head down, her long brown hair falling in a veil and effectively hiding her face.

Ellie was out of her element. Before everything happened and her life was turned upside down, whenever she'd thought about her future as a teacher, she'd known enough not to discount arguments, scuffles, and hurt feelings. But she'd planned for arguments over the purple marker, over a coveted spot in the story circle, or about whose turn it was to be first in line. When it came to affairs of the teenage heart, her planning was woefully lacking. It was tempting to ignore it all, to forget about the word game and instead show the video she'd planned for Monday introducing the upcoming nonfiction unit. Seeing as it was the last hour of the day, though, and that the kids would head to their lockers and then their buses, there would be ample time for a blowup if whatever was going on was left to fester. There was that incident that occurred a few years ago, the one the superintendent himself had discussed at orientation. Ellie took a deep breath.

"Is everything okay?"

Silence.

"Did something happen before class? Earlier today?"

Silence. Just some quick glances split about evenly between Kira and Ethan.

"We have time if there's something we need to talk about."

A snort. Ellie thought it came from behind that veil of hair. And a mumbled, 'Talk about. Right,' from somewhere off to her left.

"Or, if it's a matter that's better handled outside of class, I can excuse those who need to speak with a counselor."

More silence, but no shortage of nasty looks cast from one side of the room to the other.

Ellie debated, then decided she was obligated to at least try to nip whatever sort of situation this was in the bud. She'd go about it indirectly, however.

"Okay then, moving on. First, a quick installment of 'Adventures with Boomer.' Ellie clicked to turn on the TV and a paint-covered Boomer filled the screen. I told you I painted last weekend. Last night, I had to do a little touch-up. I opened the paint can, realized I forgot a paint stirrer so went to grab one, and when I got back, this is what I found. My silly dog stuck his nose right in the paint can. He must not have liked the smell, or the taste, or something, because he rubbed his head on the drop cloth, which meant he rubbed paint all over his head. Yes, it was a mess. Yes, he threw a fit when I cleaned him up. And yes, I learned my lesson."

There were a few laughs, a few comments, but the reactions were nothing like she would have gotten under normal circumstances.

"Since I still haven't gotten over the incident, we're not going to dwell on Boomer this afternoon. Today is going to be a fun day. Y'all worked hard on your essays and the assignments that went along with our persuasive writing unit, so I figured a break was in order. I've put you into groups of four, and today you don't have to do anything but play games. Games about words, of course."

Ellie clicked and the picture of Boomer was replaced with the groupings she'd put together, and the table each group was assigned to. She held her breath. It only took a moment for the room to erupt.

"I'm not playing a game with Kira!"

"There's no way I'm going to be in a group with Anna and Josie!"

"Ms. Hawthorne, you can't have group two and group five next to each other!"

"I don't want to play games. How stupid."

"Hey, Ethan, check out your spot!"

The shouts and complaints continued, blending into one dull roar, despite Ellie's pleas for quiet. Without thinking, she did something she swore she'd never do.

Clap, clap, clap-clap-clap.

Shocked silence, heads whipping fast enough toward the front to turn her room into a sea of billowing hair, then in response: Clap, clap, clap-clap-clap.

Maybe it was hearing that familiar pattern, something they likely hadn't heard for a couple of years, and they responded out of habit. Maybe they were shocked into a response. Maybe they'd all been waiting for something to take their minds off whatever situation at the moment seemed so dire, and were happy and relieved to be transported back to a simpler time. Whatever the reason, thirty-two faces stared at her.

"Thank you for your attention. As I was saying, I wanted today to be a fun day. Right now, I don't think we're headed in that direction. What happens outside of class is none of my business, but when what happens outside of class affects what happens inside my class, then it becomes my business. Here's what we're going to do. I'm going to trust you to know if you're involved in something that needs to be discussed outside of class. I will give a pass to anyone who wants to go to the office and work things out."

Heads turned, and accusatory glares shot like lightning bolts from one side of the room to the other.

"If I don't get any volunteers, I'm going to use my incredible powers of deduction and send a few of you at a time to speak with a counselor. Whatever happened was important. I'm not discounting it. But, whatever happened can be resolved, and that's my aim. Now, how are we going to handle this?"

Ellie waited and watched and tried to stop her hands from shaking. She wanted to think she'd sounded sure of herself, in control, but she'd barely gotten all her words out without her voice cracking.

Had she overstepped her bounds? Maybe she should have called the office first and asked for advice on how to handle things. Had she shattered the tenuous relationship she'd built with her students? They'd probably never trust her again. Were they all silently laughing at her? That seemed like a given.

No hands went up. No one pointed. Even the whispering was nothing more than a faint buzz. For as much as she'd hoped for a quick, simple resolution, she understood the reluctance to rat out a friend, even if that friend wasn't so much a friend as an enemy at the moment. She also understood she'd probably made a mistake giving carte blanche to anyone wanting to go to the office. If this was, as she suspected, an 'it's my boyfriend/girlfriend, not yours' type of situation, having the boys and girls there at the same time wasn't the best course of action.

As she was racking her brain for her next move, a voice choked with tears muttered, "I'll go." It came from behind the waterfall of hair.

"Okay, Kira." Ellie grabbed a pad of office passes and began writing one for Kira. Before she finished, two more voices chimed in. "Me too." "So will I."

Kira left first, by herself. Based on what Ellie had seen, she figured that was for the best. She held Anna and Josie back a few minutes while she called the office to give the counselor a head's up. Sara stayed in her seat. Ellie wasn't sure whether Sara hadn't been involved or just didn't want to admit it. None of the boys said a word or otherwise gave any indication they wanted any part of a chat with the counselor. Ellie wasn't surprised. While she couldn't claim to be an expert on teens, she knew enough to know that thirteen-year-old girls were much freer with their emotions than were thirteen-year-old boys.

Once the girls were gone, the tension in the room eased. Ellie did a little rearranging and got everyone into groups without any complaints, explained the game, and let her students spend the rest of the hour debating synonyms and antonyms. For her part, she collapsed into her chair and focused on her yoga breathing.

Nicole had an obligation with her father and Max had a dental appointment, so there would be no repeat of last Friday's happy hour. Probably a good thing, Ellie decided, but she was curious about how their weeks had gone. Other than a couple of lunches and a few minutes here and there, they hadn't had time for much more than a passing greeting.

Ellie straightened her room, marveling again at the astonishing amount of stuff left behind. Today the lost and found pile would grow by two sweatshirts, three water bottles, two books, and a pair of shoes. She was trying to reassure herself that it was an extra pair of shoes, that her student hadn't walked out of class barefoot, when her classroom phone rang.

"Hello, this is Ellie."

Ellie listened, unspeaking, for half a minute before her knees gave out.

"Oh, my goodness…"

Ellie lowered herself into her chair.

"I see…"

Her hand gripped the phone so tightly she began to lose feeling in her fingers.

"How is—"

She listened again.

"But can I…Okay. Yes. Okay. I…I won't. Thank you."

The handset wobbled and fell off the base as Ellie tried to hang up. She watched it bounce on her desk, coming to rest upside down alongside a framed photo of Boomer. Ellie stared at it while a million thoughts whirred in her head until the incessant disconnect tone got her attention. Gingerly, as if handling a stick of dynamite, Ellie replaced the handset. Then she folded her hands together, rested her elbows on her desk, closed her eyes, and dropped her head to her hands.

How long she sat there she wasn't certain, but the voice that sounded behind her had her lifting her head and spinning her chair toward the doorway.

"You did the right thing."

Five simple words, easy for anyone to say, but spoken with such authority, Ellie almost believed them. Almost.

"You heard?" An unnecessary question because of course Jill had heard or she wouldn't be there, but Ellie didn't know what else to say.

"I did," Jill said. "Actually, I saw. I had bus duty today."

Ellie sprung to her feet. "How bad was it? Are they okay?"

"They'll be fine."

"Be fine? They're not fine right now?"

Jill lifted one shoulder and let it drop. "A bump on the head, a few scrapes, a lot of tears."

"Are they being sent home, or do they need to see a doctor?"

"It's nothing serious enough for a doctor. Jackie checked them over, put on a few bandages, handed out ice packs, and they're with her now, waiting for their parents. At this point, discipline is a bigger concern than their minor injuries."

"It's my fault, Jill. I thought I was so smart, stepping in and trying to defuse the situation. I should have left things alone instead of sticking my nose in where it didn't belong."

Jill shook her head. "It's not your fault. You're a teacher. It's your job to stick your nose in, whether it belongs or it doesn't."

"But if I hadn't said or done anything, they may have gone their separate ways this afternoon and by Monday, it would have been forgotten."

"Maybe, but unlikely. You had to get involved. The days of turning a blind eye are in the past. 'See something, say something.' Or do something. Believe me, I know."

Ellie studied the veteran teacher in front of her. Jill was widely regarded as one of the best at Caston Middle School. Ellie had picked up on that from the start. Aside from her years of experience, there was a knack, a skill, a gift that made her a favorite among students and faculty alike. Jill hadn't been five minutes into her presentation during the back-to-school workshop when Ellie had realized she was listening to a pro. Jill's insights had been invaluable that first week as Ellie struggled with self-confidence. At the moment, though, Ellie found it hard to believe much of what Jill said.

"What happened out there by the buses? Did you see?"

"Not from the start. When the commotion got my attention, Kira and Josie were already on the ground, locked in a tangle of arms, legs, and hair. Lots and lots of hair."

Ellie groaned.

"From what I pieced together, the two came out different doors but their buses were nearby, so they met up on the sidewalk. One shouted an insult, the other responded in kind, and within a few seconds, the first backpack was heaved. It hit Josie on the shoulder instead of in the head, but things deteriorated from there, and like I said, Jackie had some scrapes and bruises to deal with."

"You said a bump on the head." Ellie told herself if it had been serious, more than just scrapes and bruises, the nurse would have known.

"I'm not quite clear on that, but I think Kira hit her head on the curb when their argument got physical and both girls ended up on the sidewalk."

Ellie paced a lap around her room. "I wanted to go down to the office, but Amanda told me not to. Do you think...am I...I deserve it, I suppose."

"You're not in trouble, Ellie. Far from it. You did the right thing. You have to believe that. Amanda wanted to keep the crowd in the office to a minimum. As principal, she'll deal with the parents, with the discipline, with all of it. If she was short on the phone, that's why, because she's dealing with it. Not because she blames you."

"You can't know that."

"I do know that." Jill sat, then pointed at Ellie's desk chair. Ellie fell into it. "I assume you heard the story at orientation about the incident we had here a few years ago? The one that ended up with police involvement? It's a favorite of our administrators when they want to make a point."

"I heard. I wasn't sure whether to believe it."

"Believe it. Those were my students. I sensed a problem, I asked a couple of questions, but then I let it drop. The following weekend the police were called when a teenager was spotted walking down the street with a gun." Jill squeezed her eyes shut and took a deep breath. "I didn't act when I should have and that was the result. Thankfully, no one was hurt, the gun turned out to be a toy, but the knife in the student's pocket was all too real."

"I hoped that story had been exaggerated to make a point."

Jill shook her head. "I've been doing this job for a long time. I've done some things right that I'm proud of, and I've done some things wrong that I regret. That's my single biggest regret. The one that still costs me sleep. Things could have ended much differently if it hadn't been for a neighbor willing to get involved."

Ellie shivered at the thought of what could have happened. Finally, she said, "I'm pretty sure today was about a boy."

"It was. I gathered that much from the things Kira and Josie were shouting at each other. Arguments over boyfriends and girlfriends may seem trivial. To thirteen-year-olds, they're anything but. You were a middle schooler a lot more recently than I was, but even I can remember what it was like to have a crush and to see that crush with his arm around someone else. I'm devastated, I'm humiliated because I probably told my friends about him, and I feel like nothing will ever be okay again. And if this boy was more than just a crush, if he was supposedly my boyfriend? Well, then the gloves come off."

"I remember," Ellie said. "Scotty Raines. I cried for days."

Jill nodded. "And usually that's all it amounts to. A lot of tears. At thirteen, it's soul-crushing, but usually it doesn't go beyond that. Sadly, there are exceptions. The stories are there, too many of them, of fights, pregnancies, kids getting their hands on weapons. You did the right thing, Ellie. Gone are the days of assuming nothing will come of a situation, only to learn later that the absolute worst has come of it.

"If I can give you one piece of advice, it's go with your gut. There's not always going to be a clear right or wrong answer. Err on the side of caution. Always. You want your students to trust you so that they'll come to you if they need help and feel like there's no one else they can or want to talk to, but you can't let the fear of maybe losing that trust get in the way of stepping in when necessary. They need you to do that too. Over the years I've had students come to me with family problems, fears, even to tell me of a case of abuse. It's heartbreaking, but I've been so grateful and so humbled when a student has confided in me and I've been able to help, even if it was just a small thing. It's one of the most rewarding parts of the job."

Gradually, Ellie started to believe Jill. She bobbed her head up and down in a nod. "It has to be easier in kindergarten," Ellie mumbled.

Jill's face broke into a wide smile. "Kindergarten? Did you want to teach kindergarten?"

It came as a shock to realize she'd said it out loud and, with those few words, had told Jill more than she'd told anyone in a long time. Chalk it up to the stress of the moment, to Jill's calm understanding and wisdom, or just to the fact that it was the end of a long week. Whatever the case, Ellie had a decision to make. Shut down, change the subject as she'd been doing for so long, or finally open up to someone. Somehow, it seemed like an easy decision.

"Most of my life."

"I taught elementary for years before switching to middle school. I miss it sometimes, especially the fun and silly projects I did with the kids." Jill smiled to herself and her eyes had a faraway look. "Once, when my fifth graders were reading Pippi Longstocking, I talked the custodians into letting us dump soapy water on the floor, don some heavy socks, and skate around mopping that floor just like Pippi did."

"No! Really? I used to imagine doing that when I was a girl. Pippi Longstocking was my favorite. All those incredible adventures! For almost a year, I wore my hair only in braids and begged Mama to let me have it dyed red." Ellie's eyes now had that faraway look. "I had so many ideas of things I could do with my kindergartners."

"Then why aren't you with kindergartners?"

Ellie sighed. "Sometimes life hands you lemons. Sometimes life hands you a cheating fiancé. Then you find yourself making lemonade, or teaching middle school in Wisconsin instead of kindergarten in

Oklahoma."

"I'm sorry, Ellie. Whoever he was, you deserve better. I hope you know that."

Ellie felt tears sting the backs of her eyes, but she fought them and this time came out on top. "It took a while, but I do."

"That's good. For what it's worth, I can tell you're going to be a good middle school teacher."

"Oh?"

"You care. That's a big part. The biggest part. Besides, I hear talk, and the kids are talking about you. They like you."

Warmth spread throughout Ellie, a welcome relief after the icicles that had filled her veins since she'd answered the phone. "Really?"

"Really. To quote one of them, 'She's cool. She tells us about her dog, and she uses funny words.' High praise, indeed."

Ellie smiled and breathed a little easier. Maybe she still stood a chance.

10

She might have felt a little better after talking to Jill, but Ellie still found it impossible to relax when she got home. Her mind raced with scenarios of how the situation with Kira and Josie would play out in the coming days, with each possibility worse than the one before. When she couldn't pace her living room any longer, when even her guitar couldn't soothe her nerves, she clipped a leash onto Boomer's collar and headed out the door.

The weather was still warm, but the sweltering heat had moved out after the rain and as evening settled over Caston, the first taste of fall was in the air. The humidity was gone, a welcome relief, and in its place, a hint of the crisper air Ellie loved. Some porches and front steps were already dotted with giant pots of mums, the sunshiny yellow and pumpkin orange blooms glowing where, just days ago, pink petunias and red begonias had tried to hold on to the last bit of summer. As she eyed the trees they passed, she spotted a few birch leaves turning golden. She was eager to watch her yard, her street, and her neighborhood explode with color in the coming weeks.

Despite the pleasant evening, and despite the lure and promise of fall, Ellie didn't take her time strolling and enjoying. Her steps were fast enough that Boomer, even with his long legs, had to jog at her side to keep up. Maybe if she walked fast enough, she could erase the images of two girls, girls Ellie knew to be friends, hurling backpacks and fists and words that hurt as much, if not more.

When Ellie came to the fork in the sidewalk where she'd always taken a left, she went right. The left route would wind around her block, making her walk only about a mile, and would have her home too soon. The day called for a long, sweaty walk.

She didn't know exactly where a right would take her, but told herself that if nothing else, she could always turn around and follow the same route home. She wouldn't get lost in her own neighborhood, or at least close to her own neighborhood. Well, she admitted to herself, it was possible, but her phone was in her pocket and if nothing else, she could call up a map and plug in her address.

After a couple of blocks, the houses got larger. They looked newer, and more similar to one another, than the houses closer to Ellie's where there was everything from tiny ramblers to farmhouse-inspired designs with sprawling porches. But for as similar as they were, the owners had added personal touches to set their homes apart from their neighbors. A bright red door, shutters at the windows, brick accents, and meticulous landscaping with everything from decorative trees to water features.

Many people were outside enjoying the evening and several said hello or lifted a hand in greeting. The small-town feel was as much a comfort as the big dog at her side. During every talk with her mother, Ellie endured warnings about taking precautions when she walked alone, especially as the days grew shorter and she'd be more likely to find herself walking in the dark. As much as Ellie tried to reassure her mother Caston was a safe place, Genevieve Hawthorne firmly believed anywhere outside Oklahoma was dangerous country, indeed.

Ellie spotted the dog in the yard of the house in front of them a moment before Boomer did. He jumped and barked.

"No," Ellie told him with a little jerk on the leash to get his attention. "You know better than that."

He usually did. His faults, of which it could be argued there were many, didn't include barking at other dogs when Ellie walked him. Just the opposite was true. No matter how much a dog barked at him, Boomer held his head high and pranced by, sparing the dog only a bored glance or two. Ellie had stopped trying to figure it out and had decided to just enjoy the fact that he was doing something right.

When Boomer barked again, Ellie stopped and ordered him to sit, but Boomer had no interest in sitting. He ducked and deked, trying to get a look around Ellie's legs.

"What has gotten into you?" Ellie scolded.

Just as she was about to leave the sidewalk and move to the other side of the street, the why behind Boomer's behavior became all too clear.

"You want to play with Bowie, don't you?" Ellie said with a sigh.

Her quick scan of the front yard didn't provide a glimpse of Zeke, but a moment before she could turn and make a run for it, he popped out of the garage. Knowing she couldn't turn around, Ellie tried again to settle Boomer, then continued her walk to Zeke's driveway.

"We keep running into one another," Zeke said.

"Why didn't you tell me you lived just a few blocks from me?" It was not a friendly greeting, Ellie was perfectly aware of that, but he owed her an explanation, and *he* should be perfectly aware of *that*.

"I didn't not tell you," Zeke explained, "it just didn't come up."

"It seems like it could have come up when you drove me home. When you told me you knew where Valley Lane was. When you told me about your friend's grandparents living in my house."

"Is it a problem that we live close?"

Ellie swiped her wrist across her forehead. If she hadn't been sweating before, she certainly was now.

"No," she said, "it's not a problem. It just seems like you would have mentioned it."

Zeke studied her until she grew uncomfortable.

"Why did you offer to keep Bowie the other day?" Zeke asked.

"Pardon?"

"Why? Why did you do that when it appears you don't like anything about me?"

Ellie closed her eyes and turned away from Zeke's dark, dark eyes that looked not only perplexed, but hurt. Not like anything about him? That couldn't be further from the truth. Not like the things he made her think about? Made her feel? That she most definitely did not like. She forced herself to turn back and face him.

"I apologize if that's how it's seemed. It's not true. You haven't given me any reason not to like you. In fact, the opposite is true. You've been nothing but friendly and considerate since I met you. You may not believe it, but I'm usually a nice person. Too nice, I've been told. It's just that…"

Ellie took a deep, shaky breath, then spilled her words in a rush on her exhale. "I'm not looking for a relationship. I don't want you to think anything different. I came to Caston alone and I intend to remain alone. If I've given you a different impression, I'm sorry."

Humor flickered in those dark eyes and pushed out most of the hurt. Feeling like a fool, Ellie yanked on Boomer's leash, wanting to put distance between herself and Zeke before he could outright laugh at her. She'd have to walk straight through the night to get her most recent disaster out of her head.

Before she'd taken a step, Zeke put his hand on her arm. "Ellie. Have dinner with me."

Ellie tossed her free hand in the air. "Didn't you listen to a single thing I said?"

"Of course, I listened. You may not believe it, but I'm a good listener."

Another thing to add to the list of things he was good at, Ellie figured.

"It's just dinner. Friends have dinner together all the time. Besides, I owe you for dealing with Bowie the other day."

"You don't owe me anything, and no. Thank you, but no. I have, um, I have…" Darn it. Why couldn't she think of a single thing she had to do?

"The grill's hot, the steaks are seasoned and ready to go, salad is in the fridge. Join me. Please."

Ellie looked down at her tank top and leggings. "I'm a mess."

"We'll eat on the patio."

"I have Boomer."

"Bowie would love a play date."

Bowie hid behind Zeke's legs, just out of Boomer's reach.

"Somehow, I doubt that."

"Bowie will tolerate a play date."

Ellie pushed back the hair that was slipping from its tie to fall in her face, frustrated not only with her hair, but with Zeke's refusal to take no for an answer. "It will be dark before long."

"I'll give you a ride home. I know where you live, remember?"

Ellie narrowed her eyes at him. "I remember."

"Then you'll stay?"

"Did I say that?"

"You were going to, I could tell." Zeke held out his hand. "Let me cook. You take the night off, relax, and tell me about your week at school."

For a few minutes, she'd forgotten, but like a giant tidal wave, it all came crashing back and threatened to drown her in guilt and sadness.

"Ellie? What is it?"

She didn't answer, didn't think she could, just stared at his outstretched hand.

"Are you okay?"

"Hmm?"

His hand moved to grasp hers. Some part of her brain told her it was a dangerous idea, even this tiny bit of physical contact, but it steadied her and she didn't pull away.

"Let's sit down."

Ellie let herself be led up Zeke's driveway, then onto the sidewalk that wound around to the back yard. Ellie kept her eyes down, focusing on the pattern in the paving stones and trying to block out everything else.

Zeke led her to a chair, then sat in the one next to it. He coaxed Ellie into her chair. "You look a little pale. Are you sure you're feeling okay?"

"Tired. I think I'm just tired. It was a long week."

"Was it a better week than last week? Last Friday at Scooter's I sensed maybe you and your friends were trying to put a positive spin on a trying week."

Ellie huffed out a short laugh. "Trying. That's one word, I guess."

"Then this week was worse?"

Ellie absently patted Boomer's head as she looked out over Zeke's yard before she answered. A faded flower garden in the back corner, a towering maple that Ellie guessed would explode with color in the next few weeks, a couple of bird feeders and a birdbath just past the deck. The grass might be a little long, the deck nearly ready for fresh stain, and the birdbath tilting a bit, but it was a yard that had seen love and care over the summer. Ellie wondered how Zeke found the time.

"It wasn't worse. Actually, it was better. Until this afternoon, anyway. I'm falling into a rhythm and not stressing about my every move quite as much as I was even a few days ago."

"That's good. What happened this afternoon?"

Rather than answer, Ellie asked a question of her own. "Do you ever second-guess yourself?"

Zeke angled his head and studied her. "In my personal life, all the time. In my professional life, I can't afford to."

"How do you do it? How do you know you've made the right decision?"

"What happened, Ellie?"

Ellie rubbed her forehead where a headache threatened. "I made a mistake today. I interfered where I shouldn't have, and the result was the sort of thing that will haunt my dreams. Nightmares, more likely."

Zeke waited, silently and patiently. He was a good listener, Ellie thought.

"Some of my students were in a pretty heated disagreement today. I didn't see or hear what caused it, but when they came to class, there were tears, taunts, nasty looks, you name it. I thought I was so smart, butting in and getting those directly involved down to the office to speak with a counselor. This was the last class of the day. I worried about things carrying over to next week and thought it best to have them hash it out sooner rather than later."

The phone call replayed in Ellie's mind. 'Ellie, there's been an incident with Kira and Josie…'

"After school, outside by the buses, two girls got into a fight. A physical fight. I didn't witness it, but I heard about it, and there were injuries, words that can never be taken back, and more tears. A lot more tears."

"I see," Zeke said. "You have to know you're not responsible for what happens between students outside of class. I'd argue you're not entirely responsible for what happens between them during class. They're their own people, Ellie. They think and act as they choose. You did what you thought best. I can't claim to have been in the same situation, but given what I've heard, I think I would have reacted similarly. You did nothing wrong. In fact, I think you did everything right."

"It doesn't feel that way. I can't stop thinking that if I'd left it all alone, they would have gone their separate ways after school and by Monday, it would have all been forgotten."

"That's unlikely. I think you know that. I could also argue that the counselor or whomever they spoke with in the office played into the girls' decision to act the way they did as much, or more, than anything you did."

"I'm not going to put the blame on someone else, Zeke."

"I'm not asking you to. I'm merely asking you to take into consideration you weren't the last person they interacted with."

Ellie gave a noncommittal nod.

"What was the disagreement about? Do you know?"

"A boy-girl thing."

Zeke leaned back in his chair. "Ah."

"I've been a teacher for all of nine days and I already have this thing hanging over me. Nine days. That's all it took for me to screw up with catastrophic results."

When Zeke laid his hand over hers, she jumped, but let the warmth from his hand seep into her ice-cold fingers. His voice was soft when he said, "I don't know that I'd call it catastrophic."

"In the grand scheme of things, I suppose not, but in the small world of Caston Middle School, and especially of Ms. Hawthorne's seventh grade language arts class? I don't know that catastrophic is a strong enough term."

"Two girls fighting over a boy? Boys fighting over a girl? Some other combination?"

"I'm not sure as they were tight-lipped all class, but my gut tells me Girl A liked Boy A, they were probably together in the middle school sense of together, then Boy A got too close to Girl B." Ellie shrugged. "I could be off base, but it had to do with relationships and some sort of inappropriate behavior, real or perceived. It's complicated."

"So it seems."

Just like that, Ellie was embarrassed. Zeke devoted his life to saving others with the weight of all that entailed on his shoulders, day in and day out. Here she was whining about how difficult her day had been because of a middle school argument.

"I know it seems foolish."

"Foolish? Not at all. It's very real, to those involved and to you."

Ellie blinked in surprise. "Yes, it is. Real, I mean. But compared to the sorts of things you see and deal with every day, it doesn't seem all that important."

"Whatever a person finds themselves in the middle of is important. For you, today, it was a situation involving students that, I'm guessing, you've already come to care about. The students involved cared about one another or the situation, the argument, never would have materialized. That makes it important to them. Just because something might not have a far-reaching impact outside of their bubble doesn't mean it's not important."

"Dr. Fahrner, you're sounding more like a psychologist than a surgeon."

Zeke chuckled. "Hardly. I just need you to understand you did nothing wrong. You asked me if I ever second-guess myself."

Ellie nodded.

"I don't, because I can't. I weigh the facts, I research, and I make a decision. I have to believe in my decision because if I don't, my patients and their families won't. I'm not claiming I'll never make the wrong decision, but I can't afford to second-guess myself when I'm in the middle of it. There's no going back. And sometimes there can be more than one correct decision. Different paths to the same outcome."

Ellie nodded again. "The principal and one of the long-tenured teachers at the school told me I did the right thing. I'm still having trouble believing that, but they reminded me I have an obligation to say something, to get involved, if I'm at all concerned for a student's well-being. I feel like they may have stretched the definition in this case, but I appreciated the sentiment. And I appreciate your words. Thank you. They helped."

"I'm glad." Zeke was quiet for a minute, and it was his turn to gaze over the yard where the shadows were already creeping into the corners.

"A few months ago, before I came back to Caston, I saw a patient with disturbing injuries. A badly broken arm, a dislocated elbow, bruising consistent with abuse. Like a teacher, a doctor has an obligation to report any suspected abuse. I asked a few questions of my patient and his mother, but both insisted the injuries resulted from a fall down the stairs when the boy tripped over a younger sibling's toy. I looked at his medical history, there were no red flags, but I had my doubts and contacted the authorities. I operated on the boy's arm, then sent him home with his mother. He was due for a follow-up visit a few days later. He never showed."

Zeke ran a shaky hand over his face. "I learned later he was treated in the emergency room for life-threatening head injuries. His father had been arrested, but too late." Zeke paused, and when he spoke, his voice was hardly more than a whisper. "He spilled a glass of milk. He was only six years old."

Ellie's hand flew to her mouth as she breathed, "No."

"Someone from child welfare followed up on my call. Apparently, the mother vouched for the father, the father put on a good show, and the investigator found no reason to remove the child from the home. She was scheduled to make another visit, but it was too late for the boy."

Their roles reversed, Ellie clamped her hand over Zeke's and squeezed. "You did the right thing. You followed protocol, you tried to help. It's not your fault."

Zeke nodded. "Just as today wasn't yours. I want you to believe that, but I also want you to believe it when I say I know how difficult it can be to do so. You can't afford to second-guess."

There didn't seem to be anything to say to that, and Zeke didn't seem to expect a reply, so Ellie watched Boomer's fur part, then fall back into place as she ran her fingers back and forth over his head. She let the day's events play over in her mind.

She'd done the right thing. Zeke was right. She had to believe in herself. There'd be more times coming when she'd have to have confidence in herself and in her instincts. Zeke's words, 'Sometimes there can be more than one correct decision,' made sense. Today she'd done what she thought was right, and the result had been painful. She could have made a different decision and the results could have been worse. She'd never know, but she'd used the information she had to make the most informed decision. It was the best she could have done, and she needed to have enough faith in herself to do the same thing the next time.

A light breeze rustled the drying leaves and Ellie shivered. The night had cooled, and now that her heart rate had slowed and she'd calmed some, her tank top provided little barrier against the chilly air.

"I'm going to get those steaks on the grill. Come inside with me while I grab them. I'll find you a sweatshirt and maybe a glass of wine."

Ellie wasn't sure which sounded better, the sweatshirt or the wine, but after unloading on Zeke, she was back to feeling uncomfortable.

"I really should be going."

"You really should be eating."

"I'm not all that hungry," Ellie said, but her rumbling stomach gave her away.

"What did you have for lunch today?"

Ellie frowned. "Some pretzels. I think." Maybe that had been yesterday. Lunch had sort of fallen by the wayside.

"Doctor's orders. You need a meal."

Zeke stood, then turned and held out his hand. Ellie grumbled, but took it and let Zeke pull her to her feet.

"You're a pediatrician. I think that means you can't offer advice to an adult, doesn't it?"

"It means nothing of the sort," Zeke said as he started for the house. "It means I can offer advice to children as well as former children."

Ellie chuckled, but stopped when she walked through the sliding glass door into Zeke's kitchen. Then she had to gasp.

"Oh, my."

Ellie turned in a circle, not sure where to look first. Maybe the six-burner gas range top situated on one end of the huge butcher block island. Maybe the shiny, stainless steel refrigerator, bigger than any she'd ever seen. Maybe the gleaming granite countertops that she itched to run her hand over to feel the cool smoothness; maybe the equally shiny wood floor. Or the custom cabinetry, the intricate lighting that hung over the island, the open shelves that glowed with recessed lights, the walk-in pantry, the deep farm sink, or the collection of cookbooks that took up three long shelves.

"Oh, my," Ellie repeated as she soaked it all in.

"It's a bit much, I know."

"It's fantastic. Like a dream." She whirled to face Zeke. "Are you some kind of gourmet chef?"

"Far from it. I enjoy cooking and like to play around in the kitchen when I have time, but gourmet isn't a term that should ever be linked to my name."

"But all this." Ellie waved her arm to encompass the vast space. "Did you do this?"

Zeke shook his head. "Came with the house, but I'll admit, it was a selling point."

"I'll say. It's incredible." And she couldn't help but wonder if the rest of the house matched the grandeur of the kitchen.

Ellie inched forward and trailed her fingers over the granite. It was as cool and smooth as she'd expected, and a far cry from the laminate countertops in her own kitchen. She stopped in front of the shelves of cookbooks and let her eyes wander. Some of the bindings were creased, some pages dogeared, and she spotted a few sticky notes poking out of the pages.

"Have you read all of these?"

"Not cover to cover, but I've looked through most of them. When I needed a break from medical textbooks, cookbooks were my go-to. My way of relaxing. I'd cook sometimes for the other med students. Hospital cafeteria food gets old pretty quickly."

Why did that warm her heart almost as much as learning he took his service dog with him to the hospital on his days off? She ordered herself to stop focusing on the feel-good stuff and instead on the tangibles.

"Where did you learn to cook?"

"My grandmother, mostly, and my mom. Both loved to cook and to pass on that love. Since my mom didn't have any daughters and my grandmother didn't have any granddaughters, they focused on me."

Her tactic backfired, Ellie realized, because all she could picture was a little boy, his hair curling on his neck, his eager, dark eyes watching intently as ingredients were measured, sifted, stirred, and hoping a spoon or a beater, heaping with gooey batter or fluffy icing was headed his way.

"Then your grandmother lived nearby?"

"Lived with us, more or less. My grandfather passed away when I was a baby. My parents turned the lower level of our house into a separate apartment and my grandmother lived there as far back as I can remember. That's just how it was. Grandma was downstairs, and I was always welcome."

"That's sweet. No sisters, you said. Brothers?"

Zeke's eyes clouded and his smile faltered. "One. I should get those steaks on the grill."

With that, he turned and headed for the enormous refrigerator. It didn't take a genius to know that line of conversation was over.

"Oh, my stars," Ellie said as she leaned back in her chair, closed her eyes, and put a hand on her stomach. "I haven't eaten steak that good since I left Oklahoma. Wisconsin does some things well—I've never met people more serious about their cheese—but the beef, in my humble opinion, is no match for Oklahoma's. I didn't think I'd find anything to rival one of my granddaddy's steaks, but Dr. Fahrner, you've come close. You've come very close."

Zeke grinned. "Why, thank you, Ms. Hawthorne, that's high praise, indeed."

Ellie opened one eye when she heard the drawl in his voice and tried to determine if he was making fun of her. She decided she didn't care, she'd just enjoy the memory of the meal that had been the closest thing to a taste of home she'd had in months.

"Your grandfather is a good cook?" Zeke asked.

Ellie laughed at that. "Oh, heavens, my granddaddy doesn't cook. I'm not sure he'd know how to make toast. My granddaddy is a rancher. Raises the best cattle in Oklahoma. The country, if you let him tell it."

"Oh. Oh, wow. A rancher. That's really cool. I've never known a rancher. Or the granddaughter of a rancher. A farmer, sure, but not a rancher. Makes me think cookouts, and brands, and rodeos."

Ellie laughed harder. "Kind of how I think year-round snow, fishing, and cabins up north when I think about Wisconsin. Although, I've always wondered why y'all say *up north* when there's not a whole lot farther north to go."

"Fair enough. But I stand by my initial statement: cool. Ranching sounds fascinating."

"Ranching is a lot of work, but I guess you could call it fascinating too. It's births and deaths, it's droughts and floods, it's early mornings and late nights. To me, it's family."

"Then your grandfather is still ranching? He hasn't retired?"

"Retired? I don't know that anyone ever really retires from ranching. A couple of my uncles are doing most of the work these days, but Granddaddy is still up with the roosters, on his horse, telling everyone what to do and how to do it. I imagine he'll do that until the day he dies."

With the lull in conversation, Ellie glanced at the oversized clock on Zeke's kitchen wall.

"It's late. I should be going."

"I could whip up dessert."

"Whip up dessert? What sort of dessert do you just whip up?"

"Probably nothing fancier than ice cream sundaes, but I do have some chopped nuts, ripe bananas and strawberries I can slice, and some cream that I could actually whip."

"As tempting as that sounds, I'm plum stuffed. I'm going to have to coax Boomer into a run on the way home as it is in order to burn some calories."

Boomer, who'd finally tired of tormenting Bowie, was on the floor in front of the sliding glass door snoring, his paws twitching as he dreamt, probably about tormenting Bowie.

"It's dark. I told you I'd drive you home."

"That's not necessary. I know the way, and it's not far."

Ellie frowned. At least she thought she knew the way.

The food, the easy talk, the glass of wine, all of it together equaled her letting her guard down, and that wouldn't do. It was all too comfy and cozy. Friendly, yes, but easily interpreted as more. No, it wouldn't do at all. She jumped to her feet.

"I'll just help you clean up, and then I really have to be on my way."

"It's only a few dishes. Nothing I can't handle on my own."

"Well, then, thank you for dinner, Zeke. It was delicious." Ellie walked backward toward the door, stepping into the shoes she'd left on the rug next to Boomer. "I hope you enjoy your weekend," she said as she clipped Boomer's leash to his collar and put her hand on the door, ready to pull it open and escape into Zeke's back yard.

"Ellie. I will drive you home."

Ellie's nerves skittered. "No, I'm fine. I'll enjoy the walk."

"I'll drive you home." The finality in Zeke's voice had Ellie deciding arguing would get her nowhere. Best to just let him give her a ride and be done with it.

"Very well. Thank you."

The ride home, though it was short, was filled with tension. At least on Ellie's part. When she stole a glance at Zeke, he seemed perfectly content, but for Ellie, every second that passed in silence seemed like an eternity. She tried to think of something to say, anything to break the silence, but everything she tried out in her head sounded wrong. Before she came up with anything, they were in her driveway.

"I enjoyed getting to know you better, Ellie. I hope I see you again soon."

"Thank you for dinner and for the ride." She pushed her door open, jumped out of the car, and closed it as quickly as she could. She wrangled Boomer out of the backseat and with a little wave, dashed up her driveway in record time.

Then, for the third time, she watched Zeke's taillights as he drove away from her house, with her feelings even more jumbled than the first time.

11

The month of October brought parent-teacher conferences, a school fundraiser, and the first dance of the year. When Ellie had first gotten a look at the calendar of events during summer orientation, she'd ranked those first big events of the year, and of her teaching career, in order of how much she feared and dreaded them.

The fundraiser, she figured, she could handle. From what she remembered from her own school days, other than providing reminders to her students to do their part, there wasn't much for teachers to do. She'd been wrong. Oh, so wrong.

The week before the kickoff, Ellie learned that the teachers perform skits, sing pop songs with the lyrics changed to play into the fundraising goals, or find other silly ways to fire up the kids during a special assembly. Somehow, she still wasn't exactly certain how it happened, she found herself dressed as an Oompa Loompa, complete with a baggy white outfit and an orange face, and singing to the students:

Oompa loompa doompety doo
  We've got a perfect challenge for you
  Oompa loompa doompety dee
  Be the one to earn the most money

What do you get if you outsell the rest?
  You get to choose the prize you like best
  Air pods, a tablet, tickets to the game
  Your name on a plaque and a moment of fame

* * *

Oompa loompa Caston is cool
  Oompa loompa we're the best school
  Oompa loompa help it stay that way
  Oompa loompa raise money every day!

At least she hadn't been roped, as Max had, into joining the group that pledged to sit in a dunk tank if the school reached their goal. Besides, she loved to sing even if the song and the costumes were cringeworthy.

Parent-teacher conferences came and went. What had scared the daylights out of her and ranked number one on her list of things she feared turned out to be not so scary, after all. She met some wonderful parents, the positive moments and conversations far outweighed the negative, and she felt she knew her students much better after meeting a mother, a father, or a caregiver. Of course, some of the parents she'd most wanted to talk with hadn't made it to conferences and the follow-up letters she'd sent had gone mostly unanswered, but overall, it had been a pleasant and productive experience.

Now, the school dance loomed. In just a few hours, Ellie would join a handful of other teachers who'd volunteered to chaperone an evening of awkward glances, nervous giggles, preening, and strutting. She looked forward to and dreaded the spectacle in equal measure.

Ellie swung into the parking lot at Top Dog. Knowing she'd be gone in the evening, she'd left Boomer to spend the day romping with the other dogs. He'd be plenty tired and ready for an evening on the couch.

Since the mix-up with Bowie, the service at Top Dog had been flawless, and she'd yet to pay for a single day. When she'd spoken with the owner, Carolyn had apologized profusely and had offered free visits in an attempt to right their wrong. She and Carolyn had left it at that, a vague reference to an unspecified number of free visits. Ellie felt confident the incident was an isolated one, and she'd felt comfortable leaving Boomer in their care several times since. Someday, she supposed, she'd be presented with a bill when she picked up Boomer, but for now, she just thanked the employee and took home an exhausted dog.

At home, once Boomer was fed and asleep on the couch, Ellie scanned her closet for something to wear to the dance. The theme was disco, complete with black lights and a disco ball, and the chaperones were encouraged to wear white or fluorescent colors that would glow under the black light.

"Fluorescent," Ellie muttered as she perused her options. "I don't have anything fluorescent." She couldn't recall ever owning anything that could be described as fluorescent and recoiled a bit at the very thought.

Boomer padded into her room and stared up at her with tired eyes.

"I shouldn't have waited until the last minute," she told her dog. "What am I going to wear?"

Boomer heaved a dramatic sigh and threw himself on the ground at her feet. His eyes closed before he made it all the way down.

"Big help you are."

"Disco, disco," she mumbled as she flipped through hanger after hanger. Then inspiration struck. She pulled open the bottom drawer on the small dresser she'd tucked in the back of her walk-in closet. A pile of exercise clothes she didn't wear any longer but hadn't yet thrown out or donated were squished together to fill the drawer to overflowing.

"There you are," she said when she pulled a pair of flared, black yoga pants from the bottom of the pile. She shook them out and nodded. The white stripe down the side would glow even if the pants themselves wouldn't, and the ridiculously wide flare would satisfy the disco requirement.

"Now for a shirt." Ellie tapped a finger on her chin as she scrutinized the other side of her closet. She selected and discarded a couple of tops. "Too flowery, more like a luau," she said as she returned a pink and white blouse to the closet. "Too fancy." Back went the blue silk. She frowned at a plaid blouse. "Maybe if it were a line dancing party," she muttered, but her frown turned to a smile when she remembered buying that blouse with her girlfriends before they'd all gone line dancing. Fun, carefree times. She'd been so confident of where her life was headed, and how it would turn out. Then, she'd been unsure of everything and she hadn't worn the shirt since.

Ellie shoved the plaid shirt back in its designated spot and with it, shoved the memories back where they belonged. She grabbed a simple white blouse, a pink tank top, and a pair of pink pumps. She'd knot the shirt at the waist and, being white, it would glow. The sort-of-bright pink was the closest she was going to come to fluorescent, and the pumps had a thick enough sole that with a little imagination, they could be called platforms. She'd gel, curl, then spray her hair into place, find some long necklaces and sparkly, dangly earrings and call it good.

And next time, she'd suggest that line dance.

The gym reeked of teenage sweat, popcorn, and way too much cologne. It was enough to make Ellie's eyes water. The flashing lights, the heavy bass, and the room of screeching kids were more than enough to make her head ache. She must be getting old.

Ellie roamed her assigned area, hoping there wouldn't be a reason to intervene. For the most part, the kids behaved like she'd expected. The boys congregated on one side of the gym, the girls on the other, and most of what passed the invisible boundary between the two sides was limited to glances, giggles, and the occasional brave soul sent to relay a message. There wasn't much dancing unless the DJ got the kids involved in a game or contest. Most of Ellie's job, she discovered, was watching for contraband snacks and drinks. The physical education teachers were protective of their gym floor, so all food and beverages were supposed to stay in the hallway. It didn't, so Ellie intercepted bags and bottles to exaggerated groans and no shortage of comments about how unfair it all was.

After thirty minutes, Ellie was wondering why she'd ever thought volunteering as a chaperone would be fun.

She was tapping her toe to a song that seemed to have no discernible lyrics when she detected the presence behind her, even before she heard the words.

"OMG, did you see Katherine and Heathcliff? They're like totally talking to each other."

Ellie couldn't have stopped the giggle if her life depended on it. She turned toward the voice.

"A *Wuthering Heights* reference in the middle of all this chaos? Who does that?"

"Someone who doesn't want to risk using names that might be actual students' names. Someone who's trying to get a smile out of a language arts teacher who looks like she'd trade her favorite pink shoes for a couple of aspirin and a nap."

Ellie laughed harder as she raised up to her toes with one foot and twisted it to get a better look at her shoe. "Wouldn't have to think twice. I can always get new shoes."

"I've got aspirin in my bag," he patted the bag slung over his shoulder, "but the nap, I'm afraid, might have to wait. And I'll let you keep the shoes. Probably wouldn't fit anyway."

"What in the world are you doing here, Zeke?"

Zeke rubbed the back of his neck, likely fighting a headache of his own.

"It's a bit of a story." Ellie raised her eyebrows, and he continued. "Jackie is the older sister of a friend."

"Jackie our nurse?"

"Yeah. She's got a sick kid. Pink eye. The stuff is crazy contagious. She was supposed to be here tonight. Apparently the school rules mandate a nurse or other qualified health care worker is present during functions like this, and since she couldn't make it, and since it was so last minute, and since she somehow knew I was back in town, she asked her brother to get in touch with me and here I am."

The DJ announced a hula hoop contest and began tossing pink, yellow, and green hoops into the crowd of kids. The hoops glowed under the lights, making the room look like the inside of a video game. Ellie stepped back from the throng of kids and the out-of-control hula hoops. Zeke followed her.

"That's nice of you to fill in. I would imagine working a middle school dance wasn't on your top ten list of things to do on a Friday night."

"No, but I don't mind all that much. Brings back memories."

"Good memories?"

Zeke chuckled. "Some, but I wonder if there's a person alive who has only good memories of middle school. Those are tough times." His smile disappeared and his eyes grew serious. "That situation a few weeks ago? That's resolved?"

Ellie looked around the crowded gym. It took her only a moment to spot Kira and Josie. They weren't arm in arm, but they were part of the same large group in matching neon green T-shirts. Things had been tense between them, they'd more or less ignored one another in Ellie's class for a week after their scuffle, but things were close to resolved.

"For the most part. There've been two more major blowups since that one, each involving a different set of friends." Ellie shrugged with one shoulder. "I'm coming to realize it's a part of middle school, and something that no amount of wishing on my part is going to change."

While she and Zeke had run into each other a couple of times at Top Dog, they hadn't done more than exchange greetings and a few words since dinner at Zeke's house. Ellie had been comfortable with that, but now, talking with him felt like talking to a friend.

And that posed a problem.

Ellie had given it considerable thought since that night at Zeke's, and she'd come to the realization that she'd never had a man as a friend. She'd had boys who were friends. As a child, there'd been far more boys around to play with than there'd been girls, so she hadn't had the luxury of being choosy. In high school, she'd had friends who were male, but those males were definitely still boys. Even in college, before she'd met Vincent, the guys she'd spent time with may have been men according to their birthdates, but in reality, they were just older, bigger boys. Once it had become clear she and Vincent were a couple, her relationships with men had become very different. The men she knew, the men she spent time with, were Vincent's friends, or in some cases, boyfriends of her closest girlfriends.

So, she had no idea how to be friends with a man. Simple, no-strings-attached, let's-get-together-once-in-a-while friends.

"I'm glad things worked out."

"Hmm?"

"With the kids. The disagreement. I'm glad things worked out."

"Oh, yes."

The hula hoop contest was in full swing and down to the last few contestants.

"Can we sneak out and get something to drink?" Zeke asked. "I was serious about that aspirin, if you need some."

They ducked out of the gym and grabbed water bottles from the coolers that lined the hallway. Ellie took a sip, then leaned back against the wall, moving the bottle from her lips to her forehead. "That's better. I think I might just make it without aspirin."

They stood in the relative quiet for a while, sipping water and recovering.

"Aside from tonight, how's school going?"

"Definitely getting easier. The panic attacks are much less frequent. How are things at the hospital?"

"Busy, challenging…perfect, I guess."

"You love it, don't you?"

"I do. I feel bad for those who don't love what they do."

Ellie nodded. She wasn't sure if she loved what she did quite yet, but she didn't hate it as she'd feared. But Max and Nicole? She wasn't sure either even liked what they were doing, and for the life of her, she couldn't figure out why they were doing it. Whenever she broached the subject, directly or in a round-about manner, they changed the topic fast enough to make her head spin.

"Ellie?"

"Oh, yes, I'm sorry. You were saying?"

"That I thought we should probably get back inside."

"Of course."

Zeke held out his arm, and Ellie walked back into the gym in front of him. It felt as though the temperature had risen twenty degrees in the few minutes they'd been in the hallway. Ellie dabbed at her forehead, then checked the time. She blinked twice at the clock when it told her she had nearly ninety minutes to go. "Oh, my stars," she sighed, but the voices of every girl in the gym singing along, at the tops of their lungs, with Taylor Swift swallowed Ellie's words. It was something to behold.

Ellie waved at Zeke, who looked shell-shocked, then wandered the gym to fulfill her chaperone duties. None of the kids paid much attention to her, no one seemed to need anything, so she was free to observe.

After the hula hoop contest, there was a bit more mingling between the boys and girls. Like before, there wasn't much dancing, more just standing around, talking, hair flipping, and giggling. So much giggling. Ellie spotted Kira and Josie talking to each other. When Kira threw her arms up in the air, Ellie tensed, ready to intervene, but then Josie did the same, they both doubled over laughing, and Ellie's best guess was they were mimicking someone's dance moves.

Assured the girls were back on friendly terms, Ellie continued her circuit. A few students said hello or smiled at her, but most tried to melt into the crowd and avoid having to interact with an adult. A group of sixth graders huddled in a corner working on some intricately choreographed dance moves. She wondered if they'd have the nerve to take those moves to the dance floor or if they'd stay hidden in their corner, rehearsing.

From t-shirts to leg warmers to headbands, the amount of neon in the room was off the charts. Ellie, with her white blouse and pants with white stripes, felt a little like a walking skeleton but she was no match for some of the kids who'd either raided their parents' or grandparents' closets or convinced those parents to find an online disco store. It was impressive, the lengths some of them had gone to. There were several girls in shiny, flared-leg jumpsuits, some in glittery sequined dresses, and boys in satin, wide-collared shirts with flared, polyester pants. One eighth grader, who stood out like a beacon under the black light, was in a white suit and black shirt and with his thick, dark hair slicked back, looked so much like John Travolta in *Saturday Night Fever*, it was eerie.

"Are you ready?" The DJ's voice boomed and Ellie jumped. "Are you ready?" he repeated, even louder. "Let's do the Hustle!"

He made those four words sound so exciting, he had most of the kids' attention. Not an easy task, Ellie well knew.

"On the dance floor. Come on, I want everyone."

The kids looked around, waiting for someone to take the lead. A few inched forward, but it wasn't the crush of bodies Ellie figured the DJ was hoping for.

"Teachers, that means you too! Let's show these kids how it's done!"

Twelve years of dance classes hadn't been for nothing. There was no question Ellie knew how to do the Hustle. Whether she wanted to do the Hustle in front of a gym full of students was another matter. She looked over one shoulder, then the other. Either the other teachers had found a way to become invisible or they'd bolted for the door at the first mention of them dancing. Then her eyes met Zeke's. He looked more confused than anything, but he hadn't made a run for it, which made Ellie's decision an easy one. A few quick steps and she was alongside him, reaching for his hand and before he could protest, pulling him toward the dance floor.

"I don't think—" Before he could finish his thought, the DJ spotted them.

"And we have our first brave volunteers. Let's give it up for…" He put his hand to his ear and waited.

"Ms. Hawthorne," someone yelled.

"Ms. Hawthorne! Way to go, Ms. Hawthorne and friend. Now, if Ms. Hawthorne can do it, you can do it. Out on the floor!"

This time, the kids took his invitation to heart and filled the space around Ellie until they were almost shoulder to shoulder.

"Okay, raise your hand if you know how to do the Hustle."

Ellie put her hand up as she looked around her. A couple of the kids had their hands up, but Zeke, like most of the kids, did not.

"That's not many. Looks like we've got some teaching to do, Ms. Hawthorne!"

Ellie smiled and gave the DJ a thumbs up.

"Here's what you need to know," he said into his microphone. "Four counts. Four counts back, four counts up, four counts with a spin to the right, four counts with a spin to the left. Once we get that down, we'll add some shimmies and some shakes," he gyrated on the stage as he spoke, "sprinkle in a little more disco," he did a 'Travolta' with his hand stabbing up, then down across his body, "but let's work on the fours first. Watch Ms. Hawthorne."

He started the music, then hopped down from his platform to stand next to Ellie.

"Here we go, everybody…and back, two, three, four."

Ellie grabbed Zeke's hand and pulled him along with her. Back four, up four. "To the right," she said to Zeke before she dropped his hand and spun to the right. "Now left."

Zeke tripped over his own feet as well as some feet belonging to middle schoolers, but he smiled and laughed through it all. By the third time through, he had a handle on the moves, as did most of the kids, so the group started to more resemble dancers than sumo wrestlers.

"Good job!" The DJ shouted into the microphone from his spot back on the stage. "Now, Ms. Hawthorne, are you up for some fancier moves?"

"Sure," Ellie said, and nodded.

"Okay. This time through, I want you to watch Ms. Hawthorne if you can see her, otherwise watch me and we'll add some shoulder shakes and a little disco after we do our spins to the left. It will make sense once we get going."

The music started again, and the crowd moved as one to the back, to the front, to the right, to the left.

"Here we go," the DJ shouted. "Travolta, eight counts." With his back to the crowd, he sent his right arm up and out, then down across his body. "Seven, eight, now Egg Beater." He rolled his arms in front of him.

Ellie did the same with her hips swaying to the beat, and realized she'd never had so much fun in a middle school gymnasium.

"Chicken!" The DJ announced. He put his hands on his hips then added, "Flap like a chicken," as his elbows went forward and backward. "Okay, from the top!"

They went through the moves a few more times, the kids getting better and better with each try. When the disco music eventually stopped, the DJ whooped his congratulations. Ellie watched several of the kids turn to their friends to show off their perfected 'Travoltas.'

Next to her, Zeke panted, and his cheeks flushed.

"You're not winded, are you Dr. Fahrner?"

"Not from the physical workout as much as the mental one. That was a lot of steps to remember."

Ellie laughed at him. "It was forward, backward, side to side. Not that hard."

"Maybe not for you, since you appear to be a professional dancer." He gave her a curious look. "Are you? I was tripping over my feet after the first steps backward. And then he throws in, what did he call it? Egg mixer? Chicken and the egg? Something like that. I was completely lost."

"Then you're not fond of dancing?"

"You could say that. This," Zeke moved his arm up and down, pointing his finger just like John Travolta, "this I can do. My parents had the Saturday Night Fever album when I was a kid."

"Very good," Ellie said. "You have a lot of potential."

"That, I do not. My parents would play that album sometimes and dance around the living room. My brother and I would almost die of embarrassment. Mom always tried to get us to join them, and eventually we'd give in, but no matter how much my mom loved me, she couldn't quite bring herself to lie to me and tell me I was any good. Isn't there a song, something about 'My feet have got no rhythm?' That's me."

Ellie chuckled. "Something like that. You just need someone to teach you. I bet I could."

"No way." Zeke shook his head. "You never answered my question about being a dancer. You looked like a natural."

"Classes. Lots of classes. From the time I was four. I loved it, but it was always just for fun." Ellie grinned when he shook his head even harder. "What about your brother? Was he the dancer your mama hoped for?"

A shadow passed over Zeke's eyes, but he was saved from answering when the DJ's voice carried through the gym. "We're going to slow it down for a couple of songs. Find that girl or that guy you've been wanting to ask to dance and hit the floor. Ms. Taylor Swift says 'Please?'"

The first notes of Taylor's latest love song bounced off the walls of the gym. Ellie turned to escape the dance floor, but Zeke took her hand. "This I can do. Dance with me, Ellie."

Ellie's stomach twisted in a nervous panic. She wanted to pull her hand away, but Zeke smiled and pleaded with his eyes. Even though her brain told her to run, every other part of her wanted to feel his arms around her, wanted to sway to the music, wanted to close her eyes and remember and forget all at the same time.

She didn't speak, she wasn't sure she could, but she nodded once and stepped into his arms. With one hand already in his, she let the other rest at his waist. She felt the cords of muscle through his slightly sweaty shirt, felt the warmth from his body radiating toward her, and smelled his cologne, a pleasant woodsy respite from her daily barrage of teenage body spray. Zeke smelled like all man, and it went straight to Ellie's head.

While he didn't have a wealth of tricky dance moves, Ellie was impressed with how smoothly Zeke moved once the music slowed. He'd lied about having no rhythm, and he definitely knew how to hold a woman, close enough but not too close. Ellie wondered how much practice he'd had.

Despite the DJ's pleas, the dance floor was sparsely populated. When Ellie caught the eye of one of her bolder seventh grade students, she called, "Come on, Evan, find a partner and join us." The boy grinned, but shook his head. "Extra credit to everyone who's out here in the next thirty seconds," she challenged.

Evan cocked his head in an 'Are you for real' sort of way, and Ellie nodded. "Cross my heart," she said as she moved her hand from Zeke's waist long enough to do just that.

Evan marched across the gym, held his hand out to Courtney, and in a moment, they were next to Ellie and Zeke.

"I want that extra credit, Ms. Hawthorne," Evan said. "Got a B minus on my last quiz. I figure this should raise that to an A, right?"

"You drive a hard bargain, Evan. Get a few of your friends out here and I'll give you that A."

Somewhat clumsily, Evan steered Courtney toward his group of friends. It didn't take long until several more couples joined them and it started to look like a school dance with arms stretched, elbows locked, and lots of rocking from one foot to the other.

"It's sweet, isn't it?" Ellie asked Zeke. "Do you remember what it was like to work up the nerve to ask a girl to dance? To have those butterflies doing the quickstep in your belly? Oh, it seems like such a long time ago, doesn't it?"

"It seems like two minutes ago." Zeke's voice was soft, yet it carried over the music loud and clear. "I had those butterflies when I asked you to dance. I really wanted to dance with you, Ellie."

He didn't have to pose the question for her to hear it in his voice. Did she want to dance with him or was she simply doing it to help the

DJ get kids out on the floor? As much as she wanted to laugh it off, to tease him about the butterflies, she couldn't because they were back, in her own belly, and dancing up a storm.

"I'm glad you asked because now I know you have plenty of rhythm." She put a hint of teasing in her voice, but guessed her eyes told the true story of her feelings, feelings she wasn't ready to admit to herself, let alone to him.

One slow song melted into the next. Zeke didn't let go. If anything, he drew her closer. Ellie felt his breath ruffle her hair, felt his hand trace tiny circles on her back. She was grateful for the distraction her students provided when they pointed, teased, or outright laughed at her dancing with Zeke. Responding to them meant she didn't have to respond to the feelings that wanted to demand her attention.

"Dr. Fahrner, you're needed outside the gym."

Though the voice cut over the music, no one except Zeke and Ellie seemed to notice.

"Duty calls," Zeke said. "Thank you for the dance."

He lifted Ellie's hand and brushed it with his lips before releasing her and heading for the exit to the hallway. Ellie stood frozen in place for a moment, every nerve ending humming, but when an over-exuberant student tried to spin his partner and sent her crashing into Ellie, Ellie stumbled back to reality. Rather than standing by herself in the middle of the dance floor, she followed Zeke to check on the situation.

"What happens is the blood vessels narrow when they get that blast of cold and that causes a pretty intense headache. Brain freeze, people like to call it. It rarely lasts more than a minute or two. You'll be fine, Nolan. Just hang in there."

Ellie watched as the boy, who based on his size she figured had to be an eighth grader, held his head between his hands and rocked and moaned. She took pity on him since she was intimately acquainted with brain freeze. It had been a favorite game with her siblings to see who could eat their bowl of ice cream the fastest and then who could tolerate the subsequent brain freeze without screaming. She'd never won.

Realizing there wasn't much she could do to help, Ellie stayed in the background. Gradually, the boy's moaning subsided. He blinked a few times, scrubbed his hand over his face, and muttered, "Wow."

"Your first time?" Zeke asked.

"Uh, yeah. I'd remember that."

"Maybe next time don't drink your slushie so fast."

"It was four slushies," the boy admitted, "in two minutes."

"Okay, then maybe don't do that again."

"Don't think I will. That was intense."

"Yes, it is intense."

"So, am I like, gonna be okay?"

"You'll be fine," Zeke assured him. "No long-term effects from slushie brain freeze, I promise."

The boy nodded. "Yeah, well thanks."

"No problem," Zeke said. They shook hands, and the boy wandered away.

"Sorry about that, Dr. Fahrner," Kelsey, one of the math teachers, said after the boy was out of earshot. "I didn't know what was wrong with him. He wouldn't talk, just writhed around on the floor holding his head."

"No need to apologize. That's what I'm here for. If it doesn't get any more serious than a case of brain freeze, I think we can call it a good night."

Kelsey tittered. "Oh, Dr. Fahrner, you're funny." She laid her hand on his arm. "I don't think we've met before. I'm Kelsey Williams."

"Nice to meet you, Kelsey."

Ellie was ridiculously pleased when Zeke tactfully bent to retrieve his bag, thereby moving out from under Kelsey's hand. When he took a couple of steps to the side, putting distance between them, Ellie couldn't hold back her smile. Kelsey, though, seemed oblivious.

"Do you work for the school district? It seems like we would have run into one another before tonight."

"No, just filling in for Jackie. Last minute kind of thing."

"Jackie's great, isn't she? She and her husband are so much fun."

Ellie didn't miss the emphasis Kelsey put on husband.

"I don't know her well, but I'm sure that's true. Anyway, I should see if I'm needed somewhere."

"Maybe we could get together sometime for coffee? If you give me your phone, I'll just put my number in there and—"

"Dr. Fahrner? There's a girl in the restroom who's not feeling well. Would you be able to come check on her?" Ellie smiled at Kelsey before turning to Zeke. "It's just this way."

"Of course. It was a pleasure meeting you, Kelsey."

Zeke spun on his heel and followed Ellie away from the crowd and to the adjoining hallway which was off-limits to students except to use the restroom.

"Is there really a girl who's not feeling well?" Zeke asked when they were alone except for the monitor keeping an eye on the hallway.

"Maybe. I'm not sure. There was a girl who rushed toward the restroom, kind of doubled over with her arm at her waist. She looked a little green."

"But you said someone needed me."

"I think what I said was 'There's a girl in the restroom who's not feeling well.' To the best of my knowledge, that's true. Whether she needs you is still to be determined."

Zeke smiled an amused smile that reached his eyes. It mesmerized Ellie the way his dark eyes seemed to sparkle when he held back a laugh. "Perhaps you should check on her."

"I'll do that. If you'll be so kind as to wait a moment, I'll be right back."

There had been a girl rushing to the restroom. The likelihood of her needing medical attention was slim, but it was worth a look. Only one stall door was closed. Ellie busied herself washing her hands and reapplying her lipstick. When she heard a few sniffles from the stall, she asked, "Everything okay?"

"Fine." But that fine came with a catch in the girl's voice.

"Are you sure? It's just Ms. Hawthorne out here. If you're not feeling well, I can help."

"I'm fine." This time, the voice quavered.

"Sweetie, what is it? You can talk to me."

The girl was silent for a long time before her feet shuffled a bit and she said, "I just want to go home."

"We've got some time until the dance ends, but if you're not feeling well, I can see your parents are called. Hopefully, they're able to come early to pick you up. What's your name, honey?"

Now there were tears in her voice. "Toni. And it's just my dad. My mom is out of town. I don't think, I mean, my dad..."

The pieces were falling into place. "You don't want to call your dad?"

"Um, no, not really."

Ellie nodded to herself. "Toni, did you get your period?"

The tears turned to sobs. "Ye—, Ye—, Yes. I don't, I mean, I, I..."

"I have a bag here. I'll hand it over the door. You take whatever you want. If you have questions, just ask."

Ellie took the small zippered bag from her purse and handed it over the door to a trembling hand.

"You know, I got my period for the first time at school too, except I didn't know until a boy, Jamie Jameson, announced it at the top of his lungs in the middle of a crowded hallway. I thought I was going to die of embarrassment. I ran into the bathroom, locked myself in, and wouldn't come out until someone finally got the school nurse. She brought me what I needed, gave me a pair of sweat pants to put on, then called my mama to come and get me. I begged Mama to let me stay at home the next day, but she told me I had to go face that silly Jamie Jameson and show him he didn't win. I wasn't sure why she was so insistent that I face him, usually Mama recommended avoiding confrontations, but she didn't waver on this one. Years later, I found out *she* got her period for the first time at school and some boys made fun of her. She tried to ignore it, but she never got over it. She didn't want the same thing for me."

Ellie kept up the chatter until the door opened and a striking girl with huge, dark eyes, dozens of black braids, and a tear-streaked face emerged. She handed the bag back to Ellie.

"Thank you."

"You're welcome. If you want, you can keep it. Do you know if you have what you need at home?"

The girl nodded. "My mom got a bunch of stuff a while ago. She put it in the closet in my bathroom. I wish this would have happened at home."

"I know, I do too, but it's going to be okay. Do you need something else to wear?"

"No. It's okay. My stomach felt funny. It kind of hurt, but I didn't really feel sick. I didn't know…I came to the bathroom…I…"

"Then no one knows but you and me?"

Toni nodded.

"That's good. It's nothing to be embarrassed about or ashamed of, it's important you know that, but it's also not something a girl wants anyone else to know unless she chooses to tell them."

The first hint of a smile tugged at the girl's mouth. "Was that boy's name really Jamie Jameson? That's kind of a dumb name."

"It most certainly was. I may have told him his parent's must not have liked him very much to give him such a silly name when I came face to face with him the next time, but I regretted my words almost before I said them. There's never cause to be mean, my mama taught me that from the time I could talk. Even though he never apologized to me for what he did, I apologized to him for teasing him about his name."

"Really?"

"Really. I apologized, but I also might have enjoyed it just a little when the next year in school Jamie told our history teacher he loved her and the entire class heard him."

"What?"

"Honest. He went to her desk to ask a question, they talked for a minute, then when they were through, he said, 'Okay, thanks, love you.' It was out of habit, as if he was talking to his own mama or gran, but it was embarrassing for him, you can be sure of that."

The girl giggled. "That would be so embarrassing."

"We all have those moments, and even though it seems like things will never get better, they always do. Are you going to be okay? Do you want to call your dad?"

"I think I'm okay. Um, can I ask you a question?"

"Of course. Anything."

"How do I know when, um, you know, I mean, is there a certain amount of time I wait…"

"You'll know." Ellie offered some advice while Toni dabbed at her face with a paper towel. When she was done, Ellie handed her a brand new tube of lip gloss. "This color will look amazing on you."

"But it's yours."

"It's yours now. I hadn't opened it because I knew it wasn't right for me. It's right for you."

Toni twisted off the top, then dabbed at her lips.

"Thank you, Ms. Hawthorne."

"You're welcome, honey. Now, how's your stomach? If it hurts, I can see about getting you something for it."

"It's okay. Now that I know what was going on, it kind of makes sense."

"Yeah. It gets easier every month, by the way."

"Really?"

"Really."

They walked back into the hallway where Zeke waited. When he started toward them, Ellie gave him a quick shake of her head and steered Toni in the other direction.

"I hope you enjoy the rest of the dance. If you need anything, anything at all, come find me."

"Thanks again, Ms. Hawthorne."

With a wave, Toni disappeared down the hallway and into the throng.

"Everything okay?" Zeke asked when the coast was clear.

"Everything's fine."

"She's not sick? You were in there a long time."

"Girl stuff, Dr. Fahrner. We handled it."

Understanding dawned on Zeke's face. "Okay, then."

They walked down the hallway. "How much longer?" Ellie asked Zeke.

"Half an hour."

Ellie looked in the gym door. "I suppose I'll make another lap, see what's happening."

"I could walk with you," Zeke said.

Ellie looked at him. He looked nervous, and it was impossibly cute.

"I imagine you could," she said.

With a deep breath, they crossed the threshold back into mayhem.

"May the force be with us," Zeke said solemnly.

12

"I heard about the hotly contested hula hoop contest, the mosh pit that was the Hustle, and about a slushie fight. What did I miss?" Max asked Ellie after school on Monday when she plopped down in a chair in Ellie's room. It seemed to have become their gathering place.

"Those are probably the high points. Or the low points, depending on how you look at it."

"Was it awful?"

"Awful?" Ellie smiled at the memory of dancing with Zeke but turned her head in order to avoid a slew of questions from Max. "No, it wasn't awful. Well, the music was awfully loud, at times. The smell of all that cologne being sweat out of a gym full of teenage boys was a bit awful. Overall, though, it was kind of fun."

"You have a weird sense of fun. I still can't believe you volunteered for it. They would've had to threaten me with hideous forms of torture before I would have volunteered for that job."

"You're going to be sitting atop a dunk tank this Friday afternoon. To me, that sounds awful." Ellie wrinkled her nose at the thought.

Max waved off Ellie's concern. "Have you seen some of those sixth graders? I don't think half of them can throw a ball that far, let alone hit a target. I don't plan on getting wet."

"Sixth graders? Oh, no, Max, it's not just sixth graders. Each grade gets to choose two students, one boy and one girl, to attempt to dunk you. Have you seen some of those eighth graders?"

Max paled. "What? No." She shook her head. "I distinctly remember being told that if a grade made their goal, they got a shot at the dunk tank. The sixth graders made their goal. The seventh and eighth graders did not."

137

"You didn't read the fine print. The sixth graders beat their goal by enough to cover the gap between what the other grades earned and their goals, so based on teamwork, all three grades reached their goals, and all three grades get a crack at dunking you."

"But…but that's not fair."

Max raked a hand through her short crop of hair. It was a sheer marvel to Ellie the way the hair fell perfectly back into place, no matter how viciously Max attacked it.

"Now you sound like our students, Max. 'That's not fair?' What would you say to one of your students if he or she complained that something wasn't fair?"

"Bite me, life isn't fair?" At Ellie's frown, Max added, "Okay, just kidding, I wouldn't say that even if I wanted to. But back to this whole 'all for one and one for all' bull. Who made that rule? And why didn't I know about it?"

"If I had to guess, I'd say it's because you weren't paying attention to the details, sweetie."

"Max? Sweetie? Have I entered the Twilight Zone?" Nicole grinned as she joined Ellie and Max.

Max turned to glare at Nicole. "How did you get out of all of it? Tell me that, would you?"

"All of what?" Nicole asked.

Max began ticking items off on her fingers. "Out of the fundraiser kickoff assembly, out of the school dance, out of lunchroom duty, out of freaking dunk tank duty! Why aren't you sitting in the stupid dunk tank with me?"

Nicole cringed and looked down at her neatly pressed linen slacks and silk blouse. "A dunk tank? Hardly."

"But how, Nic? Tell me how. What am I doing wrong?"

"I'm handling all the record keeping for the fundraiser. I'd be happy to show you the spreadsheets and the bank deposit slips if you're interested." Nicole smiled sweetly at Max.

"That sounds like stuff you enjoy doing. I don't enjoy sitting in dunk tanks."

"We all must work to our strengths, Max." Then, before Max could fire back, Nicole said, "Were you talking about the dance? Did you hear about Kelsey?"

"Kelsey? Who's Kelsey?" Max asked.

"Kelsey Williams. Ellie, you were there. Did you see her?"

"Yes, I saw her," Ellie answered carefully. "There weren't that many staff members there. I'm sure I saw everyone who was volunteering."

"No, no, I mean did you see her throw herself at some doctor? It was the talk of the break room this morning."

"Doctor? What doctor? One of the parents?" Max asked, her frustration with Nicole's skill at wheedling her way out of undesirable jobs apparently forgotten and replaced with a curiosity that comes with being starved for adult conversation.

"I don't know what doctor, maybe a parent, but I guess he was helping at the dance since Jackie couldn't be there." Nicole turned her eyes on Ellie. "Did you see her?"

Ellie busied herself with straightening a stack of papers in order to buy herself some time. How was she supposed to answer? She could claim she hadn't seen Kelsey with the doctor, that wouldn't be unreasonable, but she couldn't very well claim to not know who the doctor was. Given what Nicole had told her about Zeke's reputation, it seemed like only a matter of time until Nicole found out he was the one who'd given up his Friday evening to help at a middle school dance.

"I saw Kelsey talking to several people. She's such a social butterfly, isn't she? Did you hear about the slushie contest that resulted in a serious case of brain freeze for one of the eighth grade boys?"

"Yes!" Nicole nearly shouted. "That's when Kelsey was talking to this doctor. According to all reports, she threw herself at him, but he blew her off. Politely, I guess, but still." Nicole waved her hand in a sweeping motion. "Kelsey was none too pleased."

"Did you see that, El?" Max asked.

There was no point in acting as if she hadn't. One way or another, word would get to Nicole or Max and besides, lying wasn't in Ellie's genetic makeup.

"I guess I did, now that you mention it. It didn't seem like that big of a deal that people would be talking about it today."

"Hah! Have you met about ninety percent of the teachers we work with? They live for gossip, El. Grown-up gossip, that is. There's plenty of teenage gossip to go around," Nicole said.

"So what happened? Did she embarrass herself?" Max asked.

"I don't like gossip," Ellie replied.

"It's not gossip if you saw it happen, if you know it's true," Max countered. "It's simply relaying facts."

Ellie drew in a deep breath and closed her eyes. "Fine. It was Zeke Fahrner helping at the dance," she said on her exhale. "And I wouldn't say Kelsey threw herself at him. That's definitely an overstatement. She was chatting with him, then I needed Zeke to tend to another student, and that was the end of it, as far as I know."

Max narrowed her eyes and leveled Ellie with a laser-like stare. Nicole's eyebrows rose so high they nearly melted into her hairline. Ellie tapped her fingers together to keep herself from fidgeting when neither of them spoke, just stared. Wishing for that to be the end of the conversation, she scooped papers into her bag and shut down her computer. When she took a step toward the door, both Max and Nicole held up their hands to stop her.

Nicole still didn't seem capable of speech, but Max said, "There's no way that was the end."

"I told you, as far as I know, Kelsey and Zeke didn't talk to each other again. Maybe they did, I wasn't watching for it, but I didn't see anything more between the two of them. And that's not to imply there was anything between them earlier." Ellie huffed in frustration. "This is coming out all wrong. I'm making it sound like a much bigger deal than it was. They were both there. They spoke. That's all I know."

"It was Zeke? Zeke Fahrner? Zeke was here, at the school?" Nicole didn't blink. In fact, as Ellie watched, Nicole's eyes got wider with every word. What was the deal with Zeke, and why didn't Nicole just tell them? It was all starting to annoy Ellie.

"Yes. Zeke filled in for Jackie at the last minute. Why is that such a big deal?"

It took a moment for Nicole to answer. When she did, she stumbled over her words. "A big deal? It's it…it isn't, a big deal, I mean, it's not. It's not a big deal. It's just, well, hmm. Zeke was here. At school. In Caston. Hmm. Okay."

Even Max looked suspicious now. "What's up with you, Nic? You sort of freak out every time this guy is mentioned. I'm having a harder and harder time believing there was never anything between the two of you."

Ellie had more or less convinced herself Nicole had been honest when she'd said she barely knew Zeke and that there was never any sort of relationship—even a one-sided wishful sort of relationship—between them. Now hearing Max put her suspicions into words, seeing Nicole's still shocked and confused expression, Ellie began to doubt her instincts.

The confusion still clouded Nicole's eyes, kept them from completely focusing when she finally answered Max, but Ellie could tell Nicole was fighting to appear unfazed.

"No, no, there's nothing. There never was. That's a fact. It's just that, well, you didn't grow up here, you don't know just how...how famous, I guess, this guy was. When he left for college, no one expected him to return. He was definitely the guy most likely to succeed, you know? Not the guy most likely to wind up back in Caston."

Ellie tried to think who might have fit that description in her high school, but she couldn't come up with anyone. Sure, there were the popular people, the smart people, the nice people, a few that fit into all those categories, but no one as universally worshipped as Nicole made it appear Zeke had been. It was strange, Ellie decided, and it would seem strange to anyone, not just the outsider from Oklahoma.

"It's not that unusual for someone to come back to their hometown," Max said. "Maybe he got homesick. Maybe he realized the big, bad world was just that. Big and bad. Maybe he realized Caston wasn't quite so terrible after all."

Nicole shrugged, but Ellie noticed it was a jerky, nervous sort of shrug, and that Nicole seemed uncomfortable.

"You're probably right. I'm making too big a deal out of it," Nicole said. She turned to face Ellie. "El, I saw Jed yesterday. He said he hadn't heard from you."

"Jed?" Ellie said. "Oh, Jed. The tiling." With as busy as she'd been, she'd pushed her ideas for remodeling to the back burner. "I'm sorry, I haven't gotten around to calling him. I will. Soon."

"No need to apologize," Nicole said with a wave of her hand. "The topic came up when I talked with him over the weekend. I assumed you would have called him. You seemed eager to get the work done."

"I was. I am. I will. Call him, I mean."

"Whatever you two are talking about, I don't care, but you're not changing the subject that easily. Ellie, did you know Zeke was going to be at the dance? Did he go with you? Leave with you?"

"No, no, and no. I did not know he was going to be there, we did not go together, and we certainly," she paused and rolled her eyes at Max, "did not leave together."

Max smirked. "You never know. And if he blew off Kelsey in favor of you? Well now, that would be something to talk about in the break room, wouldn't it?"

Ellie pursed her lips and shook her head at Max. "Bless your heart, Max, you have quite the imagination, don't you?"

Max threw her head back and boomed out a long laugh. "And you southern girls know how to make an insult sound as sweet as that tea you're so fond of, don't you?"

For as much as she wanted to respond with a snappy comeback, Ellie could only laugh. Then, because she knew it was only a matter of time until Max and Nicole heard more, she said, "Zeke and I chatted, I dragged him onto the dance floor to do the Hustle, then we stayed and danced to a slower song to try to encourage some of the kids to participate. That's all there is to tell."

"Hmm, somehow I doubt that, but I'll let it go. For now," Max said as she glanced at the clock on Ellie's classroom wall. "Just know if I didn't have a meeting, I'd get it out of you. I'm that tough." Max flexed her arm muscle. "See you tomorrow." With a wave, she hurried out of the room.

Nicole still hadn't said anything more, but before Ellie could ask her about Zeke or about anything else, Nicole's phone buzzed. Every muscle seemed to tense, and the color drained from Nicole's face when she looked at the text.

"I have to run too. Bye, Ellie."

"Is everything..." But Nicole was already out the door. "Bye, Nicole," Ellie mumbled.

She had papers to grade, book club request forms to review, and an installment of 'Adventures with Boomer' to prepare, but Ellie was restless. As she wandered the house trying to clear her head, she paused outside the bathroom with the green tile. Looking worse than ever against the freshly painted grey walls, it taunted her. She needed to call Jed, and she would, but her concerns about Maddie were at an all-time high, and it was difficult to focus on much else.

Ever since Maddie had handed in her star with her parents' wedding photo attached and told Ellie her reasoning behind choosing it, Ellie had kept an eye on the girl. At times, Maddie was happy, turning in quality work, a leader in the classroom. Other times, and those times were becoming more frequent, she was withdrawn, taking part in class only if called on, and missing homework deadlines. Ellie had kept Maddie after class twice to discuss missing assignments. During their quick discussions, Ellie had tried to say without actually saying that she was there if Maddie needed to talk, needed help, needed anything, but so far, the girl hadn't reached out.

Maddie wasn't the only student causing Ellie to worry. There was

Malcom, whose teasing of the other boys over everything from their height to their lack of skill on the soccer field to the color of their shirt was a clear cry for attention—and help—in Ellie's mind. And there was Talia, who was relating well with Mr. T, but still refusing to speak to Ellie. And Sam, and Charlie, and Bridgette, and the list went on.

But Maddie troubled her the most. Feeling helpless, Ellie had broached the subject with Jill when they'd been alone in the lunchroom. Jill had assured Ellie she'd done the right thing, that she couldn't force the issue with the student, and that it was up to Maddie to come to Ellie. 'Gentle reminders, when the opportunity presents itself, are good, but don't push too hard or you'll push her away.' Ellie knew Jill was right, but it was so hard to sit back, watch and wait, and feel helpless.

"Oh, Boomer, what am I going to do?"

Boomer took her frustration as an invitation to play. He bounded from his spot next to her on the couch to grab his tennis ball and park himself in front of the door. His tail thumped so loudly and rapidly on the floor, it sounded like a toddler let loose with drumsticks and a snare drum.

"Okay, okay, we'll go play. I need a break too, buddy."

Ellie slipped on her shoes, shrugged into her jacket, and clipped the leash on Boomer's collar. While he was getting better, at least sometimes, at listening, she didn't trust him in the unfenced front yard to play without a leash. Another dog, a squirrel, even a leaf scuttling down the street would be all the invitation he needed to take off, and once he got going, catching him was practically impossible.

A couple of weeks ago, she'd made the mistake—again—of clipping the leash to his ID tag instead of his collar. They'd headed out the door for a walk, Boomer spotted a young girl and her dad on the other side of the street, and pulled like a sled dog. The ring on the ID tag gave out, Boomer bolted for the girl, and Ellie had been left apologizing to the dad who hadn't tried very hard to hide his annoyance. The girl, once she'd gotten over her initial shock of having a ninety-pound dog bounding toward her, and once she'd gotten over the fact that Boomer had stolen her sucker, hugged and played with the candy thief. No, Ellie didn't need a repeat of that.

"Just hang on while I get the mail. We forgot to get it this afternoon." Ellie coaxed Boomer to follow her to the mailbox when all he wanted to do was head to the back yard where he knew he'd be let off the leash. She pulled him along, he dragged behind her, and she felt like the sled dog.

"Would you just cooperate, please? It will only take a minute."

When he fought even harder, Ellie gave up and turned. "What in the world is the matter with you?"

She had her answer before she finished asking her question. A few houses away, a perfectly behaved lab jogged at the side of a perfectly put together man. They looked like they belonged in an advertisement. Bowie matched Zeke's pace; not pulling to get him to run faster, not stopping when an interesting scent captured his attention. Both were favorite tricks of Boomer's and the reason she and Boomer went for walks instead of runs.

Ellie debated ducking into the back yard. She told herself it was so Zeke wouldn't feel obligated to interrupt his run. She knew it was so she wouldn't have to face him. She still hadn't figured out the 'friends with a man' thing. But he spotted her, he lifted his hand in a wave, and she knew there'd be no avoiding a conversation.

"Ellie. Hi." Zeke trotted to a stop, then took a deep breath and blew it out slowly. He used the sleeve of his Northwestern sweatshirt, the one he'd given her to wear when she'd had dinner with him, to wipe the sweat from his forehead. "How are you? Recovered from the dance?"

"I'm well, thank you. No lasting trauma." Ellie wrapped Boomer's leash around one of her hands, shortening it as much as she could to try to keep her boisterous dog under control, and used the other hand to pat Bowie's head while he sat obediently at Zeke's left side. Again, the dog amazed her with his behavior. "Hi there, Bowie, you good boy."

"Are you headed out on a walk?" Zeke asked.

"No, just to the back to throw the ball for Boomer. We had a walk earlier, but he didn't seem to think that was sufficient. A game of fetch will tire him out. Sometimes I think he'd chase the ball until he couldn't stand any longer."

At the mention of the ball, Boomer jumped in place and nudged Ellie's hand with his nose. Bowie, while he didn't move from Zeke's side, twitched and followed the ball with his eyes.

"I think it's a lab thing," Zeke said. "Bowie spots a tennis ball, and he's obsessed until I throw it for him."

"But he's such a gentleman about it." Boomer, apparently thinking Ellie hadn't gotten the hint, started barking and knocking her in the leg with his head. "And then there's Boomer."

Zeke chuckled. "He's just reminding you that you promised him a game of fetch."

"Like a tornado reminds a tree that it's no match?"

"Well, maybe not quite that bad."

"I did promise him, and I'm sure you want to get back to your run. Nice seeing you, Zeke. Bowie." She gave the dog another pat.

"We could join you in that game of fetch, if you don't mind. Like I said, Bowie loves chasing a ball, and I'm about run out. I'm afraid Bowie has a lot more energy tonight than I have."

Zeke smiled at Ellie with the hopeful look of a little boy eyeing one more cookie. Ellie wished it were as simple as handing him a cookie.

"Sure," she said. "We have to play in the back where it's fenced. Boomer doesn't pay attention to boundaries that aren't hard and fast." Ellie started toward the back, and Zeke followed.

"That's smart. No matter how well-trained you think your dog is, he's still a dog. That was something Bowie's trainer drilled into us during class. She had too many stories of devastated dog owners who thought their pet would never run out into traffic, or never chase a rabbit, or never fail to follow a command. It's always better to be safe than sorry."

Ellie opened the gate in the fence, then closed and latched it once everyone was inside. She unclipped the leash from Boomer's collar and after Zeke did the same, tossed the tennis ball.

"I have no delusions Boomer will follow any command. Sometimes he surprises me, but more often, he ignores me. We're definitely playing it safe."

Zeke took a turn with the ball and the dogs legged it out in a mad race for the prize. Bowie was a step behind Boomer, but when Boomer overran the ball and tumbled head over heels, Bowie nabbed it and tore back toward Zeke with Boomer chasing behind.

"Not to imply Boomer needs it, but I could give you the number of Bowie's trainer. Valerie. She works with all dogs, not just those training to be therapy dogs. She's very good at what she does."

"Oh, he needs it. We did a couple of classes and I know what I should be doing with him—and that I should be doing more of it—but a refresher sure wouldn't hurt. Where is she located?"

"It's about thirty miles from here, so not the most convenient, but she has the perfect location for her purpose. She boards dogs and also takes in dogs for intense training, where she keeps them for a couple of weeks to a couple of months."

"Is that what you did with Bowie?"

"I did. I timed it with my move back to Caston. I sent Bowie to Valerie for his training while I dealt with moving and all that entails. When I got settled here, I went to a few sessions at her place for training with Bowie. It was an ideal situation for Bowie and for me."

Ellie's mind spun so fast, it reminded her of the ancient windmill on her granddaddy's ranch, its blades whirring when a storm rolled across the plains. How much would it cost to send Boomer for some of that intense training? A couple of weeks to a couple of months without him demanding her attention every minute, without having to rush home after school, without having to walk him in the pouring rain and the ever colder evenings. And maybe she could coordinate it with Jed tiling her bathroom. Wondering how she'd keep Boomer out of the way had been another reason for putting off calling Jed. But then she'd be without Boomer there to greet her when she got home, his tail thumping and his entire body twitching with excitement as she opened the door. Without the sense of security he provided, without the companionship to keep her from dwelling on how much she missed home. He'd come home better behaved, but would he still be her Boomer? Would she miss his naughty exuberance and his unbridled excitement when he caught a glimpse of a tennis ball or a whiff of the water? What if he came home so changed, their relationship changed?

"Valerie does a remarkable job. I think she also offers in-home classes. Maybe that's something to consider."

Ellie shifted her focus. Maybe it was. The best of both worlds, perhaps? "In-home? She'd come to me? To us?"

"I don't know much about how it works, but I'll forward her number and if you're interested, give her a call."

Zeke pulled his phone from his pocket, tapped it a few times, then smiled up at her. "Done."

"Thank you. I might just do that. Heaven knows, Boomer could stand to learn a few manners."

"Did you have a dog when you were growing up?"

"No, not of our own, Mama wouldn't hear of a dog in the house, but Granddaddy always has lots of dogs around the ranch. I spent a lot of time there and though the dogs were expected to work, most were gentle and we were allowed to play with them. We snuck them in the house sometimes when we spent the night on the ranch." Ellie smiled at the memory. "We always thought we were so clever, that we'd pulled one over on Gran, but when I got older, I figured out there wasn't a single thing that went on in her house that she didn't know about. She just chose to look the other way once in a while." Ellie rubbed her hands up and down her arms, chilled. "I miss her," she mumbled, more to herself than to Zeke.

"Will you go home for Thanksgiving? Or Christmas?"

No. As much as she missed Gran, Granddaddy, all of them, she wouldn't risk a trip home. "I haven't decided yet. We'll see."

"More than once, you've referred to 'your brothers and sisters,' or 'one of your sisters.' You have me wondering how many you have."

Ellie did her best to shake off the sadness. "Five. Three brothers, two sisters."

"That's quite a crowd. Where do you fall? No, wait, let me guess."

As Zeke studied her, his head tipped and his forehead creased. He nodded when he spoke, looking sure of himself.

"It's got to be in the middle. You don't strike me as the oldest because, as the oldest of six, you'd be bossier. More forceful. You'd want your way all the time. And not the youngest, because you definitely don't strike me as an attention-seeker; you don't expect others to do things for you." He nodded again. "Yes. Middle child. You're a peace-maker, you want to please, you relate well with everyone from young children to older folks." Then Zeke laughed. "And I could be way off, because all that was nothing but a bunch of generalizations from textbooks and if I've learned anything during my studies and my training, it's that every child, every person, is different. Plugging them into generalizations can be a very bad idea."

"In this case, I have to say your generalizations are spot on, doctor. I'm number four of six, so very much a middle child. And if I had to fit my brothers and sisters into your generalizations, for the most part, they'd fit like the proverbial glove."

"Huh. I guess sometimes those books are right. Tell me about them. Your siblings," Zeke said as he tossed the ball again.

Ellie took a deep breath, and while Zeke's back was to her, she squared her shoulders and told herself she could do it. She could talk about her family without letting sadness swamp her.

"Tripp is the oldest. His real name is Charles, same as my daddy and Granddaddy Hawthorne, but everyone calls him Tripp. Except Mama. She hates it, made Daddy swear that if they named him Charles he'd never be called Tripp, but she's been helpless to stop it. Tripp is a lawyer like Daddy. He's so much like Daddy it's eerie. Tripp and his long-time girlfriend, Shelby, were married a couple of years ago.

"Travis is next. He's the only other one to leave Oklahoma. Mama still will hardly discuss it except to say he'll be home as soon as he gets New York out of his system. He works for an ad agency there and loves it. I'd never tell Mama, no one would ever tell Mama, but I don't think Trav will be returning to Oklahoma."

Ellie paused to take a turn with the ball. A mistake, she realized, because Zeke jumped at the break in her story.

"Is she convinced you'll come back home too?"

Mama was convinced of a lot of things, Ellie thought to herself, but to Zeke, she said, "It was a little easier since I wasn't the first to leave, but she's not fond of me being away." Not an answer, exactly, but enough of one.

Before Zeke could ask anything else, Ellie continued. "Charlene is just a year older than me. She works for a real estate agent, running the office, and she's getting married next summer."

In their sprawling back yard, under the shade of the towering oaks and maples, rows of white chairs lined as precisely as soldiers... Ellie squeezed her eyes shut and forced herself to stop. Stop imagining, stop envying, and stop feeling sorry for herself.

"Though she's technically also a middle child, I think being the oldest girl makes Char think she's the boss of all of us. She's the one who starts the group texts, who arranges Christmas and anniversary gifts for Daddy and Mama and tells us what we owe her, and the one who has tried to be just like Mama since she was old enough to talk.

"Then there's Hayley, still in college, and not a clue as to what she wants to do once she's done. For as much as Char plans every single detail of every single day, Hayley has never had a plan in her life. She's the most free-spirited, fly-by-your-britches person I know. Mama prays every day Hayley will settle down, and Hayley prays every day she'll never have to. Hayley is Hayley. She loves life, she finds fun in everything she does, and I don't think she'll ever change. And last..."

Ellie had to pause and swallow over the burning in her throat. It was a struggle to keep her voice steady. "Last is Colt. The baby, and sweeter than stolen honey." And he was her heart. She missed him so much, it almost brought her to her knees. "He's eleven, determined to grow up and be a rancher, and would move to Oak Run right now if he could figure out how to make that happen." The yard blurred through Ellie's tears. She busied herself with picking up a stick and snapping it into pieces.

"Oak Run. That's your grandparents' ranch?"

Ellie tossed the bits of stick and rolled her shoulders. In her mind, she brought up memories of the ranch in an effort to push out the images of Colt, his tanned face and sweaty gold curls peeking out at her from under his dusty, worn hat, his eager blue eyes pleading with her to take him out riding, just one more time. It was far less painful to picture the acres and acres of land, the creek that bisected it in a lazy, meandering ribbon of blue, the ranch's head gate with the family brand proudly displayed, the fences that stretched for miles, the sun setting behind the porch that wrapped around the house she loved and that always felt like home, Gran standing on that porch and ringing the dinner bell.

It wasn't until she moved away that Ellie realized what she'd taken for granted and what she'd considered a way of life was what so many outside Oklahoma, and outside ranching country, thought existed only in movies. More the stuff of fairy tales than of real life. Sure the land was stunningly beautiful, but that land required hard work to keep it that way. Herds of cattle dotting the fields might look like something out of a storybook, but tons of feed, thousands of doses of vaccines, and countless hours worrying over freezing temperatures and droughts, fretting over breeding season and the risk of losing valuable calves, was all part of making that storybook picture possible. Even Gran ringing the dinner bell might seem like something from a bygone era and right out of an old western, but on a ranch, that sound carried far better than did spotty cell phone service.

"Ellie? Is something wrong?"

Ellie jumped at Zeke's voice. So deep in her memories, it had been easy to forget he was only a few feet away.

"No, nothing's wrong. Just thinking, I guess." What was it he'd asked? She racked her brain. Oak Run. "Yes, Oak Run is my granddaddy's ranch. It's been in the family for generations."

"So, through my incredible powers of deduction, I've concluded your mother's family are the ranchers. Your mother, though, may prefer life away from the ranch. Your brothers and sisters are as different from one another as night is from day, but you're close, all of you. You miss them a lot, but something's keeping you from going home. Do you want to talk about it?"

Ellie wouldn't have been surprised if she reached out toward Zeke, she'd feel the wall that erected itself between them. A brick wall, as strong as that smartest little pig built. Just like that little pig, no straw or twigs would suffice when it came to protecting herself. Though it may not have been from a wolf, it could just as well have been for as much as she could feel the claws ripping at her heart, the sharp teeth piercing her soul.

But Zeke was only being polite, being a friend she supposed, and he'd done nothing intentional, she had to remember that. And he wasn't Vincent. She had to remember that, too.

"It's just been a long time since I've seen them. I'm busy with school, so it's difficult to get home." It sounded lame, she knew that, but it was the best she could manage. What she could manage more easily, though, was to turn the tables. She forced a bright smile and brushed her hands against one another, effectively brushing away the memories.

"That's enough about me. What about you? You've mentioned a brother, but that's all I know. Is he still in town? And your parents?"

If it were possible, Zeke looked even more uncomfortable than she'd felt, and she was almost sorry for putting him on the spot.

"My parents retired several years ago and are in Florida. They claim to like it, but I know Mom, especially, misses the snow. It's probably hard for a southerner to understand, but some people actually like cold winters."

Zeke smiled, but it didn't reach his eyes. And, not for the first time, he'd avoided any mention of his brother, though she'd specifically asked. Curious, but understanding well how those brick walls worked, Ellie played along.

"We get snow in Oklahoma. Y'all seem to think it's summer year-round there. That's not the case. It gets cold, it snows, and it's windy. It's a far cry from what I'd call summer. Now, I'm not going to claim it's anything like winter here where it seems to last for half the year, but we know what snow is and I'll admit to liking it. In moderation."

"The Farmer's Almanac is calling for an especially snowy winter this year."

"Is that so? Boomer will like that."

At the sound of his name, Boomer lifted his head and looked up at Ellie with expectant eyes.

"Only Boomer?"

"As I said, snow, in moderation, is fine. Driving in it, however, is not. I had a twenty-mile commute last winter to my student teaching position. Do you know that there were days it took me over two hours to make the trip? Two hours!"

This time when Zeke smiled, it reached his eyes. "Oh, Ellie, trust me,

I know. It's a way of life here in the north country. Kind of like tumbleweed traffic delays in Oklahoma."

Ellie scoffed. "There may be tumbleweed in some parts of the state, but we don't have tumbleweed…" Zeke's grin got even bigger. "Oh, you're teasing me. Very funny, Dr. Fahrner. Maybe one day you'll make another visit to Oklahoma. I'd love to show you around, to teach you about ranching, to point out what makes Oklahoma the best place on earth."

"I'd like that."

Zeke said it softly, all the joking gone from his voice and replaced with a sincerity and a longing that Ellie didn't know how to handle. Thankfully, Boomer saved her from having to figure it out when he tore across the yard, barking all the way.

"Boomer!"

Zeke turned toward the commotion, but his eyes stayed on Ellie even as the rest of him pointed in Boomer's direction.

"It's a rabbit," Ellie said by way of explanation. "I keep thinking the silly thing will learn its lesson. Boomer nearly loses his mind every time he sees it. He barks like crazy, chases it across the yard like a maniac until I'm certain he's going to crash right into the fence, then stands there and stares at the spot where the rabbit ducks underneath, ignoring my calls, until I finally go get him and drag him back into the house. It's become an almost daily occurrence."

"I don't know that there's any amount of training that will stop a lab from chasing a rabbit. Or a squirrel. I have a squirrel that drives Bowie crazy."

"But I'll bet Bowie listens when you call him."

Boomer was flat on the ground, his nose pressed to the fence, and as still as could be. "Boomer! Come!" Ellie called. Boomer didn't so much as flinch.

"Bowie usually listens," Zeke said.

"Bowie always listens, I know that, you're just trying to make me feel better."

Ellie sighed and started for the fence. Zeke matched her stride, with Bowie sticking close by Zeke's side. By the time they reached the fence, Boomer's nose and front paws were black, the hole at the base of the fence sizable, and the look on the dog's face when he stopped digging long enough to glance at them, decidedly proud.

"Oh, Boomer, not again." As frustrated as she was, Ellie realized snapping a picture of Boomer caught in the act would make for a good story for the following day's 'Adventures with Boomer,' but she'd left her phone in the house.

"Do you think I could borrow your phone for a quick second to take a picture?" Ellie asked Zeke.

"Sure." Zeke unlocked the screen and handed it to her. "Do you always take pictures of him when he gets in trouble?"

Ellie crouched and snapped a picture. "Okay if I send it to myself?" When Zeke nodded, she did so. "And no, I don't always take pictures of my naughty dog. I'd do nothing all day long but take pictures if that were the case. This one is for school. I share pictures and stories of Boomer with my seventh graders. They're my last class of the day, the kids are tired and antsy, and I've found starting the class with a few minutes of what I call 'Adventures with Boomer' gets their attention and helps them ease into their last hour of the day."

Ellie handed the phone back to Zeke, then grabbed Boomer by the collar and pulled him away from the fence. He balked at first, straining to get back to work on the hole, but happily changed his focus to Bowie when Ellie didn't loosen her grip. She used her free hand to pick up a stick and toss it, distracting Boomer and giving Bowie a reprieve.

"I think Boomer and I need to head inside. Along with uploading the picture I just took, I have a pile of work waiting for me."

Zeke clipped Bowie's leash on his collar. "Is there always work in the evening? On weekends?"

"Not always, but often. I don't mind. I like to keep busy."

"It's a hard job, being a teacher. I might not have realized it at the time, but now I know how indebted I am to the teachers I had over the years who pushed me, who settled for nothing but my best, who, I'm sure, put in a lot of extra hours for their students. I don't think you're always appreciated."

"I don't think most teachers get into teaching in order to be appreciated."

"Probably not, but I have to believe it's still nice to feel that way. I hope you do. Feel appreciated, I mean, because I'm sure you are, whether your students tell you so, or not."

Her time outside, her conversation with Zeke, thinking about her family, had all helped push her concern for Maddie from her mind, but it came roaring back. More than appreciated, Ellie wanted to be trusted. Trusted enough that her students would come to her if they felt they didn't have anywhere else to go.

"Ellie?"

"Hmm?"

"I said thanks for helping me entertain Bowie."

"Oh, sure. Have a good night, Zeke."

Ellie opened the gate to let out Zeke and Bowie, keeping a firm hand on Boomer's collar, then closed it behind them.

"Do you want to go to a football game with me?"

Ellie had already turned and was headed for her back door when she heard Zeke, and already focused on figuring what she could do for Maddie, she was certain she'd heard wrong as the words had come out in a rush.

"Pardon?"

Zeke's cheeks were tinged pink, a boyish blush creeping up his neck to heat his face, and Ellie found herself smiling despite her inner turmoil.

"Um, I asked if you'd like to go to a football game with me."

He spoke slower this time, seeming to have to coax out each word. For the first time during one of their conversations, Ellie felt like the calm one, the in-control one. It was a good feeling. When one of Zeke's feet took a step away, almost of its own volition it appeared, and he looked torn between wanting to bolt for the street and waiting expectantly for her answer, she forgot about the worries and the stresses of school and felt her heart start to melt at the sight of the man in front of her.

"A football game?"

Zeke busied his hands with Bowie's leash. "Yes. The Packers game. At Lambeau Field. This Sunday."

"Oh, my stars. Lambeau Field? This Sunday? I don't know, there's Boomer—" Ellie gasped and her hand flew to her mouth. She stood frozen. For a minute, she couldn't speak and when she finally did, her voice was hardly more than a whisper. "But this Sunday the Packers play the Cowboys."

"I know. It's a big game. My family has had season tickets for years. With my parents in Florida, most weeks we've been giving them to friends or sometimes selling them, but it's been a long time since I've been to a game, I have this weekend off, and I thought I might make the trip. You said you're a football fan, I know you meant college, but I thought, well, I thought maybe, you know, you'd like to catch a game. With me. This Sunday. Yeah…"

Still in a state of shock, Ellie heard few of Zeke's words. A game, at historic Lambeau Field, the Cowboys versus the Packers? Her brothers would turn as green as grass with envy. As would most everyone back home.

"If you'd rather not, I understand. It's short notice, and—"

"I'd rather! I mean, yes, oh my goodness gracious, yes! I'd love to go. Maybe Max would watch Boomer." Ellie began pacing in circles and talking to herself. "Yes, Max might do it. She could run with Boomer, I'll warn her he can be distracted, but she can handle him, I'm sure. I think my jerseys are in one of those boxes I haven't unpacked…"

"Ellie? Then you want to go?"

Ellie breathed deep, trying to get her emotions under control. "Yes. If you're serious, I want to go. Thank you, Zeke, this is unbelievable. I never dreamed I'd see the Cowboys play at Lambeau. Really. Thank you."

"Wait a minute," Zeke said, and his nerves seemed to dissipate. "The Cowboys?" He slapped his hand against his forehead. "Of course. I didn't put two and two together. You're a *Cowboys* fan, aren't you?"

"Of course. America's team. The best team."

Zeke chuckled, the sound coming from deep inside. "We'll see about that come Sunday."

Ellie smiled in return, but there was no laughter in her voice. "We most certainly will."

13

Ellie had one hour of pure, unbridled euphoria before reality set in.

One hour was long enough for a video call with Colt, who was so excited at the thought of Ellie going to a Cowboys game in Green Bay he whooped and hollered and danced around the kitchen until Mama shooed him to his room. There, he'd pointed out his new Cowboys and Sooners posters, pulled out his Cowboys jersey from his closet and put it on while they were talking, and made Ellie promise to text him dozens of pictures, and to video call from Lambeau Field, preferably when the Cowboys scored a touchdown, if she could.

It was long enough to call Travis who, even given his fancy New York lifestyle, slipped back into the old Travis long enough to utter, 'Come on, Ellie, you're not joshin' me, are you?' Ellie stifled her laugh and refrained from telling him no matter how hard he tried to deny it, once an Oklahoma boy, always an Oklahoma boy.

It was long enough to call Tripp who, though he'd been to several Cowboys games in Dallas, was the most envious of Ellie being the first in the family to see the Cowboys play at Lambeau. An expert at controlling his emotions, he was the most restrained of her brothers, taking time to remind Ellie not to get carried away cheering for the opposing team and risking the ire of the hometown fans. Still, Ellie could tell he had a hard time quelling his excitement.

And it was long enough for Tripp to put Shelby on the phone, for Shelby to ask the questions none of her brothers had thought to ask, and for some of Ellie's own excitement to wane when it dawned on her what she'd agreed to.

She was going to a football game. Two-and-a-half hours away from Caston. With Zeke.

Like a date.

She hadn't been on a date in over two years and if she'd been thinking clearly, or thinking at all, she certainly wouldn't have agreed to this one. No, even the lure of seeing her Cowboys play an arch rival wouldn't have been enough to set aside her promise to herself. A promise she'd made the day Vincent had told her the truth. The truth she'd known for weeks but hadn't yet admitted to herself.

Ellie paced while she debated the pros and cons of calling Zeke and canceling. Or probably texting Zeke and canceling, since it seemed a lot less risky.

The pros were easy: she was in no way ready for a date; she didn't want Zeke to get the wrong idea; she wouldn't have to worry about what to do with Boomer; she wouldn't have to see the looks on Nicole's and Max's faces when she told them about it because she knew she'd never be able to keep it secret; she might be able to focus on something else, like her job, for the next five days.

She could only come up with one con, but it was a biggie: she'd miss out on seeing the Cowboys play in a venue that had long piqued her interest.

So, if she were basing her decision strictly on which side of the debate tipped the scales, she'd tell Zeke she couldn't make it. But she really, really wanted to go. Maybe she could make it clear it wasn't a date. Maybe Zeke didn't even think of it that way. He wanted to go, he needed someone to go with, and she just happened to be in the right place at the right time.

That didn't seem likely, though. She'd seen his cheeks turn pink, she'd heard his voice, so unsure of himself, and she'd sensed his nervousness. To him, it was a date. A casual date, maybe, but a date nonetheless.

She couldn't do it. She wasn't ready. Deep down, she knew that, but instead of picking up the phone, she picked up her guitar, and with her heart breaking in two, began to strum.

I wonder if you know what it feels like
  When he smiles and takes your hand
  I wonder if you know what it feels like
  To be in the arms of the perfect man

I wonder if you know what it feels like
  To sit and gaze at the stars

To hear him say I love you
I love you just the way you are

Ellie strummed harder, notching up the volume and fighting to keep her voice from breaking.

I wonder if you know what it feels like
  When he wants to share your life
  When he gets down on one knee
  When he asks you to be his wife

To dream about the future
  To hope, to pray, to plan
  To find the perfect dress
  To choose the perfect home

Her fingers became feather light on the strings, and her voice softened to a whisper.

I wonder if you know what it feels like
  When the rumors start to swirl
  I wonder if you know what it feels like
  To see him with another girl

Her sob nearly choked her. Her hand tightened around the neck of the guitar, turning her knuckles white. Boomer was there in a flash. He nudged the guitar out of his way and dropped his head in her lap. Ellie folded over him and let herself cry.

It had been a rough night, and Ellie was operating on precious little sleep. She had four cups of coffee in her belly. Three of them were protesting. Her hands were jittery, despite the caffeine her brain felt foggy, and her first hour students seemed especially loud. It was going to be a long day.

Bryce, the student who had been challenging her since day one, was in rare form. He announced to the class that he'd found sixteen swear words in the book he was reading with his book club and that his parents were mad about it.

"My mom said she's going to call the principal," Bryce said. He smirked at Ellie, waiting for her reaction, but she was simply too tired to react.

"Okay," Ellie answered, then moved on. "You should all have completed your list of literary devices you found in your novels, and you should have at least three questions or discussion topics to pose to your group. Get started with your discussions, please."

She glanced at Bryce out of the corner of her eye. He had his arms crossed over his chest and a perplexed look on his face. He'd obviously expected a much different reaction from her.

The morning dragged, and Ellie had taken to looking at the clock every few minutes. Fourth hour brought both Maddie and Talia. Ellie hadn't come up with any earth-shattering strategies to get through to Talia or to help Maddie, but Talia was absent and Maddie was a bit more talkative, even smiling with her group of friends, so Ellie let herself off the hook for the day.

When the bell rang signaling lunchtime, Ellie collapsed into her chair. She didn't feel up to facing the teachers' lounge, so decided she'd send that text to Zeke. But when she pulled her phone from her purse, she found it loaded with texts from Tripp, Travis, and Colt.

From Tripp, links to articles titled, *All You Need To Know About Lambeau Field*, *Your First Trip To Lambeau*, and *Lambeau Field: What Not To Do As A Visitor*. He also told her he hoped she'd have fun and that she'd cheer loudly, but within reason, for the Cowboys. Such a typical Tripp sentiment.

Travis sent a picture of the entire family, even Mama, decked out in jerseys, some even with face paint, taken about ten years ago when they'd hosted a playoff party at their home. Colt, just a toddler, waved a blue and silver rally towel. Travis had added a football emoji and an excited smiley face along with the note, 'Wish we all were going!' Ellie wished the same thing.

Colt hadn't been content with one text. There were seven, all silly GIFs of people cheering madly or of Cowboys players, and Ellie could almost hear Colt giggling as she scrolled through them.

When she finally set down her phone, she leaned back in her chair and closed her eyes. Canceling with Zeke, she realized, would disappoint more than just Zeke. Her brothers wanted the experience for her and would be eagerly awaiting her report. She hadn't called her sisters—after talking to Shelby she hadn't been able to—but they were fans too, Daddy had seen to it they all were, and they'd have the same reaction as her brothers. But in the end, it was still her decision.

"Eleanore Maureen, make up your mind," she scolded herself.

"I know it's bad when a parent uses your middle name. I'm not sure what it means when you use it on yourself."

Ellie had long quit being surprised by Max, who tended to show up in Ellie's room at the most inopportune times, so she just sighed and said, "It means you've got yourself between the devil and the deep blue sea."

Max shook her head. "You say the weirdest things. I'll just assume whatever you said means you've got some sort of problem. Well, Max to the rescue. Who is it this time? Bryce again? Or Mila? She's a feisty thing. She tried to pull one over on me the other day, but I set her straight."

"No, no, it's not the kids. It's, oh, it's nothing." Ellie pushed to her feet. "Have you had your lunch? We still have fifteen minutes."

"Uh-uh, Oklahoma. Sit yourself down and tell me what's wrong. I have my protein bar right here," she held up a hand, "and my water bottle right here," she held up the other hand. "We'll eat while you talk."

Since she knew there was no point in arguing, Ellie dropped back down into her chair. Max took the chair closest to Ellie's desk. She crossed her legs, then swung her foot while she chomped on her granola bar and waited.

Ellie figured she could stall long enough that it would be time for Max to get back to her classroom, but she knew she'd only be postponing the inevitable. She also knew she could lie, could make up a story about an issue with her family, a concern with Boomer, something dire enough that Max would believe it, but she hated everything about lying and refused to do it. So, she blurted it all out.

"I ran into Zeke last night, he lives nearby and was out walking his dog, he stayed a while so the dogs could play in the yard, then he asked me if I wanted to go with him to the Packers game this Sunday. I was excited, the Packers are playing the Cowboys, and who could say no to that?"

Max's expression stayed neutral as she mumbled, "No one, I suppose."

"Of course not. I agreed, but now I realize Zeke likely considers this a date and that's not at all what I was thinking when I said yes. I'm afraid I've given him the wrong idea, and I feel as though I should cancel." Ellie chewed on the pen she had clutched in her hand. "But I really want to go. It's a dilemma, Max. A dilemma, indeed."

Max finished her bar, crushed the wrapper and dunked it in the wastebasket, took a swig from her water bottle, then tapped her finger on the desk and eyed Ellie. Finally, she said, "I'm trying hard not to laugh because I'm sure this is a real dilemma for you, but seriously? It's just a football game, El. Go, don't go. Whatever. It's not a big deal."

"You're missing the point. It is a big deal, because I didn't agree to a date. I agreed to a football game. There's a big difference."

"In my mind, there's not, and chances are it's the same in Zeke's mind. It's just a football game."

"You keep saying that. 'It's just a football game.' First, it's not, it's the Cowboys versus the Packers, so it's an event, but putting that aside, I know it's a date in Zeke's mind. You didn't see him when he asked me. He got all quiet, kind of nervous. It was so cute."

Ellie's gaze drifted toward the window and she stared, not seeing the bright blue sky or the dried leaves dancing on the breeze and skittering across the parking lot, but instead Zeke's flushed cheeks, his darting eyes not quite able to meet hers, his foot as it started to inch away.

"Um, El? You okay?"

Ellie rubbed her eyes. "No. Not really."

For the first time since Ellie met her, Max's face softened, as did her voice. "Ellie, tell me what happened. Tell me who hurt you so badly you have yourself convinced you can't go on a simple date. I may not have all the answers, but I can listen."

And because Ellie knew Max was sincere, because this woman who acted so tough was now holding Ellie's hand and promising whatever help she could give, and maybe mostly because Max didn't know anyone involved, Ellie wanted to tell her. For the first time, she wanted to talk, to let it all out and get the perspective of an impartial outsider, at least outside Red Creek, Oklahoma.

But it was almost time for the students to return from lunch and if she got into it now, there was no guarantee she could do so dry-eyed. The last thing she wanted was for her students to see her as a blubbering mess.

"Thank you, Max, that's very sweet, but it's a long story and one we don't have time for right now. Another time."

"That's twice." Nicole's voice sounded from across the room. "Twice that you've either called her sweetie or said she's sweet. Is the world truly coming to an end?"

"It must be, because that sounded almost like a joke," Max said, "and I know for a fact Nicole Emerson is incapable of making a joke."

In spite of everything, Ellie laughed when Nicole made a face at Max and the two exchanged good-natured insults.

"Seriously, what's up? I just stopped by to see why neither of you were at lunch, but I figured you were only busy. Is it more? Is something wrong, Ellie?"

"Like I was telling Max, it's a long story and—"

On cue, the first cluster of students filed into the room.

"And we don't have time right now," Ellie finished her thought.

"Seems like we need to make time," Nicole said. "After school? Happy hour?"

"Happy hour on a Monday seems a bit desperate, doesn't it?" Ellie said.

"You know what they say about desperate times," Max said.

More kids barreled into the room and the volume rose. Ellie made a quick decision.

"I can't make happy hour but if y'all have time, my room, after the last bell? Does that work?"

"It works," Nicole said.

"It works," Max echoed.

Ellie couldn't hear what the two said to each other as they threaded their way through desks and bodies, but she could guess, as their heads were together and they both cast looks over their shoulders before they disappeared out the door.

A long morning was followed by an even longer afternoon. More than once, Ellie checked her phone when she was convinced the hands on the clock in her classroom had quit moving. When the final hour of the day arrived at last and when her seventh graders were especially receptive to Boomer's latest antics, Ellie let the conversation regarding Boomer and pets in general go longer than she normally would have. The kids debated the merits of big dogs versus small dogs, of exotic pets, and of the best way to convince a parent that a pet was a necessity. After she'd let them go for over ten minutes, she reined in the conversation and got them started on their reading assignment. At long last, the bell rang, and her class vacated her room in a thundering race for the door. She opened her mini fridge, grabbed the extra-caffeinated diet cola that was waiting for her, and popped the top. She only managed a few swallows before Nicole and Max refilled the just-emptied space.

"Okay, Ellie, what's up? I've been worried about you all afternoon.

So worried, in fact, that I let my students talk me into watching *Schoolhouse Rock* videos," Nicole said, shaking her head as if she couldn't quite believe her words.

"Oh! I remember! *Conjunction junction, what's your function*? Right? Remember those, El?" A child-like delight had Max bopping in place and seemed wildly contradictory to her normal demeanor. "Did you watch them in school? They're from the seventies, I think, but I had a teacher once who had a soft spot for them and used to have us watch them, usually when he didn't want to...Oh. I see."

Nicole shrugged. "What can I say? They hold the kids' attention, even if it's just to laugh at the outdated animation or to make fun of the silly lyrics. But those lyrics stick with them, and there are lessons in there. For the record, we did watch the American history ones. *I'm just a bill, yes I'm only a bill...*" Nicole looked expectantly at Max.

"*And I'm sitting here on Capitol Hill,*" Max finished.

"School house rock?" Ellie said. "I don't know what y'all are talking about."

"Really?" Max said. "Huh. You'll have to check it out. They're all online. Lots of them are about language arts stuff."

Ellie filed it away. Another tactic if she found herself needing to occupy her students.

"Anyway," Nicole said, "what's up?" She looked between Max and Ellie. "I'm always the last to know, it seems."

"Hey, I don't know much more than you," Max said. "Well, I take that back. I know she got asked out on a date by the famous, or maybe it's the infamous, Zeke Fahrner, and that she's freaking out about it. Why, I'm not sure, but that's what she's going to tell us, right Ellie?"

"A date with Zeke?" Nicole looked ready to launch into a lecture, but settled for a smile and said, "That sounds nice."

Again, Ellie was left wondering why Nicole had to bite her tongue every time the subject of Zeke came up. Sooner or later, Ellie told herself, she'd get to the bottom of whatever it was that Nicole knew, but not right then. Ellie couldn't let herself get sidetracked.

When Ellie didn't respond to Nicole's comment, Max said, "She told me she's worried Zeke will think of it as a date, and she doesn't want him to. She wants to go to the game—apparently the Cowboys playing the Packers is a big deal—but as badly as she wants to go, she's afraid she'll give him the wrong idea. It's a dilemma, Nicole."

Max's voice held a hefty dose of teasing, but earlier that afternoon, Ellie had heard Max's voice as sincere as she'd ever heard it, and Ellie knew that despite the teasing, Max was there to help. Nicole too. They were friends, they cared, and she needed an ear. Or two. And advice. She most definitely needed advice.

"Ellie, why is it so bad if Zeke thinks it's a date?" Nicole asked. "You don't like him, or you aren't attracted to him, or is it something else? You told us you're single, but is there someone back home?"

A loud, hysterical-sounding laugh escaped before Ellie could stop it. Max and Nicole looked a little frightened. Ellie took a deep breath. She'd need to shut off all emotion and stick to the facts if she was going to get through it.

On her exhale, she said, "There is someone back home, but not in the way you think. His name is Vincent. We were engaged. Fifty-three days before our wedding, he finally admitted to me he'd been seeing someone else." Ellie swallowed. "Piper. My best friend."

"Oh, my," Nicole muttered.

"Pig." Max didn't bother to mutter.

"It was hard, unbelievably hard, and I promised myself I'd never wind up in a position like that again. For now, that means I'm not dating. I'm not ready, I don't know when I will be, but I know myself well enough to know that it's not now. That's why I can't let Zeke think Sunday is a date. It's not fair to him."

"Ellie, you have to know that not every guy is like Vincent," Nicole said. "There are good ones out there."

"I know that. Logically, anyway. In practice, it's a little more difficult to believe."

"Well, you absolutely have to know that you can't let one jerk ruin the rest of your life," Max said. "He's scum. To say nothing of your supposed friend. Piper?" Max wrinkled her nose and snorted. "You should have known better based solely on her name."

"I don't think I'm letting him ruin my life. I've spent the past two years trying hard not to do that, but I can't deny he's been responsible for a lot of changes in my life. I think that part was inevitable."

"You haven't seen him or heard from him in two years?" Max asked.

Ellie shook her head. "No. Well, not really. He texted me a couple of times over the summer, just out of the blue, telling me how sorry he was and that he wishes we could talk."

"I hope you didn't respond," Max said.

Ellie remembered the feeling when she'd seen his name pop up on her phone after so much time. There'd been a second, just the briefest fraction of a second, when her heart had fluttered, when she'd felt a tiny thrill of excitement like she used to feel so long ago, but that feeling was over almost before it began, and in its place was more apathy than anger or hurt. She'd been proud of that.

"I didn't," Ellie said in response to Max. "After the second text, I blocked his number."

Nicole nodded slowly. "Good," she said. "And that's why you're here, isn't it? So far from home. You…I don't want to say you ran away, but you left to get away from him. And from her."

"Yes," Ellie said. "Not right away, but yes."

"Then you let him win!" Max started to apologize almost before she finished. "I'm sorry, I didn't mean that. You did what you needed to do, and that was the right thing to do. I just meant that he should have been the one to hide, for lack of a better word. To be embarrassed by his actions, to feel like the biggest loser in town. You should have been the one holding your head high. And I feel like this is coming out all wrong. I'm on your side, El, it just seems like you're the one who did nothing wrong, but who paid the biggest price."

"I know what you mean, Max, and thank you."

"Are they still together?" Nicole asked. "No, never mind, you don't have to answer that, it's none of my business. I'm sorry."

"It's okay. Both of you. I wouldn't have brought any of this up if I didn't want to talk about it. I think maybe I need to. It hasn't only been hard to trust men, it's been hard to trust anyone enough to have real friends. Girlfriends. I feel like I haven't had those in a long time, either. I know how pathetic that sounds, but it's the truth. I've been mostly on my own for a long time, but that has to end. To answer your question, Nicole, no, I don't think so. I don't think they're together."

Ellie paused and fiddled with the notepad and pens on her desk, ordering everything. "For a while, I wanted to know every single detail. When Vincent finally admitted the truth to me, after I'd suspected for months, I demanded those details. How long had they been together? How often had they been together? Where did they go? To the same places we went? All the times Vincent told me he had to study, or work late, or attend to a family obligation, was he with her? Did he love her? Did he ever love me?

"I was obsessive. It wasn't healthy, I know that now. I did the same thing when I drove to Piper's house and demanded information from her." Ellie rubbed her hands up her face. "It wasn't my best moment. I don't remember it all clearly, but I remember a lot of screaming, a lot of tears. Piper had always been sort of negative about Vincent. She made it clear she didn't much like him right from the start. She told me he was conceited, that he wasn't good enough for me, all kinds of things. That night I asked her if it had all been an act, if she'd wanted him from the beginning, if they'd been together all along. Again, I don't remember much of what I said or what she said, but after that night, I considered every possible scenario. Everything played out in my mind like some sort of horrible, twisted movie. I imagined everything from them dating before Vincent and I ever met to them laughing behind my back on the night Vincent proposed. Piper was supposed to be one of my bridesmaids."

Ellie took another deep breath. "So, no, I don't think they're together, but I also don't care. I can't care. The details can't matter any longer." With that, Ellie pushed the paper and pens on her desk all askew. She reminded herself it was okay if every detail in her life wasn't perfectly organized every minute of every day.

When she looked up, Max and Nicole were both wide-eyed. Neither had moved from their spots, but when Ellie waved her hand, they both dropped into chairs. Still, neither spoke.

"Ladies, what's your verdict? Am I completely crazy, or is there hope for me?" Ellie tried for levity, but her friends saw right through her.

"Ellie, you're not crazy," Nicole said. "Absolutely not. I hope you're kidding about that, because it's not even close to the truth. You did what anyone in your position would do. Actually, I'd say you controlled yourself remarkably well."

"No kidding," Max said. "Hey, do you know that song about taking a Louisville Slugger to the cheating jerk's truck? I probably would have done that."

Ellie laughed. "Believe me, I know every word of that song. One of the best scenes in that twisted movie in my mind was me doing every single thing that song talked about. Of course, Carrie Underwood was at my side, we filmed a new video for her song, and became best friends. She's from Oklahoma, you know. It could happen."

"I'm so sorry you had to go through all of that," Nicole said. "And as sorry as I am that you felt like you needed to leave home, I'm glad you ended up here."

She'd avoided tears while telling her story, but now they threatened. Having friends, having someone to talk to, felt good. Ellie's voice wasn't entirely steady when she said, "Thank you, Nicole, so am I."

"Me too, but why? I get why you left home, but why so far away?

And why Caston? It's the middle of nowhere. You could have gone anywhere. A beach in California or Florida, the mountains in Colorado, a big city like New York or Boston. Anywhere at all."

"I suppose, but I'm not really a big city girl, or a beach girl. Mountains maybe, that would be fun I think, but small towns suit me." Ellie shrugged. "I have an aunt who lives in Wisconsin, so it wasn't like I was completely on my own. I stayed with her while I did my student teaching. But to answer your question…"

Ellie blocked out the pain, the embarrassment, and focused on the facts. "I saw a therapist after everything that happened. He stressed making a clean break. It had been months, and I hadn't moved on. I was mired in a place where I didn't know what to do. I didn't think I wanted things to go back to the way they'd been with Vincent, or the way I thought they'd been, but I also didn't know how to move forward, how to picture a life without him. Again, I know how pathetic it all sounds. Mama insisted I see Dr. Tyson and as much as I fought her, as much as I was certain he'd never tell me anything that I didn't already know, once I gave him a chance, he helped me so much.

"While he didn't tell me I had to leave town, he told me I needed to make changes. If I continued with everything else in my life the same as always, it would be hard to see myself as anything but Vincent's fiancée. I was going to be a kindergarten teacher, working for a few years after we were married until we started our family, then staying home and being a mother and a wife. It's what I'd envisioned for years. If I started teaching kindergarten in Red Creek, seeing the same people, going to the same places, it would be like there was a hole where Vincent should have been. So instead, I went back to school, got my secondary education degree, moved away from Oklahoma, and got myself a new best friend in Boomer. He was a lifesaver. He depended on me, he needed me, he loved me. Unconditionally. But I needed him too, and he's been a big part of me being able to start over."

Ellie gave herself a shake and forced a bright smile. "Anyway, I'm sure that's more than y'all bargained for, but surely you understand now why I can't go with Zeke, why I can't let him think it's a date."

Nicole and Max looked at each other for a few moments until Nicole said, "Do you want to field this, or should I?"

"Oh, let me," Max said. She rubbed her hands together, then stretched her arms out in front of her and flexed her fingers until her knuckles cracked. "Okay. Here's the deal. You were hurt, Vincent—does everyone in Oklahoma have stupid names?—is a jerk and isn't worth you wasting a minute of your time thinking about him. We understand that what you went through was hard. Stupid, ugly hard. But, and this is a biggie, it's the past, far enough in the past that every day you let what happened affect what you do is another day you let him win."

"But—" Ellie interrupted.

"Nope. Not yet," Max said. "I'm not downplaying what you went through. Just the opposite. It made you strong. You're here, you're teaching middle school, so clearly you can do anything. That means you can date. Now, if Zeke isn't the type of guy you want to date, fine. That's your choice. But if you're not dating him because you're afraid of getting hurt again, you're not giving yourself nearly enough credit. If it doesn't work out, it doesn't work out, and you move on. You know how to do that. It won't be easy, it never is and it shouldn't be, but you know you can do it because you've already done it. Then again, maybe it does work out. What if you'd never given it a chance? Don't deprive yourself of something based on what happened in the past. You owe it to yourself to live your life. Don't let him win, El. Don't."

While all Ellie could do was stare, dumbfounded, Nicole clapped and said, "Well done, Max, couldn't have said it better myself."

"May I speak now?" Ellie asked Max.

"The floor is all yours."

"Thank you. And thank you for the vote of confidence, however misplaced. You said you think I'm not giving myself enough credit. I think you're giving me too much. I know what I can and can't handle, and I can't handle dating. Not now. I can't go on a date with Zeke, or with anyone else, for that matter."

"Of course you can," Nicole said. "You just go. You have fun, or you don't, and then you decide what happens next. Maybe it's another date, maybe it's letting him down gently, maybe it's telling him he's a jerk and you hope he suffers all sorts of horrible plagues, but whatever it is, you're in control of you. It has to be that way, El, or you're never going to be happy."

"Y'all make it sound so easy. It's not."

"I know it's not easy, but I think you might be making it harder than it needs to be. People hang out with other people all the time. Max said you want to go to the game, so go. I grew up in Wisconsin. I may not fully buy into the aura that seems to surround the Packers, but I sort of get it. You're a Cowboys fan. That I don't get, but to each their own. The game is a big deal. Go enjoy it."

Ellie doodled on a flower-shaped notepad on her desk while she mulled over Nicole's words. They were straight-forward, maybe a little harsh, when Ellie had hoped for compassion and understanding. But maybe her new friends' words were what she needed. Those girlfriends she'd still been able to call friends after the nightmare with Vincent had done nothing but soothe and console. They'd told her over and over what a worm Vincent was, how she deserved better, how she needed to take the time to care for herself. At the time, those words of support had been comforting, and she knew if she called any of those friends right now, she'd hear more of the same. Now, though, she had an inkling her new friends were right. It was time to shake off the past and move on to the future. While that didn't mean she was going on a date, maybe it meant she could go to a football game.

She looked up from her doodles which, she realized with a smile, were in the shapes of footballs and goal posts to find Max and Nicole watching her like a pair of hawks.

"I expected y'all to be a little more, I don't know, sweet? Understanding?"

Though both Max and Nicole looked ready to speak, Ellie didn't give them the chance.

"But it's okay. I think you told me exactly what I needed to hear. I may not have thought I was ready to hear it, but I think now that I was. That I am. Anyway, what I'm trying to say is thank you. I didn't need someone to cry with me. I needed someone, or two someones, to knock some sense into me."

"I'm all for knocking sense wherever the knocking is needed, and I do knocking a lot better than I do sweet, but that wasn't my intention." Max glanced at Nicole who shook her head. "Our intention."

"If not, it probably should have been. Really, thank you."

"We didn't do much, just sort of talked to you," Nicole said.

"You let me talk, you let me tell someone, someone away from home, all the ugly details. You listened, and then, with just a few words, told me what I needed to hear. I like having friends again." And that, more than anything that had to do with Vincent, started the tears flowing.

"Oh, Ellie, we like having friends too." And in a flash, Nicole's arms wrapped around Ellie and squeezed. "Get over here, Max," Nicole said when Max seemed content to stay on the sidelines.

"I'm not much of a hugger."

"Get over here." Nicole's tone left no room for argument, and Max dragged herself to the huddle.

"There, that's not so bad, is it?" Nicole asked.

"It's not so bad," Max said.

"It's as good as all get out," Ellie said, then laughed when Max rolled her eyes.

14

If Ellie had ordered the perfect day for a football game, it would look exactly like the day that greeted her when she threw open her bedroom curtains on Sunday morning. The sky was a pretty robin's egg blue painted with the wispiest, whitest clouds she'd ever seen. The air was crisp and cool, with just the slightest breeze rustling the few dried leaves that clung stubbornly to the towering oak in her back yard. As she drew in a deep breath, she closed her eyes and savored the scents of late fall on what was nothing short of a gift of a day. The forecast promised ample sunshine and low fifties by the three-thirty kick-off time. Perfect football weather.

Since her talk with Max and Nicole, Ellie had been mostly in agreement with their advice. Most of the time. She'd had moments where she'd reached for her phone, ready to cancel with Zeke, but she'd talked herself out of it. While she hadn't seen him all week, he had texted a couple of times to firm up their plans and to ask about what she planned to do with Boomer on game day. Zeke had arranged for Bowie to stay overnight at Top Dog, something Ellie had yet to do —at Top Dog or anywhere else—but figured one day she'd have to face.

She'd flirted with the idea of asking Max to watch Boomer, but before she'd been able to ask, Max had mentioned the 10K race she'd entered that was scheduled for Sunday and the planned barbecue following the race with some members of the running club she'd joined, so Ellie had nixed that idea. Instead, she'd contacted Top Dog, quizzed them about the accommodations and the care when a dog stayed overnight, and after stewing about it for two days, had made a reservation. Now that Sunday had arrived, she was more nervous about leaving Boomer than she was about spending the day with Zeke. She supposed that was a good thing, at least the fact that she'd triumphed over her nerves where Zeke was concerned, but she was worried she'd spend far too much time checking the video feed from Top Dog.

Before bed, she'd located the box that held her jerseys and hauled it up to her bedroom. She'd debated the night before which jersey to wear, but hadn't come to a decision. Now, she spread them out on her bed and studied them. Each one had a special significance.

One had been a gift from her uncle, and her godfather, Bobby, the last Christmas she'd seen him before he'd returned to Afghanistan and his vehicle had been struck by an IED. She ran a tender hand over the numbers and remembered Bobby's infectious laugh, the way he'd hauled her up on his shoulders and galloped like a horse when she'd been young, the way he'd listened to her problems when she'd gotten older and had felt alone in a house full of people.

Another she'd won by beating out a room full of rowdy college students during a heated bar trivia battle. She grinned, recalling the incredulous looks of the three guys who'd made it to the final round with her when she knew it was Kyle Orton who filled in for Tony Romo when he missed a game in the 2013 season.

One she'd saved for and bought when she'd been in high school because she had a huge crush on the dreamy player with wavy auburn hair, one was from the family portrait session a few years ago, and the last one was all about bragging rights. Three years ago, she'd been crowned champion of her family's fantasy football league, the first female to hold the title, and her prize had been an Emmitt Smith jersey. Already incredibly valuable to her, its value had skyrocketed when she'd worn it to a game Vincent had taken her to, and where they'd had seats in a fancy private box. She'd been hurrying to the restroom during a timeout, and had literally run into Emmitt Smith. After she'd stuttered and stammered like an idiot, he'd signed the back of her jersey, right above his number 22.

Ellie scooped it up, ignored the fact that she never would have gotten the autograph if she hadn't been at the game with Vincent, and decided it felt like the right one for the day. The right one to bring her Cowboys luck against the Packers.

That decided, Ellie took a quick shower, tried to eat breakfast but found she was far too nervous, then gathered up Boomer's things and hustled him into the car. When she stopped her car in the parking lot of Top Dog, a wave of guilt and trepidation swamped her. She reached over and wrapped her arms around Boomer's neck.

"You be a good boy, okay? It's going to seem like a long time, but I'll come back, I promise, and Bowie will be here, so you'll have a friend. Be nice to him so he plays with you."

Ellie gave Boomer's ears a vigorous rub, and he leaned into her shoulder.

"Are you ready?"

As soon as she let go of him, he lunged for the door. He knew where they were, and his exuberance helped ease Ellie's anxiety.

"Okay, buddy, here we go."

Ellie was waiting at the door when Zeke's car rolled into her driveway. She watched him hop from the driver's seat, then laughed to herself when she spotted his jersey.

"Brett Favre, I see," she said before he reached her door.

Zeke raised his eyebrows and grinned at her. "Emmitt Smith, I see."

"I like the classics."

"So do I."

Ellie shook her head. "Mine has more Super Bowl wins, you know."

"Mine has more MVP awards, you know."

Ellie locked the door behind her and followed Zeke to his car. "Pro Football Hall of Fame *and* College Football Hall of Fame."

"Record for most consecutive games played."

"First-round draft pick, 176 career touchdowns, and all-time rushing leader. I can go on."

Zeke laughed. "Okay, okay. What do you say we call a truce?" Zeke asked as he closed the car door behind Ellie.

"What do you say we make a bet?" Ellie countered when Zeke took his place behind the wheel.

"A bet? Interesting. What kind of bet?"

"The normal kind. If my Cowboys win…" Ellie paused and thought. "You have to buy a Cowboys jersey and wear it at Scooter's during a Packers game. And I get to witness it."

"Whoa. That's tantamount to asking for a beating, but okay, I'll take that bet. And if, rather when, the Packers win?"

"Then you get to see me wearing a Cowboys jersey at Scooter's." Ellie's laughter filled the car.

"No, I think if I win, you make me dinner. Treat me to some if that famous Southern cooking. I'm thinking biscuits, fried chicken, maybe a pecan pie. And sweet tea, whatever that is."

"Hmm. Well, I've never actually fried chicken, but I suppose it can't be that hard." And it would give her a reason to call Gran. "Biscuits and sweet tea are no-brainers. I can do those in my sleep. Now pecan pie? It just so happens you're speaking with the blue ribbon winner in the pie division of the Lincoln county fair two years in a row. My pecan pie recipe has been handed down for generations in my mama's family. Every one of us has tweaked it just the tiniest bit and it's scrumptious, if I do say so myself. Not that I'll be making it for you."

"Then it seems I have a lot riding on this bet, and I fully intend on winning."

"As do I. The Cowboys are favored, you know."

"The Packers are the better team, you know."

"Their current record doesn't do much to back up that claim."

"They're just hitting their stride. Undefeated in the last three weeks, and none of the games were even close."

"The Cowboys haven't lost on the road all year."

When Zeke only grunted at that, Ellie pulled her phone from her purse. "What size are you? I could get that jersey order started, save you time later on."

"Mmm. I can already taste that pecan pie."

Ellie laughed and reached her hand out the partially open window. The breeze was chilly as it whistled through her fingers and teased her hair. Usually, her hair whipping around her face, and slapping her in the eyes, drove her crazy, and she thought of reaching back into her purse for a hair tie. Then she realized the familiar football banter combined with Zeke's easy attitude had dissolved all her nerves and left her feeling relaxed and looking forward to the day. She leaned her head back, closed her eyes, and let her hair swirl.

She'd heard it referred to as Holy Ground. She'd heard the tailgating experience was incomparable. She'd heard about the Lambeau Leap, the Cheeseheads, and that the fans were like none other, the best fans in the league, even.

And she'd had her doubts. After all, she'd been to Cowboys games at Texas Stadium, then at its grand replacement, AT&T Stadium, and she'd soaked in the atmosphere, the electric excitement, the camaraderie. She'd been swallowed in the deafening roar when the Cowboys scored. She'd frantically waved her rally towel. She'd lived and died by the Cowboys' successes and failures, and she was certain nothing could top it.

Then Ellie arrived at Lambeau Field and strolled through lots filled with thousands of tailgaters. She was offered beer and brats by total strangers. She was whisked into dancing a polka with a man roughly the size of a mountain and covered in green and gold from the top of his head to the tips of his toes. She was the target of a near constant barrage of ribbing due to her choice of attire, but found all of it surprisingly good-natured. A foam wedge of cheese was dropped on her head by a man who must have been at least eighty years old and who told her with the cheese on her head, she was the most beautiful thing he'd ever laid eyes on.

She wanted to hate it, but that proved impossible. It was simply too much fun. Every time she looked at Zeke, he had a smug 'I told you so' grin on his face. She wanted to hate that too, but that also proved impossible.

Ellie ate a fresh-grilled brat and washed it down with an ice-cold beer when Zeke ran into some friends and they were again offered food and drinks from the heaps of it spread around their cozy tailgating tent. Once the introductions were finished, she was treated to a lengthy list of reasons the Packers were better than the Cowboys. Zeke's friends spouted what they claimed was irrefutable evidence that included statistics dating back nearly one hundred years, the fact that the Packers are a community-owned team and one that does immeasurable good for its community, as well as the loyal fan base and the fact that every home game since 1960 has been a sell-out. By the time they finished their impassioned arguments, they all had their arms around each other, and most were teary-eyed. It wasn't until one of them broke free of their huddle for a trip back to the beer cooler that they sniffled, wiped at their eyes, and pulled themselves together.

"What do you think?" Zeke asked later as they headed for the gates.

"What I think is that's a difficult question. If I say I'm enjoying myself, you'll rub it in. If I say I'm not, that it's all a bit over-the-top, that all of this is more like a carnival than a football game I'd be lying, and that's something I don't make a habit of doing, regardless of the subject matter. So, I guess for now, I'll say thank you for the experience, and I'll reserve final judgment for a few hours yet."

Zeke chuckled. "Fair enough, but start thinking of your best superlatives, Ms. Hawthorne, because you're in for a treat.

And for as much as it pained her to admit it, it was a treat. From the stirring National Anthem and Air Force fly-over, to the raucous cheers so loud their seats shook, to the nail-biting back and forth on the field, it was an afternoon Ellie would never forget.

She'd also never forget the kiss.

It wasn't intentional. That's what she told herself over and over as she and Zeke walked back to the car in awkward silence. At least it was awkward on her part. Zeke chatted about the game, about taking a different route on the drive home, about how the dogs were doing when he checked the video feed from Top Dog, and seem oblivious to the fact that Ellie could barely choke out a few syllables in reply.

It was a natural reaction, he'd been caught up in the heat of the moment, and it didn't mean anything. But he'd kissed her, and since she didn't like to lie, even to herself, she was forced to admit it had been nice.

With six seconds left in the game, the Packers down by four points, and with the ball on the Dallas 45-yard-line, the tension had been off the charts. And when the pass was tipped, twice, before finally being caught in the end zone putting the Packers ahead as time expired, cheering along with the ecstatic crowd, wrapping her in a bear hug and lifting her off her feet, then planting a kiss on her lips was nothing but instinct. Nothing but being swept up in the moment.

Before she'd had time to react, the swell of the crowd had engulfed them and hands were high-fiving one another over and around her. She was hugged by the woman seated next to her, and she'd done her best to avoid a beer shower when it began raining down as if the clouds had opened up. Then they'd followed the crowd out of the stadium and started the walk back to the car without a word about the kiss.

Given more time to think about it, Ellie was no less confused than she'd been when it happened. She should probably just ignore it, like Zeke seemed to be doing, but that didn't seem quite right. She couldn't just ask him about it, though. If simple conversation on the walk to the car was awkward, she couldn't imagine what a conversation about a kiss would be like.

Best to leave it alone, she decided, at least for the time being. Maybe Max or Nicole would have a better perspective. As long as Zeke didn't bring it up, she wouldn't either.

That decided, she took three deep breaths and tried to pay attention to what Zeke was saying as they inched their way out of the parking lot.

"The first time was nice, but the next time is going to be so much better. You'll be in charge of the details. When is good for you?"

"Wha—, nice? When…Good for me?" Ellie sputtered like an idiot.

"Yeah, I can't wait for that dinner. Don't forget, you promised chicken, biscuits," he turned toward her and winked, "and pecan pie."

"Oh yes, dinner. Um…" Of course, he'd been talking about dinner. What else would he be talking about? Ellie turned and looked out the window, though there was precious little to see except for a long line of taillights glowing in the moonless dark. And why in the world had she ever agreed to a dinner? Because she'd been certain she wouldn't lose the bet, that's why, and because she'd been caught up in the moment. Like Zeke had been caught up in the moment when he'd kissed her.

"I'm on call next weekend, but maybe the weekend after that? Or a week night if that works for you. I'm flexible."

"I'll have to check my schedule." Right. Like she had anything on her schedule besides school and walking her dog.

"Sounds good. And now, since the experience is behind you, what did you think? As I recall, you were going to reserve judgment, but it was incredible, right?"

She could talk football. That she could do.

"I don't know that I'd go as far as incredible, but it was enlightening."

When Zeke opened his mouth with a little gasp, Ellie cut him off before he could voice his horror.

"And," she said, voice raised, "and it was fun. It was a lot of fun. I will admit, you Green Bay fans know how to have a good time. One thing that struck me, and that came as a bit of a surprise, was how friendly and good-natured everyone was. I didn't expect such hospitality showing up in a Cowboys jersey."

"We Packers fans take pity on you sad, misguided souls who choose to cheer for a mediocre team. That's punishment enough. We don't need to rub it in."

Despite herself, Ellie laughed.

"I'll admit, you guys kept it close, but the outcome was never really in question."

"Never in question? The Packers were behind with six seconds to go!"

"And you doubted the Packers would score? Really, Ellie, you know better than that."

"The ball was tipped. It could have landed in anyone's hands." And that stung, because that's how close a Dallas victory had been.

Literally, a fingertip away.

"Those superlatives we talked about?"

"You talked about," Ellie muttered.

"I don't know what you came up with, but I'd like to offer the following: tensest, because, I'll admit, those last few seconds were nerve-racking; loudest, with respect to the cheering after that final touchdown; craziest, because wow, what a finish; and oddly enough, most relaxing, because even though the game was all of those other things, I didn't think about work the entire time."

She hadn't either, Ellie realized, but while her job stresses and concerns were very real, she knew Zeke's were tenfold, and something inside her wanted to comfort, to soothe.

"Is it always hard? When you're away, are you always thinking about patients?"

Zeke leaned his left arm on the car door, tilting his head sideways to rest in his hand. "I wouldn't say it's hard, it's just the job. What's difficult, at least for me, is turning it off. I usually know at least some of what's on my plate for the next day, the next week even, and I can't help but think it to death trying to be certain I'm as prepared as I can be."

"I'm sure your patients appreciate that, but surely you need some time for yourself. I would think your mental health plays a big part in doing your job well. If you're stressed, it's bound to carry over into your work."

"Spoken like every mentor I've ever had. You're right, they're right, but it's not easy. For me, anyway, but I'm working on it. It's all part of my education, as another mentor recently told me."

"What do you like best about it? Your job, I mean."

"Oh. I don't know that I've ever been asked that, at least not in so many words. I guess I'd have to say, aside from the usual wanting to help people, I enjoy being able to see something from start to finish. Sure, my patients see other doctors before they see me, but once they become my patient, once I begin working on a surgical plan, I'm able to talk with the patient, at least in most cases, to answer questions, then perform the necessary procedures, and see the patient again after surgery as well as during follow-up visits. For some doctors, patients pass through only to be directed to other doctors. I'm more the end of the line, so to speak. I like that."

"Hmm," Ellie murmured as she considered Zeke's words. "That's interesting. I've never looked at it that way. I guess teaching is a bit like the other doctors you mentioned. We see students for a year, then they move on to the next in line and we have to hope we've done our job well. With most students, I would suppose, a teacher never knows what becomes of him or her."

Ellie thought about that, about how that made her feel, and it left her feeling a little sad. It's not that she hadn't ever considered it, but when compared to Zeke's job, to know the continuity of seeing his patients through their ordeal was what made him love his job, it was all somewhat sobering.

"But you do have them for an entire school year. That's a long time in the life of a twelve-year-old, and long enough to make an impact. They'll take what they learn from you and build on it. It's a different sort of job than mine, but it's a vitally important job. I hope you know that."

"I do. I always have. It's the reason I wanted to teach."

Partly to keep Zeke from digging deeper and partly because she was curious, Ellie asked him another question.

"Other than having to be crazy smart and learn a million different things, what's the most difficult part of your job on a day-to-day basis?"

"I don't know about crazy smart. Sure, a person has to have the ability to learn, but it's more about being willing to put in the work. It's a grueling process, but I wouldn't change my decision to go into medicine for anything. The most difficult thing for me wasn't all the book learning or even the hands-on learning. It was the absolute focus needed to do the job. As a surgeon, it's vital that I'm able to focus on what I'm doing and nothing else. It was hard at first, and I've had many colleagues who've struggled more than I have."

"But doesn't that just happen? I would think that with a patient in front of you on the operating table," Ellie swallowed over the lump in her throat as the very idea was terrifying to her, "it would be hard to focus on anything else."

"Think about your day. Think about how often you do only one thing at a time. If you're watching TV, are you also scrolling on your phone? If you're talking on the phone, are you also jotting down a grocery list? That's not meant to criticize, it's just a fact of life in today's world. We're busy. There are countless devices and apps and games and distractions to draw our attention, and we've become accustomed to multi-tasking to the point where it can be difficult not to."

Ellie opened her mouth, but stopped and thought about what Zeke said. How often when she was working did she open a new tab on her computer and check social media? Or scroll through her email? Or skim headlines and read an article? But on the other hand...

"I agree, there are distractions, but in my job I don't think I'd survive if I wasn't able to multi-task. When thirty twelve-year-olds are demanding your attention and you're trying to get a video to play while an announcement comes over the PA system and those thirty students have at least thirty different comments, I need to be able to have my mind on a dozen things at once."

"Exactly," Zeke said. "I'm sure you see your students doing an assignment, listening to music, talking to their neighbor, and who knows what else all at the same time. It's how kids are programmed these days. I was too, and that's why it was a struggle to learn the focus needed to provide my patients with my best."

"How? How do you do it? Shut off everything else."

Zeke shifted in his seat and cast a quick glance toward her. It was dark so she didn't get a good look, but she was almost certain something like embarrassment flashed across his face.

"Mindfulness," he finally said.

"Mindfulness? So, meditation?"

"Yes, but I prefer to call it focusing since, for me, that's what it is. Focusing on one thing, and only one thing. Practicing, taking time every day to slow down, to focus all my senses on the here and now. I've found it helps in my job. I'm better able to block outside distractions, to keep my mind from wandering. And if you're skeptical, trust me, you won't be the first."

"No, not at all. I think, well, I think..." What she thought was that the more she learned about this man, the more she liked and respected him, and the more he intrigued her. As for meditation, or mindfulness, or whatever he wanted to call it, she wasn't skeptical in the least. She knew well what it could do for a person, because it had saved her.

But she couldn't say that, so instead she said, "I think if you've found something that helps you, whatever that is, then you're fortunate. Being willing to try different things, to work at things outside of the book learning and hands-on learning you talked about, tells me you're dedicated. It tells me you care a tremendous amount about what you're doing, and that you're the type of doctor I'd want caring for me."

"That's not what I expected to hear, so thank you. Not everyone understands, and that's okay, but it's nice when someone does."

She more than understood, and part of her wanted to tell him just how well she understood. She wanted to tell him how she'd relied on the techniques her therapist had preached. How learning to focus on the task at hand, to think of that and only that, had helped her mind from wandering to all the other places it wanted to go. How she'd had to learn to keep from thinking about Vincent, about all the signs she should have noticed and acted upon so much sooner, and about all the scenarios she created in her mind that left her feeling like a fool. About all the ways to get back at him, and just as many ways to get him back. Without learning to block out those self-destructive thoughts, she'd never have made it out of the darkness that had enveloped her for months following the break-up.

But drawing on that mindfulness, and choosing to focus on the here and now, Ellie said, "I have my list of superlatives for you. In no particular order: fastest, because the game seemed to fly by; friendliest, because I've never been hugged by so many strangers, and after I'd worried about just the opposite given I'd be wearing the opposing team's jersey; coldest, because by the end of the game, it was downright freezing. I don't know how y'all do it come December." At this, Ellie wiggled her toes and rubbed her hands up and down her thighs as she still hadn't quite warmed up. "And I guess most frustrating and most exciting all rolled into one, because it was exciting right down to the wire, but it could so easily have gone the other way."

"Well said, Ms. Hawthorne. You know, you're too polite for your own good. It's hardly any fun rubbing in the fact that your team lost."

"Aw, shucks, Dr. Fahrner, I'm certain I don't have the foggiest notion what you're talkin' about."

Zeke's rich laugh rumbled and bounced off the car's windows. "I have one more to add to my list. Most fun, because today was the most fun I've had at a football game, or anywhere for that matter, in a long time. That's because of you. Thank you for coming with me. I enjoyed spending the day with you, and seeing the game through your eyes made it even more special."

And there he'd gone and done it again. Made her like him just a little bit more. Since Ellie didn't know what to do with that, she stayed silent and simply nodded in the dark car.

15

It was so strange to wake up in a house without Boomer, Ellie's entire morning was thrown off schedule. Without a dog to let outside, to feed, and to pamper, she was ready for school so early, she had time to open her laptop and search for the dog trainer Zeke recommended. It wasn't hard to find Valerie's website, and it wasn't hard to find the dozens and dozens of glowing reviews left by ecstatic and grateful dog owners.

Valerie turned Freddy from our own 'Nightmare on Hill Street' to an absolute dream of a dog.

We were heartbroken thinking we'd have to surrender Jazzy after she'd run away for the eighth time and frightened a young child by jumping and knocking her over, but after four weeks with Valerie, Jazzy is a model canine citizen. We've already recommended Valerie to several friends.

I tried classes and training collars, I watched countless videos, and nothing worked for King. After just one session with Valerie, I saw improvement in King's behavior. A year later, the dog I thought I'd never be able to take in public just earned his therapy certification. Thank you, Valerie!

And on, and on, and on. So many of the stories sounded familiar, and so many of the pet owners had the same sort of issues Ellie had with Boomer. Like Zeke said, there were options for classes with your dog, options to board the dog for intense training, and options to have Valerie come to you. It was quite a distance to Valerie's kennel and training location, but after thinking more about it, Ellie decided sending Boomer for training and boarding wasn't the right option. Probably the most effective, but aside from being very expensive, she didn't like the idea of him being gone for so long. She sent off a quick email to Valerie asking a few questions about having her come to

Caston, then jumped when she glanced at the time.

"Now you've done it, Ellie," she scolded herself as she tossed her laptop into her bag, grabbed her purse and her lunch, and hustled out the door. She hated being late.

Ten minutes later, Ellie jogged across the parking lot of Caston Middle School, her jacket collar turned up against the frigid wind, and her hands buried deep in her pockets.

"Ellie! Hang on!" Ellie slowed to let Nicole catch up. "How was the game?"

"It was fun. I had a good time. The Cowboys lost, so that part wasn't great, but the rest of it kind of was. And thankfully it wasn't this cold!"

"I'm so glad. I was thinking about you all weekend and hoping you wouldn't change your mind and back out."

Nicole held the door. Ellie scooted inside and soaked up the blast of warm air that greeted her.

"So?" Nicole prompted.

"So what?"

"So, how did things go with Zeke?"

"It wasn't a date."

"Sure, whatever you say, but how did it go?"

"I told you, it was fun."

"Don't make this so difficult. You know what I mean. Was he sweet? Funny? Nervous? Hopefully not obnoxious, or overbearing, or pushy. Did he ask you out again?"

"Maybe I didn't miss having girlfriends as much as I thought I did," Ellie said as they arrived at the door to her classroom.

Ellie heard the sigh behind her as she slipped the key in the lock, gave it the little push and wiggle she'd found was the bit of magic it needed to unlock, then opened the door and turned on the light.

"I'm joking, Nicole," Ellie said, worried she'd hurt her friend's feelings, but Nicole didn't look hurt, merely exasperated and impatient. "Fine. He was sweet and funny, not nearly as nervous as I was, and definitely not overbearing or pushy. I suppose I could make an argument that he was a bit obnoxious when his team won, but no more than I would have been had the outcome been different. No more dates, except I owe him dinner since I lost our bet, and…" Ellie peeked over Nicole's shoulder to see Amanda coming down the hall, smiling and pointing at Nicole. "And there was just the one kiss."

With that, Ellie smiled sweetly and pointed over Nicole's shoulder.

"Amanda's looking for you."

Nicole whipped her head around to see their principal waving. Her head whipped back to face Ellie, and she said in a fierce whisper, "That's not fair."

"You best not keep Amanda waiting, Nicole. Have a nice day!"

When Amanda called Nicole's name, Nicole turned and headed down the hall, but Ellie could hear the mumbling and stuttering until Nicole was out of sight. Ellie laughed and decided she was glad to have girlfriends again.

"That was a dirty trick, Eleanore. And I know you didn't come to lunch just so I'd have to wait all day to get the details. You probably even arranged for Amanda to come to talk to me again over lunch so I wouldn't have the chance to track you down. Well, your stall tactics may have worked, but I'm here now, and you're not getting rid of me, so spill. *Girlfriend*."

Max walked into Ellie's room just as Nicole finished. "Spill what?"

"Good. You made it," Nicole said to Max.

"You didn't leave me much choice. 'Ellie's room. Immediately after the last bell. Don't dawdle.' It was hard to hear over the roar of a hallway full of seventh graders, but I'm pretty sure that's what you shouted at me. Given the look in your eyes, I was afraid to disobey."

"Yes. Fine." Nicole gave Max a nod and a wave of her hand, effectively dismissing her. Then she pinned Ellie with her stare. "You. Start talking."

Ellie couldn't help it, she giggled at Nicole's no-nonsense tone. Yes, Ellie decided, her friend belonged in a courtroom. While it was tempting to turn the tables and quiz Nicole on her life story, Ellie felt a tiny bit guilty about leaving Nicole hanging all day, so took pity on her.

"As I already told you, I had a nice time with Zeke."

"Oh, this is about Zeke," Max said, and earned herself one of Nicole's stares. Max made a face at Nicole, then folded herself into the closest chair.

"The game was thrilling, right down to the last second, and while I would have liked a different result, the entire experience was so much more than I expected. The fans were—"

"Okay, moving along," Nicole said, spinning her hand in a circle. "I'm certain the game was fascinating, but I'm here about the kiss."

"Wait. What kiss?" Max said. "I didn't know anything about a kiss?"

Again, Nicole silenced Max with a glance.

All day, Ellie had wondered if she'd done the right thing by mentioning it to Nicole. She'd known once the words were out, there'd be no taking them back, and no way she'd get out of a complete retelling of what happened, right down to the tiniest detail, but like she'd told herself the night before, maybe she needed a girlfriend's take on what it all meant.

Planting her feet to steady herself, Ellie launched into her story.

"So," she said when she'd finished, "what do y'all think? It was nothing, right? Just a knee-jerk reaction to the excitement at the end of the game, I'm sure. He could just as well have kissed anyone else around us."

Max, now up to speed, was the first to jump in with a response. "No, El, I don't think so. Maybe that's an Oklahoma thing, kissing everyone around you when something good happens, but I don't think it's a normal thing, at least not at a football game. A high-five, a hug maybe, but a kiss? On the lips? With the woman who caused you to wage war with your nerves to even invite her to go with you to the game? No, it wasn't a knee-jerk reaction. It was a kiss, plain and simple."

That hadn't been what Ellie'd expected to hear from Max. Out of the two of them, she'd expected Max to be the one to agree that it had been nothing more than a way of celebrating. Maybe she'd had it wrong and Nicole would be the one to agree with her.

"Nicole?" Ellie pleaded, and even to her, it sounded desperate.

"I need a few more details before I weigh in." Nicole paced in a circle. "Answer yes or no, please. Did he kiss anyone else during his celebrating?"

"No," Ellie mumbled.

Nicole nodded, and her next questions came in rapid-fire succession.

"Did he look you in the eye before, during, and after the kiss?"

"Yes."

"Did he hold on, however briefly, to you afterward?"

"Yes, but—"

Nicole held up her hand to stop Ellie, then asked the next question. "Did he smile at you?"

"Yes."

"Did you like it?"

"Yes." Ellie gasped. "Wait! You tricked me!"

Nicole crossed her arms, a self-satisfied look on her face. "My conclusion is that he kissed you because he wanted to, and the celebration was just an excuse. You admitted you liked it, so whether you knew it, or not, you were hoping he'd do it."

"Hoping? No. It hadn't even crossed my mind."

Had it? Maybe, but only briefly, and not seriously. Like any number of bizarre thoughts that cross a person's mind dozens of times in any given day. To prove it to herself, Ellie cleared her mind and let her eyes wander the room. They landed on an open magazine left out by one of her students. *That man looks just like my fifth-grade teacher.* On the page opposite, *her skin tone isn't right for that shade of yellow.* On to the kids' stars, which still hung from a bulletin board and were heavy on pets. *I have to remember to look up a recipe for homemade dog biscuits.* And there was Kaede's origami. *I'll probably never be able to fold a fitted sheet the right way.* To her phone on the corner of her desk. *I wanted to find that song...Oh, what's it called? It's from that movie, it played when we were driving home from the game, after Zeke kissed me.*

Ellie sighed. Maybe she'd proved her point to herself that thoughts jumped into a person's mind with only the slightest trigger, but her thoughts had led her to Zeke. And to the kiss. And not for the first time that day. Or even the second, or the third.

"Fine. Maybe I'd thought about it," she admitted, "but I'm still not convinced Zeke meant anything by it."

"He meant something, Ellie," Nicole said. "He meant to kiss you. In fact, I think you can be certain you weren't the only one who'd been thinking about it. It wasn't simply a reaction on his part."

"Okay," Ellie said, still not quite convinced. "But what do I do about it? Isn't a first kiss usually something a little more special? Something you both remember? This was...oh, for heaven's sake. I don't know why I'm fretting about it. It was nothing. I shouldn't have mentioned it."

"Shouldn't have mentioned it? To us? Of course, you should have," Max said. "That's what girlfriends do, right? I can't claim to have a lot of experience, but it seems like something girlfriends do." She looked to Nicole for help.

"Of course, it's what girlfriends do. Tell each other things like this and help each other analyze things like this. You can't possibly look at the situation objectively, El, only we can. And therefore, my conclusion stands. There was nothing 'spur of the moment' about it." Nicole nodded once, then dropped her hip onto the desk next to her.

"But—"

"Let's assume Nic is right and move on," Max said. "As far as kisses go, how was it? Is he any good at it?"

"How am I supposed to know? I told you, it was so fast, it was over almost before it started. Although…"

Ellie remembered that moment of warmth she'd felt, and it had nothing to do with the throng of people around her. It could have been just the two of them, standing on the fifty-yard-line of a frozen Lambeau Field in the middle of a blizzard, and she would have felt that warmth all the way to her toes. In all the times Vincent kissed her, she couldn't remember ever feeling that way.

"Although?" Max said.

"Although, for that brief second, it was nice. Better than nice, if I'm being honest."

"Hah! I knew it." Nicole looked as if she'd scored a victory, but then, in a flash, that look was gone and her entire demeanor changed. She pulled her lip between her teeth and chewed on it. "What's next, then?" She sounded afraid to hear the answer.

"I don't know what's next. Probably nothing." Nicole had taken to biting on the end of a pen and tapping her fingers on the desk. "Nicole, what's wrong?"

Nicole fisted one hand to quiet the tapping and set down the pen she had clutched in the other hand. "Nothing. Nothing at all. So, you don't think you'll go out with Zeke again?"

"No, I don't think so." Saying the words left her feeling so much sadder than she'd expected, but she told herself it was for the best. "I told y'all I'm not looking to date."

"Okay," Nicole said. "Okay."

"I thought we were trying to convince her she *should* date," Max said to Nicole. "Now we're not? This girlfriend thing should come with an instruction manual."

"We're not trying to convince her not to date, we're just, um, we're just…"

"Trying to convince me not to date Zeke? Not that I plan on it, but why? I'm with Max on this. You did a one-eighty, Nicole."

Nicole twirled her hair around her finger. "I'm sorry. I don't know what to say. I'm not telling you not to date Zeke, I just want you to be prepared, I guess. And careful."

"Prepared? Careful? I don't follow. Careful of what? Of Zeke?"

This time, Nicole rubbed her fingers on her forehead as if fighting a sudden, intense headache. "A lot of people you'll run into know Zeke, and know his family. I want you to be prepared..." Nicole sucked in a breath and when she blew it out, the papers left behind on the desk next to her fluttered. "Oh, I really hate this."

Nicole got up and walked across the room, her hands flying as if arguing with herself. Ellie looked at Max who shrugged, though she had the hint of a grin on her face, no doubt finding some humor in whatever sort of inner turmoil Nicole was facing.

"Nicole, what has gotten into you?" Ellie said.

Nicole walked back and stood in front of Ellie. Ellie didn't think she'd ever seen a more apt example of someone 'torn in two.'

"I lost sight of what was going on here, and I'm sorry. I wanted to prove to you that the kiss meant something, that you needed to trust yourself enough to date again, that you should let yourself be happy again, but I forgot, in the heat of the moment, that it was Zeke Fahrner we were talking about." Nicole's hand found her hair again and twisted it tight enough to knot it. "I'm not going to go into detail, it's not my place, but if you plan on seeing more of Zeke, I wish you'd ask him why he left town. Ask him what happened just before graduation. And please, ask him soon, before you hear things I'm afraid you won't like."

"What in the world are you talking about? Was Zeke in some sort of trouble?"

"Please, El, please don't ask me anything more. There was so much confusion back then, so many people who thought they knew what they were talking about but probably didn't. I don't know for certain what's true and what's not, but I don't want to see you hurt. Not by this. Maybe I should have said something right from the start, but I didn't want to spread rumors and lies. Honestly, I don't know the whole truth, I don't know that anyone besides Zeke does, so please ask him. Don't wait until it's too late."

"You're not making any sense at all. If Zeke did something, if I should be afraid..." Ellie refused to believe there could ever be a reason to be afraid of Zeke, but Nicole's behavior let the doubt creep in.

"No, no, it's not like that. You don't need to be afraid of him, but I don't want you hearing things that might upset or concern you before you've had a chance to talk to him and hear the truth. Please."

"This sure isn't what I expected when I walked in here," Max said. "Small town secrets, Golden Boy's image tarnished, rumor and innuendo. Wow. I can hardly wait for the next chapter."

"It's not what I expected, either," Ellie said. "Not at all what I expected." She grabbed her things. "Thank you, ladies. I appreciate you talking this out with me. I need to go pick up my dog. Will you please lock the door behind you?"

Ellie's heels snapped on the floor as she walked as fast as she could without running.

"Ellie, wait!" Nicole called after her, but Ellie kept walking.

Once she was inside her car, Ellie dropped her head to the steering wheel and fought for control. She wasn't sure if she felt angry, or shocked, or scared, or some combination of all three. Whatever it was, it hurt, and while she knew it hadn't been Nicole's intention, that didn't make it hurt any less. She'd counted on her friends to make things clearer.

Confused, she decided. She was confused. Nicole had made no sense whatsoever. Not that Ellie knew many people in town, and not that the topic of Zeke Fahrner was likely to come up with those she did know, but assuming it did, what was it she might hear that had Nicole in such a state?

Nicole had acted weird about Zeke from the start, some strange combination of fascination with the fact that he was back in town and a reluctance to say much about him. Ellie had assumed it was, like Max had guessed, because Nicole'd had a crush on Zeke. The kind of crush a freshman has on the most popular senior. Definitely a one-sided, daydream kind of crush. But maybe there was much more to it. Maybe there was some reason Ellie needed to be wary of Zeke.

"Oh, it's all nonsense," Ellie muttered to herself, and decided she'd put it all out of her mind and go pick up Boomer. He'd be excited to see her and would keep her busy all evening. Exactly the distraction she needed.

Just as she went to start her car, her phone buzzed with a text. She was sure it was Nicole apologizing or asking Ellie to wait so they could talk. When she glanced at the screen, it was a number she didn't recognize, and words that made her cringe.

I still love you. Please give me another chance.

Something like a growl sounded from deep in Ellie's throat. Vincent must have gotten a new phone number, or texted from someone else's phone, because she'd blocked his number months ago. As quickly as she could, Ellie blocked the new number and deleted the text. The last thing she needed, on top of everything else, was Vincent.

* * *

Boomer was overjoyed to see her, and he did distract her, but it was short-lived. Once he ate, lapped up two bowls of water, and sniffed everything in the house, apparently to make sure she hadn't made any unwelcome changes while he'd been away, he threw himself down on the couch, clearly not intending on moving again anytime soon.

When her phone buzzed with a text, Ellie's stomach gave a nervous lurch. The more she'd thought about receiving a text from Vincent, the more it had upset her. Why, after all this time? The couple of texts she'd gotten over the summer had been more along the lines of apologizing, definitely not asking for another chance, and they'd been enough to lead to her blocking his number. She didn't want any contact from him, let alone texts saying he still loved her.

But she'd blocked the new number, so unless he was using yet another number, the text was unlikely to be from him. Ellie leaned over and craned her neck to peek at her phone screen without touching the phone. Just before it went dark, she caught enough of a glimpse to see it was from Nicole. She picked up the phone and opened the text.

I am so sorry I upset you. Please don't worry about what I said. Can we talk tomorrow? Lunch?

Ellie had moved past hurt to just plain curious. Nicole's reaction had been so out of character that once Ellie thought more about it, she'd decided Nicole was likely making more out of the situation than necessary. Knowing Ellie's past, and wanting to protect her from any more hurt, Nicole erred on the side of caution. That had to be it. Based on everything Ellie knew about Zeke, he wasn't the kind of person to have something sinister enough in his past that it need worry her.

Sure. See you tomorrow, Ellie typed, and hit send on her reply to Nicole. She'd smooth things over with Nicole, because if she had to worry about Vincent, she didn't want to have to worry about anything coming between her and her new friend.

That settled, Ellie used her phone to snap a picture of Boomer sprawled out on the couch with his head nestled in a pillow, and uploaded it to her computer to share with her students the following day. She'd share the picture and the report she'd gotten from Top Dog that Boomer had done well on his extended stay, but that he'd spent all Monday following Bowie around and trying to snuggle up next to him every time Bowie tried to lie down.

"Poor baby," Ellie whispered as she stroked Boomer's head. "You were lonely, weren't you?"

Boomer twitched, but never opened his eyes.

Ellie'd been unable to sleep Sunday night after the game, so had gotten a big head start on her school prep for the week. That meant once she was done with readying the next day's installment of 'Adventures with Boomer,' she didn't have any other school work to occupy her, and her mind wanted to drift to the unexpected, and upsetting, text from Vincent.

He couldn't be serious. Not after all this time, not after all that had happened. Was it some sort of cruel joke intended solely to upset her? No matter how much Vincent had hurt her, no matter how many things he'd done wrong, he'd never been cruel, and she couldn't imagine him being so now. But she also couldn't imagine him being serious and thinking she'd come back to him.

"Ugh," Ellie groaned. Why could he still get to her? Why did she let it bother her? It was aggravating to know he still had that sort of power over her. She'd worked so hard to take that away from him.

She turned her phone over in her hand. It was tempting to call one of her friends in Red Creek. She figured she could work the conversation around to Vincent without making it seem like that's why she called. Tenley would be her best bet. She'd be the one to know all the latest gossip about Vincent, and given the smallest opening, she'd be only too happy to tell Ellie every last detail.

Maybe Vincent had been drinking? He didn't drink often, at least he hadn't when they'd been together, but when he did, he made mistakes. A lot of them. If he'd been drinking and had, for some reason, thought of her, that could have very well been what led to him texting her.

On a Monday, though? It seemed odd. "Oh!" Ellie said it loudly enough that Boomer's head popped up. "It's his birthday, Booms. It's Vincent's birthday. I didn't think of it all day! Good for me!" She rubbed Boomer's head, and he dropped it back down on the pillow.

His birthday most definitely could mean he'd been out with friends for an early happy hour, he could have had a drink too many, and he could have made one of those mistakes. Chances were good he'd regret it in the morning, he may even text and try to defuse the situation, but she'd already blocked the number and had no plans of changing that, so whatever he did, it wouldn't matter to her.

Deciding that was settled, Ellie coaxed Boomer off the couch and outside one last time before bed. A warm bed, maybe a silly movie on TV, and early to sleep sounded like the perfect end to a very strange day.

16

The morning passed with only one hitch, but it was a big one.

Her sixth graders were due to hand in their first five-paragraph essays. They'd been working on them for the past two weeks, some of them harder than others, but Ellie had monitored their progress, and all of them had something ready to submit. She'd learned she had writers of all abilities, from those who struggled with proper sentence structure to those who wrote at a high school level. With her goal being to have each student see some progress and improvement in their writing over the course of the year, she set her expectations differently for different students. Some she'd had to encourage every day just to finish the assignment. Others she'd pushed to challenge themselves, to do more than what came easily, to craft an essay that concisely stated their thoughts and used strong words. Something that, when finished, would be a source of pride. Ellie was certain she was far more nervous about the results than her students.

She started both her first and second hour classes by telling her students they had one more chance to ask her questions or to read through their essays a last time, then the rest of the class time was for reading their novels.

Danny wanted Ellie to check to see if his concluding paragraph restated his thesis. It did, she assured him, and with the press of a button and a proud smile—one he tried unsuccessfully to hide—Danny submitted his essay. Mira was frustrated by the fact that the online spelling and grammar check didn't like 'there' in one of her sentences when it was spelled correctly. Ellie explained Mira had used the wrong form of the word and needed 'their' instead. Mira changed it, but seemed unconvinced. Ellie made a mental note to spend part of a class on homophones. She knew of a game the kids would hopefully enjoy and that would make the lesson seem less like learning something they should have already learned.

"Good morning," Ellie said to her fourth hour class. "Take your seats, please. Your essays are due today. If you're ready to turn yours in, go ahead and submit it. We have class time if anyone has a last-minute question or wants to read over their work once more. Take your time and be sure you're turning in your best work. Once you've submitted your essay, the rest of the class is reading time for your new novels. You can move around to the reading nook or find another comfy spot, whatever you choose, as long as you're reading. If it gets too chatty in here, y'all will be back in your seats in the blink of an eye."

There was some murmuring and screeching of chairs as students began shifting from one spot to another. A couple of hands waved to get Ellie's attention.

Then there was a roar.

"I forgot it!"

Before Ellie could look to see where the sound had come from, a desk chair bounced and clattered across the floor. The shrieks from two of the girls in the chair's path made Ellie's ears ring. Then everything seemed to happen at once. Talia pounded her fists on her desk and screamed over and over, "I forgot it!" Toby spread his huge hands over Talia's tiny clenched fists. Talia fought to free her hands, but Toby didn't budge. He bent his head closer to Talia and spoke to her, though whatever he said was drowned out by her screams. Ellie began weaving her way toward Talia, whispering to her students, and in some cases, giving them a gentle nudge to hurry them to the opposite side of the room.

For over two months, Ellie had been trying with Talia. They'd take a small step forward only to take two back. Toby felt Talia was making progress, and Ellie concurred, for the most part. Talia's class work had gone from almost nonexistent to being done quite regularly with more and more effort put in on the girl's part. Talia still rarely acknowledged the other girls in the class, but a few times had talked and even laughed with a couple of the boys. And until now, Ellie had seen no sign of the violent outbursts she'd read about in the reports from Candace, the school district's psychologist.

Ellie eased closer to Talia. "Talia, what did you forget? Your essay?"

Since Talia struggled with typing on her laptop, she often turned in hand-written copies of her assignments.

"Don't talk to me!" Talia shouted. If it hadn't been for Toby's powerful arms over Talia's, Ellie was certain Talia would have lunged at her. As it was, Talia strained and twisted against Toby's hands and continued shouting. "I don't have to listen to you! Don't look at me!" Her face was scarlet, and her small, thin body shook from head to toe.

Talia's voice bounced off the walls of the room and engulfed Ellie, wrapping her in an unsettling combination of empathy and fear for Talia's safety. Terrified the girl would hurt herself, Ellie took a step forward intending to help Toby calm her, but Toby gave a quick shake of his head and Ellie retreated, feeling utterly helpless.

Toby never stopped talking to Talia. His voice stayed even, calm, and though Talia kept screaming, Toby's low voice carried over Talia's shrill one.

"Okay, Talia, you're okay. Quiet your voice, please, remember we're inside. You're okay. Sit down please, it's going to be okay."

Little by little, Talia's screams slowed, then stopped. She fell back into her chair, her body rigid and her eyes glassy.

"That's good, Talia. You're okay. Let's go for a walk. Can you get up and go for a walk with me?"

Talia didn't get up, instead went limp and sank lower and lower in her chair, like a balloon deflating in front of Ellie's eyes. Toby glanced at Ellie and, with a nod of his head, directed her to the closed classroom door. While Toby helped Talia to her feet, Ellie opened the door. When Toby guided the now deathly pale girl from the room, Ellie was certain Talia wasn't aware she was moving. With each step, she leaned more on Toby until he was almost carrying her. When Ellie closed the door behind them, she saw Talia's eyes close.

Ellie stood facing the door and took three deep breaths before turning to face the rest of her students. A few whispered to one another, some looked confused, but most looked sad.

"Okay, everyone, back to your work. Try not to worry about Talia. Mr. T will take good care of her."

"What's wrong with her?"

Ellie wasn't sure who asked, but she was sure the question was on everyone's mind. And how to answer it?

"Talia got upset. Everyone gets upset sometimes, but once in a while, it becomes more than we can handle. Talia will be fine. Our job will be to make her feel welcome when she comes back to class, whether that's later today, tomorrow, or another day."

Bless their hearts, every one of her students accepted Ellie's explanation, nodded, and got back to their essays or their books.

For her part, Ellie needed a minute. Or maybe a lot of minutes.

"She's fine. She's asleep in Jackie's office now. It was unsettling, that's for sure. I felt so helpless, but Toby had everything under control. He is amazing with her. He stayed so calm that after a few minutes, he was able to calm her."

Somehow, Nicole got word of the incident with Talia before the end of fourth hour, so she'd grabbed Max and headed to Ellie's room for lunch instead of meeting up in the teachers' lounge. Now, Max stared at Ellie, her eyes drawn together, her forehead creased, and Ellie figured, trying to decide if Ellie was really okay.

Nicole just looked terrified.

"I told you, I'm okay, Max. If anything, I'm ashamed that after over two months, I still haven't made any progress with Talia."

"I haven't either," Max said. "I try to engage with her, but at the same time, try not to push. It's like walking on a balance beam. I never was any good at that."

"But weren't you frightened?" Nicole asked. "I heard she tried to attack you."

Ellie shook her head. "I don't know where you got your information, but she most certainly did not. She got upset with herself, it escalated, and I think she reached the point where she didn't know how to stop herself. At least that's how it seemed to me. I'm meeting with Candace this afternoon to go over what happened. Hopefully she'll have some advice for me about what to do when Talia comes back to class, and what to do in the future. I feel like I've failed her."

"No," Max said. "You haven't failed her, El. You've done everything right. She's been hurt, she has things she has to work out and overcome. I spoke with Candace before school started. She told me not to expect too much too soon or I will feel like I'm failing. Those were her exact words. It's going to be a long road for Talia. One day at a time is the only way to approach it."

"I suppose you're right, but it was hard watching her go through what she went through today and sit by, helpless to do anything to comfort her."

"Is it horrible of me to say that I'm glad she's not in my class? Nevermind, you don't need to answer that, because it is. I know that, but I also know that I'm not equipped to give her the support she needs."

Nicole trembled, though she tried to hide it by shifting in her seat and straightening the crease in her pants. Not for the first time, Ellie sensed the barely concealed fear Nicole seemed to still have when it came to her students.

"How did the other students react? Did things get out of hand?" Nicole asked.

"They were incredible, bless their hearts. At first, they were startled, especially the two girls seated closest to Talia. When the chair tumbled, it was enough to startle anyone, but after a moment, they were all silent."

Nicole blanched. "A chair tumbled? What does that mean?"

"I didn't see what happened, so I'm not sure if Talia pushed it, or threw it, or just bumped into it, but it sort of bounced across the floor. Anyway, once it was all over and Toby took Talia out of the room, it was mostly concern I saw on the faces of the other students. They may poke fun at one another, they may say unkind things with or without thinking, but deep down, they've got such good hearts."

Nicole nodded, but still looked unsure. Ellie understood. She'd been unsure herself, she'd been shaken, but already now, less than an hour later, things were clearer.

"No one was hurt, the other students were never in any sort of danger, so I'm choosing to look at it as a learning experience for them. Everyone is different, everyone handles situations differently. It's not the first time, and it won't be the last, that the kids have someone in class with different needs, different learning styles, different abilities. It's good for everyone, don't you think, when we can learn from each other? We'll all be better for this minor little ripple in our day today."

"You still have your pompoms, don't you? You pull them out every night and do a little cheer to psych yourself up, I just know it."

"Hilarious, Max. And no, for the record, I do not have them, though I wish I did. I'd come over to your house tonight and do a special 'Max' cheer out on your front lawn. It would be so loud all your neighbors would come outside to see what was happening. I'd get them fired up, they'd all join in, and before you knew what hit you, everyone would be cheering for Max."

Max slapped her hand down on the desk. "There you go, Oklahoma. I've been waiting for a little sass out of you."

The atmosphere in the room was lighter, but Nicole still chewed on one of her perfectly manicured nails.

* * *

She may have shown a little sass to Max, but by evening, that confidence was long gone. Ellie found it impossible to do anything but rethink her reaction to Talia. No matter what Max said, no matter what Candace told her, no matter what she herself might know to be true, she couldn't shake the feeling that she should have done more. A lot more.

Because what had she done? She'd made a feeble attempt to talk to Talia that had accomplished nothing but upsetting Talia more than she already was. If it hadn't been for Toby, if she'd been there alone with Talia, well, it was almost too terrifying to think about.

Ellie flipped over one of the books Candace had given her and glanced at the back cover. She could read all three of them, study facts and statistics until she knew the data backward and forward, and end up with no guarantee she'd handle the next incident any better than she'd handled this one. And that left her with that helpless feeling again.

She alternately paced and thumbed through the books, nothing helping to ease her anxiety. She had herself so tightly wound that when the doorbell rang, she jumped a foot into the air. Boomer flew from his spot in the corner of the couch and ran for the door, barking and dancing in place. And he used his low-pitched, 'It's my job to guard this house' bark. While Ellie was grateful for her protector, she had to laugh at her dog's antics. She wondered if, when she opened the door, a masked and armed intruder stood on the other side, what, exactly, her protector would do. Lick the intruder into submission?

When she opened the door, she found Zeke standing on the other side, and that was enough to send Boomer into ecstatic fits. Poor Zeke never stood a chance. Before Ellie could grab Boomer's collar, Boomer jumped up and proceeded to put some of that licking power to the test, covering Zeke's face in slobbery kisses.

"Oh! Oh, Zeke, I'm so sorry." Ellie apologized, and she meant it, but it was hard to get the words out over her laughter. Zeke's face twisted in a sort of shocked horror.

"Boomer! No!" She pulled her dog down and commanded him to sit at her side. After a few failed attempts, he did.

When Ellie finally got Boomer under control, and when it seemed the dog would stay at her side, Zeke used one hand, then the other, to wipe his face, only to look at his hands, look at Ellie, and in the end, use his jacket sleeve to swipe across his face.

"I really am sorry," Ellie said, this time not laughing. "He's never acted quite that crazy before. Let me get you a towel."

"Don't worry about it. It's not the first time I've been covered in dog kisses. I guess I just wasn't expecting it."

Ellie went to the kitchen and dampened a towel, then returned and handed it to Zeke.

"And I wasn't expecting you. What brings you by?"

"I know I should have called," Zeke said as he handed the towel back to Ellie. "I meant to, several times today, but the hours got away from me. I decided to take my chances that you'd be home." Zeke handed Ellie a pair of sunglasses. "You left these in the car on Sunday."

"I did? Thank you. I hadn't noticed they were missing. It's been so cloudy I haven't needed them." Ellie smiled up at Zeke, and when he smiled in return, nerves danced in her stomach. With everything that had happened with Talia, she'd forgotten about Nicole's strange behavior, but it all came thundering back.

'Ask him why he left town. Ask him what happened just before graduation. And please, ask him soon, before you hear things I'm afraid you won't like.' The words didn't make any more sense than they had when Nicole uttered them the day before.

"You didn't need to make a special trip. It's supposed to stay cloudy. I think that's what the forecast said this morning."

To give herself something to do, Ellie opened the closet door, found her purse, and tucked the sunglasses inside.

"It's not exactly a special trip. You're on my way home. Besides, I wanted to see you again."

"Oh?"

"Yes. I had a really nice time on Sunday."

"I did too. Thank you again." And she wanted to say more, so much more, but the very idea terrified her, and she didn't have the faintest idea of how to begin.

"There's still that dinner…"

Despite her nerves, Ellie relaxed some. "You're right. A bet's a bet." Ellie's mind whirred. Maybe a conversation would be easier over dinner, a glass of wine… "Thursday. Does that work for you?"

"As in the day after tomorrow?"

"Yes. I know it's short notice, so if you're busy—"

"I'm not. Thursday is perfect. And I'll bring the wine. The game could have gone either way."

"Glad you're admitting that. Okay then, Thursday. Fried chicken, biscuits, and pecan pie. It's too cold for sweet tea, so we'll stick with the wine."

"I'm looking forward to it. Very much. But there's something I need to…well, I guess it can wait until Thursday," he said, and the smile he'd had on his face just a moment earlier disappeared when his jaw clenched.

If Ellie thought she was tense, she didn't know what to call the vibe she was getting from Zeke. Before she could try to get to the bottom of whatever it was, even before she could say anything, Zeke was reaching for the door.

"I'll see you on Thursday, Ellie. Good night."

And just like that, he was out the door.

Ellie took a step toward the window and watched as Zeke hurried to his car. She saw him give his head a sharp shake and saw his lips move ever so slightly, almost as if he were scolding himself.

"Why am I always left staring after you, Zeke Fahrner?" Ellie muttered as Zeke's car backed out of her driveway and rolled down the street.

Boomer looked almost as confused as Ellie felt.

"I don't know, boy. I don't know what that was all about, I don't know what I'm supposed to do with what I heard from Nicole, I don't know what to expect on Thursday, and I really don't know how to fry chicken. That I can solve, though," she said with a smile. "It's been too long since I talked to Gran, anyway."

Boomer tilted his head and studied her.

"I get it. All you really want to know is why Bowie wasn't here too, isn't it?"

In reply, Boomer yipped and jumped straight up into the air.

Despite worrying about Talia, and despite worrying about the mystery surrounding Zeke, Ellie had enjoyed a night of deep, uninterrupted sleep. She should have known talking to Gran would be just the thing she needed.

Their conversation had lasted over an hour. Her grandmother had brought Ellie up to speed on everyone in the family and on everything happening at the ranch. Granddaddy had twisted his ankle over the weekend when he'd been working with a young horse that had 'more attitude than sense' according to her grandfather. Gran told Ellie she felt the same could be said about Granddaddy. 'He's too old to be fightin' with those horses, and he knows it. But does he listen to me?

Of course not. Never has, never will.'

That wasn't true, and both Ellie and her grandmother knew it. Granddaddy always said Gran was the boss in their house, and Gran always grinned and denied it, but only half-heartedly. Theirs was a relationship built on love, respect, and lots of fun. Ellie wondered if she'd ever have something even close to that for herself.

Gran had reported that Granddaddy was supposed to be using a cane, but that he'd tossed it aside the moment he'd walked back inside the house after Gran had dragged him to the doctor and hadn't touched it since.

'Stubborn old thing,' Gran said. 'He'd rather hobble around like a lame horse for weeks than use that cane for a few days and help that ankle heal.'

Just listening to her grandmother's voice had been the salve Ellie had needed to soothe every ache, every worry.

They'd eventually gotten around to her grandmother's instructions for frying chicken, and Ellie felt reasonably confident she could do it. She might be cleaning up the mess for days, but she'd show Zeke a real southern home-cooked meal even if it meant scrubbing oil splatters off her ceiling afterward. She'd also added glazed carrots to the menu after Gran told her a meal wasn't complete without a suitable vegetable.

There'd been a few moments at the end of their call when her grandmother had asked Ellie about her plans to visit over the holidays. Ellie's heart had nearly broken in two. Ellie knew how much her grandmother missed her, and how badly she wanted her entire family together, so Ellie was thankful when Gran didn't push too hard.

Even with the thought of missing not only Thanksgiving but also Christmas with her family, Ellie had focused on the happy part of the chat with her grandmother and had fallen into a deep, dreamless sleep.

So, the next morning, she was bright-eyed when she bounced into school, ready to face the day, even whatever fallout there may be from the incident with Talia. She was still shrugging off her jacket when Nicole poked her head in the room.

"Ellie. I'm glad I caught you. I wanted to call you last night, but I was worried you wouldn't want to talk to me. I'm so sorry about the other day. I didn't mean to sound so dramatic, and at the same time, so evasive. It's not that I think you shouldn't see Zeke, or that you need to worry about seeing him, or—"

"Nicole, it's okay. Really. Don't worry about it. I'm not."

That wasn't entirely true, but Ellie felt it was the right thing to say to Nicole.

"But you were so upset. I planned on talking to you yesterday but after everything that happened with Talia, it didn't seem like the right time."

"I said it's okay. Please, let's just forget it."

"Then you're not angry with me?"

"Of course not. There's nothing to be angry about."

Nicole looked relieved, but wary. "Have you talked to Zeke?"

"I've talked with him, yes, but not about what I assume you're asking about. I didn't question him about his past."

"I see."

"I know what it's like to have things in your past you'd rather not talk about, so I don't think it's my place to ask Zeke about his past. If he wants to tell me something, anything, he's free to do so. If not, he's free to do that, as well."

Nicole nodded. "Okay." She fussed with the strap on her bag, then took a few steps into the classroom. "Are you going to see him again?" Almost before the words were out, she shook her head and said, "Never mind, that's none of my business."

"Nicole, we're friends. That's the sort of things friends ask one another."

"Under normal circumstances, I suppose, but this doesn't feel like normal circumstances."

"I don't know what happened back then. I'm not going to ask you to tell me anything more than you've already told me. I am, however, going to ask you to relax and just be my friend. I need a friend a lot more than I need to know ancient history."

Nicole flew across the room and wrapped Ellie in a hug. "You're right. I am your friend, first and foremost, so this stuff is all forgotten." To prove her point, Nicole released Ellie from the death grip and waved her hand as if to clear the air.

Ellie smiled. "Forgotten."

Looking relieved, Nicole changed the subject.

"As your teacher friend, what's the latest on Talia? Do you know if she'll be here today?"

"I don't know. I haven't had time to check with the office or with Candace to see if anyone has any updates. I can't decide if I hope she's back today or not. Does that sound horrible?"

"Not at all. You want what's best for her, but also what's best for the rest of the students. If Talia needs some time, then hopefully she can take it, maybe stay home for a day, if that's what's best for her. If it's best she gets back on the horse, so to speak, then I hope she's back. You'll know how to handle the situation, whatever it may be."

"Sometimes I think you give me more credit than I deserve."

Nicole had made her way back across the room and was ready to head out the door, but stopped in her tracks. "First, you deserve whatever credit I may give you. You're doing a remarkable job. Second, I *have* to believe that you have all the answers. Please never tell me you don't. If I stand a chance at making it in this teaching gig, if I'm to believe I have *any* of the answers, I need you as my role model. Don't burst my bubble. You're so much better at this than I am. I'm hoping a little of you will rub off on me." Nicole gave her a wistful smile. "Have a good day, Ellie."

Ellie stared after her friend. A role model? Ellie wanted to laugh, but Nicole had seemed sincere, desperate almost. Ellie knew Nicole sometimes struggled, that she wasn't doing what she thought she'd be doing with her life, whatever that may be, but Nicole seemed sure of herself in so many other areas, it was strange to think of her as vulnerable as she'd just appeared.

It was all Ellie could do to keep herself from running after Nicole, convincing her—shouting if she had to—that Nicole needed to find someone else to look up to. Most days, Ellie felt inadequate, at best. At worst, like an abject failure.

But she didn't chase down Nicole. Instead, she purposefully hung her jacket on the coat rack she kept tucked in the corner next to her desk, unzipped her bag, removed her water bottle and her laptop, and lined them up on her desk. She took a deep breath and lowered herself into her chair. Then she closed her eyes and told herself to think. To think about what she'd done right over the past three months; about the times she had, in fact, bolstered Nicole or Max when they'd been discouraged; about the times she'd gotten through to a student and had seen the metaphorical lightbulb flash to life; and about the times she'd known, if just for a minute, that she was in exactly the right place.

It was easy to focus on the negatives, to think about all the should haves and could haves, but the positives were there, if she looked hard enough. And if Nicole noticed them, if somehow Ellie was giving off the impression that she knew what she was doing, then maybe she did. More importantly, if she could help Nicole by giving off such an impression, then she just better keep doing it.

Feeling a little uncomfortable with her revelation, Ellie ordered herself to focus on the coming school day and on the kids who'd start arriving in a few minutes. Before she could do anything, her phone rang. When she hung up after the short conversation, she was left to ponder her feeling of relief at the news Talia wouldn't be in school that day.

The school day was uneventful; just what the doctor ordered, as far as Ellie was concerned. Since her sixth graders had just turned in their essays, they were beginning a new unit that focused on the differences between writing news articles and opinion articles. Ellie devoted the first lesson to studying examples and having the students try to determine which were strictly factual and which contained opinions. It was a fun exercise and most of her students enjoyed it.

Her seventh graders were in the middle of their poetry unit and it was still a struggle. With most, the idea of poetry was a hard sell. When they'd first started the unit, she'd asked them all to take out a sheet of paper and write their definition of poetry. Most hadn't had the first idea of what to write other than something about rhyming words.

Then, she'd read several poems to them, from Emily Dickinson, to Shakespeare, to Langston Hughes, to Bob Dylan. They'd spent several class periods analyzing poems, looking for the meaning behind the words that at first glance didn't seem to make any sense. When they finally did make sense, when it clicked for a student, Ellie's reward was a spark in that student's eye. While they still may not love it, after a week, at least they didn't all hate it any longer.

"Today you're going to write your own poem. We've looked at many types of poetry, from short and silly limericks, to lengthy sonnets, ballads, and elegies. Some poems rhyme, some don't. Some follow a pattern of syllables, some don't. Some are happy, some are sad. Some tell a story, some make a point, some are so heavy on symbolism, it's hard at first to know the author's meaning. I want you to decide on one type of poem, any type you want, and write a poem for me. We're going to write it in just this one class period, so put on your thinking caps."

Chloe's hand shot up in the air.

"I know what you're going to say, Chloe, and yes, I know forty minutes won't be long enough for many of you to write the poem you want to write. What I'm asking you to do today is to write something that you can finish in forty minutes. My goal is to show you it's possible to have fun with poetry. Then those of you that want extra credit can write another poem outside of class and turn it in by the end of the week. That, too, can be any type of poem you choose."

Now Sam's hand stabbed the air.

"No, Samantha, you don't have to write another poem. Like I said, it's extra credit."

After almost three months with her students, Ellie had gotten pretty good at predicting their reactions.

"Refer to the notes you've taken on the different styles of poems and start writing. Remember, even though we're doing this quickly, you still have to follow the guidelines for the type of poem you choose. For example, if you want to write a haiku, how many lines will your poem be? Chloe?"

"Three."

"Right."

"And how many syllables on each line? Someone other than Chloe?" Ellie nodded at Evan when he raised his hand.

"Five, seven, and five."

"Very good. Okay. Let's get started."

By the time the bell rang, Ellie had a poem from each of her students. As she said goodbye to them while they crammed their belongings into their backpacks, she glanced at a few and grinned. It was going to be interesting reading.

On her way home, Ellie stopped at the grocery store for everything she'd need for the following evening's dinner. Armed with her list organized by sections of the store, she began plucking items from the coolers and shelves.

"Chicken, check," Ellie said to herself as she pushed her cart and scanned her list. "Carrots, check. Flour, baking powder, pecans, brown sugar, corn syrup, shortening, vegetable oil, vanilla, check." She hadn't done any baking since moving to Caston, so her baking cupboard needed a serious boost.

She gave her cart a once-over and nodded to herself. "On to dairy."

Unsalted butter and eggs joined her rapidly filling cart. "Now, buttermilk, buttermilk…" Ellie's eyes roamed the refrigerated shelves, then she frowned as her eyes landed on the small, empty spot on the far end. The spot where the buttermilk should be. Frustrating, but not a catastrophe. She'd make do. Gran had told her if she couldn't find buttermilk, she could make her own with milk and a little lemon juice or vinegar. She'd go that route rather than make a trip to the grocery store on the other side of town. She needed to get home to Boomer.

Satisfied that she had everything she needed to tackle the menu she'd promised Zeke, Ellie pushed her cart to the check-out line. Now it was just a matter of putting all those ingredients together and ending up with a meal.

17

The pie was done. Ellie had baked it the night before, and it was perfect. At least something was. The biscuit dough, made from the recipe she'd used countless times, the recipe she knew backward and forward and inside out, looked a bit off. Maybe it was due to the different brand of flour, maybe it was the different climate, but sitting there on the baking sheet, the biscuits didn't seem quite right. Then again, maybe it was her imagination. An imagination that was working overtime, given her tightly wound nerves.

The carrots were prepped and ready for the skillet, the chicken was battered and resting, just as Gran had instructed. Ellie glanced at the clock. She'd have to start the chicken soon, and even though she had her grandmother's instructions memorized, she was regretting not having a backup plan. What if the chicken was undercooked? What if Zeke ended up with food poisoning? She should have put a roast in the slow cooker just in case. Grabbing her phone, she made sure she had the number for Pizza-n-More saved. If things really took a turn, she'd make a call.

With a deep breath, and after wiping her sweaty palms on the legs of her jeans—jeans she'd fretted over for twenty minutes before deciding that, paired with her red, cashmere sweater struck the right balance between dressy and casual—Ellie picked up the tongs, grabbed the first piece of chicken, and with the confidence of one walking into a den of lions, lowered it into the hot oil.

It sizzled and spit and splattered. Gran had warned her, but it still came as a shock. Ellie jumped back from the stove, grateful she'd remembered her apron or she'd be back in her closet searching for another outfit she could deem appropriate. After a moment, the sizzling slowed, and Ellie inched forward, ready to add the next piece of chicken. The process got easier with each piece, and by the time the pan was full, Ellie felt reasonably sure she'd survive, though she wished Zeke hadn't offered to bring the wine, because she sure could use a glass.

Keeping one eye on the chicken she half expected to burst into flames at any moment, Ellie popped the biscuits in the oven. She'd no sooner closed the oven door than Boomer barked and a moment later, the doorbell rang.

"Oh, boy," Ellie muttered. "I hope I'm ready for this."

The chicken was good, not as good as her grandmother's, but Ellie hadn't expected that. Zeke devoured two pieces. The biscuits weren't quite as round as she would have liked, but for all her fretting, they tasted as good as she remembered, and she was certain Zeke hadn't noticed their slightly lopsided shape. The carrots were cooked just right, sweet and not too hard, not too soft. Overall, Ellie gave herself a solid B-plus.

When she took her first bite of pie, though, she couldn't stop the self-satisfied smile. It was perfect. The crust was firm, but flaky, with just the right amount of buttery flavor, and the edge fluted and browned to perfection. The filling was just the right amount of gooey sweetness, offset by the crunch of the toasted pecans.

"Wow, Ellie, this is fabulous," Zeke said as he forked up a second bite. "I can see why you won a blue ribbon."

"Thank you. I'm glad you like it."

"Like it? I think I'm in love. I'm not always a big fan of sweets, mostly because I've trained myself to believe that, but if I had this around all the time, I'd have to rethink my entire life."

Ellie laughed. "I don't want to be responsible for something so drastic, so we'll keep the pie to just once in a while. How's that?"

Ellie hadn't paid attention to her words, but when Zeke was quiet for what seemed like a long time, she replayed them in her mind and heard what Zeke must have heard.

"Then there will be a next time? And a next time?" Zeke asked.

"Oh, I didn't mean...I just meant..."

"I'd like there to be a lot of next times."

She busied herself swirling her fork through the ice cream that was melting on her plate, but then slowly raised her eyes and met Zeke's. Her heart thudded so erratically she swore it missed a beat or two before making up for it and hammering away at double-time.

How was she supposed to respond to that? She liked him, she was far past trying to convince herself otherwise, but she wasn't past the hesitation and the fear that came with anything approaching a relationship. Regardless of what Max and Nicole told her, regardless of what she might have said in reply, when faced head-on with the possibility of something more than a casual friendship, she was as scared as a deer caught in the headlights of an oncoming truck.

Suddenly the pie she'd been sure was worthy of another blue ribbon tasted sickeningly sweet. What was already in her stomach jumped and jumbled until all she could do was push the plate away from her and pray she wouldn't have to excuse herself from the table.

"I hope you feel the same way, but regardless, before this goes any further, there's something I need to tell you."

Zeke, too, pushed away his plate that held the last bites of pie. Ellie thought he looked nearly as sick as she felt. What a pair they made. Both apparently scared to death of something, but both also too scared to do anything about it. For her part, it was infuriating to think Vincent still held that sort of control over her. Just like Max and Nicole had told her, she reminded herself she was in charge. If she wanted to date Zeke, she should date Zeke. If it turned out they weren't right for each other, so be it. She'd deal with that if, or when, she had to, but she'd deal with it. She wouldn't fall apart, wouldn't hide away like she'd done after Vincent. She had the feeling Zeke was worth fighting for, even if that fight was against herself.

"I think I—"

"Before you say anything, may I ask you a question?"

Maybe Zeke was ready to fight too, but when Ellie looked more closely at him, there was fear and a sad sort of resignation in his eyes.

"Of course," Ellie lied, because she was afraid his question was the last thing in the world she wanted to hear.

Before Zeke could say anything more, Ellie's phone chimed. A text. "I'm sorry, I thought I silenced it."

"No problem. Go ahead and check it." Zeke leaned back in his chair with a sigh that sounded a lot like relief.

"I don't have to. It's probably nothing." But a shiver shook her as she said the words.

"Really, check it."

Ellie nodded, then stood. "I'll just turn it..." Ellie's words died on her tongue when she saw the text. *I want you back and I'll do whatever it takes to get you.*

Ellie's hands fumbled with the power button, unable to vanish the words and silence the phone fast enough. Before she'd achieved her goal, the phone fell to the floor.

"Ellie, is it bad news? Is there something I can do?" Zeke was on his feet and moving toward her.

"No, it's nothing. It's just school. A situation with a student." She hated herself for lying, but she wasn't ready to talk about Vincent with Zeke. "It's okay, or it will be."

"You're sure? If you need to go, need to do something, I understand."

Did he sound like he welcomed the interruption? Ellie told herself she was imagining things. He was concerned, that's all.

"It's fine." Ellie set down the phone, now not only silenced but turned off, and smiled up at him. "You wanted to tell me something."

"Yes. I guess I did." He shifted his feet. He put his hands in his pocket, then pulled them out again, before finally asking, "Have you heard things about me? Things from your friends, from other teachers at school, from anyone?"

"Um, no, I...what do you mean?" She could feel her cheeks heat as she failed spectacularly in acting as though she didn't know what he was talking about.

"You have." Zeke nodded. "I figured. I'm surprised it didn't happen sooner. Although, maybe it did, and you were simply being polite, not asking questions. Either way, I owe you an explanation."

"No!" Ellie surprised herself with the forcefulness of her answer. "No," she repeated at a more reasonable volume. "You don't owe me anything. Believe me, I know what small towns are like, and I know how people in small towns like to talk. Sometimes, back home, I would have sworn talking about others was a more popular pastime than football. And I know what it feels like to be...Let's just say I understand. Honestly, I haven't heard much of anything about you aside from the fact that you grew up here, that you were a star athlete and scholar, and that you left after high school. When I first mentioned you, after we met following the mix-up with the dogs, Nicole seemed surprised that you'd come back, but she didn't say more than that. Then, just the other day when I was telling the girls about the football game, she hinted at something in your past, but she didn't go into detail and, anyway, like I said, it's none of my business."

"It is if I want to keep seeing you, and I do. I really do. I'm not very good at this, I haven't dated much, and never seriously, and I'll probably say the wrong things, and I'm not sure about all the latest dating rules, but I'd like to spend more time with you. If you still want to, that is, after, well, after."

With those few words, any remaining doubt she may have still had about letting Zeke become more than a friend melted away like the first few snowflakes hitting the still-warm ground. Something in her heart cracked open and feelings she hadn't felt, or hadn't let herself feel, in years flooded out. But that didn't mean she knew how to answer him, because for as much as he may *think* he wasn't very good at it, she *knew* she wasn't.

When she didn't respond right away, Zeke's shoulders sagged. "You're nervous, that's obvious, so that means you've heard more than you've let on."

"No, really, Nicole just acted strange, and said I should talk to you."

"She was right. Ellie, I'll answer any questions you have. I'll try to answer them all as honestly as I can, but there may be some I can't answer and if that bothers you, I'll understand. The last thing I want to do is to make you uncomfortable."

"What I am is confused. Nicole was very vague, and you're not making any more sense than she did. You know, why don't we just drop the whole thing?"

The dishes, the food left on the table, the melted ice cream, the mess she knew waited for her in the kitchen all seemed to demand her attention. Whatever Zeke had to say, she got the feeling he was afraid of her reaction. If she expected to concentrate, to have a sensible conversation, it couldn't happen over the messy, chaotic table. Ellie began gathering dishes.

"I'm just going to clean up a bit. I've never been able to relax when there's a mess around me."

She could tell Zeke wasn't in favor of her stall tactics, but he nodded and began helping her clear the table. They worked mostly in silence, only the occasional question about what he should do with the chicken or where he'd find containers for the leftovers shattered the unnatural quiet. Once things were cleaned and straightened enough that Ellie knew any further fussing on her part would be downright rude, she folded the dishtowel, hung it over the oven door, and with a wave of her arm, directed Zeke to the living room.

"Would you like another glass of wine?" Zeke asked her as they passed the table where the bottle and glasses still sat.

"Yes. Thank you."

Zeke poured, then handed her the glass. When his hand brushed hers, Ellie felt the tingle all the way from her fingertips to deep in her belly. Another thing she'd have to get under control if that sensible conversation stood a chance of happening.

They sat in the living room, Ellie on the couch and Zeke across from her in a chair. Trying to settle her nerves, Ellie took a far bigger gulp of her wine than she intended, sending her into a coughing fit.

"Are you okay? Can I get you some water?"

"Fine. I'm fine," Ellie managed between her coughs. "I don't think I'll need any medical treatment." She offered Zeke a weak smile.

Zeke waited until her coughing slowed, then said, "I always wanted to be a doctor. From the time I was a little boy, it's all I imagined doing. My brother and I would pretend to operate on our toys, using words we heard our father using. It was one of our favorite things to do. Sometimes, Dad would join in and though it seemed like play, I soaked up everything he said, every movement he made. Caleb, my brother, too. At least for a while. As we got older, Caleb's interests turned more toward computers, electronics, that sort of thing.

"Your friend, Nicole, may have told you I was a good student, that I was a decent football player, and I suppose those things are true, or they were at one time, but that's not the impression I left most people who remember me from those days. There's a cloud over my name in Caston. I got into trouble in high school, just before graduation. A lot of trouble. My dad was pulled into the mess, and it hurt a lot of people. Mostly my family, and that's something I've had to live with ever since."

Zeke quieted, and his gaze drifted to the dark window. He looked unbearably sad and completely alone. Ellie pressed her hands to her thighs and ordered herself to stay put when all she wanted to do was go to his side, to wrap her arms around him, and to ease his pain.

Shoplifting, cheating, vandalism. Ellie tossed around ideas, but couldn't reconcile any of them with the man she knew. "It couldn't have been that bad. You were young. Everyone makes mistakes."

He shook his head and kept his eyes fixed on the blackness outside. When he finally responded, it was as if she hadn't spoken.

"One of the things I learned from my dad, or gleaned is maybe the better word, was the power of his prescription pad. With a few illegible scribbles and his signature, he could heal illnesses, he could relieve pain, he could give someone more time. I respected it, I did, until I didn't."

Zeke pulled his eyes away from the window and met Ellie's. "I stopped by my dad's office one day, he stepped out for a minute, I was there alone, and I tore some sheets from his pad. I wish I could tell you it was a spur-of-the-moment thing and that I regretted my actions immediately, that I never did anything with what I stole, but I told you I'd be honest with you."

The desire to comfort was still there, but a sense of unease began overshadowing it. Ellie felt a little ill. He'd forged prescriptions? He'd had a drug problem?

"I needed money. A lot of money. I forged prescriptions and sold them."

It seemed so out of character, so very opposite from everything she knew about him that Ellie waited a beat, and then another, for Zeke to recant what he'd said, to say it was all some sort of horrible joke, but he didn't. Instead, he slumped back into his chair, his shoulders rounded, and he seemed to shrink before her eyes. Had Ellie not known him, had she not seen him running past her house with Bowie, splitting firewood in his yard when she'd walked past with Boomer, she'd have been certain he was ill, perhaps even with physical disabilities, he looked that defeated and vulnerable.

"I can't believe you did that. I have to admit, it's not what I expected to hear." Not in any of the countless scenarios she'd dreamt up. "Why, Zeke?"

"Money, like I said."

"Money. Money for what? No, never mind that, but you felt like you needed money so badly you did something that went against everything you believed? Something that put all your dreams at risk? Medical school. How did you think you'd get into medical school with something like that in your past? How did you get into medical school?"

"It never became a police matter. I've thought about that a lot over the years, and I have a lot of different feelings about it. I broke the law, clearly, but, well, there really are no buts."

Ellie's head spun. "I don't understand, Zeke. Any of it. I don't understand what you did, why you did it, or why you're telling me."

Zeke rubbed his hand over the back of his neck and moved his head from side to side as if trying to work out a kink that would never quite go away.

"I'm telling you because I know you've heard, or will hear, things.

It's inevitable."

She had a million questions and hardly knew where to start.

"I still say it's your business, but if you insist on talking about it, explain how it was never a police matter, yet you say you got into a lot of trouble."

Zeke pushed to his feet with a groan more befitting an eighty-year-old man than someone his age. He wandered to the window again and stared for so long, Ellie's anxiety skyrocketed.

"The summer before my junior year of high school, I injured my shoulder. Not my throwing arm, but it was serious, very painful, and required a lot of therapy. The doctor prescribed me pain medication. I tried it but didn't like the way it made me feel, so I settled for over-the-counter meds instead. One day at a team workout, I mentioned something to that effect. It was just talk, just passing the time while we were in the weight room. Later, one of my teammates got me alone and asked me for some of the pills. He claimed he had a knee injury and that he hadn't been able to get any relief with over-the-counter products. I knew he didn't have an injury. I refused, he wasn't happy, but we put it behind us. Twenty months later, I sold that same guy a forged prescription. Some of his friends, as well."

Zeke wandered to where Boomer was curled up in the corner of the couch and crouched to pet the dog. Long, rhythmic strokes elicited a contented groan from Boomer and seemed to do double duty as Zeke was steadier when he stood again.

"One day, my dad got a call. At home. I was in the room when he answered. I only heard his side, of course, but later learned the details. It was a pharmacist in town, one who knew him well. She was suspicious of the number of prescriptions she'd filled in a short amount of time for oxycodone, all for teens, all written by him. My dad didn't say too much after the call. Later he told me he was confused by what he learned from the pharmacist, but had an inkling things would get worse. At first, he thought perhaps they were old prescriptions he'd written that had never been filled and then had the date or the names altered. He painstakingly reviewed his records, didn't find anything that fit with what he'd heard, so started to try to puzzle it out. He considered everyone he worked with who would have access to his office, who might do something like forge his signature, and he also looked closer to home.

"It's a long story—a long, ugly story—but in the end, I admitted to my dad that I'd done it. Never in my life had I seen my father so angry, so disappointed, and so shocked all at the same time. We talked for hours. I told him what I'd done, I told him how sorry I was, I swore to him I would never do anything like it again, and in the end, my dad only said he needed time to think.

"He took time. Almost a week. It was the longest week of my life. To this day, I don't know how much he told my mom as she and I have never talked about any of the details, even though I know she knew something was very wrong. After a week, my dad called me back into his study and laid out his decision. I was to drop out of school effective immediately. I would, of course, finish my classes, but I would do it from home. There wasn't much of the school year left, so the academic side of things wasn't a problem. I would also do nothing but go to my part-time job, to church with my family, and perhaps some other family outings. I would not see any of my friends, I would not participate in the graduation ceremony, I would not have a social life."

Zeke paused and looked at Ellie for the first time since he'd started his story. His face was remarkably blank. Pale, but blank of any emotion. Ellie, on the other hand, figured just about every emotion there was, at least every sad, every shocked, every horrified emotion, was visible on her face.

"My dad told me his decision not to turn the matter over to the police was the hardest decision he'd ever made. It went against everything he believed in, it went against all that he swore upon when becoming a doctor, and it went against what he believed as a parent. But, he said, I was underage, he believed I was truly remorseful, he also believed I would never do such a thing again, and he felt I deserved a second chance.

"The next day, my father and I met with the principal, Mr. Keller, and explained I wouldn't be returning to school. My father said only that there'd been an incident involving drugs, that he was aware of all the details, and that nothing occurred on school grounds. This was true, because the other people involved were all a year older than me and were out of high school by that time. My father told Mr. Keller the police were not involved, and that there was nothing to involve the school in the matter. Mr. Keller had never been in a situation quite like it, and he didn't know what to say or what to do. He asked some questions, mostly to be sure he and the school were protected should anything get out about the incident. He tried to word his questions to get more information out of my dad, but my dad wouldn't budge. In the end, Mr. Keller checked my transcript to be sure I was on track to finish all my credits. I was, so his concern then was finding a replacement to give the valedictory address at commencement.

"There was never any kind of announcement from the school about what happened, just that there'd be a new graduation speaker, but it didn't take long for rumors to circulate. I didn't have much contact with anyone, but still, I heard things: a nervous breakdown, a major cheating scandal, a drug problem. That was closest to the truth, I guess, but still miles off. There were other stories, I heard about them later, that I had done something illegal, but I don't know that anyone believed that. It sounds incredibly conceited to say, but up to that point, my reputation had been spotless and I don't think anyone believed I'd fallen that far. There were those who may have been a bit envious of me, who maybe took some delight in my plight, whatever it was, so I'm sure there were some ugly rumors."

Zeke shook his head as if now, years later, he still couldn't quite believe all of it. "Anyway, that's about it. I spent my time that summer prepping for my first year of college, reading the textbooks, doing whatever I could to show my dad I was serious about school and that I wouldn't let him down. I spent every summer after that staying at school, taking courses, and ended up graduating in three years. The rest, I guess you know."

Ellie felt like she didn't know a thing. No matter how Zeke explained his story, she couldn't make sense of it.

"When I moved back last year, there was talk, some of which you've heard. Or at least have gotten wind of. When someone would recognize me at the store, or at a restaurant, even once or twice at the hospital, there were whispers, a lot of questioning glances. Some of my friends who were still around called me up. I reconnected with a few, but I've made it clear any talk of what happened back then is off limits. They've respected that, though I'm sure there are still questions. A lot of questions. Small towns, you know?"

Small towns, she knew. What to do with the information she'd heard, she had no idea.

"You don't have to say anything, Ellie, and if you decide you'd rather not see me again, I'll understand. Honestly, I will, and with no hard feelings."

"I...I don't know. I don't know what to say. I don't know what to think. It's a lot to take in. It seems so out of character."

Zeke nodded, but said nothing.

"Can I ask you one question?"

"Of course."

"You and your father. Is your relationship okay? Have you reconciled with one another everything that happened and put it in the past?"

Zeke drew in a shaky breath and Ellie saw his eyes glisten with unshed tears. Her heart raced, and she wanted more than anything to take back her question.

"After all I told you, that you would ask about my relationship with my father..." Zeke shook his head. "Ellie, I don't deserve your friendship. You're an incredible person. You have an incredible heart."

Zeke reached for the jacket he'd draped over the back of the chair when he'd arrived and slipped into it. "Good night, Ellie. Thank you for the best meal I've had in a long time." He reached down and patted Boomer's head. "Bye, Boom-man. Take care of Ellie."

When he got to the door, he turned. "We're okay, my dad and me. We're okay."

For a moment, he looked as though he wanted to say more, but then he was out the door, pulling it shut behind himself, and Ellie was left staring at a closed door.

18

As the minutes and the hours ticked by and Ellie lay with her eyes wide open, staring at a black ceiling while her mind whirled and replayed events from the past few days—each one, it seemed, worse than the last—she was grateful for one thing. The next day was a teacher workshop day. She'd be exhausted, she didn't know how she'd get through the three meetings she had on her schedule, and she didn't see any way she'd get through reading all the essays and poems she'd told herself she'd read and grade, but at least she wouldn't have to face sea after sea of expectant faces and try to figure out how to teach them anything meaningful. And Monday was a day off for students and staff, so that gave her even a little more time to get her act together.

Lingering concern for Talia, frustration and growing concern over the bizarre texts from Vincent, and so many questions about what she'd heard from Zeke. She'd alternated between fretting over and pondering each in turn, with no answers or brilliant insight anywhere. She tried reading the books she'd gotten from Candace, but concentrating on the medical and technical jargon proved impossible. She couldn't help but think how much she'd like to discuss the situation with Zeke, to get his opinion, maybe to even ask him to help her better understand some of what she read. She wouldn't, of course, give him a name or any other information that would identify Talia, but she figured she could provide enough of a character sketch to get him up to speed that he could help without compromising Talia's privacy.

But that just made her wonder if she'd ever see Zeke again, let alone have anything resembling a serious discussion.

She'd been blindsided by what she'd heard, there was no denying it, and the thought of Zeke doing something like that had upset her, also no denying that. Still, the more she thought about it, the more she recalled the little details of his voice, his body language, his refusal to make eye contact for most of the time he was talking, the more odd and confusing his story seemed. She wondered if there was more to it, if he'd left out something important.

Maybe the police *had* been involved? He'd been arrested? But that begged the question of how he'd been accepted to medical school. Maybe it hadn't been just the one time? But she felt his father would have figured that out and wouldn't have decided upon the punishment he'd decided upon. Maybe Zeke had built a story based on lies to protect himself? He'd said there might be things he couldn't discuss. But she'd never gotten the feeling, in all the time she'd known him, that he was anything but honest. Maybe she was wrong about him?

And that, more than anything, made her uneasy. She'd been wrong about someone before, and it had resulted in a kind of hurt she'd never known. A kind of hurt she swore she'd never put herself in a position to feel again.

Since sleep wasn't going to happen any time soon, Ellie climbed out of her warm bed and put on a cozy robe and her fuzzy slippers. Boomer lifted his head, gave her a long, sleepy look, then dropped his head back down on the bed and closed his eyes.

"I'm glad someone can sleep."

Ellie went down to the kitchen where the lingering smell of fried chicken brought on a barrage of emotions. In one short evening, she'd felt happy and afraid; nervous and shocked; confident and confused. Hours later, the jumble of emotions made no more sense than they had while Zeke sat across from her. Ellie wished someone would give her the answers to all the questions that seemed impossible.

It was tempting to brew a pot of coffee, but that meant admitting there'd be no sleep in her future, and she wasn't quite ready to give up. It was nearly two o'clock; her alarm was set for six. The possibility of a couple hours of sleep was still there, so she decided on hot chocolate.

While the milk heated, Ellie told herself she was a much better judge of character than she'd been when she'd met Vincent. She'd had plenty time since their breakup to look back at their relationship and see the red flags. With a clearer eye, they weren't hard to spot.

He'd lied about the littlest things, things that didn't even matter. At the time, she'd told herself he was trying to impress her and that he'd stop once they were more comfortable around one another. He'd stop lying about his grades, the number of hours he worked at his part-time job, even what he'd eaten for lunch, because there'd be no reason to once their relationship evolved into a comfortable one. Ellie recalled the times when for her, the topics had been idle chit-chat, but for him, had been like some sort of competition. He'd fabricated stories, and he'd told outright lies.

It had gotten better as their relationship grew more serious. For a while. With the things that didn't really matter. He stopped lying about school, his job, that kind of thing, but it had taken far too long for her to realize the lies were still there, they were just about much more serious things.

Ellie frowned while she stirred the chocolate into her milk. She'd been a fool, she knew that, but she also knew she couldn't change the past, and she had to believe she was a better person because of her past. That told her she was a better judge of character, which told her she'd know if Zeke was lying to her. He wasn't. Even so, there was something. She couldn't put her finger on it, but something about his story didn't ring true.

She should probably just forget about it. After all, she'd told Zeke it was his business, and she'd meant it. If someone mentioned his past to her, if someone asked her questions looking for the true story, they wouldn't get anything from her. Not her business. Not their business.

Her hot chocolate was gone, but she felt no closer to sleep. Her mother used to tell her, on those nights Ellie couldn't sleep and had fretted about it, that she should close her eyes and rest, that rest was almost as good as sleep for her body and her mind. Her mother had been right about most things, so Ellie figured the smart thing to do would be to go back to bed, to close her eyes, to relax, and hope sleep would come. She rinsed her mug, then started up the stairs when she got a text. A text in the middle of the night was never good news, so her hands weren't entirely steady while she read the words. *Why won't you talk to me? I miss you. I know you miss me.*

"No," Ellie muttered, "no more, Vincent."

On top of everything else, she couldn't deal with Vincent and whatever had gotten under his skin. As she blocked yet another number, she had to shake her head in wonder at the lengths he was going to. How many phones did he have? Or have access to?

Ellie wondered again if she should be worried, or frightened, that he'd continue to escalate things, but put the thought out of her mind almost as quickly as it had entered. Vincent was too concerned with his career to risk anything so foolish. Then it hit her that maybe his concern for his career meant trying to win her back. She'd like to think he wouldn't stoop that low, that he wouldn't use her to get ahead in his career, but he'd always set his sights high, had always been determined to be hired by the best law firm, and to quickly make partner. Ellie's father was a key to that success.

While they'd been dating and during their engagement, Vincent had done everything he could to prove himself to Charles Hawthorne. After the breakup, Vincent had tried his best to stay in her father's good graces, though he'd had an uphill battle. Of course, Ellie had since realized part of his attraction to her was because of her father. Maybe all, but she'd thought a lot about it, and was confident when they'd first met, he didn't know who her father was. Whether they would have dated for years, whether Vincent would have proposed, and a hundred other questions had all, at one time, dominated Ellie's thoughts, but no more. It was the past, and it would stay in the past.

Just as Zeke's past should stay in the past. Probably, anyway.

Knowing sleep, or even rest, was out of the question, Ellie turned and headed back to the kitchen. She may as well try to get a start on reading those essays. Maybe it would help keep her mind on something other than everything that wanted to cause her worry.

This time, she brewed the coffee.

The day was a brutal one. Ellie could function on little sleep, but no sleep was another animal entirely. The morning went reasonably well, the caffeine fueling her through her first two meetings, but after lunch, Ellie struggled to keep her eyes open. Her third meeting was a one-on-one with the seventh grade language arts teacher. Ellie got through by mumbling a word here and there, and by nodding and agreeing to whatever Kent suggested. She left certain he now considered her the biggest waste of space in the school. She'd redeem herself, but it would have to be another day. After she got some sleep.

Ellie ducked out after that meeting. She'd spend the weekend catching up on grading and on her lesson plans. With Thanksgiving the following week, then only a few weeks until winter break, she'd have to put some spark into those lesson plans if she hoped to keep her students' attention. Teaching during holiday time was a challenge, and she'd need a trick or two up her sleeve in order to survive.

She drove home with her window wide open, hoping the frigid air would work like a slap to the face and keep her awake for the few miles she needed to travel. It did the job, and before she knew it, Ellie was pulling into her driveway. As quickly as she could, she lugged her things inside, clipped the leash on Boomer, and took him outside. A walk would just have to wait, maybe until the next morning, and he'd have to be okay with that, because there was no way she had the energy.

"Okay, Boomer, let's go. I'm freezing."

Ellie tugged on the leash and tried to convince her dog he'd had enough outside time. He didn't agree, and Ellie reminded herself she needed to answer the email from the dog trainer. As soon as the holidays were over, she was going to schedule some in-home training sessions.

Ellie was walking backward, pulling Boomer along as she went, when a car rolled slowly down her street, almost coming to a stop in front of her house before turning into her driveway. Ellie didn't recognize the car, but that wasn't saying much as there weren't many cars in town she would recognize. She figured it was someone at the wrong house, but the car stopped and the engine cut. Ellie squinted and held her hand against her forehead to shade her eyes, but the afternoon sun glinted on the windshield and Ellie couldn't make out any details of the driver, or even if there was more than one person in the car.

She took a couple of steps toward the car, Boomer at her side, his curiosity piqued as much as hers. When the passenger door opened, when Ellie saw the perfectly smooth blonde bob and the tailored red wool coat, she gasped, then squealed. Without realizing she'd done so, she dropped Boomer's leash and flew the rest of the distance to the car.

"Mama! Oh, Mama! I can't believe you're here! Why didn't you call? What in the world are y'all doing here?"

Ellie threw her arms around her mother, nearly knocking the petite woman off her feet.

"Eleanore. My dear." For as much as her mother prided herself on her poise, there was no missing the catch in her voice as she fiercely hugged her daughter right back.

Half laughing, half crying, Ellie pulled herself away from her mother. Ellie had dozens of questions on her tongue, but when she got a good look at her mother's face, at those kind, understanding eyes that looked back at her, the dam broke and all Ellie could do was fall back into her mother's embrace.

"Oh, my baby, Mama's here. Whatever it is, we'll figure it out together."

And they would. Ellie hadn't a doubt. She'd tried so hard to be strong. She'd been determined to prove to everyone back home—and more so, to herself—that she could do it, that she could navigate her life without running back to the comforts of home and of her family, but she needed her Mama. And she wasn't too proud to admit it.

Ellie swiped at her eyes, and when she could finally speak, said, "I don't know why you didn't tell me you were coming, but I am just so happy to see you, Mama, you have no idea. I've missed you so much. Come on, come inside, you'll catch your death out here."

And then it hit Ellie. Her mother hadn't been driving. She'd gotten out of the passenger door. Ellie's eyes flew back to the car, a thrill bubbling up inside her. "Daddy? Is Daddy with you?"

"No, sweetheart, he's not. This was a spur-of-the-moment decision and your father couldn't get away."

"Then who?" Her mind raced. It couldn't be Trav, he was in New York. It wouldn't be Tripp, he wouldn't leave Shelby, and Shelby would have long since jumped out of the car. "Did Char come with you? Or Hayley? Oh! Is Coltie here?" Never mind that her youngest brother couldn't be the one driving, her heart leapt at the thought of seeing him.

"It's just me, I'm afraid."

"You made the trip by yourself? That's not like you, Mama."

"I wasn't exactly by myself. Now, this is just for the sake of convenience. Keep your head about you, Eleanore."

"Whatever are you talking about, Mama?"

As if in reply, the driver's-side door opened. As much as she wished she wouldn't, Ellie would recognize that head anywhere too. The sandy brown hair, expertly cut with not a strand out of place, as if even the hairs on his head knew to listen to Vincent Cunningham.

"Mama, nooo..." Ellie breathed.

Vincent turned and nodded at Ellie, but then crouched down and whistled to Boomer. In all the excitement, Ellie had forgotten her dog was loose in the front yard. Apparently the commotion was enough to hold Boomer's interest and keep him in the yard rather than bolting off down the street as was his usual modus operandi. Boomer charged toward Vincent, who gave the dog a vigorous rub in greeting.

Ellie took the opportunity to whirl on her mother. "I can't believe you brought him here. Mama, what were you thinking? You can't

possibly believe there's anything…that there's a chance…you can't…
you just can't!"

"Oh, Eleanore, pull yourself together. I told you, it's merely a matter
of convenience. There's some sort of conference in Madison. Your
father decided not to go, but I got wind that Vincent would be
attending, and after our last phone call, I thought it would be a good
idea to come and see you. The pieces fell into place. I was able to get a
last minute plane ticket, Hayley is home from school to stay with Colt
during the day, and Vincent was considerate enough to drop me here
so I didn't have to think about driving myself or taking a long taxi
ride." Genevieve closed her eyes and gave her head a shake with her
words.

"But Mama, I don't want to see him."

"You don't have to see him. Well, you have to *see* him, but he'll be on
his way shortly. We agreed on that ahead of time."

"Oh." She didn't like it, not one bit, and she'd see to it that Vincent
held up his end of the bargain. She'd have him back in the car and on
his way so fast his head would spin.

As if he'd overheard their conversation, a moment later Vincent
said, "I'll get your bags, Mrs. Hawthorne, and then be on my way."

"Thank you, Vincent. I'd like to head inside sooner rather than later.
However do you put up with this weather, Eleanore?"

"I don't know," Ellie muttered to her mother's retreating back.

Vincent held Boomer's leash in one hand while he used the other to
punch the button that opened the trunk on the rental car. It annoyed
Ellie to no end that Boomer sat, calmly and patiently, at the end of the
leash. Where was the dog that jumped straight up in the air? The dog
who delighted in wrapping his leash around the legs of the unlucky
holder of that leash?

"I'll just take these to the house," Vincent said.

"I'll do it."

"Ellie, let me carry the bags. Here, you take your dog. At least, I
assume he's your dog?"

"He is."

Ellie reached for the leash.

"You look good, Ellie. You're happy here?"

"I'm fine."

Vincent nodded, but said no more.

"You need to stop texting me."

Vincent was already on his way to the house, but stopped and turned to face her. "Texting you?"

"Yes. Stop. I don't have anything to say to you."

"I haven't texted you, Ellie."

"Oh, Vincent, stop it! Stop the lying." Ellie's hands shook, and she knew she was dangerously close to losing whatever dignity she'd managed to hold on to where Vincent was concerned.

"I'm telling you the truth. I have not texted you. Not for a very long time."

"But I got your texts! Don't act like you don't remember doing it. Did you drink too much on your birthday? Is that what started all of it? Whatever your excuse is, I'm telling you, it has to stop."

Vincent cocked his head and studied her as one might study a particularly uncooperative child. "I swear to you, I don't know what you're talking about."

Given his history of lying, Ellie was loath to believe him, but something in his expression was different, and his body language told a different story than it had on all those many other occasions. He was genuinely confused and, Ellie was forced to admit to herself, possibly telling the truth. Since she didn't want to make a scene in her driveway, she let it go.

"Whatever you say. Take Mama's bags to the door, if you insist, and then continue on your way." Though the words wanted to stick in her throat, Ellie added, "Thank you for getting Mama here. She never would have made the drive herself."

Vincent said nothing, just did as Ellie asked and took the bags to the door. Ellie stayed rooted to her spot. She watched as Vincent opened the door, set the bags inside, then walked back toward the car.

He put his hand on the door handle, but before he opened it, he turned to her.

"For what it's worth, I'm sorry. I'm truly very sorry for what I put you through, for hurting you. I wish I had the words to take away the pain, the embarrassment, all of it, but all I can tell you is that I'm sorry. You didn't deserve any of it."

They'd only spoken, face to face, twice since the night Ellie learned the truth. Once was the day following that fateful night when Ellie, still raw and reeling and against the advice of all her friends, had stormed to his apartment, pounded on the door, and demanded the whole story. The other time was much more civilized, but no less painful. They'd run into one another by chance, at the mall of all places, when Ellie's sisters had dragged her there thinking shopping would help take her mind off her pathetic life.

On both those occasions, Vincent had said he was sorry, but she hadn't believed him. Now, something had changed. As it had to, Ellie realized. After nearly three years, there'd be no reason for Vincent to lie any longer. Just as there was no point in her holding onto whatever anger and heartache still resided inside her. It was time to move on. Really move on.

"Thank you," Ellie said, and realized she meant it.

"Are you happy here, Ellie? Truly happy?"

"I—" She stopped herself and stopped the automatic response she'd gotten so used to giving. "I'm getting there," she replied instead.

"I don't want to be the reason you stay away from home. If you want to come home, I wish you would. I won't bother you, and I'll do all I can to make sure everyone knows you were innocent in everything that happened between us. I want you to be happy, Ellie."

Ellie opened her mouth to reply, another one of those automatic replies, but closed it again and pressed her lips together as she thought. Ellie knew the importance Vincent put on appearances, how important his reputation was to him, so she knew what it took for him to say the words he'd said.

"Thank you, but I think I need to stick it out here. For a while, anyway, and for me. I need to do this for me. I need to prove to myself that I can do it, that I can manage, that I can make a life for myself, and that I can be happy. Like I said, I'm getting there. If I were to go home now? Then I'd never know if I could have done it, would I?"

Vincent nodded. "You really are amazing, Ellie. I always knew that, but I guess I lost sight of it somewhere along the way. If this is what you want, living here, working here, then I know you'll do more than just manage. A lot more. You'll thrive. This town and your school are lucky to have you."

It was more than she'd bargained for, and Ellie found herself tongue-tied, so instead of responding, she took a moment to study the man in front of her. The polished good looks, the poise, the intelligence that lived behind dark and mysterious eyes. It was all still there. More so, if she were being honest, as a couple of years had served to fill out his face and his once-lanky frame, and he was more striking than he'd been when they'd met. But she didn't have feelings for Vincent any longer, not even deep-down-admit-to-no-one feelings, and that felt good. To be able to stand in front of him, to look at him, and to know the past was really in the past felt unbelievably good, and it was freeing. So much so that she was being completely honest when she returned Vincent's sentiment.

"I hope you're happy too, Vincent. And I know that wherever you land, whether it be with Daddy's firm or somewhere else, they'll be lucky to have you."

When he smiled, it was the smile she remembered from their earliest days together.

"I told your mother I'd be back for her on Tuesday. If anything changes with her plans, she knows how to get in touch with me. It was nice to see you, Ellie."

"Okay, and thanks again for getting her here. I'm sure she'll be in touch regarding the plans."

Get in touch meaning with his phone number. Ellie wasn't ready to give up, so as Vincent opened the car door, she tried once more.

"The texts. You sent them, didn't you?"

He shook his head. "I told you, I haven't texted you. Not since last summer. What's going on? Is someone harassing you?"

What was going on? If not Vincent, then who?

"No, I'm sure it's nothing." Then, because she felt better than she had in a long time, Ellie rose to her tiptoes and hugged Vincent with her free arm. "Drive safely."

Vincent hugged her back, but it was a hug between friends, nothing more. When he backed out of the driveway and she turned to watch the car leave, Ellie saw a man and a dog—a man that could only be Zeke and a dog that could only be Bowie—turn themselves around and jog the other way.

"No, Zeke, no," Ellie mumbled, but she could only watch them turn the corner and disappear from view.

"Eleanore, what in the world is keeping you?"

"Coming, Mama." And because it had been a day, and because she needed her mama, she headed for the house.

Time with her mother was the perfect remedy. They shopped, they cooked, they chose tile for the bathroom, and best of all, they talked. For hours and hours. They drank tea or wine, depending upon the time of day, and they talked about everything under the sun. Ellie heard the details, as far as her mother knew them, on everyone in the family. And since there wasn't much Genevieve Hawthorne missed when it came to her family, Ellie figured she was as up-to-date as she could be.

Grandaddy was still limping, but was doing better, and no amount of threatening from Gran would keep him from what he still saw as his chores on the ranch.

Charlene's wedding plans were coming along, despite Charlene changing her mind on the colors. Ellie's heart ached a little listening to the details, but she smiled, asked all the right questions, and deep down, was thrilled for her sister.

Colt was as happy as could be. With breaks from school coming up, he was begging to spend more time at the ranch and while Mama pretended like she wouldn't let him, Ellie knew she would. She'd do just about anything Colt asked.

Hayley was still undecided about school, something that irked Mama to no end, but Ellie, as gently as possible, told Mama Hayley was Hayley, and no amount of fretting or pleading would change the way Hayley looked at life. She'd figure things out in due time.

Tripp and Trav were both happy, working hard. Mama didn't say much about Travis and his life in New York, and Ellie knew her mother was still hoping Travis would come back home one day soon. Genevieve refused to entertain the idea that he was settled for good in New York.

And when the conversation turned, as it did so many times over their four days together, to Ellie and what was going on in her life, Ellie tried to be honest with her mother. She talked about school, about her students, about the ups and the downs. She talked about her fears and insecurities, and about her friends, Nicole and Max. Ellie knew it wasn't her imagination when she spotted a bit of disappointment on her mother's face as she listened to Ellie's stories that involved her new friends. Ellie knew that in her mother's mind, friends made it easier to stay in Caston.

What Ellie didn't do during those four days was talk to, or hear from, Zeke. She knew it had been him in the road when she'd given Vincent a hug, and she knew Zeke had seen that hug. Whether the fact that it was nothing but a friendly sort of farewell and be well sort of hug translated to someone watching from a hundred yards away was unclear, but the more time that passed without hearing from Zeke, the more she figured it hadn't.

Of course, she hadn't made an effort to contact Zeke either. In the dark of her room, after she and her mother said their good nights and Ellie fell, exhausted, into bed but before her eyes closed, she thought of Zeke and of what he'd told her. When her eyes opened in the morning, before she started another busy day, he was her first thought. But she didn't contact him because she didn't know what to say, and because she didn't know if he wanted to hear from her.

He'd said he wanted to tell her his story, to tell her the truth, because he wanted a relationship with her and he didn't want there to be any secrets in that relationship. Or something to that effect. But it was very possible he'd changed his mind. She recalled the last few words he'd said before leaving, when he'd said goodbye to Boomer and had told the dog, 'Take care of Ellie.' That sounded final, as if Zeke wouldn't be back. No matter how often she mulled it over, the situation remained unresolved in her mind.

It shouldn't have come as a surprise. Her mother had always known when something was on Ellie's mind, but nonetheless, Ellie was caught off guard on Monday evening when her mother brought up Zeke.

"You've mentioned the man who took you to the football game more than once, but you've yet to tell me why the very idea of him seems to upset you so much. Tell me about him. Tell me about Zeke."

Tell her about Zeke? If only she knew how. Zeke was everything Ellie wanted, and everything she didn't. Or at least everything she was afraid of. He was kind and funny, he was patient and intelligent, he was caring and considerate. Still, she was afraid, even when she tried to tell herself it was foolish to feel that way, because she'd thought she'd had all those things once before.

"There's not much to tell, Mama. We've seen each other a few times, he's nice, but he's busy."

It was a feeble comeback, Ellie knew that, and she knew her mother wasn't buying it when, with one flick of her wrist, Genevieve dismissed Ellie's comment.

"Everyone's busy. His being busy doesn't explain why you seem upset whenever his name comes up." Her mother reached and put her hand over Ellie's. "Tell me," she added, her voice taking on the gentle tone Ellie knew so well, and that had the power to make everything better.

"I'm afraid, Mama." Ellie leaned her head onto her mother's shoulder and curled her legs underneath her, cocooning herself in comfort. "No matter how many times I tell myself it's silly, that it's not healthy, no matter how many others tell me the same things, I can't completely forget about the hurt and the betrayal with Vincent. I feel like it broke me, and that I'll never be fully put back together."

Ellie had expected more of that gentle voice, more of the

reassurances and comforting words Mama was so good at. Instead, she got a jolt. A physical one when her mother pulled away and Ellie's head jerked from her mother's shoulder, and then an audible one when her mother raised her voice. Genevieve Hawthorne never raised her voice.

"Eleanore Maureen. I will not listen to another minute of this nonsense."

Ellie's eyes went wide as she watched her mother shoot to her feet and stand, hands fisted on her slender hips, and facing Ellie with fire in her eyes.

"I raised my daughters to be strong, and you, Eleanore, are just that. You were hurt, hurt badly, but you are strong enough, and smart enough, to know that one incident cannot define your life. You needed time, you needed to heal, and you've done that. Look at what you've accomplished. You went back to school, you earned another degree, you committed to a job and a home far outside of, and away from, your comfort zone, and you've crushed it. I believe that is the term Colt likes to use. Now, it's time to take the next step and put everything that happened with Vincent behind you, chalk it up to a learning experience, and move on. There will always be people who hurt you, situations you can't control, obstacles to overcome, but how you handle those people, those situations, and those obstacles is up to you. I know you are more than capable of handling them all with aplomb."

Ellie wanted to argue that no, she couldn't handle all of it. She wanted to tell her mother that since she'd never gone through it, she was in no position to tell Ellie what to do. Mostly, though, she wanted her mama to come back to the couch, to put her arm around Ellie's shoulders, and to say in her mama voice that everything would be okay. But the longer Ellie went without speaking, the more that look crept into her mother's face, the one that said, 'You know I'm right, so let's just get on with it, shall we?'

"But, Mama, maybe I'm not as strong as you think I am. Maybe this has all been an act. Maybe—"

"As I said before, nonsense. Believe in yourself, Eleanore. Everyone else does."

Ellie tried for a reply, a snappy comeback maybe, but all she could manage was a series of unintelligible grunts. Her mother shook her head, then softened her stance and returned to the couch where she did, in fact, put her arm back around Ellie's shoulders.

"Now, tell me about Zeke." And the voice Ellie wanted to hear was back.

So Ellie did. She told her mother about the first time they met following the mix-up with their dogs, and about all the times they'd seen one another since. She told her mother how intelligent and compassionate he was when he talked about his job, how kind and fun he was at the school dance and at the football game, and how he loved his dog and tolerated Boomer. Her mother was quiet, listening and nodding, but not saying anything until Ellie lifted her hands in a shrug.

"I guess that's about it."

"What aren't you telling me?" her mother asked. "Not that I expect you to share every detail, but you've left out something. Something important."

"I don't think so." Ellie kept her eyes steady, but as much as she fought it, she couldn't help shifting and moving her legs. She may as well have held up a sign for as easily as her mother read her. It earned her a narrow-eyed stare from her mother.

"Fine. I'm afraid he's not been completely honest with me. He told me something, something about his past, after insisting he had to tell me just so there weren't any secrets or any surprises down the road, but I don't know. I was left with the feeling that, despite all his assurances, he didn't tell me the truth. Or not the whole truth, anyway."

Her mother sighed. "And that's the one thing you cannot, and will not, abide. Nor should you."

"I told him he didn't have to tell me anything, that his past was just that, the past, and had nothing to do with me, but he said he didn't want me to hear things from someone else and be unprepared. What I don't understand is why, if he was so determined to tell me, did he not tell me the truth? Because the more I think about it, the more I'm sure he didn't."

"I can't answer that, only Zeke can, and without knowing what it is he told you, all I can think is that perhaps the entire story is too painful. Perhaps he's not ready to risk reliving whatever caused him pain the first time around. And that, my darling, is something I think you should understand."

"I do. Of course, I do. But..."

"I know." Genevieve took Ellie's hands in hers and turned Ellie to face her. "Listen to me. Risking your heart isn't easy, but the alternative, never taking a chance? That is even harder. It isn't often that the first person you fall in love with, or think you've fallen in love with, is the right person. You were young, only eighteen, when you met Vincent. Still a child, really. You are not the same person you were then. You've grown in so many ways and have become a strong, intelligent woman who knows what she wants and who has the ability to decide whether she's going to go after it. If you think Zeke is worth it, nothing should hold you back. If you have questions, ask him those questions. You'll know soon enough what to do from there."

"You make it sound so easy."

"Easy? Goodness, no. Nothing about love is easy, but what it is, is worth it. Worth the worry, worth the pain, worth the not-so-good times, because the good times? Well, the good times make you forget all the rest."

19

The next morning, Ellie asked her mother once more about Boomer.

"I'm happy to take him to day care today if you'd rather not deal with him. He's a handful. I don't want you to be worrying about him all morning until Vincent gets here."

"Boomer and I have come to something of an understanding. He knows what I'll tolerate and what I won't. If he steps out of line, he knows the consequences. We'll be just fine."

Ellie wanted to protest, but Boomer chose that moment to jump down from the couch and go to Genevieve, dropping his head on her lap and looking up at her with adoring eyes.

"Oh, brother," Ellie muttered.

Genevieve put a hand on Boomer's head and patted before pulling her hand back and wiping it on the napkin next to her coffee cup.

Ellie put her hand over her mouth to hide her grin. Her mother may insist she wasn't a ranch girl, she may have left the ranch for college and claimed to have never looked back, but there was no denying it was in her blood. She had a way with animals, from the dogs she pretended to barely tolerate, to the birds with broken wings Colt seemed to have a knack for collecting, to the horses she admitted she loved, because 'A girl can love horses and not be a rancher.' If she had Boomer listening to her after three days, she could tame anything.

"If you're sure," Ellie said. "I wish I could stay home today and we could have a little more time, but being it's a holiday week, teachers aren't allowed to take personal days unless it's a downright emergency."

"Of course. We had a lovely visit. You know, there's still time to find a flight home for Thanksgiving, still time to book a spot for Boomer at that place you take him."

"No, Mama, I can't. Not this year. As much as I'd like to see everyone, to spend Thanksgiving with y'all, I'm going to stay here."

"Christmas, then."

There was a finality in her mother's voice that left no room for disagreement and since the last thing Ellie wanted to do right before they said their goodbyes was have an argument, she kept her reply simple.

"Maybe. Now, you said Vincent will be here around noon?"

Her mother looked like she maybe wanted that argument, but let the matter go. "That's what his latest text said."

Ellie gathered up her things and started toward the closet for her coat, but stopped midway across the living room.

"Mama, did Vincent really have a conference in Madison?"

"He did."

"A conference he wanted to, or needed to, attend?"

Her mother lifted her hands and let them fall. "Your father mentioned the conference to me. You know how he feels about those sorts of things."

"He hates them."

"He does, but this one was so close to you that if he could have found a way to attend, he would have just to sneak in a visit with you."

It warmed her heart, thinking of her father suffering through something he considered unbearably boring just to have a reason to visit her.

"Anyway, your father had a meeting he couldn't change, but he put the idea in my head. I contacted Vincent, asked him if he was planning on attending, and things worked out."

"It seems a little fishy to me, Mama. Vincent just happened to be attending? His plans just happened to fit with getting you here, attending the conference, and picking you up again?"

"Perhaps I suggested he could make his plans fit, but he was more than willing. It turns out he has law school friends in Madison, so he came early to spend the weekend with them. He attended one day of the conference yesterday and will fly home today. I think this was his small way of trying to make amends."

Ellie only nodded. If nothing else, things made a little more sense. Then something hit her.

"Mama, what number does Vincent use to text you?"

"I don't know. His regular number, I assume."

"What is it? Can you find it on your phone?"

"I suppose, but whatever for?"

Genevieve reached for her purse and pulled out her phone. Ellie tapped her toe while she waited.

"Here. This must be it." She held the phone out toward Ellie.

Ellie took the phone. She looked at the number, but couldn't recall if it was the same number Vincent had used while they were together. She compared it with the numbers she'd blocked and found it didn't match. Still, she jotted it down, just in case. Vincent had seemed sincere, but there was still a little part of her that wasn't quite convinced.

"Eleanore?"

"Sorry, Mama, it's nothing. Just curious. Anyway, I need to run."

They'd been so busy, and Ellie had enjoyed the visit so much, she had managed to put out of her mind any thoughts of her mother leaving. Now, faced with it, with the idea of not knowing when they'd next see each other, it was crushing.

"Mama…"

"I know."

Her mother wrapped her in a hug and for a minute, just held her.

"Christmas. We'll see each other in just over a month. Come home, Eleanore. Everyone misses you. In fact, Colt told me to tell you that you wouldn't get any Christmas presents if you didn't come home. He seemed to think that would seal the deal."

Ellie pulled away, dabbed at her eyes, and forced a smile.

"I'll do what I can. Give everyone hugs. Have a safe trip, Mama, and thank you. Thank you so much for coming."

"Where my children need me, that's where I'll be."

It may not have been her best teacher day, but it wasn't her worst. She was distracted, watching the clock, and thinking first of her mother home alone with Boomer, then of her in the car with Vincent and what they might talk about. Mixed in with all of that were the recurring thoughts and questions about Zeke. That led to her missing the fact that two boys she normally wouldn't have let out of the classroom at the same time managed to both finagle restroom passes and Ellie getting a call from the office when they were found trying to sneak out of school through the gymnasium door. Still, she managed to introduce quick, fun lessons to both her sixth and seventh graders that would take them through the short, two-day week leading up to Thanksgiving break.

A brief chat with Maddie brightened her day when the girl rushed to Ellie after class to report her parents weren't getting a divorce, but were thinking about moving because of a new job for her mom. The arguing, which after listening to Maddie's whirlwind report Ellie figured was more discussing than arguing, had been about whether it was worthwhile to uproot the family again—there'd already been two moves for job changes—and had nothing whatsoever to do with divorce. Maddie was bouncing on her toes as she reported the news to Ellie. Not only did her parents assure her they were very happy together, they had also decided they wouldn't be moving. Maddie was thrilled.

Moments after the last bell, Max stuck her head inside Ellie's classroom door.

"How was the long weekend? I hope you didn't spend it all working."

"As a matter of fact, I didn't. I had company."

"Company? Do tell."

"Tell what?" Nicole asked as she followed Max into the room.

"Mama surprised me. She showed up out of the blue on Friday afternoon."

"Oh, Ellie, how nice for you," Nicole said. "I would have loved to have met her."

Ellie felt a pang of guilt. "That's so sweet. She would have loved to meet the both of you, but we had so much to squeeze into just a few days, the time got away from me. How about y'all? Did you enjoy the weekend?"

"Errands," Max said. "Who knew ignoring everything for two months could mean so many errands?"

Ellie shook her head. "Max, you've got to be the most organized disorganized person I've ever met."

"I'll take that as a compliment."

"How about you, Nicole?"

Nicole looked tired, Ellie thought. She'd done a good job with her makeup, but the dark circles under her eyes were there.

"Same. A lot of errands." Then, as if sensing Ellie was ready with more questions, Nicole changed the subject. "How did it go with Talia? I heard she was back in school today."

One of these times, Ellie was going to get to the bottom of whatever it was that was upsetting Nicole, but it would have to be the right time, and Ellie sensed this wasn't it.

"It was fine. I guess that about sums it up. Fine. No better, no worse. No more or less friendly with me. In fact, it was almost as if nothing ever happened. The other students didn't react to her being back, just as I hoped, and Talia was the same as always. I had a minute to talk with Toby after class. All he had to report was that Talia hadn't wanted to discuss what happened when he and Candace met with her this morning. He said she didn't seem to recall much of the incident, so he and Candace felt it was best, at least for the time being, to let it go."

"Candace knows better than I do, but it seems like ignoring what happened might backfire. Don't they think talking it out would be beneficial?" Nicole asked.

"I don't know. Candace gave me a few books to look at, but with Mama here, I'm afraid I've hardly cracked them open, and what I did read left me plum confused. I thought maybe..." Ellie had been ready to say she'd wanted to discuss it with Zeke, but thought better of it. "I have a meeting scheduled with Candace early next week. I'll see what she can tell me then. If there's something I can do to help Talia, I'm ready to try."

"Were your kids out of control today?" Nicole asked. "I suppose it's the two-day week, they're excited for the break, but wow, they were wild."

"They were antsy," Ellie agreed. "I have some easy, almost silly activities for them to do these two days, hoping that will help keep their attention. It's mostly review, and I looked up some of those *Schoolhouse Rock* videos y'all told me about. That's on the schedule for tomorrow."

"*Y'all, plum confused.* I would have loved to have met your mama just to listen to the two of you talk to each other," Max said, and winked at Nicole, who smiled in return.

"Very funny," Ellie said, but told herself Max was probably right and she better watch how she spoke to her students or any progress she'd made, she'd lose. "Anyway, what are ya—, you two doing for Thanksgiving? If you don't have plans, I thought you might like to come over to my place for dinner. I was going to sort of ignore the holiday, but spending a few days with Mama got me hungry for a real Clayton Thanksgiving dinner. I know I won't do it as well as my gran, but I can give it a try."

"Sorry. I'm heading out right after school tomorrow. Have a friend I haven't seen in a while. Thought it was time," Max said.

"Oh, where—"

"What about you, Nic," Max interrupted.

Ellie frowned at Max, but turned to look at Nicole.

"I'm sorry, Ellie, I have to take my dad somewhere. We've had it planned, otherwise I'd love to join you."

"Don't fret about it, either of you. It's too late to buy a turkey and thaw it, anyway. I'll use the time to catch up on all the work I should have done while Mama was here. I hope y'all…I hope you both have a nice Thanksgiving."

"You too, El," Max said.

Nicole smiled and nodded, but seemed distracted. When her phone buzzed, she ducked out of the room with a wave, and Max followed her. Ellie was left wondering how long it took for new friends to become the kind of friends that shared. Really shared.

Wednesday was a whirlwind of a day. If the kids had been excitable on Tuesday, it was nothing compared to Wednesday. The idea of a four-day break had them bouncing in their seats. For the most part, the *Schoolhouse Rock* videos did their job and kept the kids entertained, with them laughing and repeating the ditties back to the screen. It may not have been the most productive of days, but Ellie headed home that afternoon certain her students wouldn't soon forget that a conjunction's function is 'hooking up words and phrases and clauses,' or that an interjection shows emotions and is 'generally set apart from the sentence by an exclamation point, or by a comma when the feeling's not as strong.'

Ellie knew she'd have the songs in her head for days.

When she got home, she changed clothes, bundled up in the new jacket she'd bought while shopping with Mama, her warmest hat and mittens, and grabbed Boomer's leash. It was cold, well below freezing, and Ellie couldn't help but think it was a good thing the temperature had been milder while Mama was there, or she might have pushed Ellie right into the car with her and dragged her back to Oklahoma. Mama was not a fan of the cold.

Ellie wanted to take advantage of what was left of the daylight to get Boomer some exercise. They headed out, alternately walking and jogging, until Ellie figured her nose looked like Rudolph's. They'd gone farther than she'd planned, getting all the way to the woods, and would have a long trek back home.

"Let's go, Boomer."

Ellie tugged on the leash, but instead of following, Boomer froze. His ears perked, and for a moment, he wouldn't move a muscle. Then he moved just his head, back and forth, tilting it from one side to the other as if trying to solve an especially difficult puzzle.

"Boomer, I'm freezing. Come on!"

Ellie tugged again, but Boomer wouldn't budge. When he finally did move, it was to head into the woods, not back down the trail with Ellie.

"No way, buddy. We're going home."

Boomer, however, was determined, and once he decided he was going into the woods, and pulled in that direction, no amount of resisting and pleading on Ellie's part was going to change his mind. Figuring he must have heard an animal, Ellie decided the easiest thing to do would be to indulge him for a minute or two. When he'd sniffed all there was to sniff, she'd get him turned for home.

Once Boomer realized Ellie was going to follow, he seemed relieved, if that was possible, and led her away from the path and deeper into the woods. They'd never ventured off the path before, and with the dark settling in, it wasn't the time Ellie would have chosen to go exploring, but a few yards into the trees couldn't hurt. They'd be quick about it.

Twigs and dried leaves snapped and crunched under their feet while low branches slapped at their faces. Boomer didn't seem to notice. He kept his nose pointed forward and didn't stray from his course. Ellie ducked and dipped, trying to avoid the largest branches and at the same time, trying to watch the ground for rocks or divots that could lead to a fall. The last thing she needed was to hobble home on a twisted ankle.

She gave Boomer a couple of minutes, then decided enough was enough.

"Okay, my friend, you've had your fun. Let's go."

She tugged on the leash and tried to convince Boomer to change direction, but he put his nose to the ground, sniffed, and then let out a loud bark.

"What in tarnation has gotten into you?"

Her patience all but gone, Ellie grabbed Boomer by the collar and pulled him along with her back in the direction they'd come. She shivered and used her free hand to pull her hat further down over her ears.

Boomer heard it a second before she did and once again stopped in his tracks. A sob. That was the only way Ellie could think to describe the noise they'd both heard, because it didn't sound like an animal, but like a person.

Terrified, Ellie quickened her pace. Boomer followed for a couple of steps, but then jerked and pulled Ellie back toward the sound.

"No, Boomer!"

She intended on sounding firm, leaving no doubt that Boomer was to obey, but her voice came out as more of a desperate plea. If her dog was determined, Ellie feared there'd be no way she'd get him to follow her. Instead, she'd be the one doing the following.

Then she heard it again. Definitely a sob, but cut short, as if the person responsible for the noise was also afraid of being heard. Ellie's concern for herself switched to concern for the person who must be in some kind of trouble.

Summoning her courage, courage bolstered by the ninety-pound dog who was now glued to her side, Ellie called, "Hello? Is someone there?"

There was no response, but while they stood as still as statues, she heard the unmistakable crack of a twig.

"Do you need help?"

Ellie reached into her pocket for her phone. She wasn't stupid. She'd try to help if someone needed help, but she'd also be ready to call for assistance if it turned out she was the one in need of help. Measuring every step and scanning the surrounding area, Ellie ventured deeper into the woods with Boomer a step ahead and guiding her.

"Hello?" Ellie tried again. This time, she got a response.

"Leave me alone."

A child. Not a young child, but definitely a child. And a very frightened one, from the sounds of it.

"I want to help you. Are you hurt?"

"I said leave me alone."

Boomer turned in the direction of the voice, but Ellie would have been able to follow it herself this time. It sounded like a girl, and it sounded like they were getting much closer.

"Don't be frightened. I'm not going to hurt you. If you're lost, or you're hurt, I can help." Ellie decided it might be best to keep talking. "I'm a teacher at Caston Middle School. I don't have any way to prove that to you, and I'm sure you've been taught to be careful around strangers, but you can trust me. My name is Ellie. How old are you?"

There was no answer. Ellie could hear more rustling, more twigs snapping, and worried the child was trying to get away.

"Please stay where you are. Do you like dogs? My dog is with me. His name is Boomer. He's big, but he's friendly. If you don't like dogs, I'll keep him away from you, but he's the one who heard you and guided me to you. I think he'd like to make sure you're okay."

There was a gasp and a sharp but muffled scream. Ellie's stomach dropped. She and Boomer quickened their pace. Then, it was just a flash, but Ellie was sure there'd been movement a few feet ahead. The trees were thick, and it was getting dark, but there'd been color. Red, or maybe pink.

Choosing not to talk, not to let the girl know they were as close as they were, Ellie stepped lightly. After a few more steps, Ellie heard the soft crying, and a moment later, the girl came into view.

She was crouched into a ball, on her side with her arms around one of her legs. Her back was to Ellie. Wanting to help, but not wanting to frighten the girl any more than she already was, Ellie spoke softly.

"Did you hurt your leg?"

The girl whirled, and Ellie wasn't sure who was more shocked, she or Talia.

"No!" Talia shouted, and tried to crawl away from Ellie. "Leave me alone!"

Ellie backed away, but Boomer strained to get to the girl.

"Talia, I want to help you. If you're hurt, you need to let me help you."

"Get away from me! I don't have to listen to you cuz we're not at school!"

Ellie saw the girl's slender shoulders tremble. The incident in the classroom was too fresh in Ellie's memory for her to dare get any closer. Not knowing the extent of Talia's injury and not wanting to be responsible for the girl trying to run and injuring herself further, Ellie backed up a couple of steps.

"Please just let me help you. I can call someone, or try to get you home."

For the first time, Talia looked at Ellie. Even in the waning light, Ellie could see the color drain from Talia's face, and could see the fear in her eyes.

"No! I'm not going home! You can't make me!"

Ellie hadn't considered the possibility that someone at home could be responsible for Talia's injury. Sick at the thought, Ellie racked her brain for a way to get through to the girl, sensing time was not on their side. So far, Toby was the only one Ellie had seen have any success with Talia, but Ellie had no idea how to get in touch with Toby. As terrified as the girl was, suggesting a call to the police seemed out of the question. Max or Nicole? Ellie knew they'd come and try to help if she could get in touch with them and direct them to her location, but that seemed like a big if.

Zeke.

"Talia, I won't get any closer, but you need help. I have a friend. He's a doctor. How about if I call him and see if he can come and check out your leg? It looks like it hurts a lot."

She got only a sniffle and some more crawling in response. Deciding it was her best bet, probably her only bet unless she dialed 911, Ellie took a few more steps away and pulled out the phone she'd dropped back in her jacket pocket.

Fear and nerves were making her sweat, but when Ellie pulled off her mitten and tried to unlock her phone, she realized just how cold it was in the now dark woods. Who knew how long Talia had been on the ground? She must be freezing. Before Ellie tried Zeke, she tried once more with Talia.

"Talia? My dog wants to come and see you. Do you like dogs?"

It was mostly a moan, but since Talia didn't yell, Ellie risked it. She crouched down next to Boomer.

"Boomer, I need you to be a good boy." He licked her face in response, quivering as he did so. "Go help her, buddy. Go help Talia."

With no idea what to expect, Ellie held on to the hope that Boomer sensed Talia's pain, her desperate situation, and would respond accordingly. Praying she wasn't making a huge mistake, Ellie released Boomer.

It took only three loping strides, and he was alongside Talia. He didn't jump, he didn't sniff and lick, he merely nudged her, then lay down alongside her.

"Good boy," Ellie whispered over her tears. Then she called Zeke. "Please be home, please be home."

"Ellie! Are you okay? Tell me you're okay. I was just reaching for my phone to call you!"

"What? I'm okay." How did he know? "It's not me. It's a girl, a girl from school, she's hurt. Can you come? Please? Are you home? She's scared, really scared. She won't let me near her, but I think it's her leg. She doesn't trust me, hopefully she'll trust you—"

"Ellie? What are you talking about? Is he there? Where are you?"

"I'm sorry, I'm not making any sense, am I? Is who here?" Zeke wasn't making any more sense than she was. Ellie shook her head, took a deep breath, and tried again. "I was out walking with Boomer. We were by the woods, on the other side of the park, and he dragged me into the trees. He heard something. It turned out to be one of my students. She's hurt." Ellie lowered her voice. "She doesn't particularly like me, but she needs help. I'm hoping she'll let you help her."

"I'm not sure I followed all that, but if someone is hurt, you should call 911. Right away."

"I know, and I would, but she's, well..." Ellie lowered even more. "It's a special situation, Zeke. She needs special attention."

"I see. Tell me where you are."

Ellie did her best to explain, then told Zeke she'd turn her phone's flashlight on in a few minutes in an attempt to guide him. Zeke said he'd call when he got close.

Having done all she could for the moment, Ellie inched closer to Talia and Boomer. She could hear Talia whispering to Boomer and though it was too dark to see much, the rhythmic swooshing sound told her Talia was likely stroking the dog. An occasional gasp or sob mixed in with Talia's words to Boomer, and Ellie's heart ached for the girl.

With some of the adrenaline wearing off, Ellie shivered. It felt like the temperature had dropped ten degrees in the last few minutes. If she was that cold, she couldn't imagine how Talia must be feeling. Boomer was probably providing some warmth, but Talia wore only a sweatshirt and jeans.

Ellie inched closer to Talia.

"Talia, I'm going to toss my jacket toward you. I won't get any closer than I have to, but please pull the jacket over yourself. It's important you stay warm."

Talia didn't agree, but she also didn't protest or try to move away. Ellie took it as a positive sign. Slipping out of her jacket, Ellie took one more step, then risked turning on the flashlight on her phone to help her toss the jacket in the right direction. She flung it as far as she could. It didn't quite reach Talia, but there was enough light to see Talia reach for it. The rustling sounds told Ellie the girl must have pulled it over herself. Ellie breathed out a sigh of relief. Then she began jogging in place to try to stay warm, praying Zeke would hurry.

It took less than five minutes for Zeke to call her.

"I'm at the edge of the woods. I'm not sure where you went in, though."

"I know. Um…" Ellie tried to think. "We were past the garbage can, the one with the smiley face painted on it? We'd passed that, but not far past, heading…heading west."

"Okay."

Ellie could hear Zeke's breath and could tell he was running. "Hurry," she whispered.

"How far into the woods?"

Now she heard him crunching through the branches and the leaves. The sounds echoed in her ears like thunder.

"I don't know. Not too far. I don't know."

"Wave your phone. I'll do the same."

Ellie held up her phone and waved her arm back and forth, then she caught a glimpse of light. To her left, just a flash, but she was sure she'd seen it.

"Zeke! Over here!" She realized her phone was still high over her head, so pulled it back to her ear. "Zeke! I saw your phone. You were to my left." Then she held her phone up again and waved it.

"Ellie!"

This time the sound didn't come through the phone, but through the trees that, if Ellie let her imagination get the better of her, looked like black fingers reaching out and wanting to wrap themselves around her.

"Ellie!" Zeke said again, and this time, emerged from the trees to stand in front of her. "You're okay?"

"Fine, I'm fine. It's Talia. She's over there."

Ellie pointed, and Zeke's eyes followed her arm.

"Do you know what happened?"

"No. She won't talk to me, but I can tell she's hurt. And scared. She was holding her leg. Boomer's with her. He seems to have helped calm her."

"Boomer? Calm?" Zeke managed a quick grin.

"Go figure."

"I'll take a look. Talia, you said?"

"Yes. Go easy with her. She needs a very gentle touch."

Zeke nodded. "But you're sure you're okay?"

"Yes, yes, I'm fine."

"You don't have a coat."

"I gave it to Talia. She was shivering."

Zeke took off his coat and wrapped it around Ellie's shoulders. Then he wrapped his arms around her.

"I'm so relieved you're okay."

Before Ellie could get over her shock and react, Zeke released her and jogged toward Talia.

Ellie wanted to get closer so she could see, but didn't want to risk upsetting Talia, so stayed away. She could hear Zeke speak calmly and slowly to Talia as he got closer. Talia answered, only short, one word replies, but at least she was talking.

Ellie paced and ran her hands up and down her arms. Ever so slowly, she was warming up inside Zeke's thick jacket. It smelled like him, she noticed. A trace of menthol, a bit of what smelled like antiseptic, and when she raised her shoulders to bring the jacket up higher around her neck, the clean, woodsy scent that she knew to be his aftershave.

"No!"

Talia's scream broke through the dark like the first heavy chord opening up a rock concert.

Ellie couldn't make out Zeke's words with Talia's scream echoing in her ears, but she could make out the soothing, calming tone of his voice. Ellie felt utterly helpless and took to pacing faster, wringing her hands as she did so.

There were more words from Talia, and when Ellie heard her name, she stopped pacing and listened.

"I don't want her here!" Screaming again, but Ellie thought maybe it wasn't quite as loud, maybe not quite as angry.

There were more mumbled words from Zeke, then Ellie heard Zeke's voice, louder and wanting to be heard.

"Ellie? Will you come back here, please?"

"No, no, no." Ellie muttered. The only reason she could think Zeke would ask her to join them would be if Talia was in such bad shape he needed help, and he decided to ignore Talia's insistence that Ellie stay away.

"You're sure?" Ellie called.

"Yes, we're sure."

More mumbling, more soothing.

Ellie wanted to help but knew she was scaling a very slippery slope. If Talia rebelled, tried to get away as Ellie got closer, the chance of Talia injuring herself further was very real.

Ellie had to believe Zeke wouldn't let that happen, that he had things under control. She tiptoed forward, worrying each step would be the step that was one too far. Then she scolded herself for not giving Zeke more background on Talia, on the strained relationship between herself and her student.

"Ellie, would you shine your phone down here near Talia's left leg?"

"Okay." Ellie crept forward, inch by inch, unable to see much, but listening intently for any sort of reaction from Talia. The girl stayed silent.

"Right here," Zeke said, when Ellie got close.

Ellie didn't make eye contact with Talia, thinking it best if she focused only on Zeke's instructions. She did her best to shine the light where Zeke indicated. Zeke reached, adjusted the angle of the phone by an inch, then ran his hands over Talia's ankle and shin.

Talia drew in a sharp breath, and Ellie couldn't help but turn to look. She saw Talia bury her face in Boomer's side and heard a sob escape. Boomer's eyes met Ellie's and his tail wagged, sweeping a path through the brittle leaves.

"Good boy, Boomer," Ellie whispered, but turned her attention away from her dog, afraid if she talked too much to him, he'd leave his spot at Talia's side.

Instead, she whispered to Zeke. "What is it?"

Zeke spoke so Talia could hear. "Talia's got a sprained ankle and possibly a broken leg. She's being incredibly brave. A broken leg hurts a lot. I told her I needed you to help me get some light on her leg so I could have a look, make sure things look okay, and decide if we think we can carry her out of here."

"Don't you think we should call her par—, call her father?"

"Don't call my mom! Don't!"

"I won't," Zeke said, as calmly as if Talia hadn't just screamed at the top of her lungs and tried to twist away from him. "I told you I won't, and I never lie to my patients. Right now, I'm going to talk to Ms. Hawthorne for a minute, and I need you to stay right where you are and let Boomer keep you warm, okay?"

It took a moment, but Talia answered with a weak, "Okay."

Zeke stood and motioned for Ellie to follow him. When they were a few yards away, Zeke stopped and Ellie got a look at his face. Even if she'd never before seen him, she'd know it was worry in his expression.

Though she feared the answer, Ellie said, "There's more. More than just a sprained ankle and a possible broken leg."

"She definitely has a sprained ankle, and her leg is definitely broken. I didn't want to frighten her, but once you brought the light and I examined her leg more closely, I found what I was afraid I was going to find. She has a compound fracture of the tibia. The bone has protruded through the skin. I need to get her to the hospital, and I'm reluctant to do that without contacting her parents. Or parent."

Ellie's knees felt weak. She leaned on a nearby tree for support. She thought of the conversation she'd had with Max and Nicole about student privacy and the very clear rules that prohibited discussing anything pertaining to a student, but decided in this case, Zeke needed whatever knowledge he could get to help him deal with an injured, frightened child who was now his patient.

"Talia lives with her father. Her mother, at least according to what I know, is in prison. There's speculation she abused Talia. Talia's reluctance to have us contact her father, though...you don't think he could have, I mean, do you think she was hurt before she got here, that she was running away?"

"I think she most certainly was running away, but I don't believe she was hurt before she got here. At least not the injuries to her ankle and leg. She tripped, there are tears and mud stains on her jeans, mud and scrapes on her palms, so I'm certain she hurt herself when she fell, just as she told me."

The vice around Ellie's heart loosened some. "I don't know how to reach her father." Ellie's mind raced. "I could try to reach Max or Nicole, I have their numbers, ask one of them to try to get in touch with the principal, or maybe her secretary. That would take time, and even if I could get Max or Nic, and if they could reach someone, I don't know if that contact information would be readily available. It will take too long."

Zeke nodded. "We don't have that kind of time. Okay, I'm going to try talking with her again. If I can't get her to give me her father's phone number, I'm going to call 911."

Zeke didn't wait for Ellie to agree or disagree. He wound his way through the trees and crouched down alongside Talia. Ellie followed, but stayed a few steps back.

"Talia, you need to go to the hospital. I know that sounds scary, but I'll go with you, and I promise I will stay with you."

In what could only be a testament to the pain and the fact that it was now pitch-black and colder than ever, Talia gave Zeke a shaky, "Okay."

"It would be much better if we could have your father meet us there.

The people at the hospital will have some questions for him."

"But...but..." Talia stuttered. Then, as if it were too hard to continue fighting, she simply whispered, "Yeah, 'kay."

While Zeke called 911 for an ambulance, Ellie called Talia's father who was frantic and wanted to come to them. It took some convincing, but in the end he agreed it was likely the ambulance would beat him to his daughter and agreed to meet her at the hospital.

"With the injury as serious as it is, I don't want to move her," Zeke told Ellie. "I explained our location as best I could, but I think it would be helpful if you could get back to the path and watch for the ambulance. I want to stay with Talia."

"Of course." Ellie looked down at the girl whose eyes had gotten very heavy and threatened to close.

"She's going to be okay, right?" The alternative was too horrible to consider.

"She'll be okay, but the sooner the paramedics get to her, the better. Her pulse is rapid, her breathing is shallow. She needs more care than I can give her right now."

Ellie's own pulse raced as she nodded and turned to thread her way back through the trees to the path. Zeke took hold of her arm.

"Take Boomer with you. I don't want you to be alone."

"Alone? I'll be fine. Besides, I think Talia needs Boomer."

"Take Boomer. I'll feel a lot better if he's with you."

"Why? It's not exactly a high crime area."

"Ellie, please."

"Fine, but I don't know that he's going to come to me."

Zeke gave her arm another squeeze, but said nothing more. With a little bit of moonlight, Ellie could make out Zeke crouching next to Talia, then taking Boomer's leash and leading him away from the girl. Ellie called her dog, and he came barreling through the twigs to her.

"Boomer, you're full of surprises tonight. Come on, boy."

The wait seemed interminable, but finally Ellie saw the flashing lights and heard the siren. She jogged along the dark path to flag down the ambulance. The driver eased the ambulance onto the walking path and drove until she'd maneuvered the vehicle alongside Ellie who then directed them into the woods and to Talia.

It seemed like an eternity, but the entire process took only about ten minutes. Zeke briefed the paramedics on Talia's condition, what he'd been able to do for her, and the extent of her injuries as far as he'd been able to determine.

"I promised Talia I'd ride with her and stay with her at the hospital." Zeke dipped his head to nod at the pocket of his jacket that was wrapped around Ellie. "My car keys are in the pocket. Take my car and please, go straight home and stay there. Don't answer the door unless you're certain who it is. I'll be there later tonight or first thing in the morning."

"Why can't I answer my door? Zeke, what's wrong with you tonight?"

Zeke looked over his shoulder at the paramedics who were making their final preparations to transport Talia to the hospital.

"Texts. You've gotten strange texts, threatening even, haven't you?"

On top of everything that had happened that evening with Talia, it was too much to take.

"How? How could you know? I never said anything." And then it hit her. "No. Oh, no, Zeke. No." Ellie backed away from him. "Why? How could you?"

"Dr. Fahrner, we need to go." The words sounded far away, like they'd traveled through a long, hollow tunnel before reaching her ears. From somewhere farther away, car doors opened and slammed shut.

"No, Ellie, not me. I swear, not me. I have to go, but I'll explain later. Please, just go home and stay there."

Then he was gone, running toward the back of the ambulance. Everything felt like slow motion as Ellie turned, watched Zeke climb into the ambulance, then watched the doors close, hiding him from her view. When the flashing lights disappeared and nothing was left but the dark surrounding her, she fingered the keys in Zeke's coat pocket. With no idea what she'd hear from him later, but with his warning ringing in her ears, Ellie coaxed Boomer into a run, and they hurried toward his car.

20

It was a long night. Every creak of her house, every car that happened down her street, was cause for concern. While she'd figured out on the drive home Zeke couldn't be responsible for the odd texts she'd been receiving since she'd gotten one during their dinner together, not even the long hours since had been enough for her to figure out how he knew about them.

With nothing to do but worry, whether it be about Talia or about whatever it was Zeke was warning her about, she tried to recall every word he'd said to her, and how he'd said them.

'Strange texts,' he'd called them. He'd added 'threatening.' He'd sworn he wasn't responsible, but had given her no indication who was. He must know, or must at least have an idea, but he had said nothing other than warning her to be careful.

A lot of help that was.

She got one text, a text that nearly stopped her heart when the phone she was white-knuckle clutching vibrated, but it was from Zeke. An update on Talia. She was doing well, but was headed into surgery soon. He'd be assisting, so he wouldn't be able to contact Ellie or get to her house until very late that night. More likely, the following morning. He added another reminder to be careful. The relief she felt at finding out Talia was okay was like having a hundred-pound weight lifted off her. Still, the questions, the lingering fear, ate at her and kept her from sleeping, or reading, or watching TV, or doing anything but driving Boomer crazy with her pacing and her almost constant barrage of chatter of which he was the unlucky recipient.

Hours later, Ellie sat wrapped in the worn pink quilt her great grandmother had lovingly stitched before Ellie was born. As she watched the chilly dawn tinge the sky orange, Ellie fell into an uneasy sleep.

Flashes of terrifying images, snatches of disjointed conversations, and scenes from the night in the woods flitted in and out of her over-tired brain and left her tossing on the couch, effectively cocooning her in the quilt. When the doorbell woke her and she stumbled to her feet, any memory of those dreams disappeared from her mind as quickly as the quilt fell to the floor and her feet flew toward the door.

Just before she reached to open it, Zeke's words replayed in her mind and she pulled her hand back, fisting it and shoving it in her pocket to keep it from reaching once more for the doorknob. She stretched to her toes and peeked out the window high in the door. Only the top of a head was visible, but when a hand ran through the disheveled hair and Ellie glimpsed the watch Zeke always wore, she breathed easier.

"Zeke?" she said, more for his sake than hers.

"It's me, Ellie."

She pulled the door open. If she'd expected him to look worse than she did, with exhaustion and strain on his face, she was very much mistaken. While the lack of sleep showed in the faint circles under his eyes, those eyes were alert and lively. His hair may have looked as though it wasn't the first time he'd raked his fingers through it, but he stood straight and looked ready for anything. Ellie hoped it meant good news regarding Talia.

"How is she?"

"She's fine. She was sleeping when I left. It was a long night—and a long day, I guess—but she's going to be just fine."

"Oh, good," Ellie breathed. "I was so worried."

She stepped back and motioned Zeke inside. His eyes darted from one corner of the room to the other, taking in everything at once.

"And you're okay? Nothing happened?"

"I don't know what you thought was going to happen, but other than being worried sick and not being able to sleep, it was an uneventful night."

She decided not to tell him how many times she'd nearly jumped out of her skin at the smallest noise.

Zeke nodded, and kept looking around the room as if he didn't quite believe her.

"I have about a million questions for you, but first you have to tell me what you know about Talia. Did her father come to the hospital?

Did you talk to him? Do you have any idea what she was doing out in the woods?"

"I have a few answers, probably not all that you want, but I'll tell you as much as I can. I did talk with her father. I told him about your part in the situation, and he gave me his okay to discuss some of the details of Talia's situation with you."

"Good. I was worried about how much I could tell you last night, but decided with you being her doctor, it was okay. It's a fine line, isn't it?"

"You did the right thing."

Zeke rubbed his hands up and down his arms, much like Ellie had done out in the woods.

"Your coat. I'm sorry, I should have given it back to you before you left with Talia, but everything happened so fast. Sit down. Let's get you warmed up. Coffee?"

"If you have some."

"Not yet, but believe me, I need it."

Zeke didn't sit, but followed her to the kitchen.

"You had a rough night. I'm sorry. I know I'm part of the reason."

Ellie busied herself with the coffee. "I have questions for you, but first, Talia."

"Right. Her father told me she ran away. He thinks it's likely she overheard a phone conversation he had with her mother. She's due to be released from prison in a few months. Her father knows Talia is afraid of her mother coming back home, though he was very insistent he's doing everything he can to prevent that from happening. I don't know the details, but I gathered Talia is afraid of her mother."

"Yes. There was mention of that in her school file. She tends to not trust women in general. I keep telling myself that's why I haven't been able to make any headway with her, but it could just be me."

"She wanted me to tell you thank you."

"Talia did?"

"Yes. Right before her surgery. The sedative probably had her talking more than she would have otherwise. I've found a lot of patients like to talk once they're calm. She said she was glad you found her, and that you had a dog. She told me to tell you she likes your dog. There was more, but most of it was mumbling and half thoughts."

"I took a route I don't normally take, and I tried to coax Boomer away from the woods when he wanted to investigate. It was getting so cold, and edging toward dark, I was eager to get home. If I wouldn't have gone that way, or if I wouldn't have indulged Boomer…"

Ellie's body convulsed with a shiver that had nothing to do with the cold. She turned away so Zeke wouldn't see the tears that flooded her eyes.

"But you did." Ellie felt Zeke's hand on her back between her shoulder blades. He rubbed as if knowing she had a knot the size of Oklahoma right there. "You took that route, you followed Boomer into the woods, that's what matters. Talia's going to be fine. Don't think about what ifs."

Ellie nodded once, then turned to face him. "You're right, I know you're right, but it's hard. So many things could have happened to her. Terrible things."

"They didn't. She's got some recovery time and therapy ahead of her, but she's young, she'll heal, and in no time, will be better than ever."

"I wonder, do you think she'll be in the hospital long? Could I visit her, or would that be a mistake?"

"She should go home this evening unless there are complications," Zeke said, "which I don't expect," he added before Ellie could ask the question on the tip of her tongue. "I have a shift today, but I think I'll try to bring Bowie by before it starts."

"You have to go back? But you were there all night! You need to rest."

"I'm used to little to no sleep. I'll catch a few hours before I'm due back."

Ellie yawned. "I don't know how y'all do it." Then her eyes opened wide. "I know! I can follow you to the hospital when you take Bowie. I'll wait outside while you visit with him, then take him home. That way, you won't have to go as early. You'll get a bit more sleep."

Zeke frowned, but behind it, looked relieved. "Only if you're sure. It would help, I'll admit, but it's Thanksgiving. You must have plans."

"Thanksgiving?" Startled, Ellie looked around her as if there would be clues as to whether that was true. "Thanksgiving," she repeated. "Oh, my stars, you're right. The shortened school week, everything that happened with Talia, I've lost track of the days. And it still seems like yesterday. Oh," she repeated. She'd be alone on a holiday for the first time in her life. It was unsettling and more than a little depressing, and for some reason, she didn't want Zeke to know.

"No plans until later." Not entirely untrue because she had plans for a video chat with her family later in the day. "I'm happy to help. Just tell me when."

Zeke's expression changed to something unreadable, confusing Ellie. Maybe after all the talk about Talia, he'd just remembered his dire warnings of the night before.

"What was it you wanted to tell me last night? You had me plenty worried, you know."

This time, his expression was as plain as the pumpkins on the napkin he'd picked up with his cup of coffee and now crushed in his fist. He was angry, and he was afraid.

"I didn't mean to worry you. Actually, that's not true. I meant to worry you enough that you'd be careful." He raised his arm and bent it at the elbow, forcing his sleeve to pull back enough that he could glimpse his watch. Then he sighed, though he tried to hide it when he lifted his coffee cup and sipped.

"How did you know I was getting texts, Zeke? I've been over it and over it, and I can't come up with any logical explanation. I must admit, at first I thought you'd been the one sending them, but I realized that didn't make any sense. Still, I can't come up with anything that does."

"Can we sit? For just a minute?"

He looked tired now, all the energy he'd had when he arrived washed away in a sea of worry.

"Of course."

Ellie took her coffee and returned to the living room. When she sat on the couch and Zeke in the chair across from her, it wasn't lost on her that they were in the same spots they'd been in the week before when Zeke had been so determined to tell her something, but so troubled at the same time. Ellie was afraid of what was coming this time.

"I only found out yesterday. When you called about Talia, I was telling you the truth when I said I'd been reaching for my phone to get in touch with you. To warn you."

Ellie waited, both her hands wrapped around the coffee mug, willing the heat to seep into her and to take away the chill that had settled in her bones.

Zeke dropped his gaze. "My brother showed up at my house yesterday. I hadn't seen him in over a year, not since I've been back in Caston. At first, I wondered how he knew I was here since we hadn't been in touch, but I realized how foolish that was. Caleb has a way of finding out whatever it is he wants to find out."

"Your brother." Ellie had no idea what Zeke's brother had to do with her, but figured Zeke would get there eventually. "You don't talk about him."

"It's hard to talk about him."

Zeke looked at his watch again, and Ellie felt guilty.

"I'm keeping you from sleep. You should go."

"Caleb sent you the texts."

"Caleb? Why?"

"It's such a long story, the whole story anyway, and you're right that I need some sleep. Suffice it to say, it was his way of trying to get what he wanted from me."

"I don't understand."

Zeke gave a rueful laugh. "I don't think there's a person alive who understands Caleb. Including Caleb. He needs money. Again. I've given it to him in the past. Reluctantly, but I've done it, which keeps him coming back for more. The last time, over a year ago, I told him that was it, that I absolutely would not do it again. He must have believed me and that forced him to come up with a way to change my mind. You."

"But if you haven't seen him, haven't talked to him, how did he even know about me?"

"Like I said, Caleb has a way of finding out anything. Everything. He's a...I don't know what the best term is. He's a genius, to be sure, and I don't know that there are many better when it comes to knowing how to use a computer, but he's also troubled? Sick? Paranoid? Probably schizophrenic, though he's never been diagnosed, and his ability to function at an extremely high level, when he wants to, might make that diagnosis tough to pin on him. Regardless, he can't fit himself into what I would consider a normal life the way he is, and instead, lives on the fringes, doing things that put him in danger."

"Oh, my. I'm so sorry, sorry for you, your parents."

Zeke closed his eyes for a long moment and nodded slowly, as if he'd heard it all before, but it did nothing to soothe.

"I still don't understand how I fit into any of it. He wants to use me to get to you?"

Zeke opened his eyes, then lifted his hands, only to let them drop back to his lap. "In his mind, it must make sense. I don't know what he texted you, but I got the feeling it was something to do with a past relationship, with making me think there was still something there, so I'd be free to help him."

"But—"

"Like I said, it doesn't have to make sense to anyone else for it to make sense to him."

"And you're worried about me because…"

"Because I've never seen him quite this frantic. In the past when he's come to me, he's asked, he's begged, he's told me wild stories I didn't know whether to believe, but he's never looked as scared as he did this time. He's in trouble, and I'm afraid that will make him desperate. I don't know what that means, or how he'll handle the fact that I told him no."

"I see."

"I'm so sorry to have to drag you into this mess. Before I came over here I tried calling him, but the most recent number I have is no longer in service. I don't know where he is or what he'll do next. He's unpredictable, to say the least."

Ellie had to stand, to walk. It wasn't Vincent, it had never been Vincent. He'd told her the truth. Somehow, that mattered. What to make of the new information, though, Ellie had no idea. She wasn't frightened, exactly, but she was uncomfortable with the idea of someone knowing such personal things about her.

"How did he know? How did Caleb know about Vincent?"

"Vincent?" Ellie thought Zeke looked sad, defeated, but knew more likely exhaustion was to blame. "Caleb finds things. Whatever he wants. If he wanted to track my movements, he'd track my movements. My guess is he tapped into my texts, saw your number, decided you were important to me, researched what he needed to know about you to serve his purposes, and sent the texts to you."

"He can do all that?" Ellie was horrified, but couldn't help also being impressed.

Zeke nodded. "He can."

"And you don't know where he is? What he'll do next?"

"I wish I did. I wish I could tell you that you don't have anything to worry about, but I can't do that. Caleb has never hurt anyone. He abhors violence, always has, is afraid of any kind of physical altercation, and I don't think that has changed. I don't believe he'd try to hurt you, but as for harassing you, trying to use you to get what he wants from me? That I'm very much afraid he'd do."

"Now that I know, I can handle it."

"You shouldn't have to. I'm sorry."

"I'd say I could change my phone number, but that wouldn't matter, would it?"

"It wouldn't."

"Well then, I can't fret about it. I'll delete any strange texts, and do my best to ignore whatever they say."

"Tell me, though, won't you? Tell me if you hear from Caleb? And keep your guard up?"

"Yes, to both."

Zeke stood. He took a last sip of coffee from his mug before setting it down again on the table.

"I need to get a few hours of sleep. You don't have to help me with Bowie. I know you were just looking for a way to help Talia. I can manage today, but thank you."

"I want to help. What time?"

"You're sure?"

"I'm sure. Let me do something."

"I'd argue that you've already done everything, but if you insist, maybe you could meet me at the hospital around two o'clock? I'll take Bowie over for a visit around one, then you can take him home before I start my shift. Unless that interferes with your plans for the day?"

"No. I'll bring Bowie here. He can spend the day with Boomer and me."

"Oh, no, please just drop him off at my house. I've made arrangements with Blake. He'll be over in the evening to feed Bowie and let him outside."

She felt Zeke pulling away. Whether from her or from the situation, Ellie wasn't sure, but it also felt as though they'd never land on the same page.

"Okay, if you're sure."

Zeke nodded. "I'm sure. Thanks, Ellie. See you this afternoon." He opened the door, took a step outside, but then turned back. "I guess I need my keys if I want to take my car home."

"Of course. I forgot. How did you get here?"

"Someone who was leaving the hospital at the same time I was dropped me off." Zeke took the keys Ellie held out to him. "Happy Thanksgiving, Ellie."

"Happy Thanksgiving, Zeke," Ellie said, though it seemed anything but happy.

Though she was exhausted, Ellie still found sleep elusive. Boomer needed a walk, but Ellie couldn't bring herself to do it. She wasn't sure if it was due more to the incident with Talia or what she'd learned from Zeke, but an uncomfortable mixture of fear and foreboding had her sticking to the back yard. She threw a tennis ball for Boomer until her arm threatened to fall off, then herded the dog back inside and hoped he'd be ready for a nap.

Ellie tried again to sleep, but every time she felt her eyes close for more than a minute or two, she grabbed her phone and checked the time. Fear of sleeping through the promised pickup time had her double and triple checking that she had the correct alarm set.

Though she hoped there wasn't one, she also wanted to make sure she hadn't missed a text.

When she finally admitted to herself she wasn't going to get any sleep, Ellie dragged herself into the shower and willed the hot water to wash away the stiffness and tension. When the water ran cold, she wrapped herself in a thick robe, twisted a towel around her hair, and went to her room to sit on her bed. She looked at the colorful paper chain that hung around the ceiling. Shorter now than it had been, but depending on the day, and on her mood, it could be nothing more than a few links waiting to be torn in two, or it could seem miles long. Today, it could have stretched all the way to Oklahoma.

She was so confused. Like that paper chain, depending on the day, she loved her new life in Caston, or she dreaded the next day and every one to follow. Max and Nicole helped notch more days in the 'loving her new life' column, but they had secrets of their own, and Ellie feared those secrets would take them away from Caston. Zeke had been responsible for many of the good days, but also responsible for some of the not so good.

So much of the confusion, she realized, was because of him. Or due to him, was maybe more accurate. One minute, she convinced herself it was worth the risk. He was worth the risk. She believed what Nicole and Max told her, what her mother told her, and what she'd told herself, over and over. She could risk her heart, because what was the alternative? Not one she wanted, she knew that. And she could take the risk because she was so much stronger than she'd been before.

The next minute, she didn't believe a word of it.

Ellie sighed and tightened the towel that slipped loose on her head. She looked to the corner of her room, the corner where her guitar sat propped against the wall, and reached for it. Along with Boomer, her guitar was the one thing that could always bring comfort. It was solid, it was familiar, and when she played it, she was in control.

Her fingers found the chord, and she began playing. After a moment, she began to sing the familiar words.

* * *

I wonder if you know what it feels like
When he smiles and takes your hand
I wonder if you know what it feels like
To be in the arms of the perfect man

I wonder if you know what it feels like
To sit and gaze at the stars
To hear him say I love you
I love you just the way you are

I wonder if you know what it feels like
When he wants to share your life
When he gets down on one knee
When he asks you to be his wife

To dream about the future
To hope, to pray, to plan
To find the perfect dress
To choose the perfect home

I wonder if you know what it feels like
When the rumors start to swirl
I wonder if you know what it feels like
To see him with another girl

I wonder if you know what it feels like
When your world falls all apart
When you have to make the phone calls
When each 'I'm sorry' breaks your heart

I wonder if you know what it feels like
I wonder if you know what it feels like

I hope you don't

As she strummed the last note, sang the last word, her hands stilled, and she blinked in surprise. It was the first time she'd played the song all the way through to the end. Though she'd written it, or the beginnings of it anyway, within days of the break-up, and though the end had always been there, somewhere in her mind, she'd never been able to get to the end. Now that she had, it was freeing.

Sure, the song hurt, but not like it had. And sure, it reminded her of Vincent, but that didn't seem to matter so much any longer. Now, it was just a song. Maybe a good one, maybe not, but just a song. No longer the sad, sad story of her life, a story without an ending.

Ellie jumped up from the bed, pulled the towel from her head, and decided she'd spend a little time on her hair and make-up, and she'd wear that blue sweater she'd bought while shopping with Mama. It brought out her eyes. Then she'd watch some football, text her brothers about the games, and when it was time, go pick up Bowie.

21

Ellie hadn't seen Zeke since Thanksgiving when he'd stopped by early in the morning with news on Talia. He hadn't come out with Bowie when she'd gone to the hospital, but had sent out one of the hospital volunteers with the dog and with an explanation that he was running behind schedule.

She hadn't received any texts, at least not the texts she'd been dreading. Silence, as far as she knew, from Caleb. She supposed, based on what Zeke had told her, that Caleb could be monitoring her phone calls, her texts, even listening in somehow on everything she did. She had to tamp down those ideas to save her sanity.

What it all meant for Zeke, she didn't know. Other than one text telling her Talia had gone home as scheduled, she hadn't heard anything from him, either.

He was busy, she knew that, working double shifts throughout the holiday weekend, but she couldn't help feel a little neglected. More than a little disappointed.

They'd shared something in the woods while working together to get Talia the help she needed. Ellie thought of it like a bond between the two of them, but when she didn't hear anything from Zeke, realized to him, it had probably been nothing more than another medical situation, another patient he could help.

Sunday was long and boring. She had her lesson plans done, all the work she needed to grade, graded, and several days' worth of 'Adventures with Boomer' ready to go. Even though she knew Talia wouldn't be back at school for a while, Ellie had also delved further into the books she'd gotten from the school psychologist. They were still confusing, but once she'd slowed down and read them in a

259

different, calmer frame of mind, she learned a few things. She felt more confident in dealing with Talia.

Still, she was bored and restless. She wanted to call Nicole or Max, but since they'd both mentioned Thanksgiving plans, she figured they were both either still busy with those plans or were playing catch-up with their school work after being busy most of the weekend. She didn't want to interrupt them, but for the first time in a long time, she longed for girlfriends to talk to, to bounce ideas off, and to just be with.

She hadn't walked Boomer farther than around her block—lap after lap around her block—but was just debating taking him on a longer walk when the doorbell caught her by surprise. When she peeked out the window, she saw Zeke, tired beyond measure, and holding the jacket she'd given to Talia that night in the woods.

"Zeke, come in. You look exhausted."

He shook his head. "I am, and I can't stay. Bowie's been home alone for too long. Here." He held out her jacket. "I'm sorry, I've had it for a few days but haven't had a chance to get it back to you."

"No problem. Are you sure you can't come in? Just for a minute?" She had so many things she wanted to say to him. So many things she wanted to ask him.

Worry creased his brow. "What is it? Have you heard from Caleb? I asked you to text me."

"No, I haven't. Have you?"

"Not a word. I don't know what to make of it."

"You're worried."

Zeke bent his head and rubbed the back of his neck. "I am. I don't want to be, but I am."

"I could make you something to eat. You probably haven't had a decent meal—"

"No, I really have to go."

He looked sad and defeated as he turned and plodded toward his car. Concern for his brother, Ellie figured, but more than that? She had her answer when he paused before climbing into his car.

"Bye, Ellie. If you hear from Caleb, please let me know. Otherwise, I hope you're happy. You and Vincent."

Before she could recover from her shock, before she could utter, "Wait," he was inside the car, the door closed, and was backing down her driveway.

The days seemed eternal. School was a brutal seven-and-a-half-hour-long torture session, day after day, as the holidays and the long winter break loomed ever closer. The kids wanted no part of lessons on letter writing. The assignments Ellie had thought might be fun, like writing letters to the kids' favorite companies telling why they liked or didn't like a product, turned out to be anything but. The only thing that seemed to hold their attention were the stories about Boomer, so Ellie had started sharing them with her sixth graders as well as her seventh graders.

The sixth graders had gotten wind of 'Adventures with Boomer' and had been asking for months to be included. Ellie had resisted, wanting to keep that one thing special for her seventh graders. She was realizing they often felt lost in the shuffle between the sixth graders who seemed to get special attention just for being the youngest, and the eighth graders who got special attention for being the oldest, or because their less-than-stellar behavior demanded it.

Eventually she gave in. The 'Adventures with Boomer' segments of class grew longer every day. Besides giving her a few minutes of peace, it gave her an idea for an end-of-the-year project in which the kids would write and produce their own video production. Most of them did better with at least some aspect of technology as part of their assignment, so she thought it could be a fun way to end the year. She told herself she'd think more about it when she could actually hear herself think.

On a Friday, the last Friday before break, just after the final bell, Nicole dragged herself into Ellie's room.

"Oh, my gosh. I don't think I can do it, El. I can't come back next week. I don't care if it's only three days. That's more than enough to be the death of me."

Ellie considered her friend. Her hair was disheveled, her gorgeous sweater had a smear of something green on one sleeve, and her manicured nails were chewed and jagged.

"You know, Nicole, normally I would sit here and tell you, of course you can do it. You're an amazing teacher, your students are lucky to have you, and it can't be as bad as you think it is, but I can't. I can't do it. It's horrible, there's no denying it, and I'm running out of ways to put a positive spin on things. All I can offer you is a large drink at Scooter's or, if you want, at my place, where you can spend the night if that one large drink turns into two. Or three. Or more."

Nicole had fallen into a chair at one of the desks and had dropped her head onto her folded arms. She raised one elbow and peeked underneath. "Really? I can come over?"

"Of course! Will you stay? Like a slumber party?"

Nicole sat up and stared at Ellie. "I think that's the best idea I've heard in a long time. Oh, I know. We should challenge each other to see how many super hot peppers we can eat. That's what I heard a group of eighth graders talking about doing at their sleepover tonight."

"Peppers? I'm in," Max said when she joined them. "Sounds stupid, but at this point everything does, so why not?"

"They really do act stupid sometimes, don't they?" Nicole said. "Exponentially stupid, like the more of them that are together, the more stupid they act. And they think they're so funny. And so original." She dropped her head down again, muffling her next words. "I can't take much more."

Max hooked her thumb in Nicole's direction. "What's up with her?"

"It's been a long week," Ellie said.

"I'll say." Max fell into the seat next to Nicole. "I bought six gigantic bags of candy on Tuesday. They're gone as of this afternoon. For the past three days, I've tried to bribe kids to be quiet and at least pretend to do some work. All I accomplished is contributing to a slew of future diabetics."

Nicole turned her head sideways to look at Max. "Join us. We're having a slumber party at Ellie's. There will be drinks. Hopefully no peppers, but I can't promise."

Max's laugh echoed off the walls. "A slumber party? Wow. Can you imagine? What a..." Her head turned back and forth from Ellie to Nicole and back again. "Wait. You're serious? A slumber party?" She laughed again, but this time it was subdued, nervous even.

"Of course, we're serious. It'll be fun. Y'all have only been over once or twice, and that was just to pick me up or drop me off, and you never stayed more than a few minutes. You hardly know Boomer. He was at day care today so he'll be tired. That will help. Maybe we can order pizza? Oh, we're going to have so much fun!"

Ellie twirled in a circle, once, then again, the tiredness, the frustration, the helplessness she'd felt for the past couple of weeks dissipating with each turn like ripples on the water.

"I'm sure y'all need to run home first, but come over as soon as you can. I'll get some things ready. Maybe by four-thirty? Anything special you want to eat or drink? We could make margaritas? Or maybe not, seeing as it's so cold outside. Ooh, maybe mulled wine?"

"Hang on a minute," Max said. "You guys are serious?"

Nicole lifted her head again, and her eyes bored into Max. "You've never been to a slumber party, have you?"

Ellie giggled. "Oh, Nicole, everyone's been to a slumber party. We used to have the most fun. Sometimes Daddy would set up a tent in the back yard and we'd sleep under the stars, telling ghost stories and eating candy, laughing until our bellies hurt."

"And having pillow fights, and talking about boys?" Max added.

Lost in her memories, Ellie didn't pick up on Max's sarcasm. "Sure, we talked about boys. Pillow fights, I don't know. Maybe. Popcorn fights, though, for sure. One time—"

"Ellie," Nicole interrupted, "she's never been to a slumber party."

"But...no. Max, is that true?" The question came out as a whisper, a mixture of shock and sadness.

"Yeah, and I can't believe I've gone twenty-some years without being in a popcorn fight."

"How is that even possible? Didn't you..." Ellie glanced at Nicole and caught the almost imperceptible shake of her head. "Oh, Okay. Well, tonight, we remedy that. Go pack your pillows and sleeping bags, girls. This is going to be more fun than a fiddle at a square dance!"

"We're really doing this?"

"Geez, Max, you look like you've just been told there'll be school all weekend," Nicole said as she pushed herself to her feet. "We're doing this. We need this. All of us."

"Oh, man," Max grumbled, but Ellie saw the hint of a smile hiding behind Max's scowl.

"And I was kidding about the sleeping bags and pillows. I have plenty. You'll both be there soon?" Ellie watched Max, afraid she'd back out.

Max took an enormous breath, then blew it out in a huff. "With bells on, Oklahoma."

Ellie considered an impromptu cheer, but was afraid it would scare off Max. She settled for, "That's the spirit!"

It took a couple of hours, and a couple glasses of wine, but as they sat on the floor in Ellie's living room, cozy in pajama pants and sweatshirts, eating pizza and popcorn, laughing, and sharing horror stories, their bond was forged. The hugs were genuine, as were the occasional tears, and Ellie was confident that even Max was glad she'd come.

Max threw a piece of popcorn up in the air and caught it in her mouth. "You know, this isn't so bad. I guess I can see how a person might think it's fun."

Nicole reached over and shoved her. "Admit it. You like girl things."

"I used to hear the boys in school talking about sleepovers. I don't think it's a girl thing."

"This is," Nicole corrected. "Boy sleepovers are sweaty, and smelly, and full of insults and contests to see who can make the most disgusting noise. Trust me, a slumber party is a girl thing."

Ellie laughed. "Our den smelled for days after my brothers had sleepovers. Mama used to go in there armed with a can of Lysol. She'd open the windows, didn't matter if it was the dead of winter or if it was pouring rain, then spray and spray." Ellie let herself remember for a minute, then reached for Max's hand. "I can't believe you've never been to a slumber party. Why not?"

Max shrugged. "We moved around a lot. I guess I never had a chance to make the friendships that would lead to a slumber party. Got invited to a birthday party once. It was a huge deal with those big blow up things you jump around in, a snow cone machine, some woman who did this elaborate face painting, and so much food. We left with treat bags that were better than the gel pens and notepads I brought for the girl's gift. Crazy."

"That's a little over the top. My birthday parties were usually slumber parties," Nicole said. "We'd have snacks and stay up all night, or we tried to anyway, and I thought it was the best thing ever. I can't imagine something like that party."

"Once?" Ellie said. "You said you got invited to a birthday party once. There must have been others."

"No, just the one."

Ellie could name dozens she'd been to with hardly a thought. "Max, I'm sorry."

"Sorry? Why? It's not like I knew everyone was invited but me, it's that I just didn't know. I didn't know when kids were having birthday parties, or going on vacations, or getting puppies, or any of that. Sure, once in a while I'd hang out with someone long enough to hear a little, but it never lasted. I went to four different schools in fifth grade."

Ellie glanced at Nicole to see if she looked as shocked as Ellie felt. Nicole tried to cover by leaning over and petting Boomer who'd taken up residence at her side, but Ellie saw the surprise in Nicole's wide eyes.

Ellie had lived in the same house, even slept in the same bedroom, until she left for college. She'd gone to one elementary school, one middle school, and one high school, and had many of the same friends since she'd been able to toddle to a playgroup. The type of life Max described was as foreign to her as, she supposed, her life was to Max.

"What was that like?" Ellie asked.

Max leaned back against the couch and looked up at the ceiling. "Honestly? I guess when I was young, it was confusing, but then it was normal. I can remember being really young, five or six, and waking up in the middle of the night. The house we were in was big. I don't know what we were doing there, why we had such a huge house, but that's where we'd landed that time. I woke up in the middle of the night and had to go to the bathroom. I got that feeling. You know, when you first wake up and you have no idea where you are? Not a new feeling, it happened all the time, but this time, even when that feeling passed, I didn't know where I was. I left my room, started wandering around, and got lost. I couldn't find a bathroom and ended up in the kitchen. I crawled under the table and cried."

Ellie didn't know what to say. To her, it sounded awful. No stability, no place to call home.

Max must have sensed Ellie's unease, because her voice was upbeat when she spoke again. "It was always an adventure, though. I've lived in dozens of places, seen most of the country, learned everything from surfing to snowshoeing, eaten everything from crawfish to cheese curds. Now, from what I know about slumber parties, we're supposed to be talking about boys, right? So, Oklahoma, tell us about Zeke."

The abrupt change of topic caught her off guard. Zeke? She'd been trying hard not to think about him. "There's not much to tell. He's certainly not my boyfriend."

"But what's going on? You've hardly talked about him lately, not since telling us about the whole thing with Talia." Nicole frowned. "Not that we've had a lot of time to talk about anything but school."

"Like I said, not much to tell. We've seen each other twice. No, three times. Twice when we've been in and out of Top Dog at the same time, but never for more than a minute or two. Just long enough to say hello, ask about the dogs, that sort of thing. Then once when I was walking Boomer past his house. He was in his driveway and waved, but he was talking on the phone, so I didn't stop. That's it."

"Why, El? Why don't you talk to him?"

"And say what, Max? I get the feeling neither one of us is ready for more than just a casual friendship."

"Bull. I'm sure I don't know the half of it, but from what I do know, from what you've told me about the time you've spent together, there's more than a casual friendship there. And you're ready, right? You told us that much. You're over everything that happened with Vincent, but you haven't cleared the air with Zeke over what he thinks he saw between you and Vincent. That seems really stupid. You need to talk it out. You need to tell him how you feel. Call him. Text him. Do something."

"I don't think I can do that. I'm not really that type of person."

"What type?" Nicole asked. "The type who knows what she wants and goes after it? I'd say you're exactly that type of person."

"Then you agree with Max? You think I need to talk to him? To make the first move?"

"Of course. You can't sit around and wait forever. *Carpe diem*, Ellie, *carpe diem*."

"*Carpe diem*. Hah. What about *abundans cautela non nocet*? Or *actum fieri infectum non potest?*" Ellie sat up straight and squared her shoulders. *"Hic sunt dracones?"*

The room was quiet, with both Nicole and Max narrowing their eyes at Ellie. Finally Max asked Nicole, "What is she talking about?"

"How should I know?"

"What I said was, instead of seize the day, your words of wisdom, what about *abundans cautela non nocet*? Abundant caution does no harm. More loosely translated, one can never be too careful. Or *actum fieri infectum non potest*. It is impossible for a deed to be undone. Meaning, once I send a text, I can't un-send it."

"How do you know all that?" Nicole asked.

"I studied Latin in college."

"That sounds hard."

"Kind of. I certainly haven't mastered it."

"There was a third one," Max said. "You said three things."

"Oh, yes. That one just means here there are dragons. I always thought it was funny."

"You're an odd one, Oklahoma."

Ellie stretched one arm out and bent the other, putting her hand on her stomach. She bowed. "Why, thank you very much."

Max threw a handful of popcorn at her and Ellie laughed; slowly at first, then harder until she could barely catch her breath. It was contagious. Nicole and Max joined her until all three were gasping for breath and had tears running down their cheeks. It took Boomer circling from one to the next, whining and licking their faces for them to calm enough to talk.

"Oh, my stars. I haven't laughed that hard in ages," Ellie said, swiping a hand under her eyes.

"Me neither," Nicole said. "Felt good, though I'm not sure what was so funny."

"I've never laughed that hard. Well, maybe the time this guy who thought he had such an awesome car wanted to race me. I left him in the dust. That was pretty funny."

The quiet returned, this time with Ellie and Nicole both staring at Max, but it didn't last long before laughter again won out.

It took the ding of the oven timer to quiet them. Ellie jumped to her feet. "Brownies!"

Max and Nicole followed her, and their noses, to the kitchen.

"I love brownies," Max said. "I once baked a pan and ate the whole thing in one afternoon. Not my proudest moment, but," she shrugged, "I was a teenager."

"The most you can have tonight is a third of a pan," Nicole said. "As long as I've already eaten pizza, and popcorn swimming in butter, and had half a bottle of wine, what's a few brownies?"

"Right. No rules at slumber parties. That's the rule." Ellie laughed at herself.

Max reached for a knife from the block on Ellie's counter and aimed it at the pan. Ellie slapped Max's hand away.

"They're too hot."

"No, they're just right."

"They'll fall apart."

"They'll taste the same."

"You'll burn your mouth."

"It's my mouth."

"Max, you're impossible." Ellie rolled her eyes, then handed out forks. They all dug in.

After they'd eaten their fill, Max said, "I think red wine goes with chocolate, right?"

"Everything goes with chocolate," Nicole said, and held out her glass.

Max filled all three, then they went back to their cozy spots on the living room floor.

"Okay, Ellie, we got sidetracked, but back to Zeke. You need to contact him. Tonight," Max said.

"Tonight? No way."

"Max is right. We'll help you write the perfect text, find the perfect emojis. If you don't do it tonight, you're just going to chicken out again."

Ellie knew they were right about that, at least. Whether sending it after three glasses of wine was a good idea? They were probably wrong about that.

When Ellie didn't argue right away, Max took it as agreement. "All right, then. Let's figure this out. You want to talk to him—tomorrow, we decided—and you need to make sure he knows it's important. Not like it's something about the dogs, or the weather, or something."

"The weather?" Ellie said. Max ignored her.

"Tell him you love him." Nicole giggled. Max joined her and nearly started a third round of laughing fits.

"Wait!" Ellie held up her hand. "We have to figure this out. I'm not saying I love him."

Nicole giggled again, but put her hand to her mouth and stopped herself.

"What do I say? For real?" Ellie asked Nicole.

"Tell him you want to talk to him. Tell him it's important, and that it's not something you can text or discuss over the phone. You have to talk in person. Tell him your relationship with Vincent is over, kaput, dead in the water. There's nothing there, and whatever he thinks he saw, he was wrong."

"That's a lot to text."

"You can abbreviate," Max said.

"And you have to ask him to come over tomorrow. Don't leave it at 'we need to talk soon' because then it won't happen. It will be too easy to let it slide, and you'll be right back where you are now."

"Okay. So I tell him, *It's over. Vincent is dead in the water. You need to come here tomorrow.*" Ellie typed as she spoke, afraid if she didn't, she'd lose her nerve again.

"That sounds good. Say tomorrow morning, though. Don't leave it open-ended," Max advised.

Ellie went back and added *morning* to her text. "Wait a minute. What time is it? Is it already tomorrow? If it is, and I say tomorrow morning, he's going to think Satur-, I mean Sunday morning. Right? Is that right?"

Max leaned her head into her hand and screwed up her face.

"Um…"

Nicole looked around her, then grabbed Ellie's phone and looked at that. She held it close to her face, then stretched out her arm and squinted, before pulling it closer again. "Nope. It's still today. Tonight. Friday. You can say tomorrow morning." She tapped the phone, then handed it back to Ellie. "There. Done. That's a relief. What should we do now?"

Ellie held her hand over her eyes and squinted against the blazing sun. It had snowed overnight, just an inch or so, but enough that the light that morning was as bright as a thousand suns. At least it was to her bloodshot eyes. With her free hand, she waved to Max and Nicole as they eased out of her driveway and then out of sight.

"What a night," Ellie said to Boomer when she coaxed him back inside. "So much fun, though." Ellie rubbed at her temples. "Maybe a little too much fun."

They'd fallen asleep on the living room floor, snuggled in blankets and quilts Ellie had rounded up, and watching *Grease*. Max's story of racing the guy at school had them talking about the movie, and after some digging, Ellie found her DVD copy. They'd sung and danced along until they'd been too tired to do anything but curl up and watch.

The floor wasn't as comfortable as it had been during those slumber parties twenty years ago, which meant they'd woken early. After a cup of coffee and leftover brownies, Max and Nicole were on their way. Ellie desperately wanted a shower and a nap. And maybe some aspirin.

She got the shower, a quick one, and the aspirin, but before she could think about the nap, her doorbell rang.

Ellie looked around the living room. "Do you think one of them forgot something, Booms?"

She pulled the door open without thinking. An agitated Zeke stared back at her.

"Oh, sorry, I was supposed to look to see who was there, wasn't I? Nicole and Max just left a few minutes ago. I thought it was one of them."

Zeke just stared at her as if she were from another planet.

"What?" She ran a self-conscious hand over her damp hair, her face. Had she washed her face in the shower? She couldn't remember. "Do I have chocolate on my face?"

"Ellie, what is going on with you? Chocolate? That's what you're worried about?"

"Well, I'm sure I don't look great. It was a long night. I showered, but maybe I missed some."

She couldn't put her finger on it, but something was there, on the edges of her mind, something about Zeke. She'd been hoping to talk to him, that was a fact, but he hadn't seemed to have time for her lately. She'd been trying to tell herself it was his job, it was lingering concern for his brother, it was any number of things, but it was getting harder to believe those excuses. Maybe that was it. It was awkward now that he was there, and she didn't know what to say. But why was he there? Had she agreed to help with Bowie? No, he hadn't asked for weeks.

Then those vague memories started to take shape.

Her hand flew to her mouth as she gasped. The air was frigid, but she felt her face heat, hot enough to melt the ice from her front step. She'd sent a text. Max and Nicole had convinced her it was a good idea. What did it say? What did it say? Her hand itched to grab her phone, to look, but she was too horrified to move. Zeke just stood and stared.

"What happened last night, Ellie? I woke up this morning to a text from you." He looked over her shoulder and around the inside of her house, shifting to get a better view. "You said I should come this morning."

Ellie felt beads of sweat form on her forehead. The hand that was still over her mouth began to tremble. "Oh...oh, no..."

Zeke took her shoulders in his hands and marched her backward into the house, pushing the door shut behind him. Ellie barely noticed.

"Are you in trouble? You didn't do anything rash, did you?"

Wine, pizza, popcorn, brownies, coffee—all of it rolled and rumbled in her stomach and she felt a burning at the back of her throat.

"What did I say?" The words thundered in her ears, but given her dry throat and the fact that each syllable burned like fire, she wasn't sure Zeke heard her.

"Your hair's wet."

"A little."

"Is there anyone else here? Anywhere?"

"No, I told you Max and Nicole just left."

"And Vincent?"

"Vincent?"

And then it hit her. Like a Mack truck. *It's over. Dead in the water.* How had that ever sounded like a good idea?

"I'm so embarrassed." She had to turn away. Facing him was too much. Not even the night she stormed to Vincent's after their break-up and ranted like a lunatic could rival this for embarrassment. She closed her eyes and tried to tell herself it was all some sort of horrible dream.

"Embarrassed?"

Not a dream, then. All too real. She still couldn't meet Zeke's eyes.

"Yes. I'm sorry I texted you. I wasn't exactly thinking clearly."

"But what happened? Was Vincent here? *Is* he here? Did something happen? Does he need a doctor?"

Now she whirled around. "Oh, my stars, Zeke! A doctor! No! You didn't think…"

Then, against all reason, she laughed. Her brain told her there was nothing remotely funny about the situation, but she couldn't help herself. *Dead in the water*! Zeke thought she killed Vincent! Max and Nicole would never believe her.

"Ellie, you're going to have to give me something."

When she saw him raking his hand through his hair, she sobered.

"You're right. I'm sorry. I've made a mess of things, haven't I?" Suddenly she had a kind of confidence she never would have believed possible even a day ago. "Do you have time to sit? Have a cup of coffee? Stay a while? I promise you I'm not a murderer."

22

"So it really was just a poor choice of words. I'm not sure why it seemed like it made sense last night. Okay, I guess the empty wine bottles have something to do with it, but still, you'd think one of us would have noticed."

"You'd think."

At least he was smiling now. It had taken some convincing, even an offer to search her house, but Zeke had stopped thinking he was at a murder scene.

"They were trying to help me work up the nerve to tell you I wanted to talk to you."

"You needed to work up the nerve? We see each other all the time. We talk."

"We haven't seen each other much lately, not since the night with Talia, and we don't talk. Not about anything important, anyway."

"What is it you want to talk about?"

"Us."

"Us?"

Ellie tried to read his expression. She wanted to think it was hopeful, pleased even, but Zeke was doing a remarkable job of keeping his emotions hidden. Under the table, she clasped her hands together and told herself she could do it.

"Yes, us. As in, I want there to be an us."

"When you say us…"

"You're making this difficult. I like you. I think you like me. If I'm mistaken, then maybe you can tell me sooner rather than later, because I'm close to making a complete fool out of myself."

A grin. Quick, then gone in a flash, but she'd seen it and it gave her hope.

"Making a fool out of yourself? Maybe I'll stall and see what that entails."

Ellie clicked her tongue. "There is nothing between Vincent and me, if that's what you were thinking. We were together, years ago, and it ended horribly. He lied, over and over, he made a fool of me, and I was broken. It all left me reluctant to get involved with anyone, but lately I've realized, with a little help from some very important people, that I'm only hurting myself by not trusting myself enough to live. And love. To give love another chance.

"Whatever you think you saw with Vincent, because I know you saw me hug him that day out by the car, you were wrong. It was a goodbye, a thank you for giving Mama a ride so she could come for a visit, and, I guess, a forgiveness sort of thing. Forgiving him, forgiving myself, and moving on. That's all."

"That's a lot."

"I suppose it is."

"And you mentioned something about giving love another chance?" Zeke's eyebrows rose with his question.

"I did."

"I like the sounds of that, Ellie. I like it a lot."

Her heart swelled. "You do?"

Tentatively, she put a hand up on the table and slid it halfway across. Zeke did the same. When their hands met, he closed his over hers.

"I do. Outside my house, the day I convinced you to stay for dinner, you told me, in no uncertain terms, that you weren't looking for a relationship. Ever since, I've been hoping to change your mind. Especially since the afternoon at the football game. Watching you cheer for your Cowboys, seeing you smile, watching how you talked and laughed with the die-hard Packer fans, how gracious you were in defeat."

"Hah!"

"How you grinned and held up in defeat."

"Better."

"Mostly, though, it was the hours in the car, talking with you, learning about you, realizing you have the biggest, kindest heart of anyone I've ever known."

That heart pounded now in her chest, and she felt tears sting the backs of her eyes. The good kind of tears, she reminded herself. The good kind.

"I do have to tell you something, though. You said you were hurt before by someone who lied to you. I will never lie to you, and I will do everything in my power to never hurt you. They're words, I know, and words can be easy, but I back up my words. That's a promise. The most serious kind of promise I know how to make."

There was a 'but' coming, Ellie could tell. She held her breath.

"But, before I go any further, before this goes any further, I have to tell you something I didn't tell you earlier. When I told you about my high school days, about getting in trouble, I left something out. Something I've never told anyone."

"It wasn't you." Ellie surprised herself with her words, but at the same time, she wasn't surprised at all. Finally, it all made sense. The story that didn't quite fit, the reluctance to meet her eyes when he'd told her, the way he never wanted to talk about his brother.

"It was Caleb, wasn't it? He's the one who stole from your father."

Shock registered in Zeke's wide eyes. "How did you know that?"

"It makes sense, knowing what I now know. You've been covering for him since you were kids."

Very slowly, Zeke nodded. He breathed a deep breath, like he hadn't taken one in years.

"Caleb is the one who needed money back then. He got himself in trouble and he was desperate. He stole the prescription pad, he forged the prescriptions and sold them. He was on his last chance, with my parents and with school, so I made him promise that he'd never do anything like it again."

"It never fit, what you told me before. I knew something wasn't right, but couldn't quite figure out what."

"I'm sorry I lied to you."

Ellie shook her head. "That's not something you need to apologize for. Not to me. It didn't involve me. I wonder, though, what about your father? Have you ever told him the truth?"

"Last week."

That surprised Ellie. "Why now?"

"After a couple of weeks of not hearing more from Caleb, I called my parents to let them know he was looking for money again. He went too far involving you, and I worried he might try something with them. He's gone to them for money over the years, they've given it to him sometimes, but as far as I know, he'd never done anything like what he tried to pull with you. While I was talking to my dad, I decided it was time to tell him the truth about what happened all those years ago."

"How did that go?"

"I only got a few words out before he stopped me. He told me he knew, that he's known since it happened. Not right away, but during the week he took to think about it, to decide how to handle it, he figured it out. He said he took that full week to give me time to tell him the truth, or better, for Caleb to come clean, but when a week passed and neither of us said anything, he did what he did. That's why he didn't go to the police, that's why he let me off with the punishment I got and not something much worse, or something more fitting the crime. As for why he didn't turn in Caleb, he wouldn't talk much about that. It's such a painful subject for him, for both my parents, to have one of their sons turn his back on them, to hear from him only when he's in trouble, when he needs something. It's a kind of hurt I don't think a person understands unless they're in that position."

"I'm so sorry, Zeke, for all of you. What happened to Caleb this last time? Do you know? Is he okay?"

"I don't know. It seems he's gone, but I don't know where. He was really scared this time. More so than before. I don't know what he did, but it has to be something big. My gut tells me he's either gone into hiding, or he's made a new identity for himself and we may never see him again."

Ellie was dumbfounded. "He could do that?"

"He could do just about anything he wanted to do. I wasn't exaggerating when I told you he's a genius. He has the skills to make something incredible out of himself, but he keeps using his skills in the wrong way."

Zeke looked at her, and she felt his inner war.

"He steals from people. He does it all online, mostly just for the challenge. Then he turns around and donates the money anonymously to a charity that never saw it coming. Don't ask me how he manages all of that without ever having his name attached to any of it, because I don't completely understand. Suffice it to say, there's not much he can't do with a computer.

"He gets a real job once in a while to make some money to cover living expenses, but then quits after he figures he can get by for a while. To the best of my knowledge, he's never kept anything he's stolen. None of it makes much sense, obviously. I can't tell you how many times I've wondered why, with the brain he has and with all that he can do, he doesn't use it for good. I don't know that I'll ever have an answer to that, and it's frustrating. I also don't know why he is the way he is. I don't know what happened to make him the way he is. He was a good kid when we were young."

Zeke looked down at the table, lost for a moment in his painful memories. "When Caleb gets in trouble, it's when someone figures out what he's doing. He's been caught a few times. I don't know the details, but from what I've gathered, he returns the money, plus some, in order to keep himself alive. The people he steals from aren't good people. He's not taking money from someone's grandma, or stealing from a hospital, or anything like that. He finds criminals. Loan sharks, illegal gambling operations, drug runners, that sort of thing. It's dangerous business, so on the rare occasion he's caught, these people can't exactly go to the police. They threaten him, and like I said, he's afraid. He can't always hide behind his computer if someone's after him with a gun or a knife. So, he returns the money, he has to come up with extra to keep himself safe, and that's when he's come to me. Or to Mom and Dad. It's almost unbelievable, I know, like something out of a movie, but I've been living it for years. I wish it was a movie I could turn off, or a book I could close."

As if drained by finally telling the entire story, Zeke rested his elbows on the table and dropped his head onto his fists.

"I don't know what to say. I'm so sorry that you and your parents have to live with this."

Zeke raised his head, then shook it.

"There's nothing to say. I've been trying to come up with something for years, but there's just nothing. I needed you to know the whole story, the whole truth, because, like I said, from this point on, there will never be anything but the truth from me."

"I know that." And she did. In her heart, she knew. "And I can say the same. There will be only truth from me."

Zeke's smile held a hint of mischief. "Then I can ask you a question and you'll answer truthfully?"

"Of course."

"It's something I've wanted to ask you since I met you. Actually, I suppose you could say I've wanted to ask since before I met you, though that doesn't make much sense, does it?"

"Not really."

"Before I met you, I was out for a run with Bowie and passed this house. It was a nice day, the windows were open, and I heard music."

"Music?"

"Yes. A song. A sad, but beautiful song that I'd never heard before."

"Oh?" Ellie figured she knew what was coming, but hoped she was wrong.

"I stood outside and listened, but only caught part of it. I tried searching the lyrics to find out the name of it, or the artist, but I was never able to find it."

"I see."

"I did finally figure it out. Since then, I've been waiting for you to tell me you play the guitar, or for you to sing along with the radio so I could again hear the most beautiful voice I've ever heard."

"You probably heard something off my playlist. Maybe I could find it for you."

"Ellie, you promised the truth."

"I can't be certain what you heard."

"That's true, but I think you have a pretty good idea."

"Not really…"

"Okay, if you're going to be difficult, this is your fault," Zeke said with a laugh in his voice. He cleared his throat, then sang, "I wonder if you know what it feels like…"

When Ellie squeezed her eyes shut, Zeke stopped.

"I'm sorry. Ellie, I'm sorry, I didn't mean to upset you. We don't have to talk about it. Forget I ever mentioned it."

It would be easy to forget about it, to get back to the happy they'd had just a minute ago, but Ellie told herself that was the coward's answer, so she opened her eyes and smiled at Zeke.

"You didn't upset me, you just caught me off guard. I've never played that song for anyone."

"Then it is your song? You wrote it?"

"Yes."

"Wow. I guessed, but having you confirm it, wow. It was incredible. The small part I heard was incredible. So much emotion, so much… oh." Understanding dawned, dousing his excitement like a bucket of water poured over a campfire. "You wrote it when your heart was broken."

Like she had the other day when she'd sung it all the way through for the first time, Ellie felt nothing but free. Free from the sadness, free from the heartbreak, free from remembering what had been. None of it mattered any longer, and while she'd never considered herself a performer, she found she was comfortable with the idea of someone hearing the song.

"I did, but that doesn't matter any longer. Now, it's just a song. It has no more hold on me than any other song I've written."

"There are others?"

Ellie wrinkled her nose. That had slipped out. "Yes, there are others."

"Will you play one for me?"

"Now? Are you serious?"

"I'm very serious. I've been waiting months to hear that voice again. You know, it's possible when I heard you sing, I fell in love with you before I met you."

"I'm not that good, I mostly just sing for fun, I...wait, what did you say?"

Zeke's smile touched every inch of his face, from his lips to his dimples to his eyes that held her in his gaze. "I said a lot of things, but for the sake of time, let me boil it down. I love you. I do. I love you, Ellie."

Ellie had dreamed of hearing those words from Zeke, and every time she'd imagined it, she'd imagined herself crying. Happy tears, of course, the kind a person cried when they got good news, but tears nonetheless. She surprised herself when she found crying was the last thing she felt like doing. Instead, she smiled, then she laughed, then she got up and circled the table to stand in front of Zeke. She put her hands on his shoulders and leaned over to press her lips to his.

There was a moment of surprise, she sensed it in the rigidity of his lips and his jaw, then everything went soft, his arms went around her, and she felt the tingle from her lips to her toes as he kissed her back.

She loved him too. She was certain, because everything felt so different from the way it had before. With Zeke, it was real love; true, honest, we're-in-this-together love. That kind of love didn't want tears, it wanted to be celebrated.

"I love you too, Zeke. I never thought I'd say this, but I'm glad Top Dog mixed up our dogs. We may never have met if they hadn't, and meeting you is the best thing that's ever happened to me. You're the best thing that's ever happened to me."

She kissed him again.

"I started writing another song a few days ago. It's not done yet, but if you want to hear it, I'd like to play it for you."

Zeke looked a little dazed, but said, "I'd love to hear it."

Ellie wasn't sure her feet touched the ground as she dashed up the stairs to her room to fetch her guitar. When she returned to the living room, Zeke hadn't moved. He still sat at the table with a grin plastered on his face. If Ellie had any nerves at playing and singing for him, they disappeared when she saw how he looked at her. When she *knew* that he loved her.

She sat across from him and strummed. No more minor chords. When the beginnings of the song had come to her a few weeks ago, it had demanded C major. For as comfortable as she may have gotten playing in a sad key, the much happier C major felt natural. Felt like her.

Love is a miracle
A wild and crazy ride

The music reverberated off the walls and filled the room with happy. Nothing but happy.

If you enjoyed reading *Leaving Home*, please help other readers find and enjoy it by leaving a review on Amazon or Goodreads or wherever you review books. Just a few words will do and will be very much appreciated.
Thank you!

Margaret Standafer lives and writes in the Minneapolis area with the support of her amazing husband and children and in spite of the lack of support from her ever-demanding, but lovable, Golden Retriever. It is her sincere hope that you enjoy her work.

To learn more about Margaret and her books, please visit www.margaretstandafer.com

Manufactured by Amazon.ca
Acheson, AB